MARVEL

AN ORIGINAL GRAPHIC NOVEL

MS. MARVEL
STRETCHED THIN

WRITTEN BY
NADIA SHAMMAS

ILLUSTRATED BY
NABI H. ALI

LAYOUTS BY
GEOFFO

LETTERS BY
VC's JOE CARAMAGNA

graphix
AN IMPRINT OF
SCHOLASTIC

LAUREN BISOM, EDITOR

CAITLIN O'CONNELL, ASSOCIATE EDITOR

JAY BOWEN, PUBLICATION DESIGN

JENNIFER GRÜNWALD, SENIOR EDITOR, SPECIAL PROJECTS

SVEN LARSEN, VP LICENSED PUBLISHING

JEFF YOUNGQUIST, VP PRODUCTION & SPECIAL PROJECTS

DAVID GABRIEL, SVP PRINT, SALES & MARKETING

C.B. CEBULSKI, EDITOR IN CHIEF

MICHAEL PETRANEK, EXECUTIVE EDITOR, MANAGER AFK & GRAPHIX MEDIA, SCHOLASTIC

JEFF SHAKE, SENIOR DESIGNER, SCHOLASTIC

WITH SPECIAL THANKS TO **SANA AMANAT** AND **DAN BUCKLEY**

ISBN 978-1-338-72259-8

10 9 8 7 6 5 4 3 2 1   21 22 23 24 25

Printed in the U.S.A.   113

First edition, September 2021

Art by Nabi H. Ali
Letters by VC's Joe Caramagna

To every daughter trying her best, under a mountain of expectations—you are so valuable, and I write for you. Also, for my father, who always wanted a dedication on my first book. Thank you for everything, Baba. —NS

~

To Ms. James, for introducing me to Kamala's world. —NHA

CHAPTER ONE

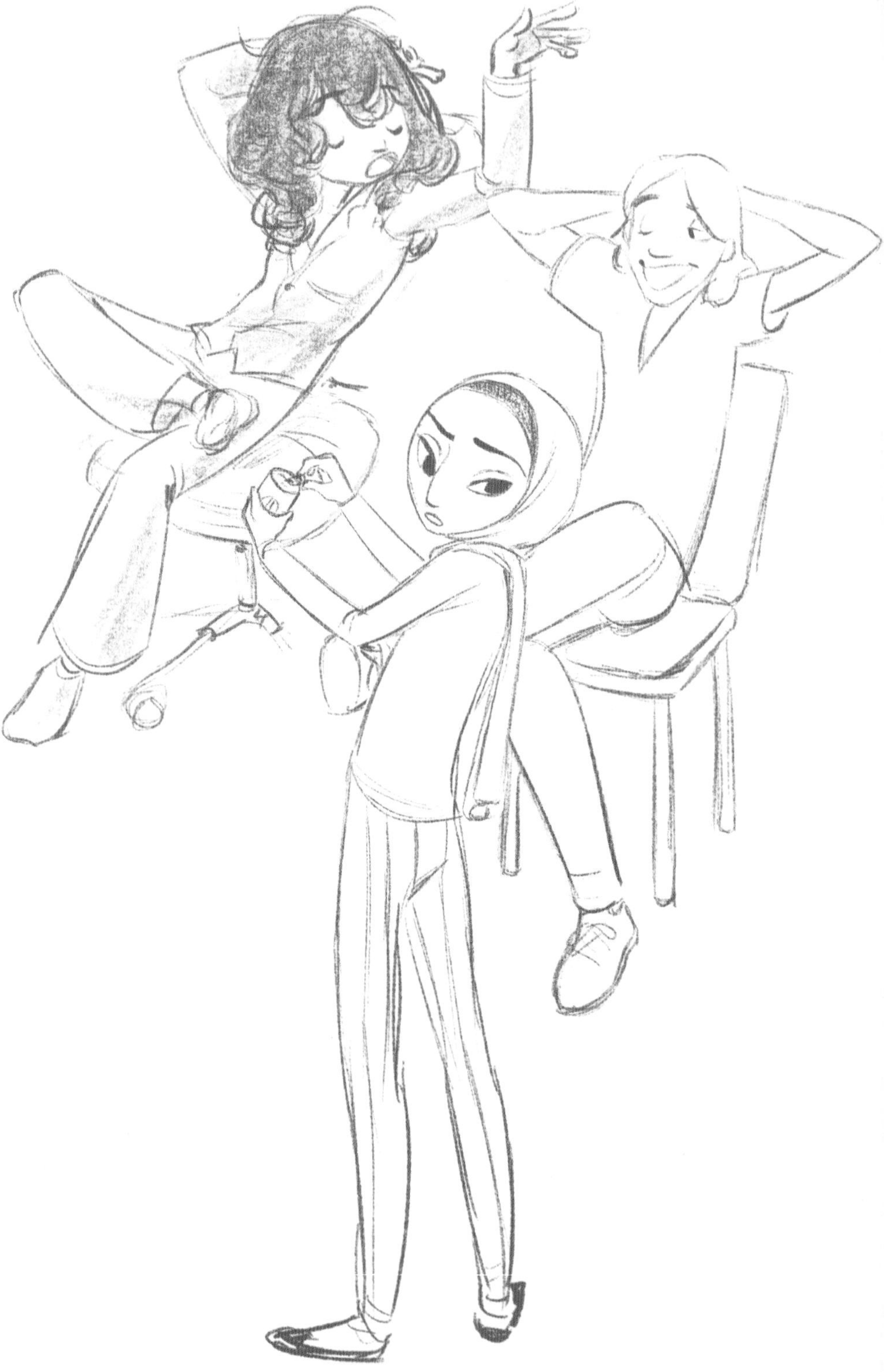

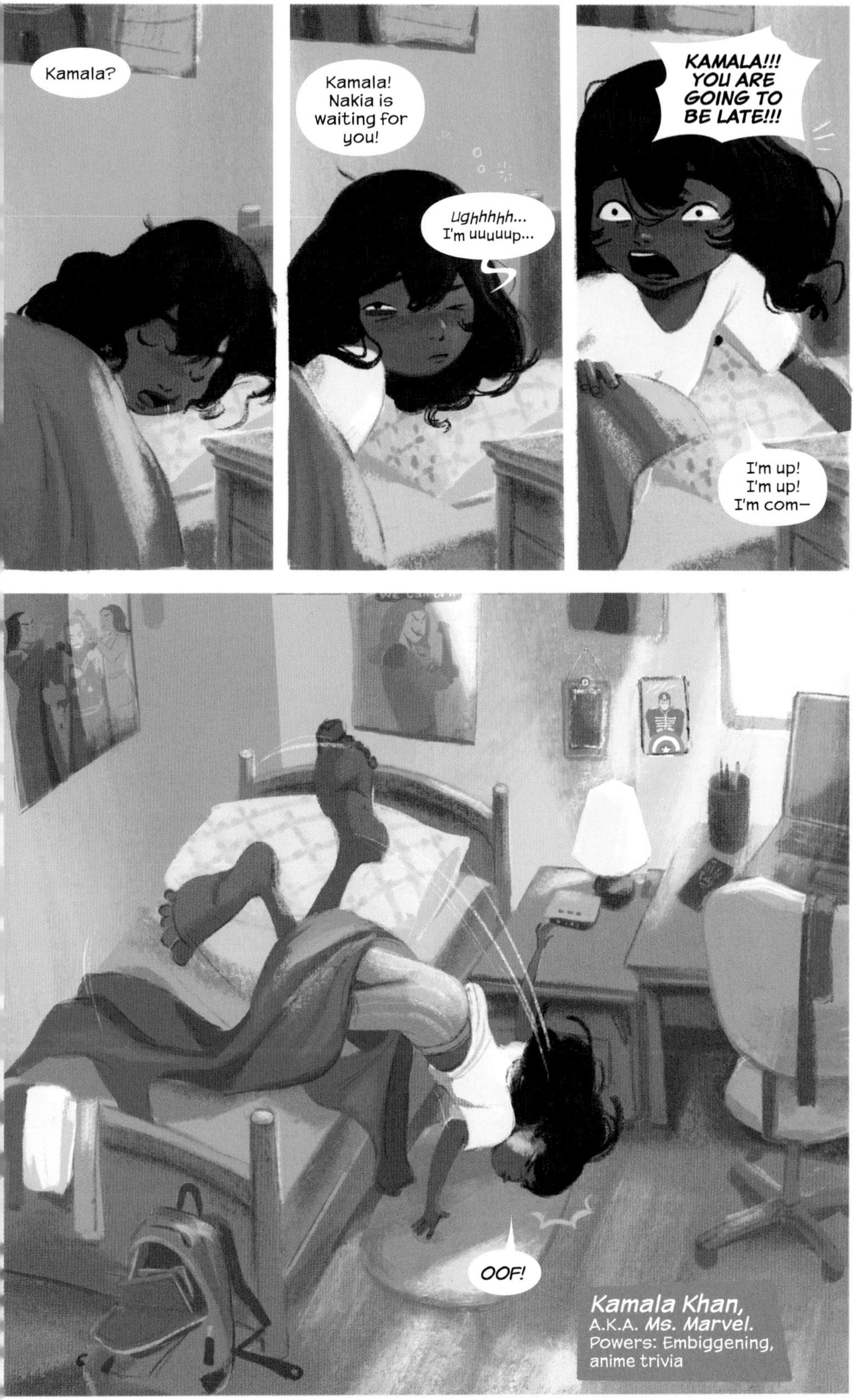
Kamala?
Kamala! Nakia is waiting for you!
Ughhhhh... I'm uuuuup...
KAMALA!!! YOU ARE GOING TO BE LATE!!!
I'm up! I'm up! I'm com—
OOF!
Kamala Khan, A.K.A. Ms. Marvel. Powers: Embiggening, anime trivia

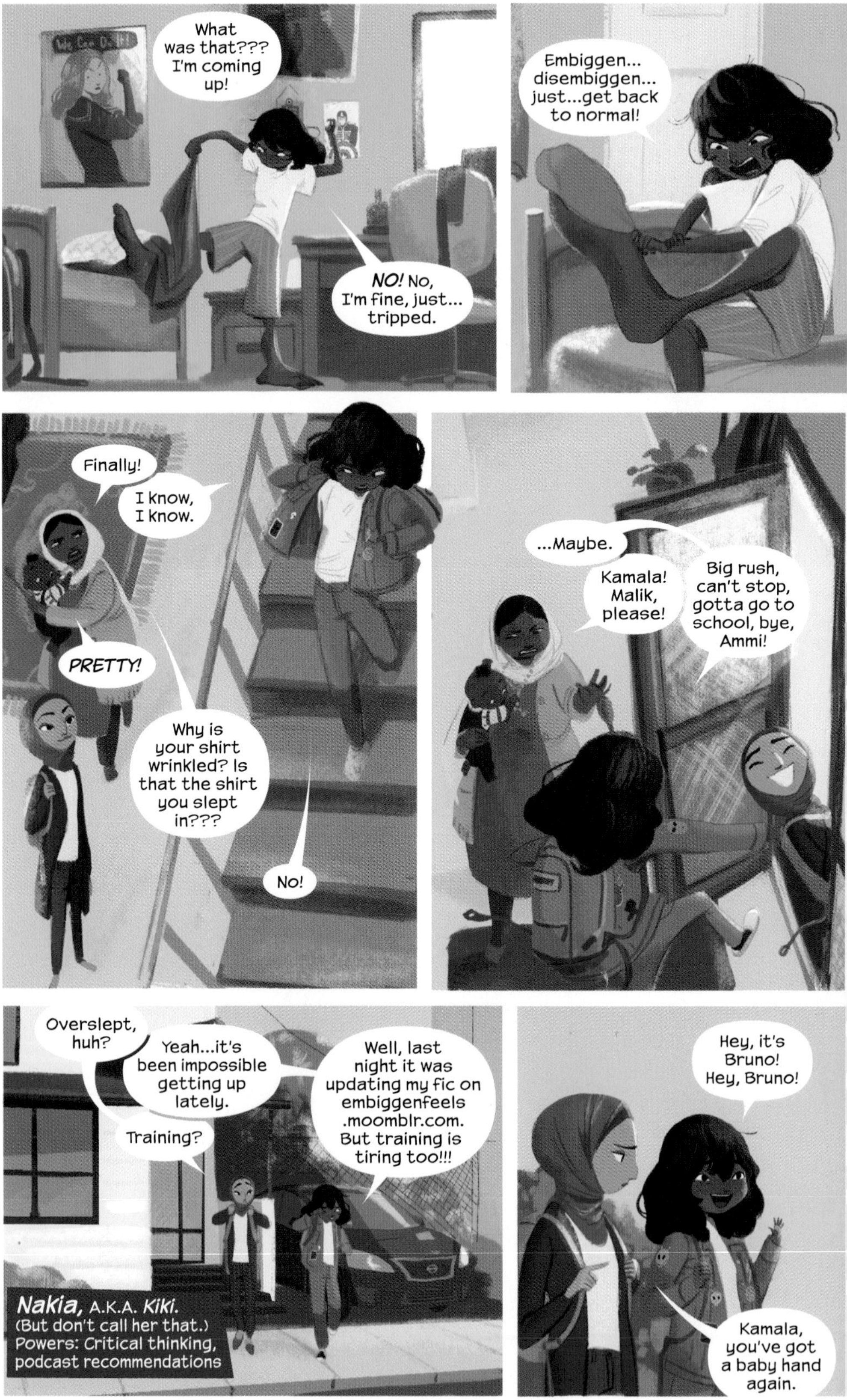

What was that??? I'm coming up!
NO! No, I'm fine, just... tripped.
Embiggen... disembiggen... just...get back to normal!
Finally!
I know, I know.
PRETTY!
Why is your shirt wrinkled? Is that the shirt you slept in???
No!
...Maybe.
Kamala! Malik, please!
Big rush, can't stop, gotta go to school, bye, Ammi!
Overslept, huh?
Yeah...it's been impossible getting up lately.
Training?
Well, last night it was updating my fic on embiggenfeels .moomblr.com. But training is tiring too!!!
Nakia, A.K.A. Kiki. (But don't call her that.) Powers: Critical thinking, podcast recommendations
Hey, it's Bruno! Hey, Bruno!
Kamala, you've got a baby hand again.

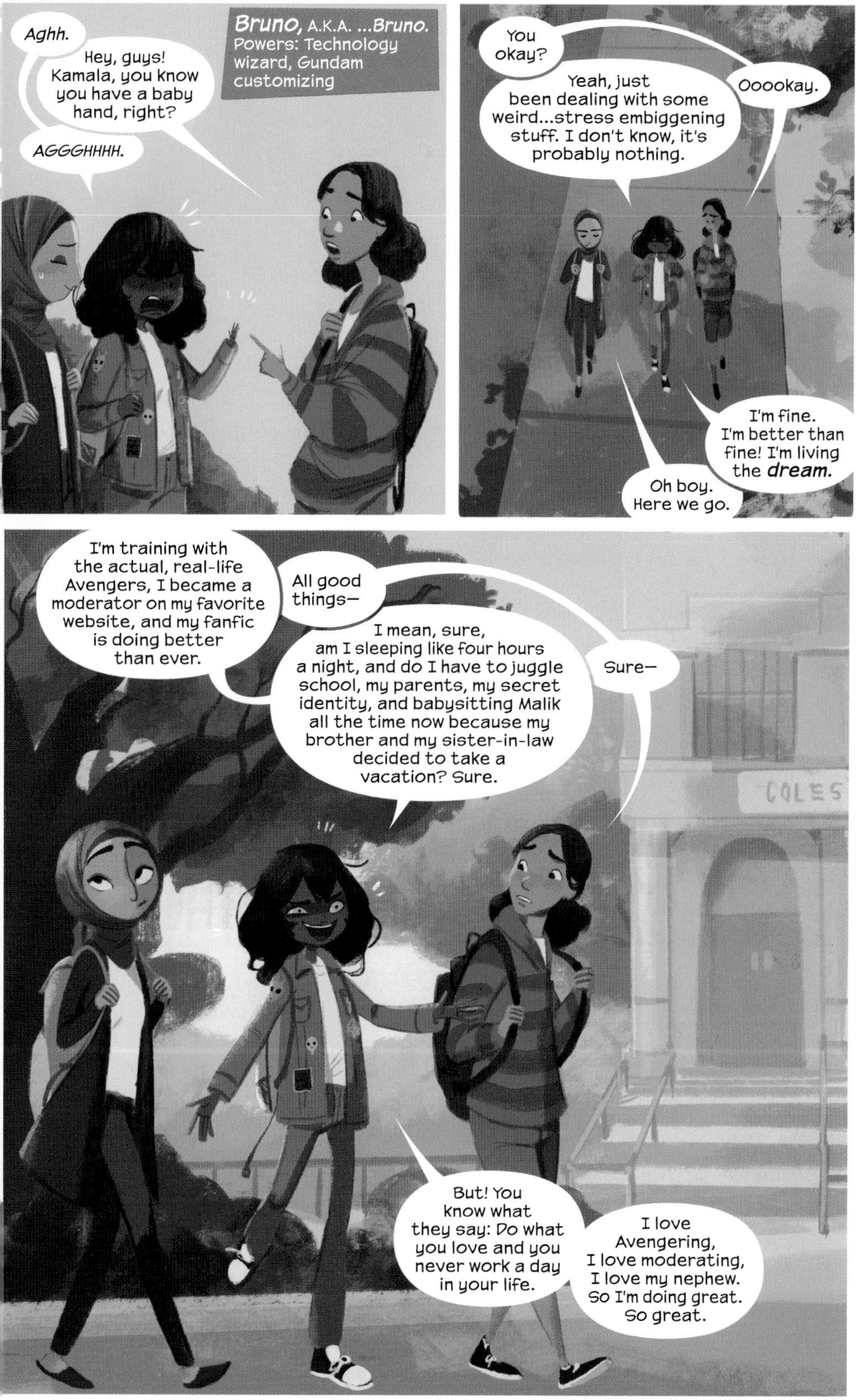
Aghh.
Hey, guys! Kamala, you know you have a baby hand, right?
AGGGHHHH.
Bruno, A.K.A. ...Bruno. Powers: Technology wizard, Gundam customizing
You okay?
Yeah, just been dealing with some weird...stress embiggening stuff. I don't know, it's probably nothing.
Ooookay.
I'm fine. I'm better than fine! I'm living the **dream.**
Oh boy. Here we go.
I'm training with the actual, real-life Avengers, I became a moderator on my favorite website, and my fanfic is doing better than ever.
All good things—
I mean, sure, am I sleeping like four hours a night, and do I have to juggle school, my parents, my secret identity, and babysitting Malik all the time now because my brother and my sister-in-law decided to take a vacation? Sure.
Sure—
COLES
But! You know what they say: Do what you love and you never work a day in your life.
I love Avengering, I love moderating, I love my nephew. So I'm doing great. So great.

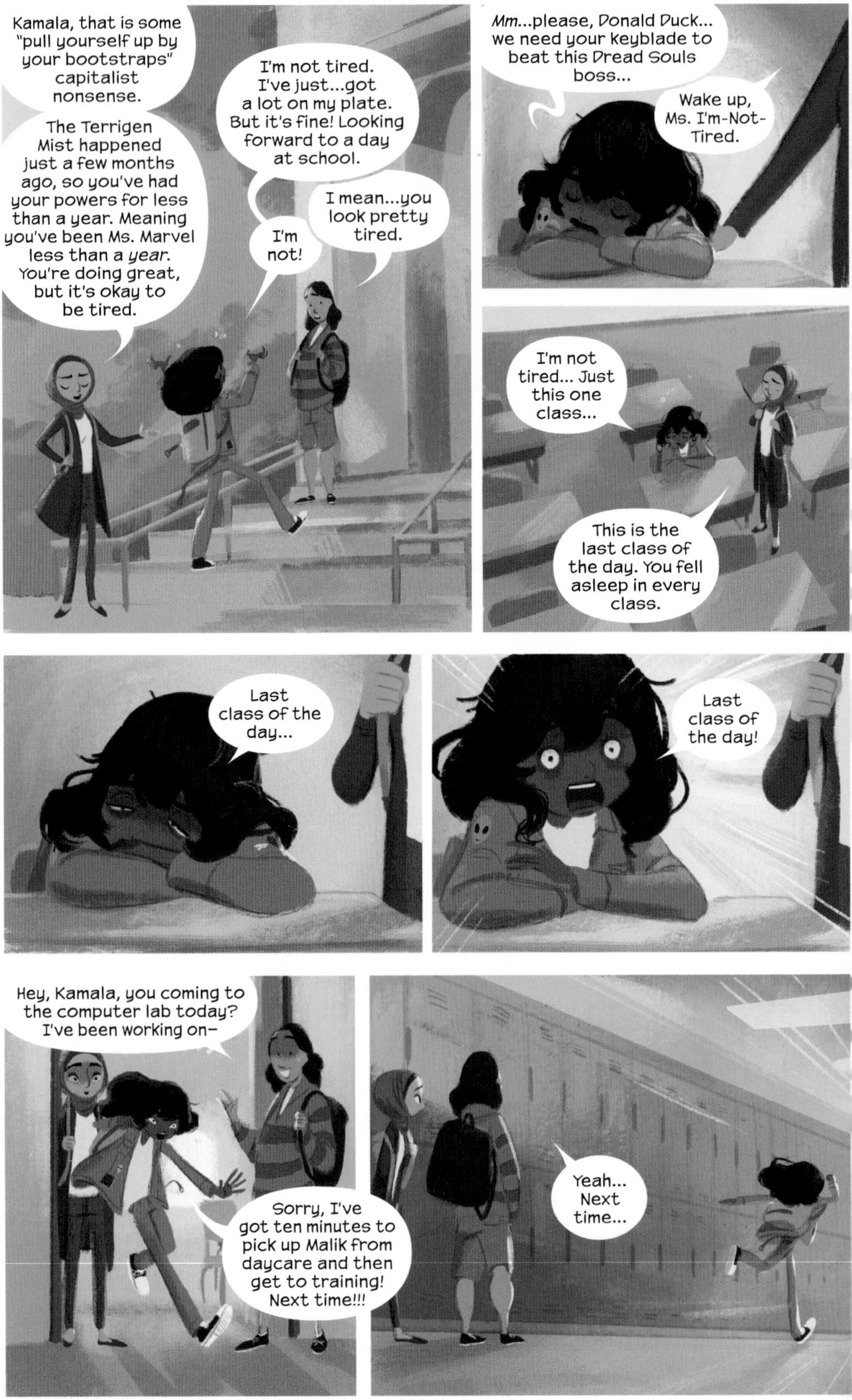
Kamala, that is some "pull yourself up by your bootstraps" capitalist nonsense.
The Terrigen Mist happened just a few months ago, so you've had your powers for less than a year. Meaning you've been Ms. Marvel less than a *year*. You're doing great, but it's okay to be tired.
I'm not tired. I've just...got a lot on my plate. But it's fine! Looking forward to a day at school.
I mean...you look pretty tired.
I'm not!
Mm...please, Donald Duck... we need your keyblade to beat this Dread Souls boss...
Wake up, Ms. I'm-Not-Tired.
I'm not tired... Just this one class...
This is the last class of the day. You fell asleep in every class.
Last class of the day...
Last class of the day!
Hey, Kamala, you coming to the computer lab today? I've been working on–
Sorry, I've got ten minutes to pick up Malik from daycare and then get to training! Next time!!!
Yeah... Next time...

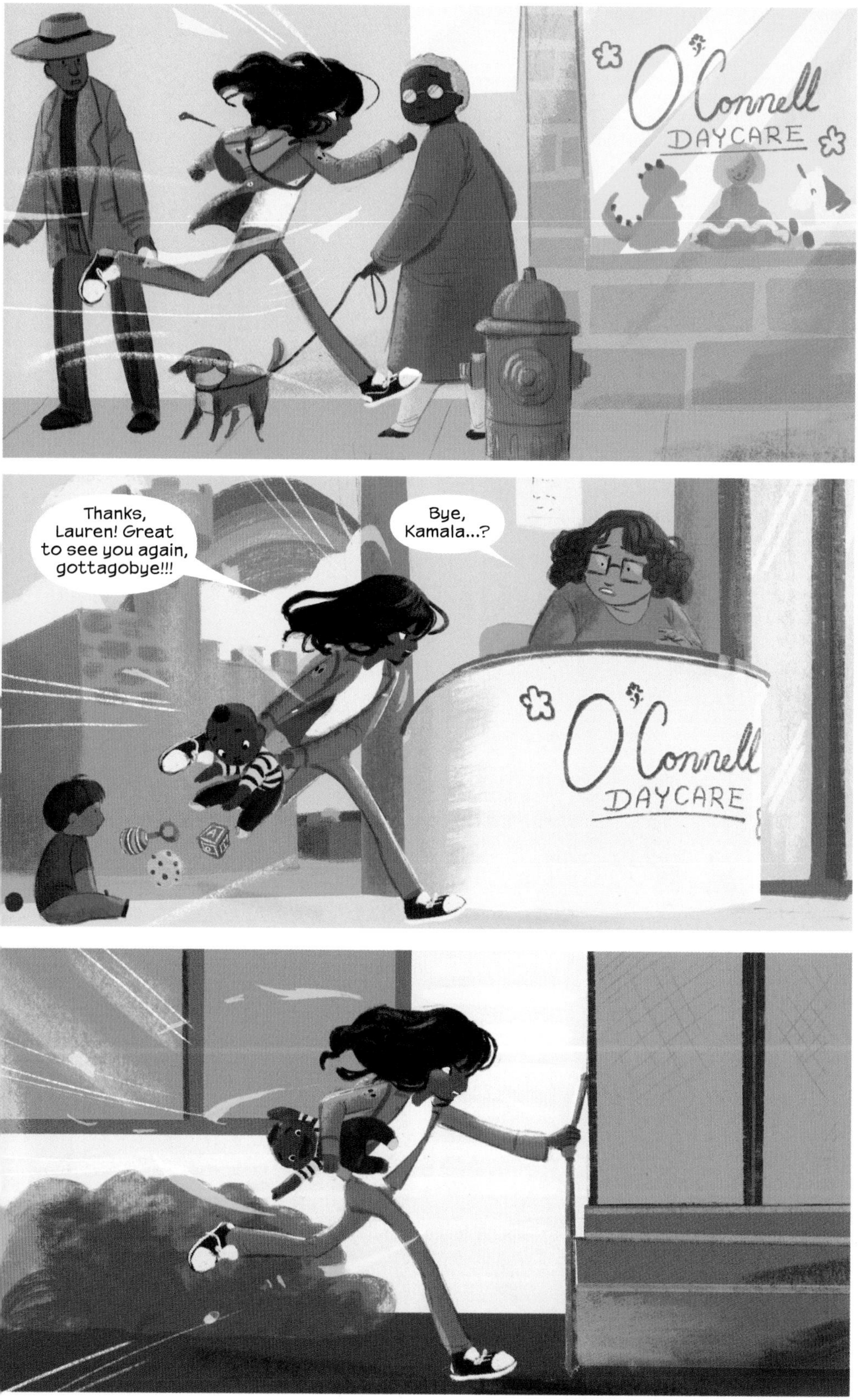
O'Connell
DAYCARE
Thanks, Lauren! Great to see you again, gottagobye!!!
Bye, Kamala...?
O'Connell
DAYCARE

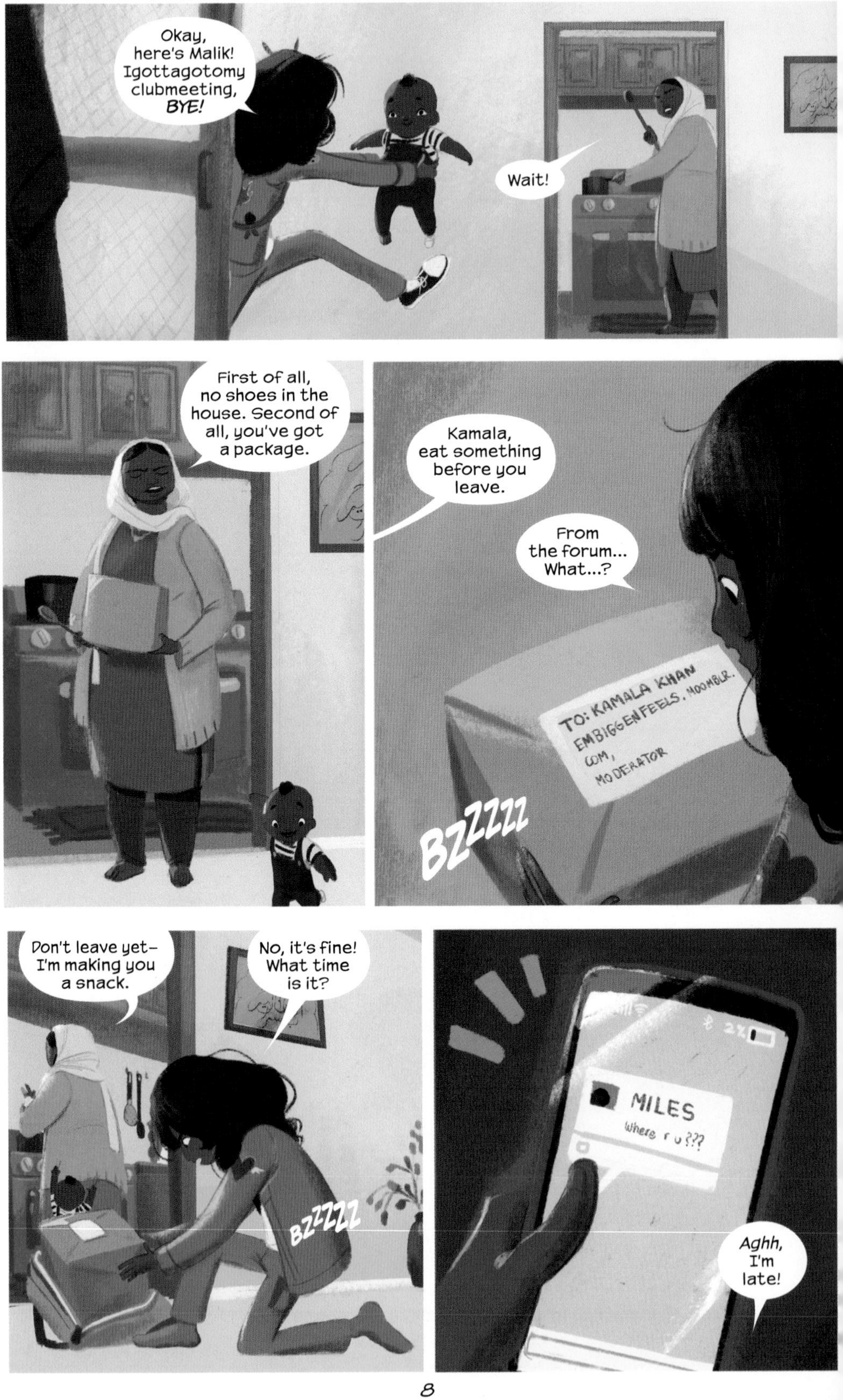
Okay, here's Malik! Igottagotomy clubmeeting, BYE!
Wait!
First of all, no shoes in the house. Second of all, you've got a package.
Kamala, eat something before you leave.
From the forum... What...?
TO: KAMALA KHAN EMBIGGENFEELS. NOOMBLR. COM, MODERATOR
BZZZZZ
Don't leave yet– I'm making you a snack.
No, it's fine! What time is it?
BZZZZZ
2%
MILES
Where r u???
Aghh, I'm late!

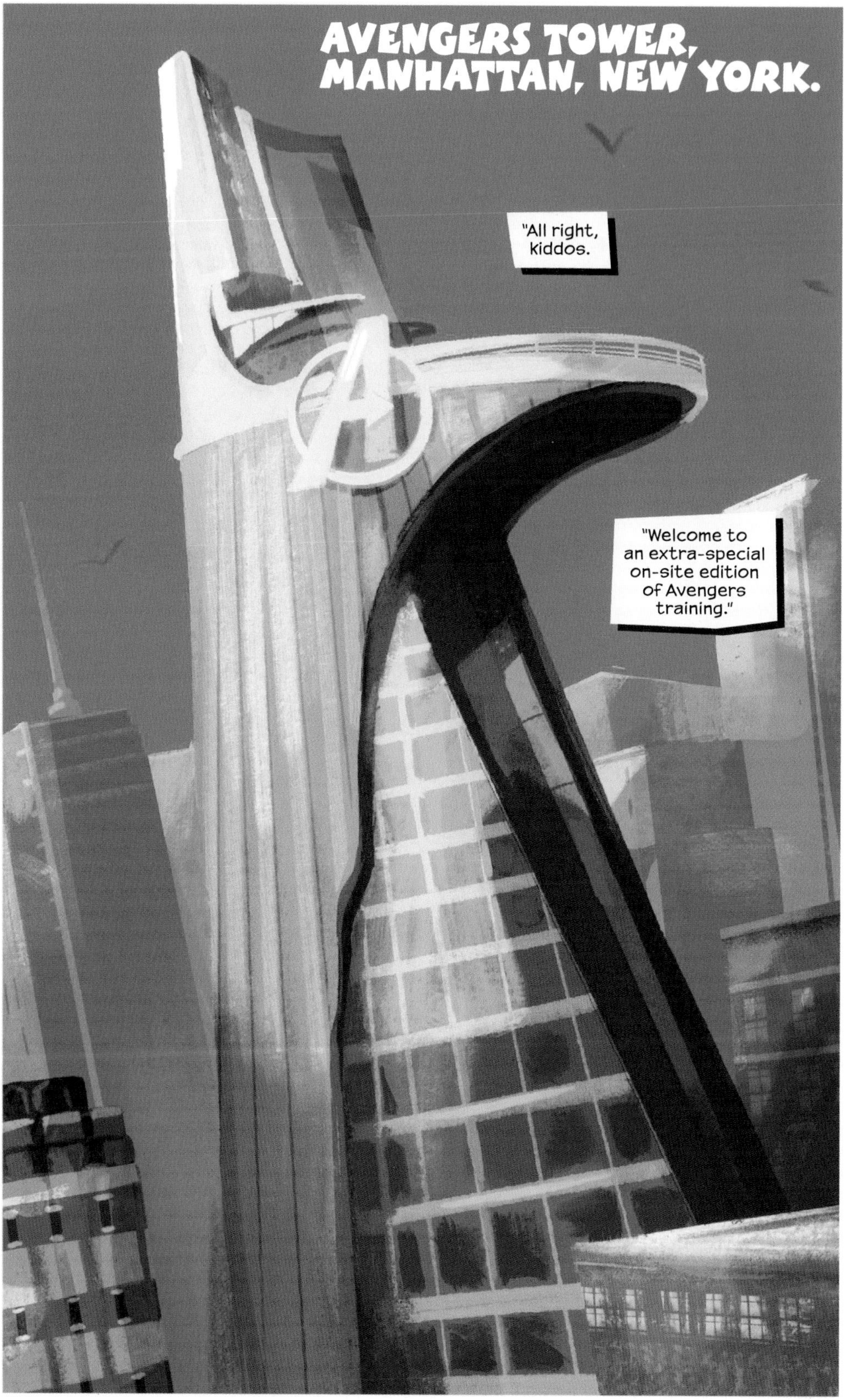
AVENGERS TOWER, MANHATTAN, NEW YORK.
"All right, kiddos.
"Welcome to an extra-special on-site edition of Avengers training."

Doreen Green, A.K.A. Squirrel Girl. Powers: Superhuman speed and agility, cool tail, can talk to squirrels
Miles Morales, A.K.A. Spider-Man. Powers: Web-slinging, invisibility, playlist making
Tony Stark, A.K.A. Iron Man Powers: Genius inventor, robot suits, being very rich
Tippy Toe, A.K.A. That Squirrel with the Bow. Powers: Stealing food from park picnics
As I have a policy of managing only three preteens at a time, maximum, you're all lucky to be here.
So, robots. Don't know what it is about robots, but the bad guys just love making you fight robots. So that's what we're gonna do.
Nice.
Without much ado: the robots.
NICE.
MS. MARVEL, SPIDER-MAN, SQUIRREL GIRL (A.K.A. TEAM AWESOME NEXT-GEN SUPER HEROES)
VS.
RANDO TRAINING BOTS (A.K.A. TEAM TOTALLY GOING DOWN)
CRASSHHH!!
Uh-oh. That's not supposed to happen.

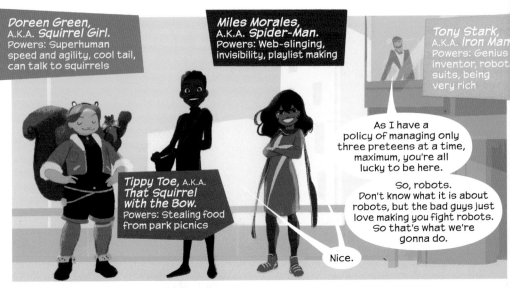

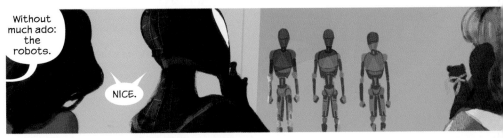

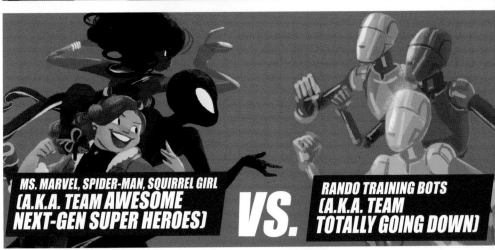

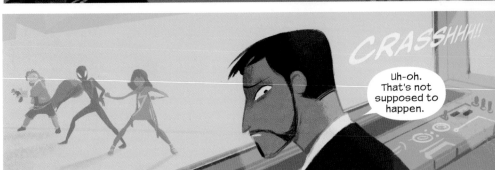

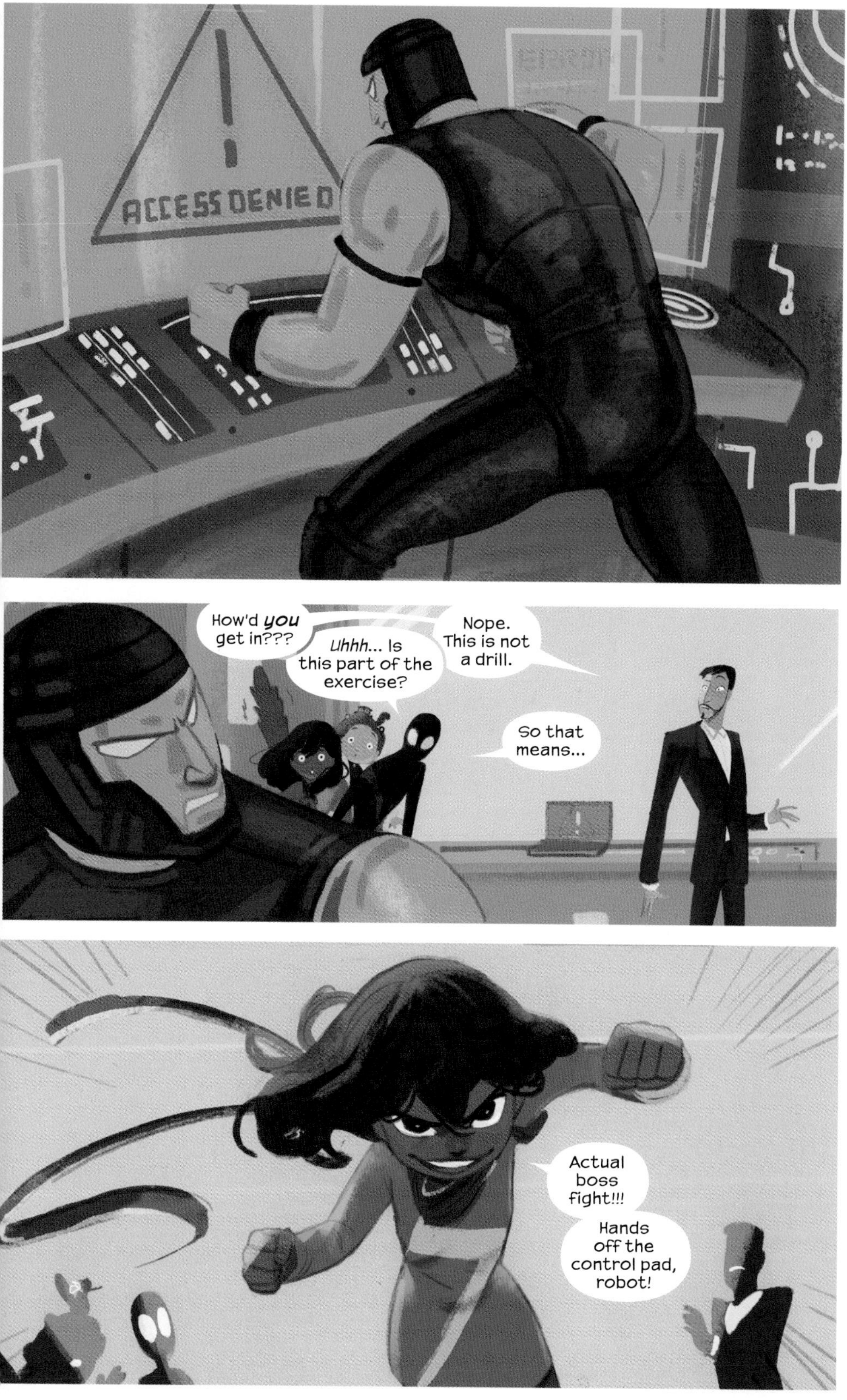
ACCESS DENIED
How'd *you* get in???
Uhhh... Is this part of the exercise?
Nope. This is not a drill.
So that means...
Actual boss fight!!!
Hands off the control pad, robot!

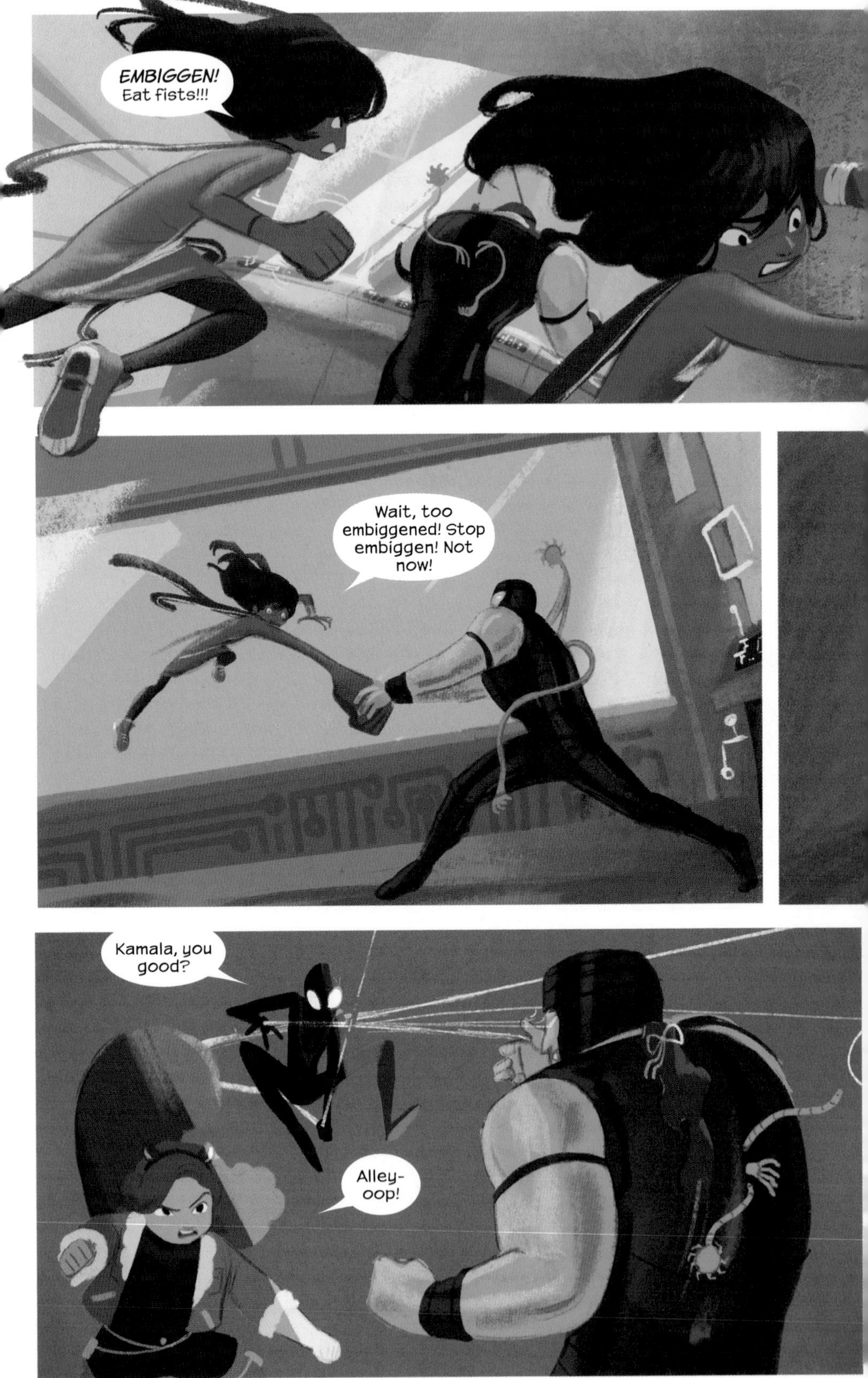
EMBIGGEN! Eat fists!!!
Wait, too embiggened! Stop embiggen! Not now!
Kamala, you good?
Alley-oop!

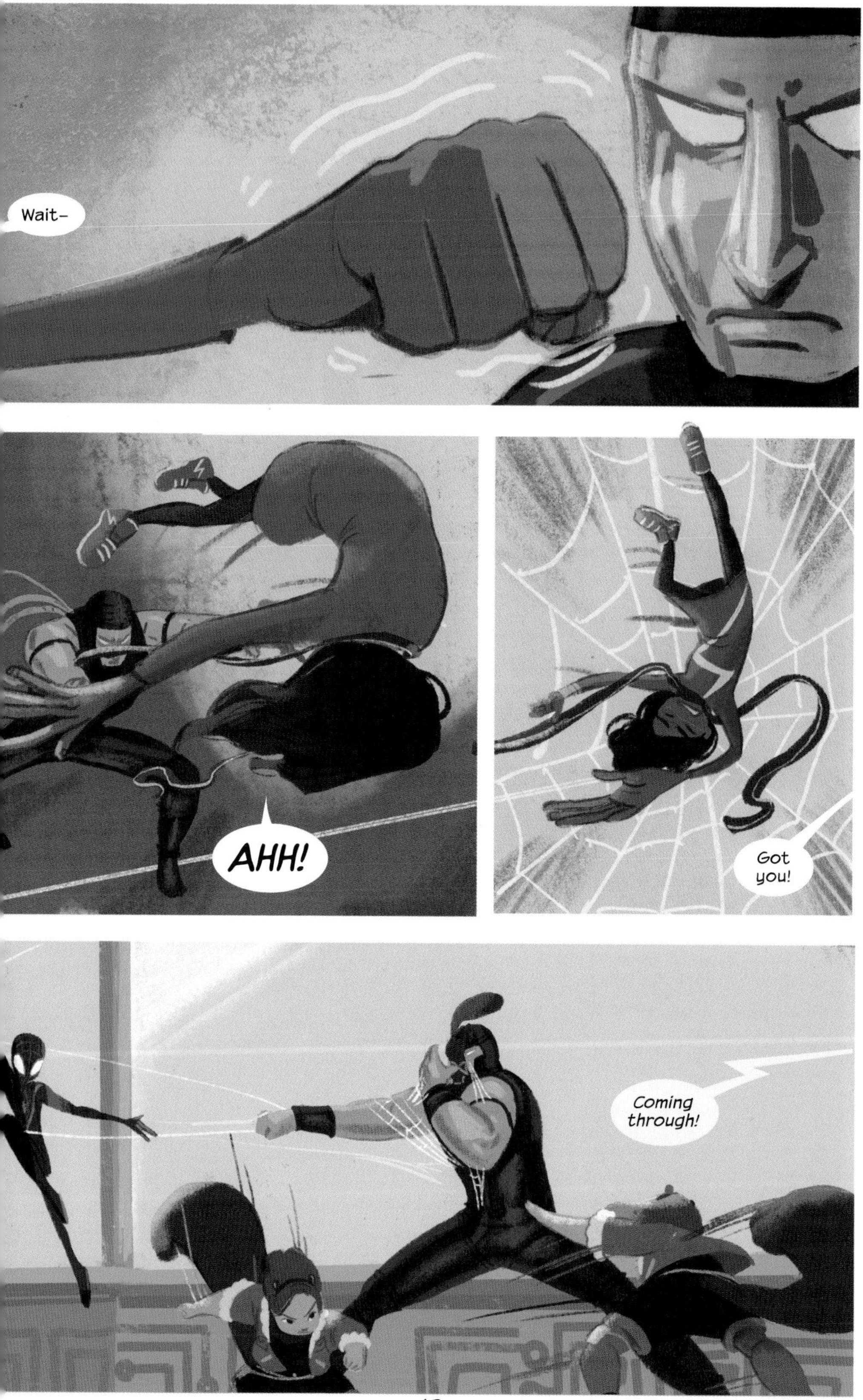
Wait–
AHH!
Got you!
Coming through!

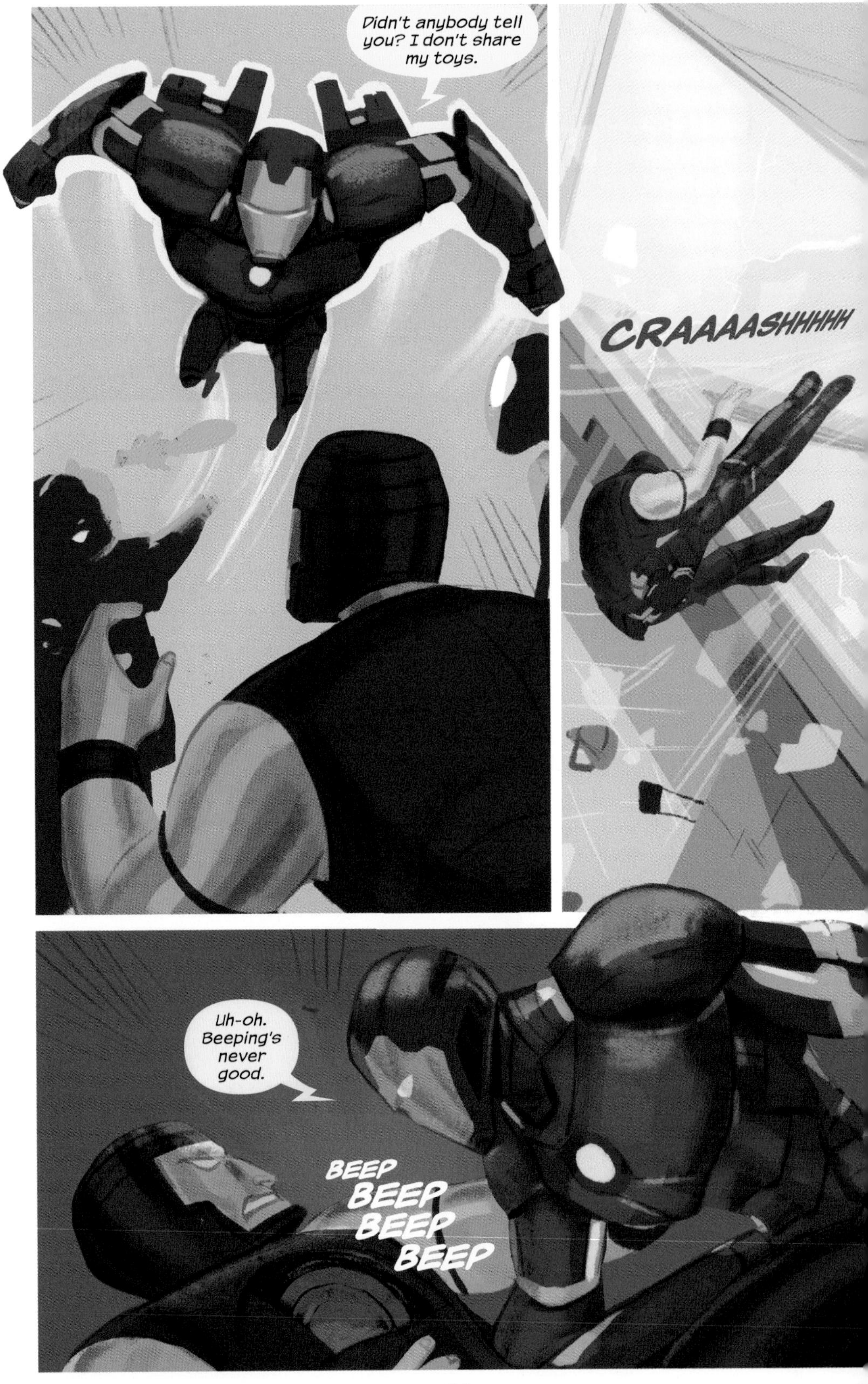
Didn't anybody tell you? I don't share my toys.
CRAAAASHHHHH
Uh-oh. Beeping's never good.
BEEP
BEEP
BEEP
BEEP

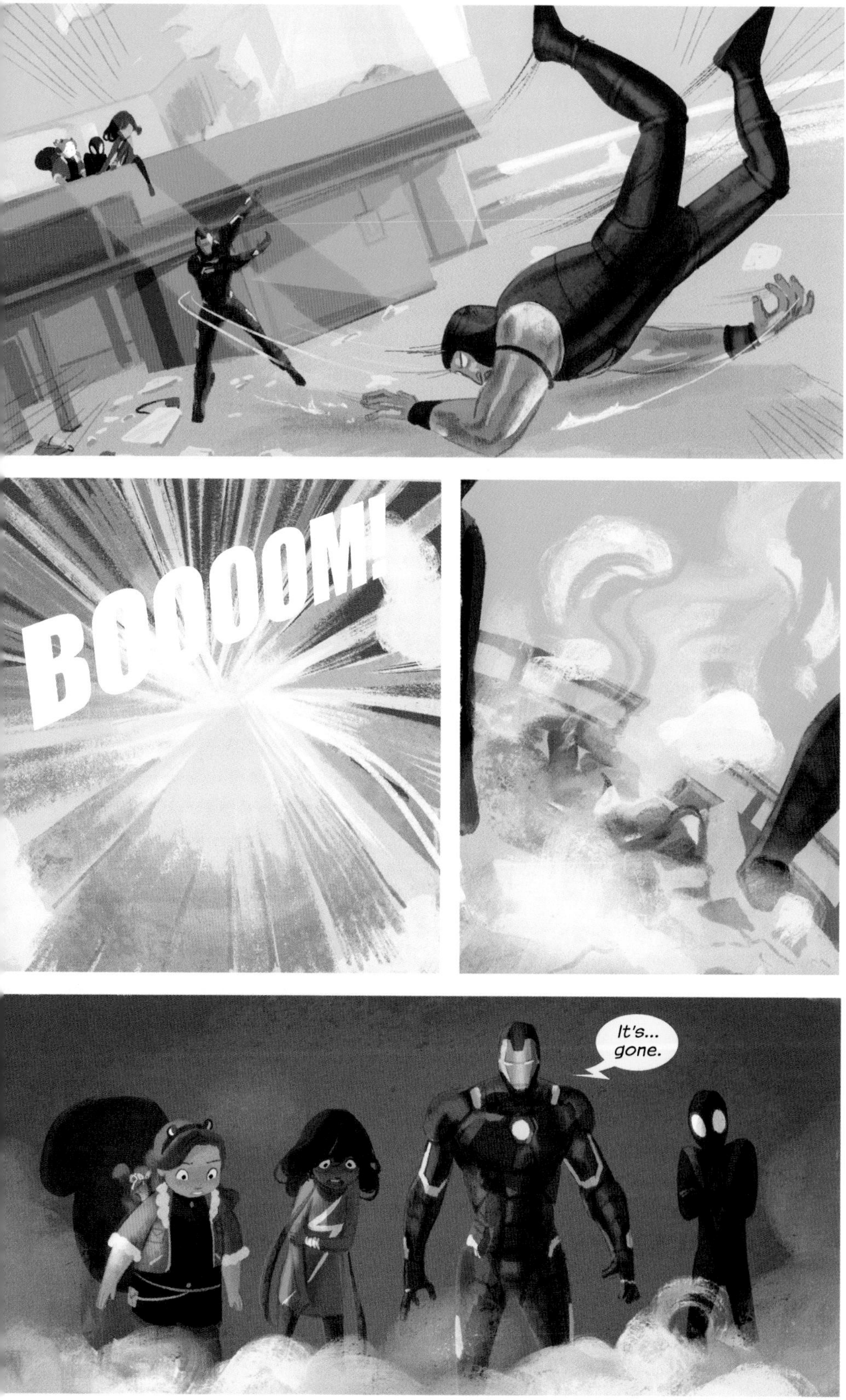
BOOOOM!
It's... gone.

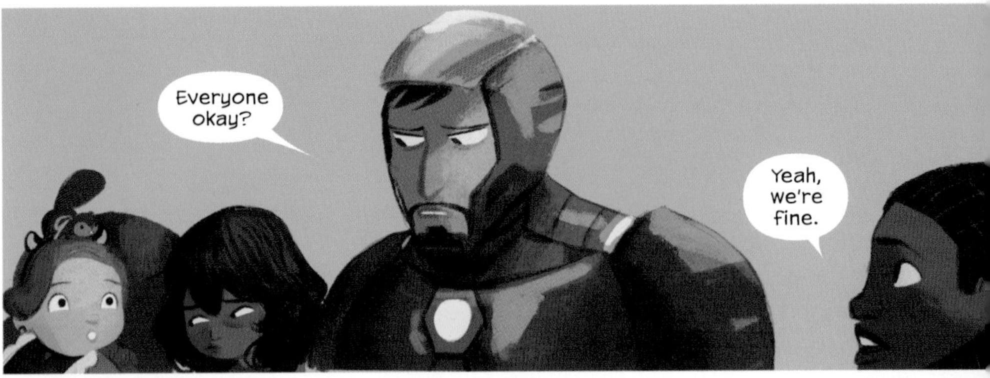
Everyone okay?
Yeah, we're fine.

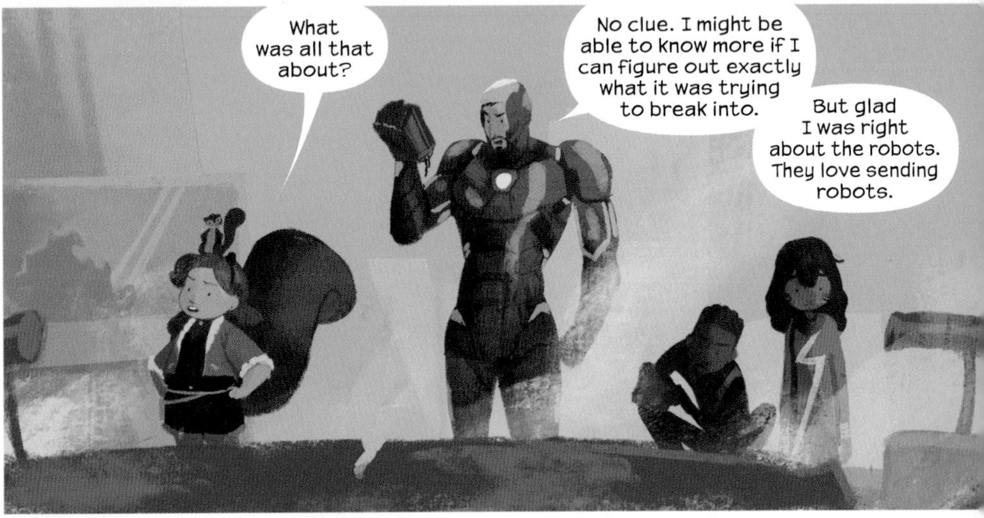
What was all that about?
No clue. I might be able to know more if I can figure out exactly what it was trying to break into.
But glad I was right about the robots. They love sending robots.

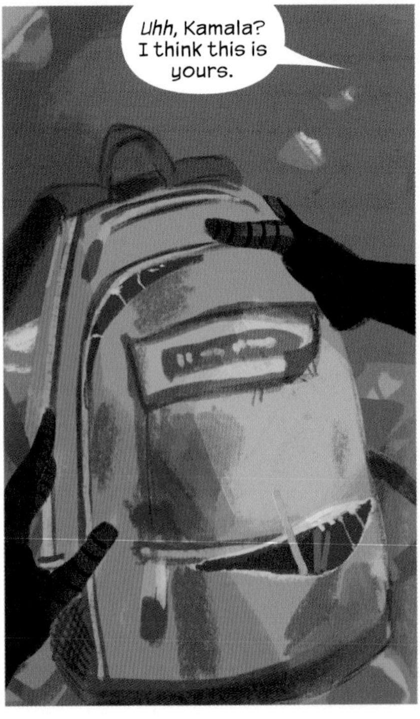
Uhh, Kamala? I think this is yours.

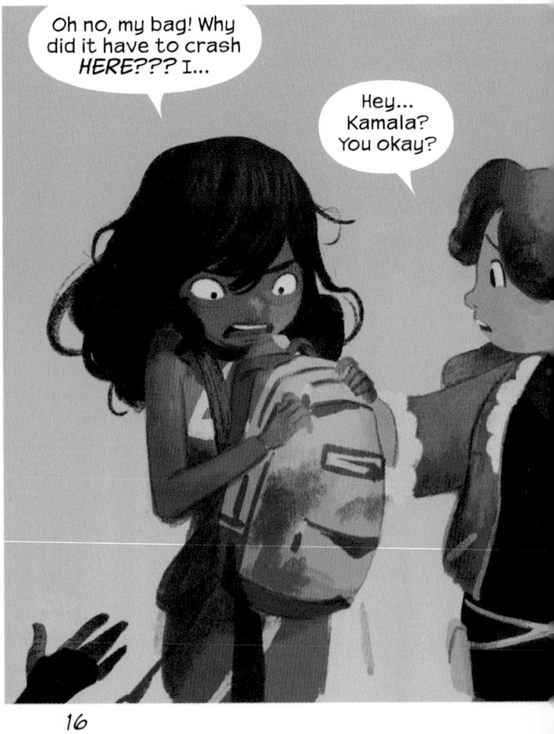
Oh no, my bag! Why did it have to crash *HERE???* I...
Hey... Kamala? You okay?

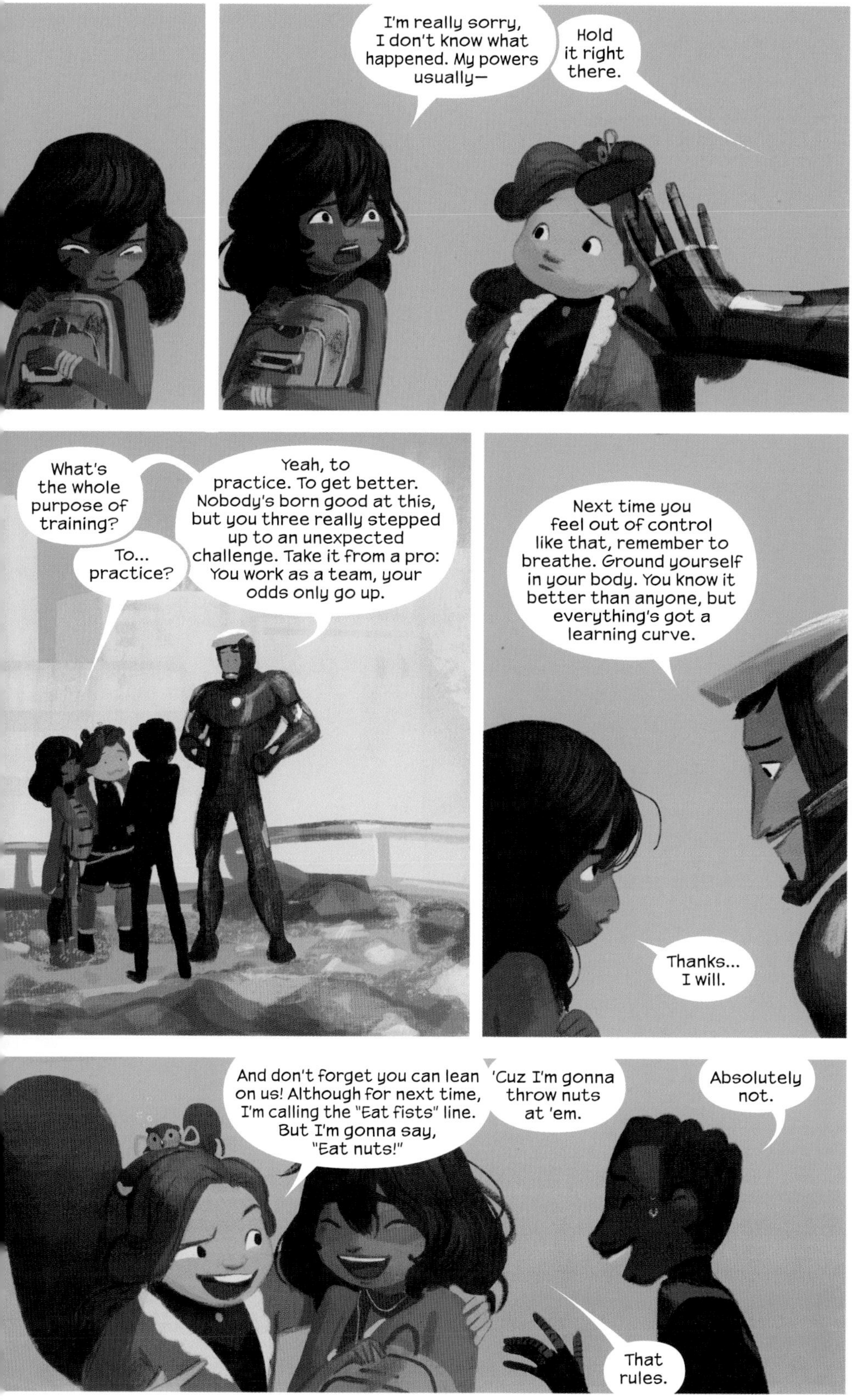
I'm really sorry, I don't know what happened. My powers usually—
Hold it right there.
What's the whole purpose of training?
To... practice?
Yeah, to practice. To get better. Nobody's born good at this, but you three really stepped up to an unexpected challenge. Take it from a pro: You work as a team, your odds only go up.
Next time you feel out of control like that, remember to breathe. Ground yourself in your body. You know it better than anyone, but everything's got a learning curve.
Thanks... I will.
And don't forget you can lean on us! Although for next time, I'm calling the "Eat fists" line. But I'm gonna say, "Eat nuts!"
'Cuz I'm gonna throw nuts at 'em.
Absolutely not.
That rules.

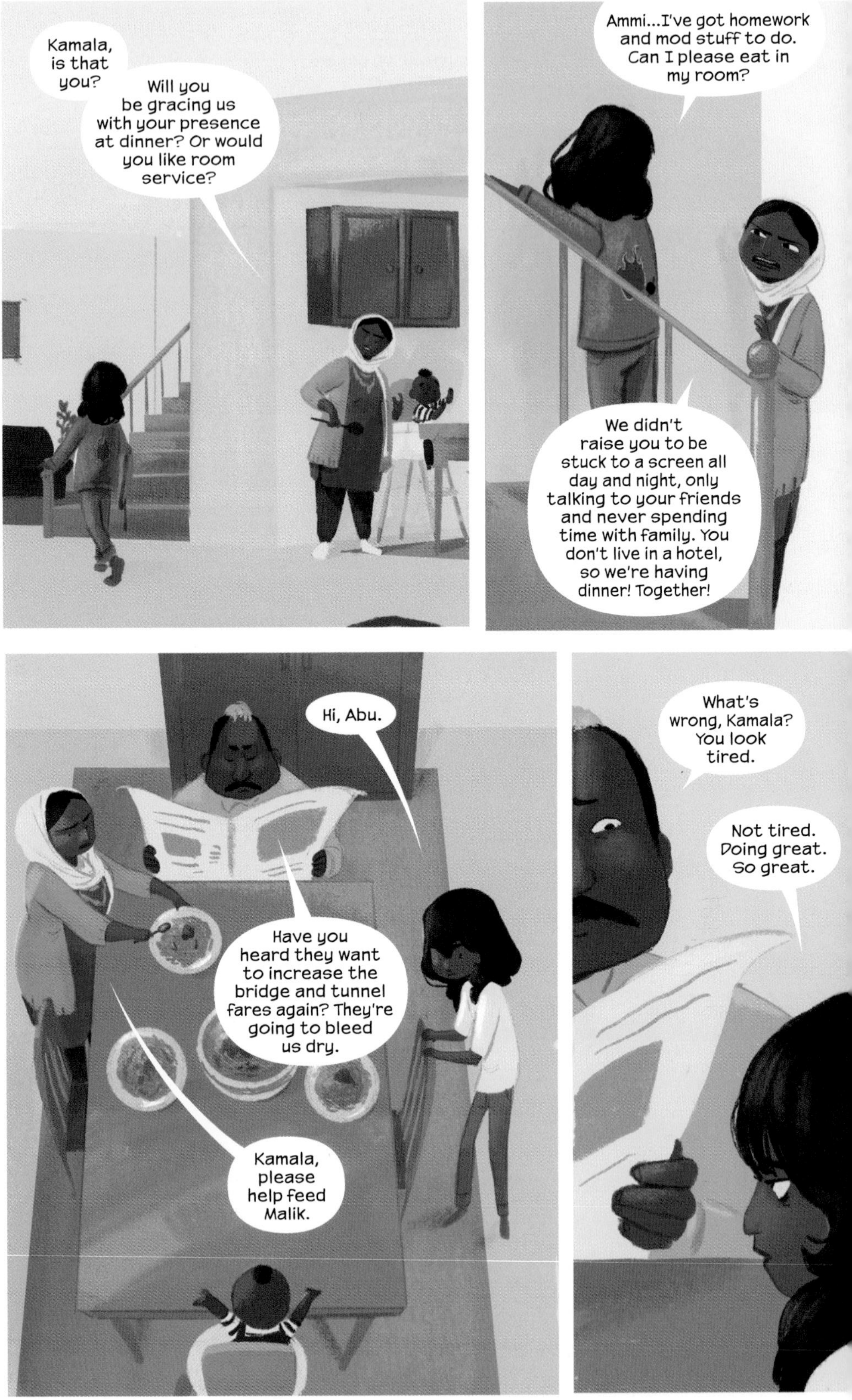
Kamala, is that you?
Will you be gracing us with your presence at dinner? Or would you like room service?
Ammi...I've got homework and mod stuff to do. Can I please eat in my room?
We didn't raise you to be stuck to a screen all day and night, only talking to your friends and never spending time with family. You don't live in a hotel, so we're having dinner! Together!
Hi, Abu.
Have you heard they want to increase the bridge and tunnel fares again? They're going to bleed us dry.
Kamala, please help feed Malik.
What's wrong, Kamala? You look tired.
Not tired. Doing great. So great.

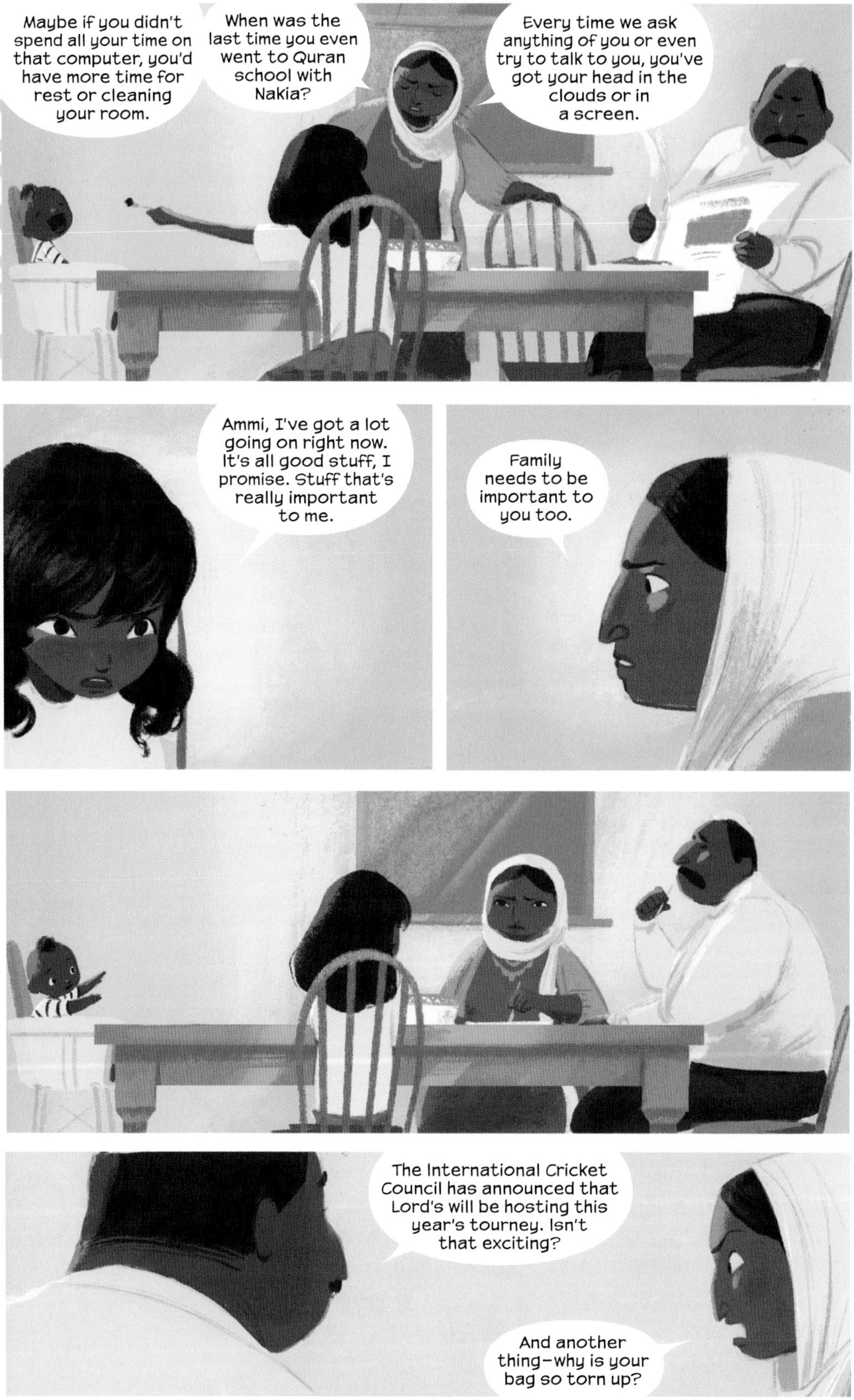
Maybe if you didn't spend all your time on that computer, you'd have more time for rest or cleaning your room.
When was the last time you even went to Quran school with Nakia?
Every time we ask anything of you or even try to talk to you, you've got your head in the clouds or in a screen.
Ammi, I've got a lot going on right now. It's all good stuff, I promise. Stuff that's really important to me.
Family needs to be important to you too.
The International Cricket Council has announced that Lord's will be hosting this year's tourney. Isn't that exciting?
And another thing—why is your bag so torn up?

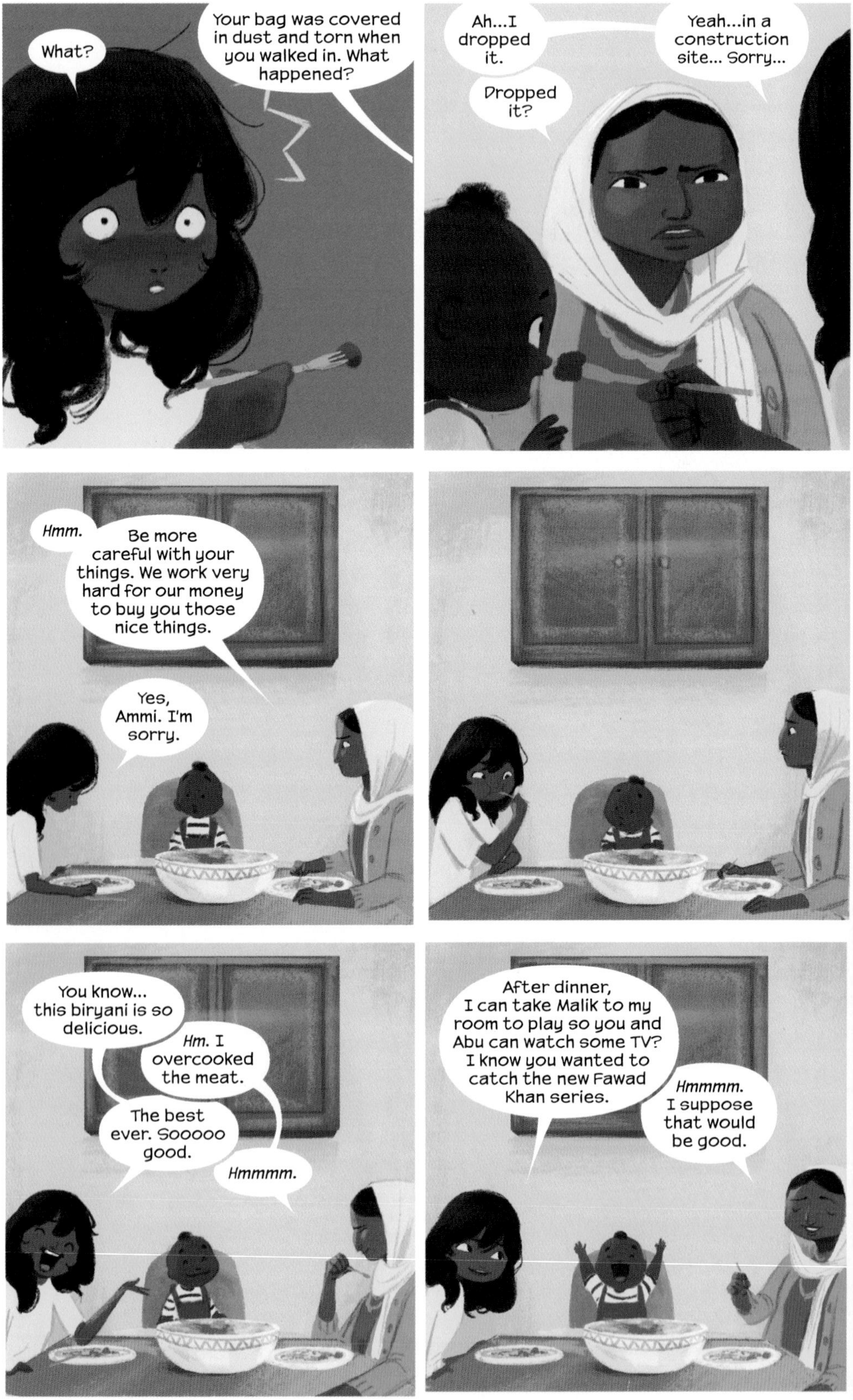
What?
Your bag was covered in dust and torn when you walked in. What happened?
Ah...I dropped it.
Dropped it?
Yeah...in a construction site... Sorry...
Hmm.
Be more careful with your things. We work very hard for our money to buy you those nice things.
Yes, Ammi. I'm sorry.
You know... this biryani is so delicious.
Hm. I overcooked the meat.
The best ever. Sooooo good.
Hmmmm.
After dinner, I can take Malik to my room to play so you and Abu can watch some TV? I know you wanted to catch the new Fawad Khan series.
Hmmmm. I suppose that would be good.

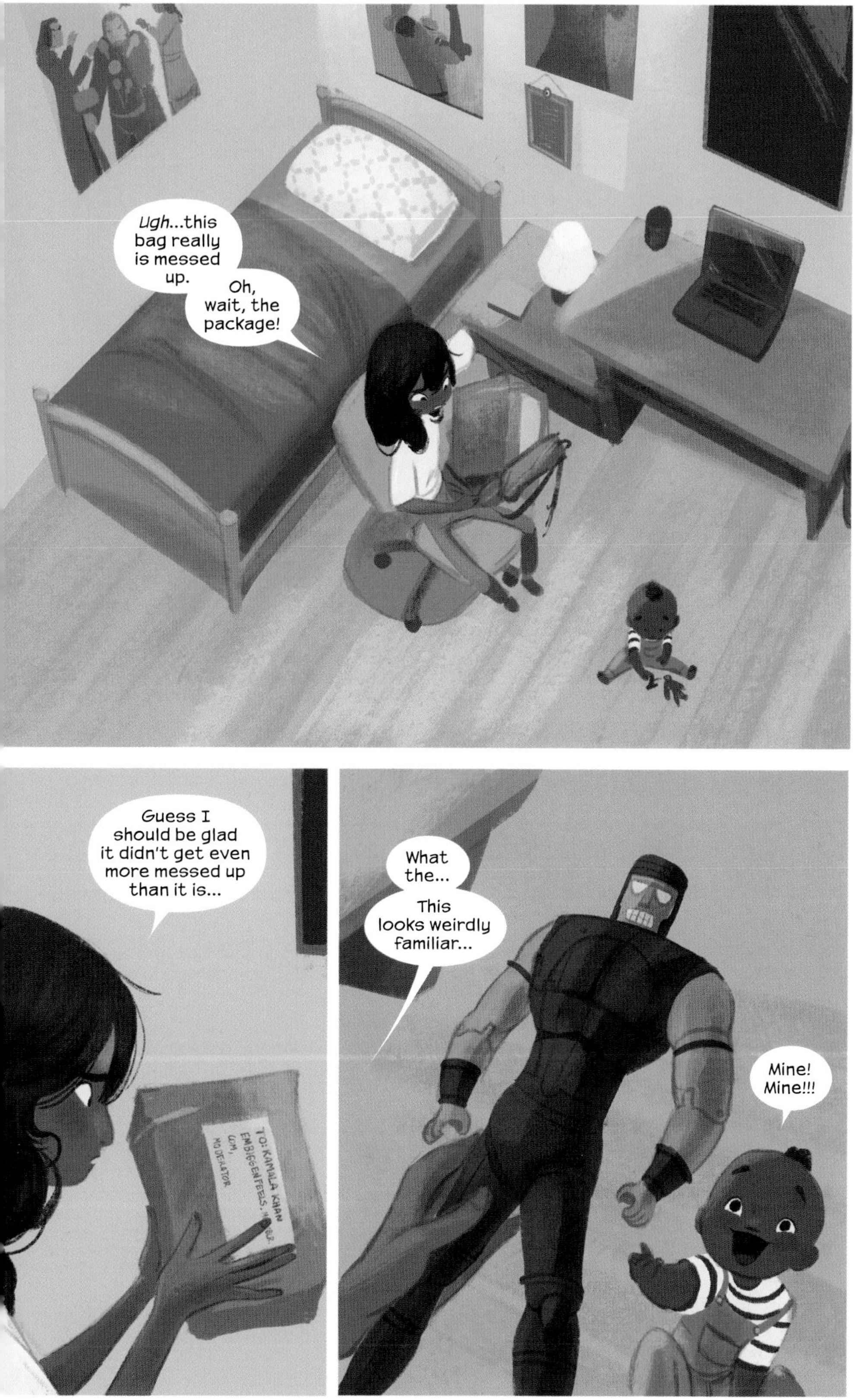
Ugh...this bag really is messed up.
Oh, wait, the package!
Guess I should be glad it didn't get even more messed up than it is...
What the...
This looks weirdly familiar...
Mine! Mine!!!

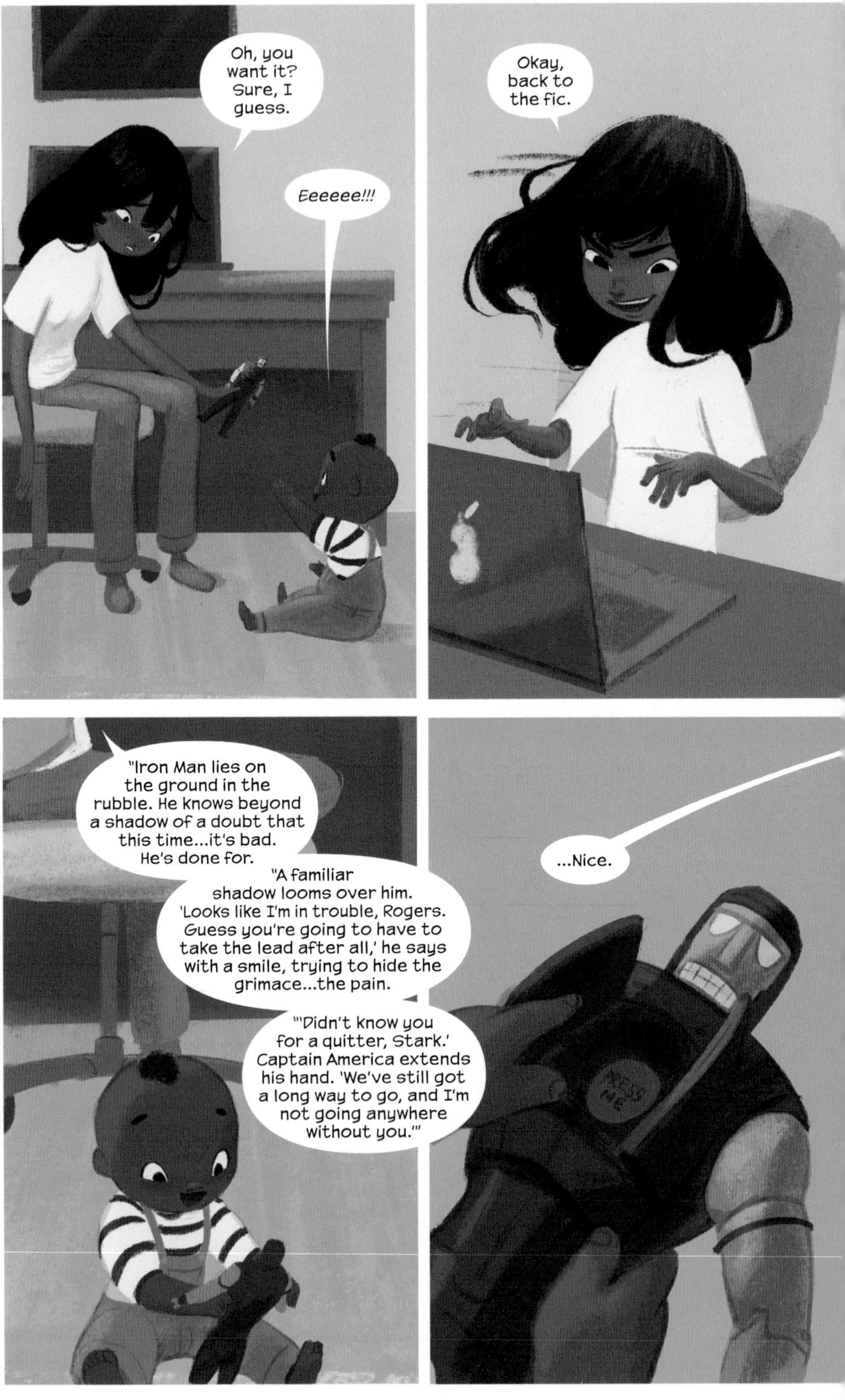
Oh, you want it? Sure, I guess.
Eeeeee!!!
Okay, back to the fic.
"Iron Man lies on the ground in the rubble. He knows beyond a shadow of a doubt that this time...it's bad. He's done for.
"A familiar shadow looms over him. 'Looks like I'm in trouble, Rogers. Guess you're going to have to take the lead after all,' he says with a smile, trying to hide the grimace...the pain.
"'Didn't know you for a quitter, Stark.' Captain America extends his hand. 'We've still got a long way to go, and I'm not going anywhere without you.'"
...Nice.
PRESS ME

CHAPTER TWO

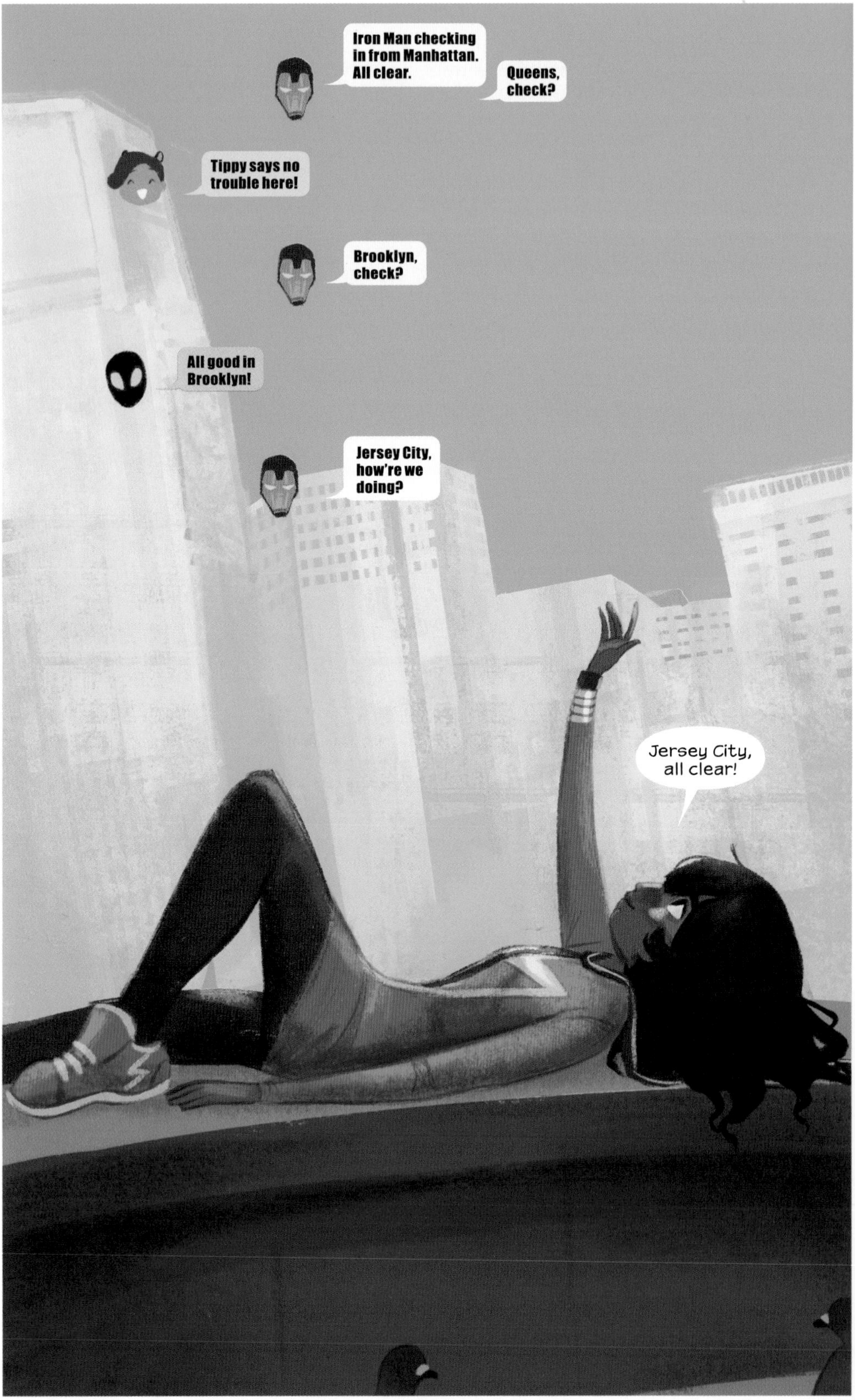

Iron Man checking in from Manhattan. All clear.
Queens, check?
Tippy says no trouble here!
Brooklyn, check?
All good in Brooklyn!
Jersey City, how're we doing?
Jersey City, all clear!

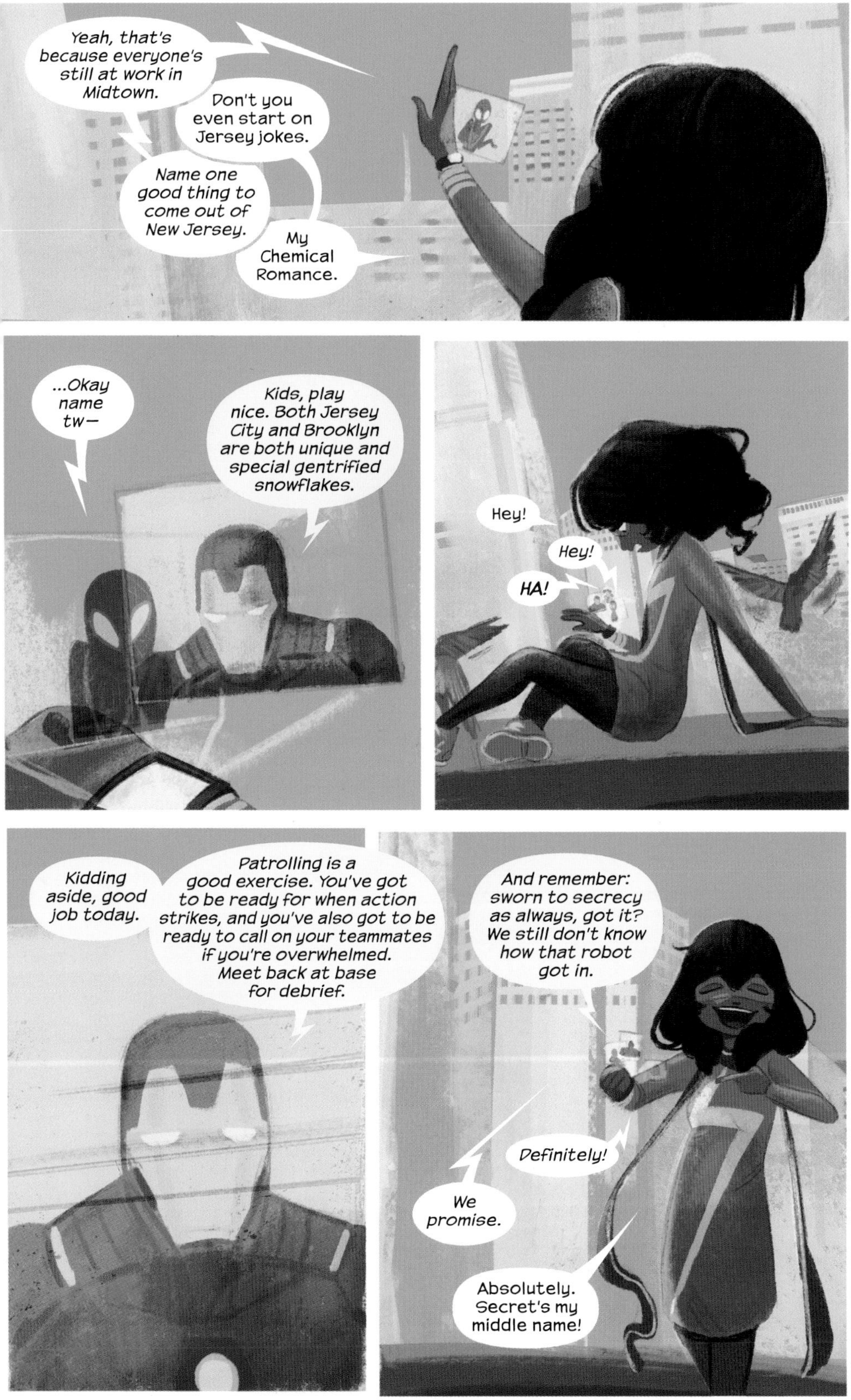
Yeah, that's because everyone's still at work in Midtown.
Don't you even start on Jersey jokes.
Name one good thing to come out of New Jersey.
My Chemical Romance.
...Okay name tw—
Kids, play nice. Both Jersey City and Brooklyn are both unique and special gentrified snowflakes.
Hey!
Hey!
HA!
Kidding aside, good job today.
Patrolling is a good exercise. You've got to be ready for when action strikes, and you've also got to be ready to call on your teammates if you're overwhelmed. Meet back at base for debrief.
And remember: sworn to secrecy as always, got it? We still don't know how that robot got in.
Definitely!
We promise.
Absolutely. Secret's my middle name!

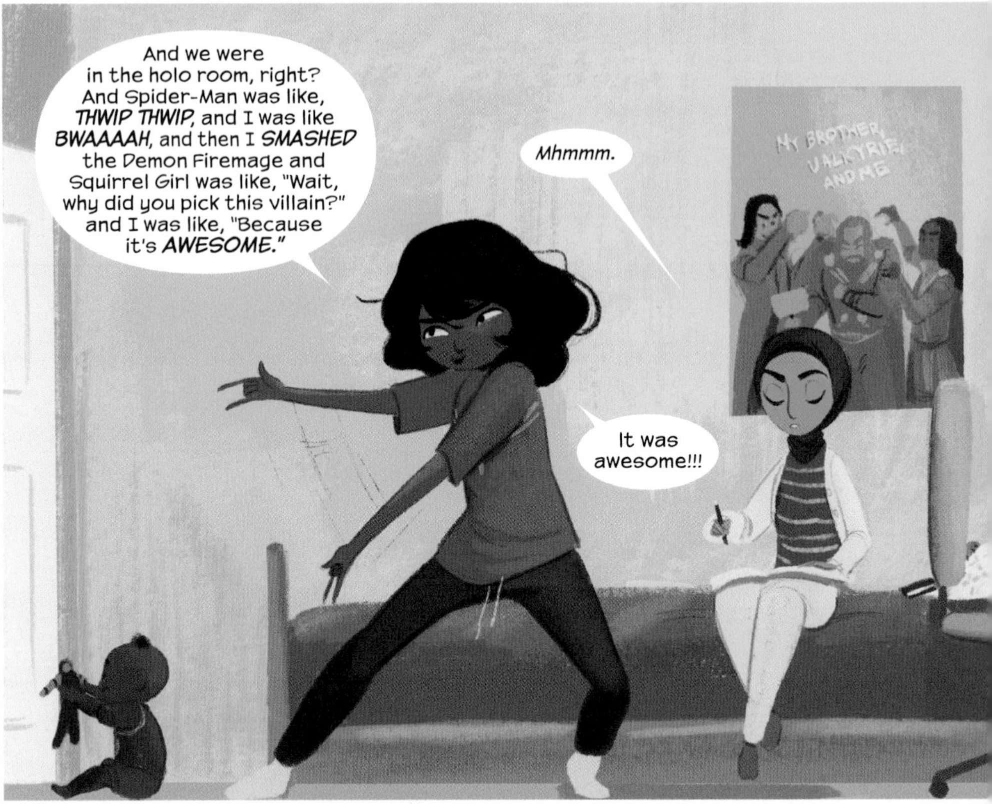
And we were in the holo room, right? And Spider-Man was like, THWIP THWIP, and I was like BWAAAAH, and then I SMASHED the Demon Firemage and Squirrel Girl was like, "Wait, why did you pick this villain?" and I was like, "Because it's AWESOME."
Mhmmm.
MY BROTHER, VALKYRIE, AND ME
It was awesome!!!

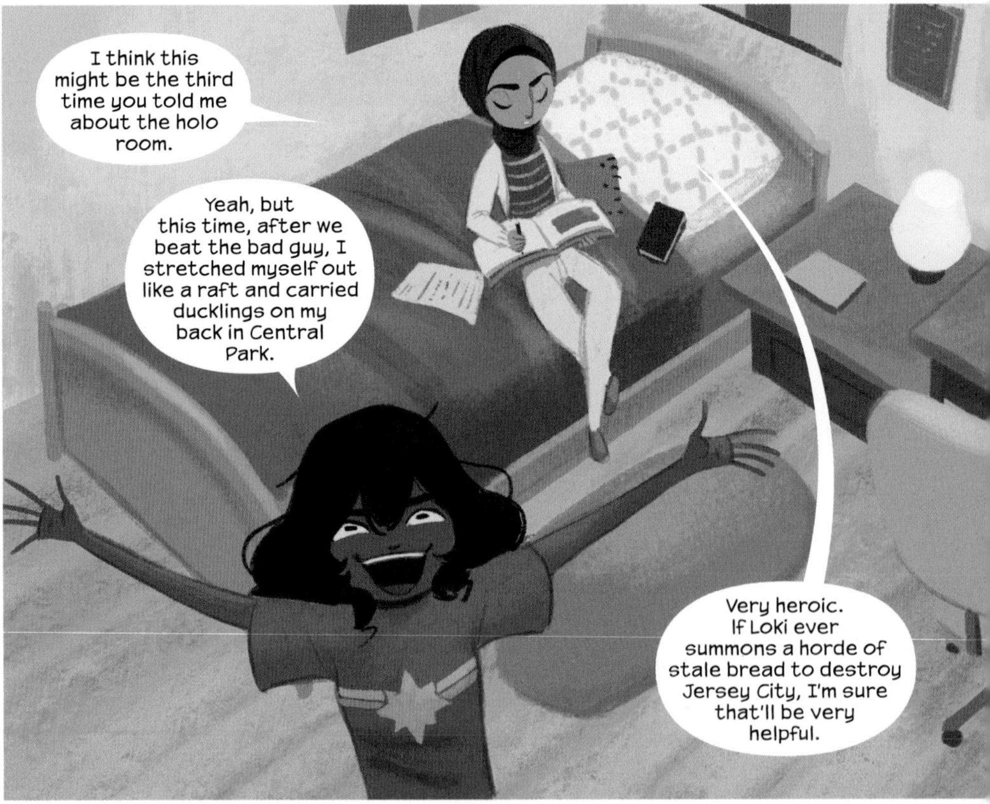
I think this might be the third time you told me about the holo room.
Yeah, but this time, after we beat the bad guy, I stretched myself out like a raft and carried ducklings on my back in Central Park.
Very heroic. If Loki ever summons a horde of stale bread to destroy Jersey City, I'm sure that'll be very helpful.

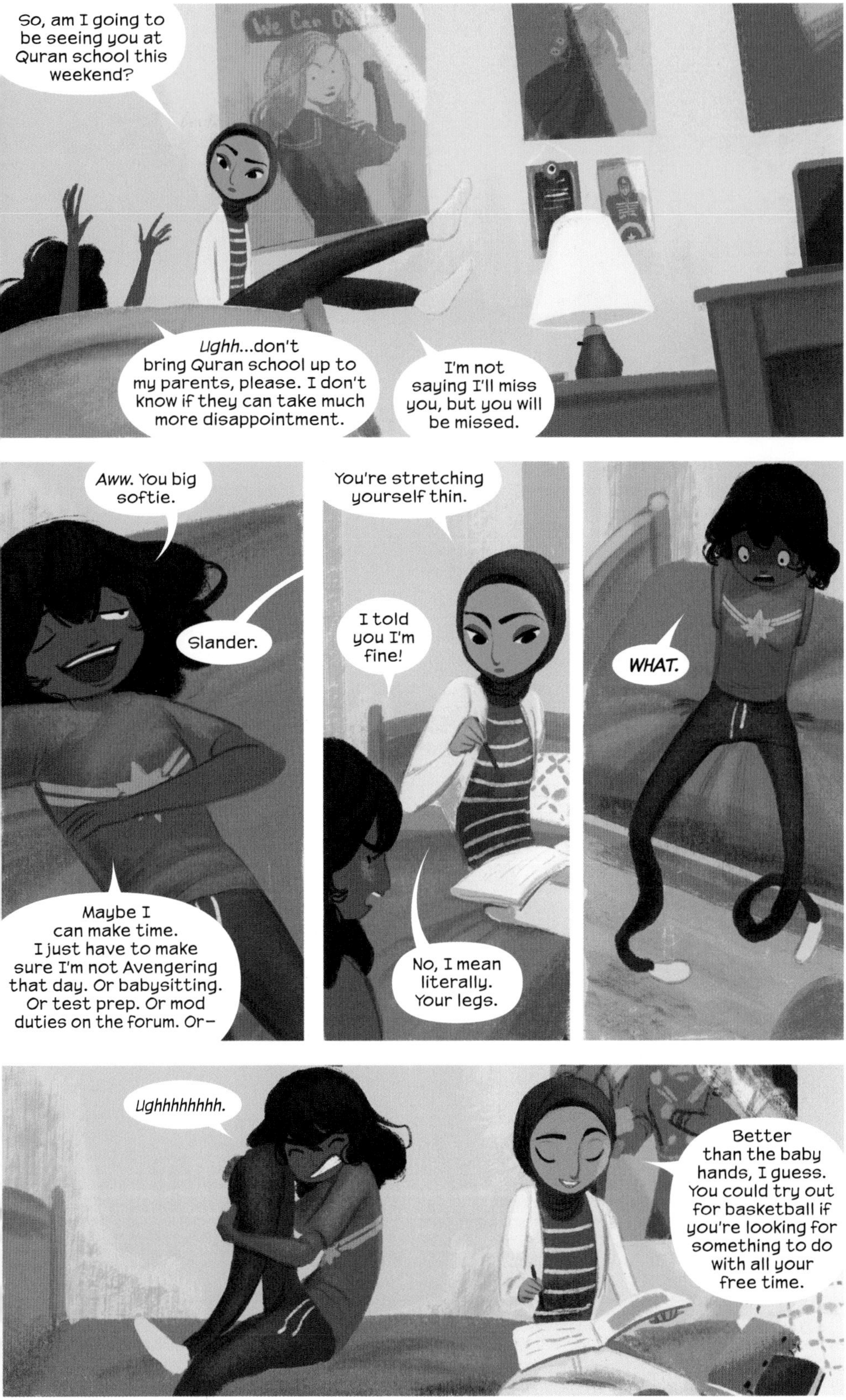
So, am I going to be seeing you at Quran school this weekend?
Ughh...don't bring Quran school up to my parents, please. I don't know if they can take much more disappointment.
I'm not saying I'll miss you, but you will be missed.
Aww. You big softie.
Slander.
Maybe I can make time. I just have to make sure I'm not Avengering that day. Or babysitting. Or test prep. Or mod duties on the forum. Or–
You're stretching yourself thin.
I told you I'm fine!
No, I mean literally. Your legs.
WHAT.
Ughhhhhhhh.
Better than the baby hands, I guess. You could try out for basketball if you're looking for something to do with all your free time.

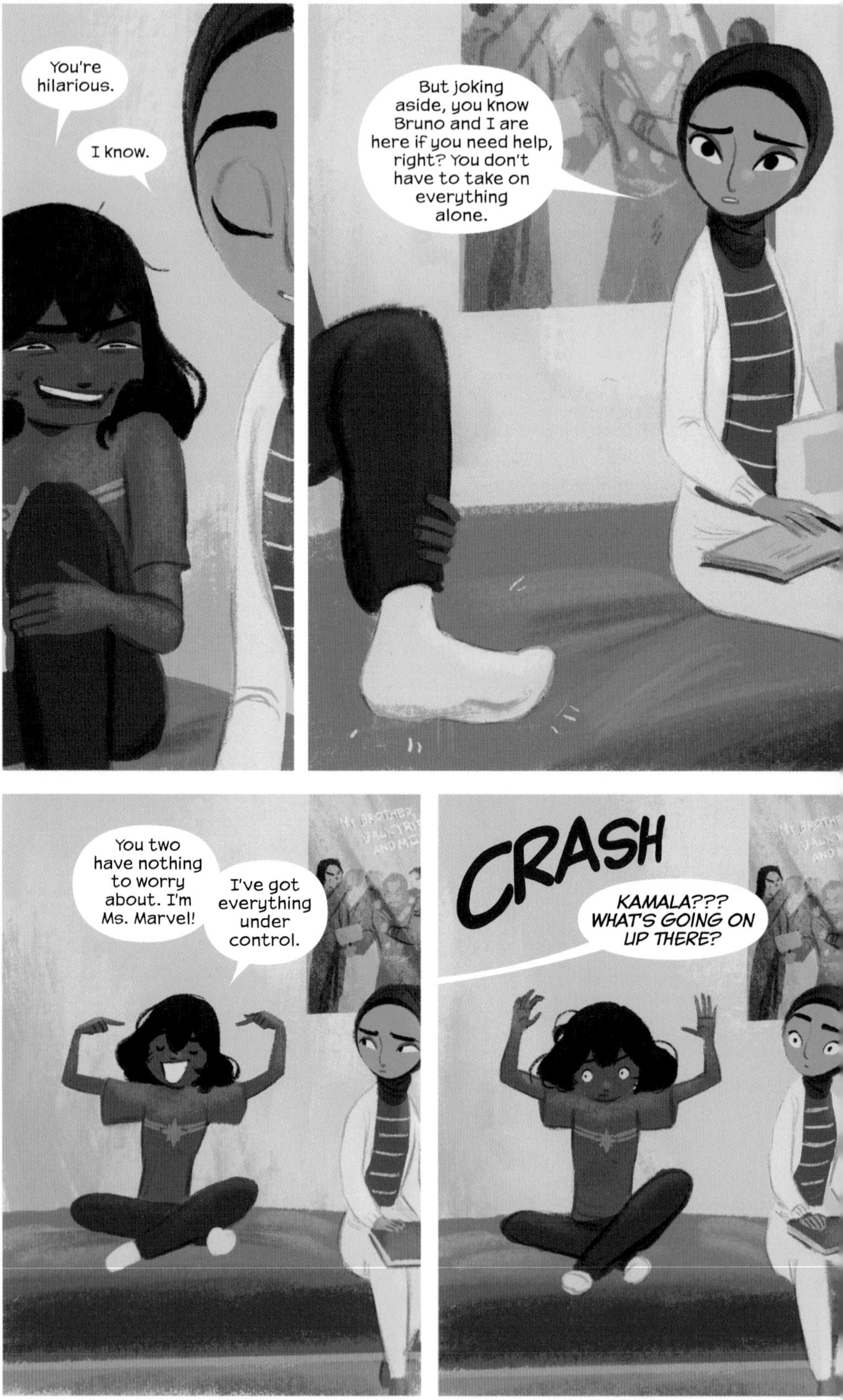
You're hilarious.
I know.
But joking aside, you know Bruno and I are here if you need help, right? You don't have to take on everything alone.
You two have nothing to worry about. I'm Ms. Marvel!
I've got everything under control.
CRASH
KAMALA??? WHAT'S GOING ON UP THERE?

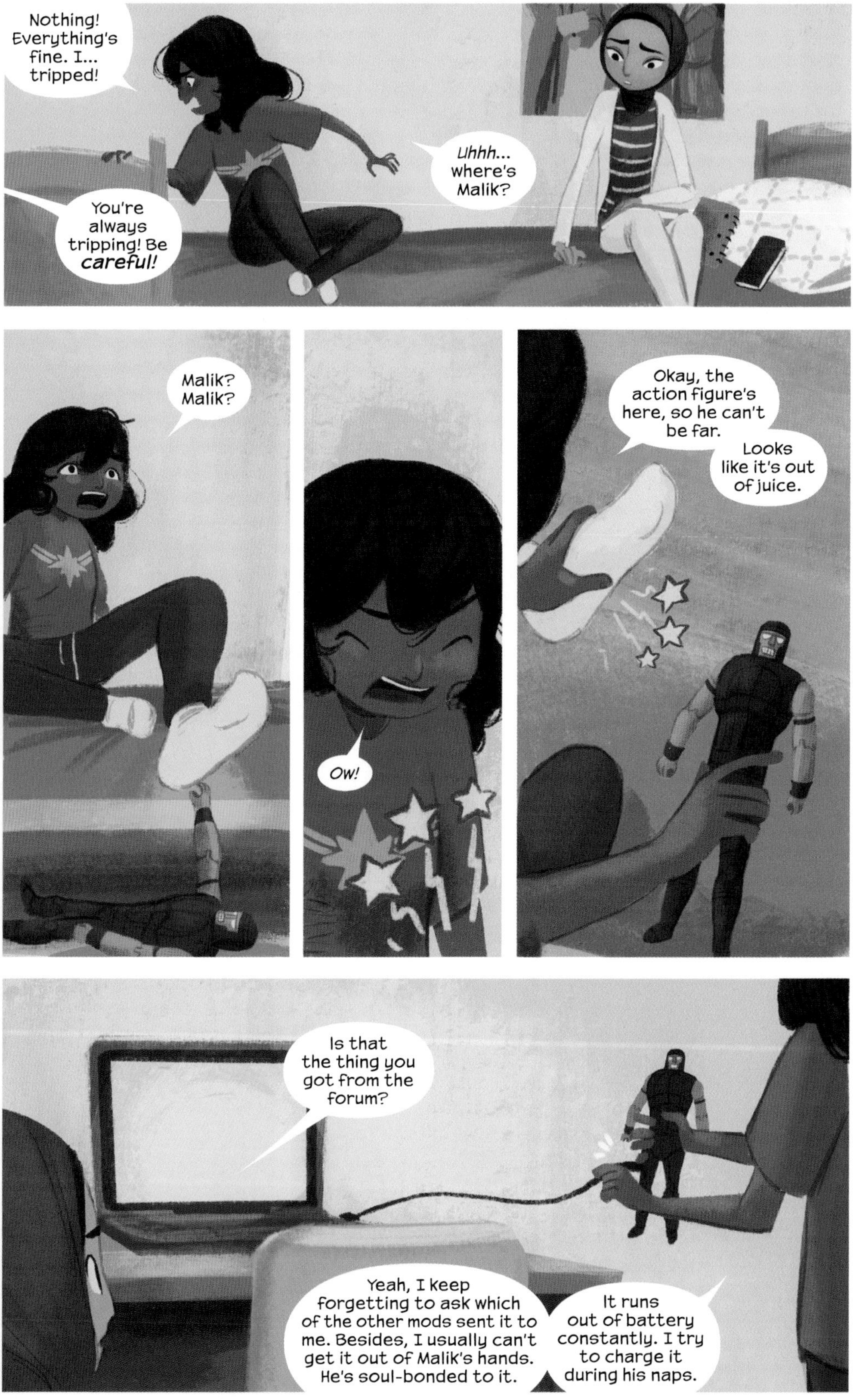
Nothing! Everything's fine. I... tripped!
You're always tripping! Be *careful!*
Uhhh... where's Malik?
Malik? Malik?
Ow!
Okay, the action figure's here, so he can't be far.
Looks like it's out of juice.
Is that the thing you got from the forum?
Yeah, I keep forgetting to ask which of the other mods sent it to me. Besides, I usually can't get it out of Malik's hands. He's soul-bonded to it.
It runs out of battery constantly. I try to charge it during his naps.

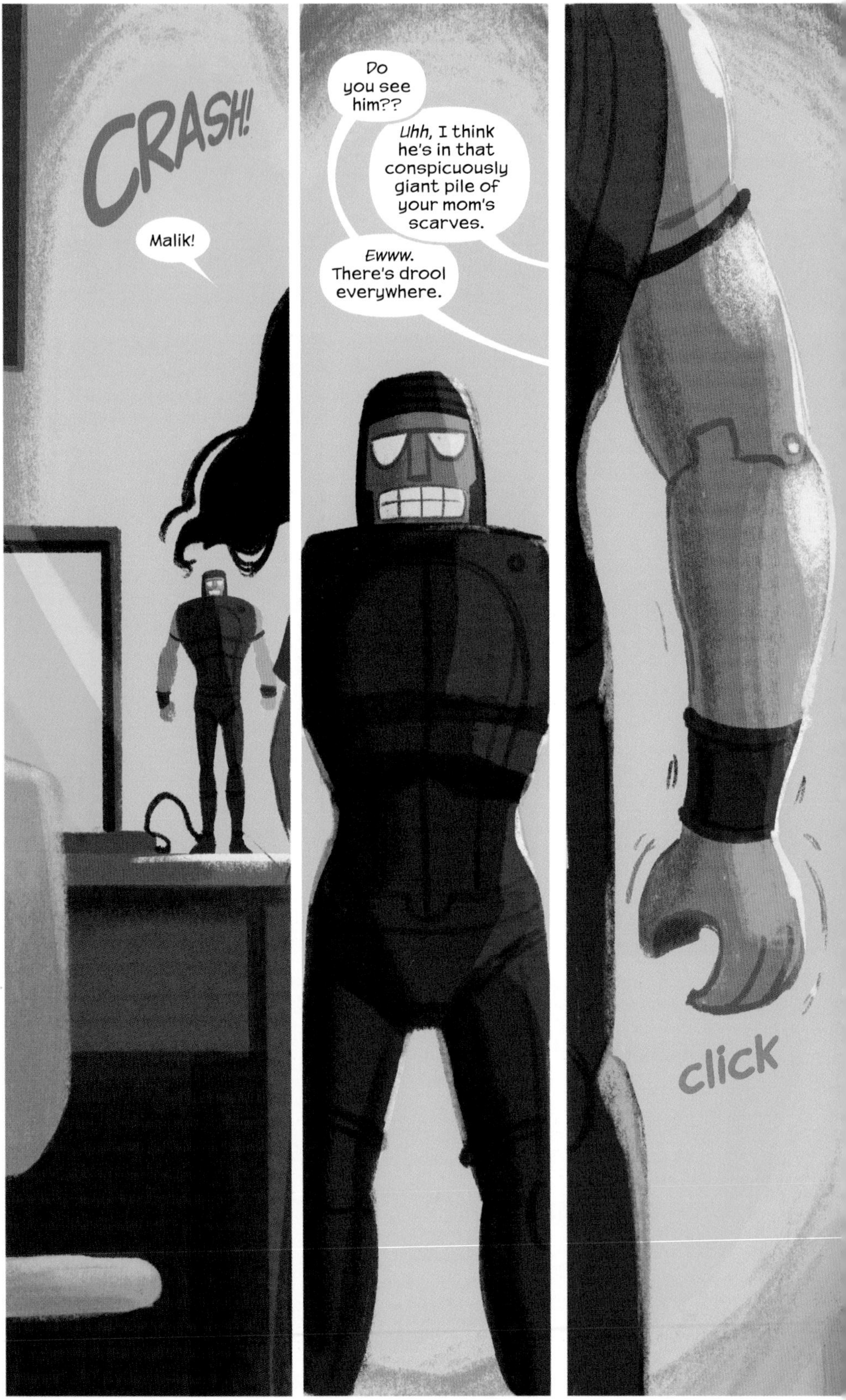
CRASH!
Malik!
Do you see him??
Uhh, I think he's in that conspicuously giant pile of your mom's scarves.
Ewww. There's drool everywhere.
click

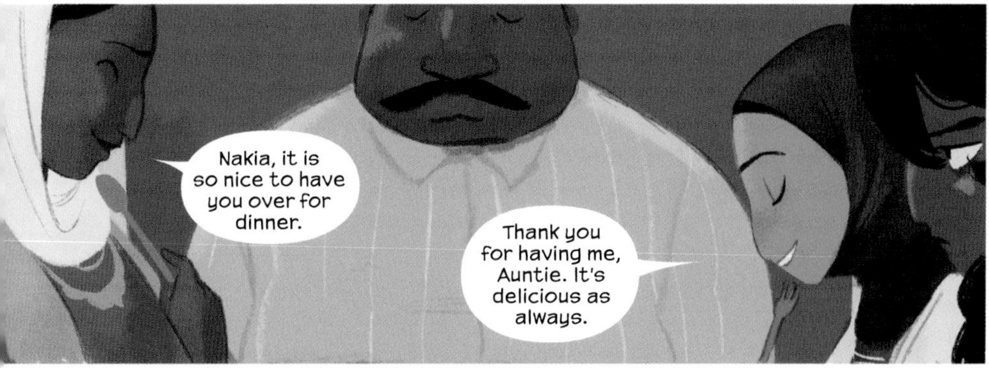
Nakia, it is so nice to have you over for dinner.
Thank you for having me, Auntie. It's delicious as always.

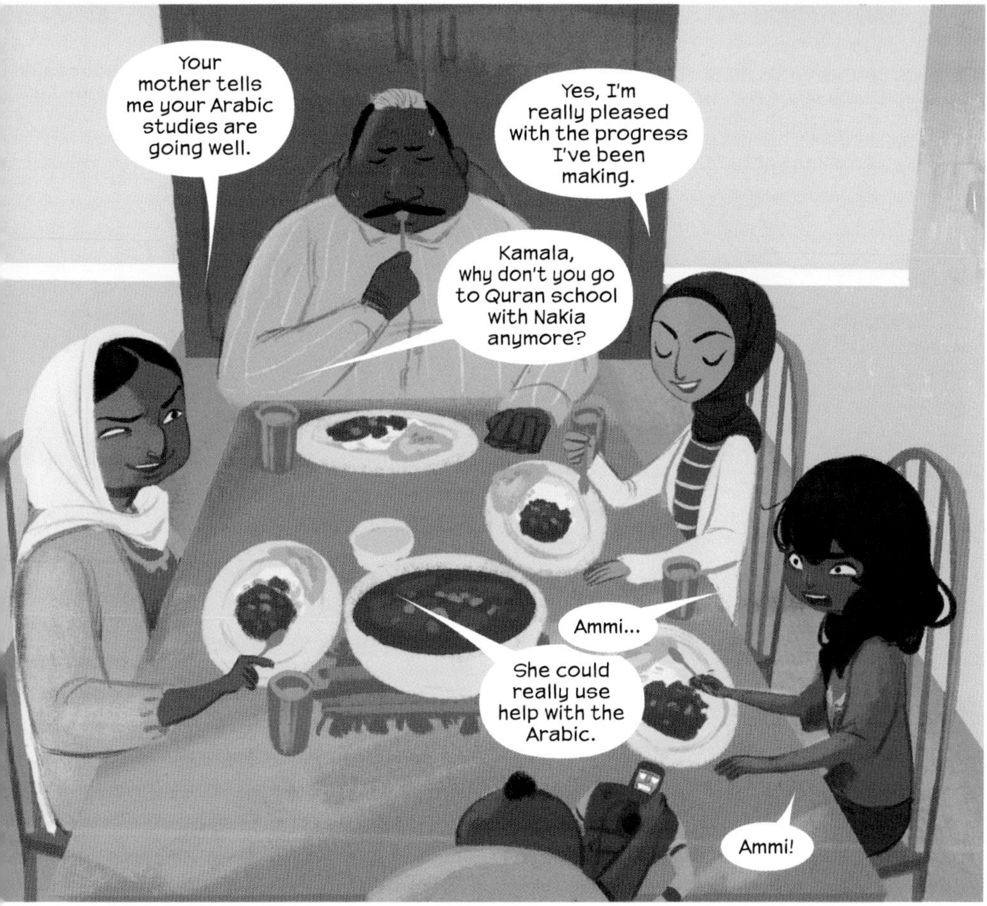
Your mother tells me your Arabic studies are going well.
Yes, I'm really pleased with the progress I've been making.
Kamala, why don't you go to Quran school with Nakia anymore?
Ammi...
She could really use help with the Arabic.
Ammi!

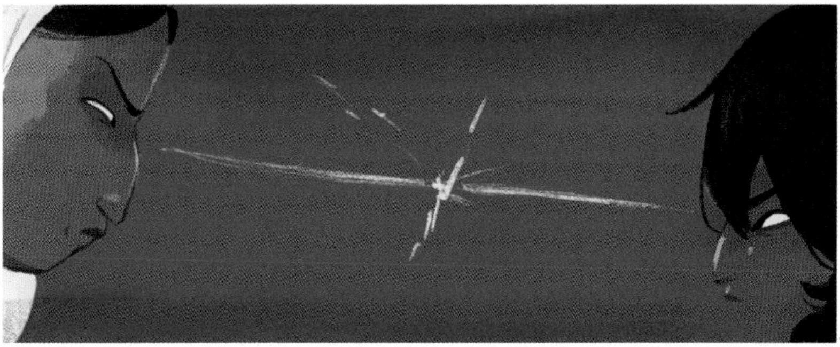

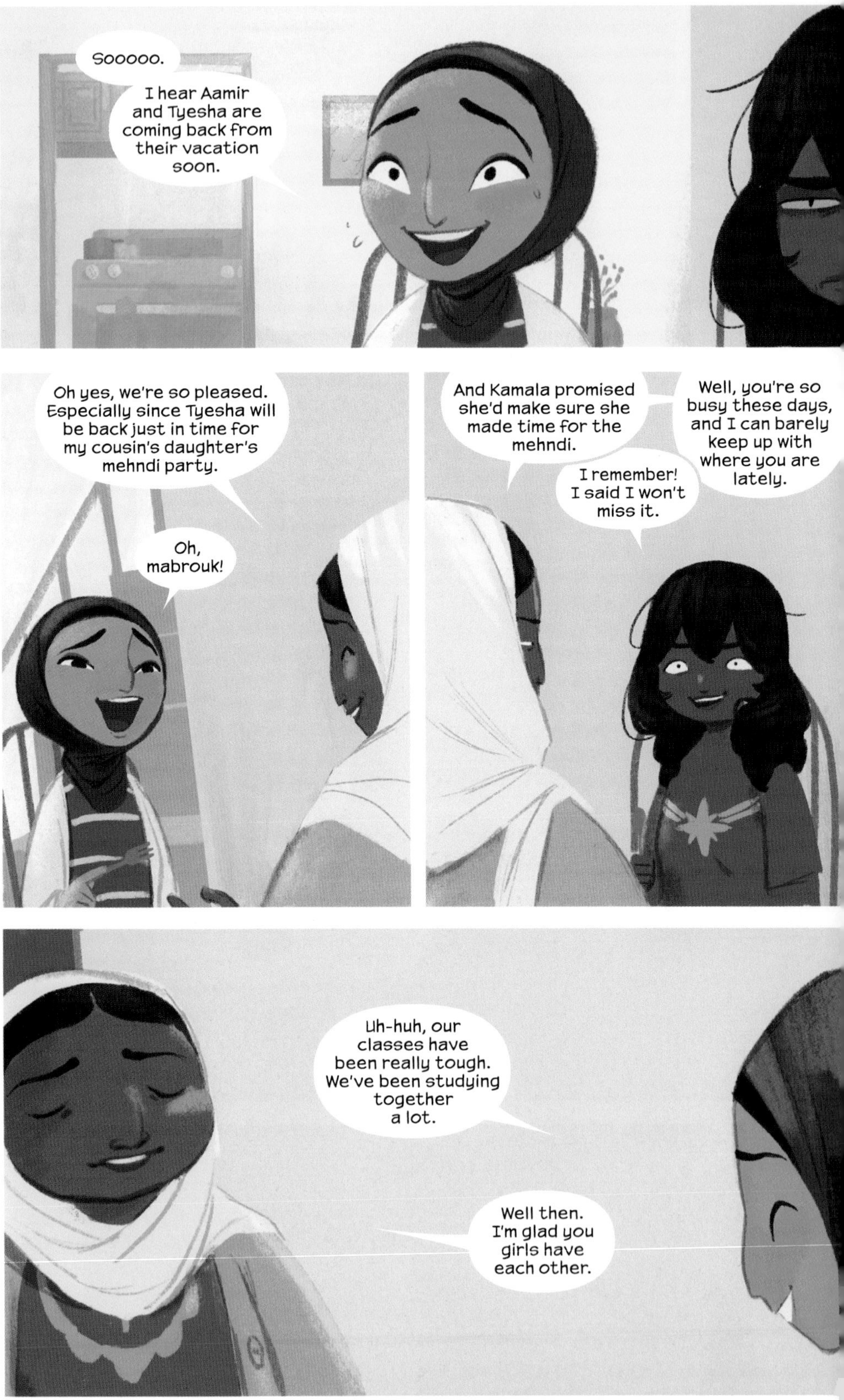
Sooooo.
I hear Aamir and Tyesha are coming back from their vacation soon.
Oh yes, we're so pleased. Especially since Tyesha will be back just in time for my cousin's daughter's mehndi party.
Oh, mabrouk!
And Kamala promised she'd make sure she made time for the mehndi.
Well, you're so busy these days, and I can barely keep up with where you are lately.
I remember! I said I won't miss it.
Uh-huh, our classes have been really tough. We've been studying together a lot.
Well then. I'm glad you girls have each other.

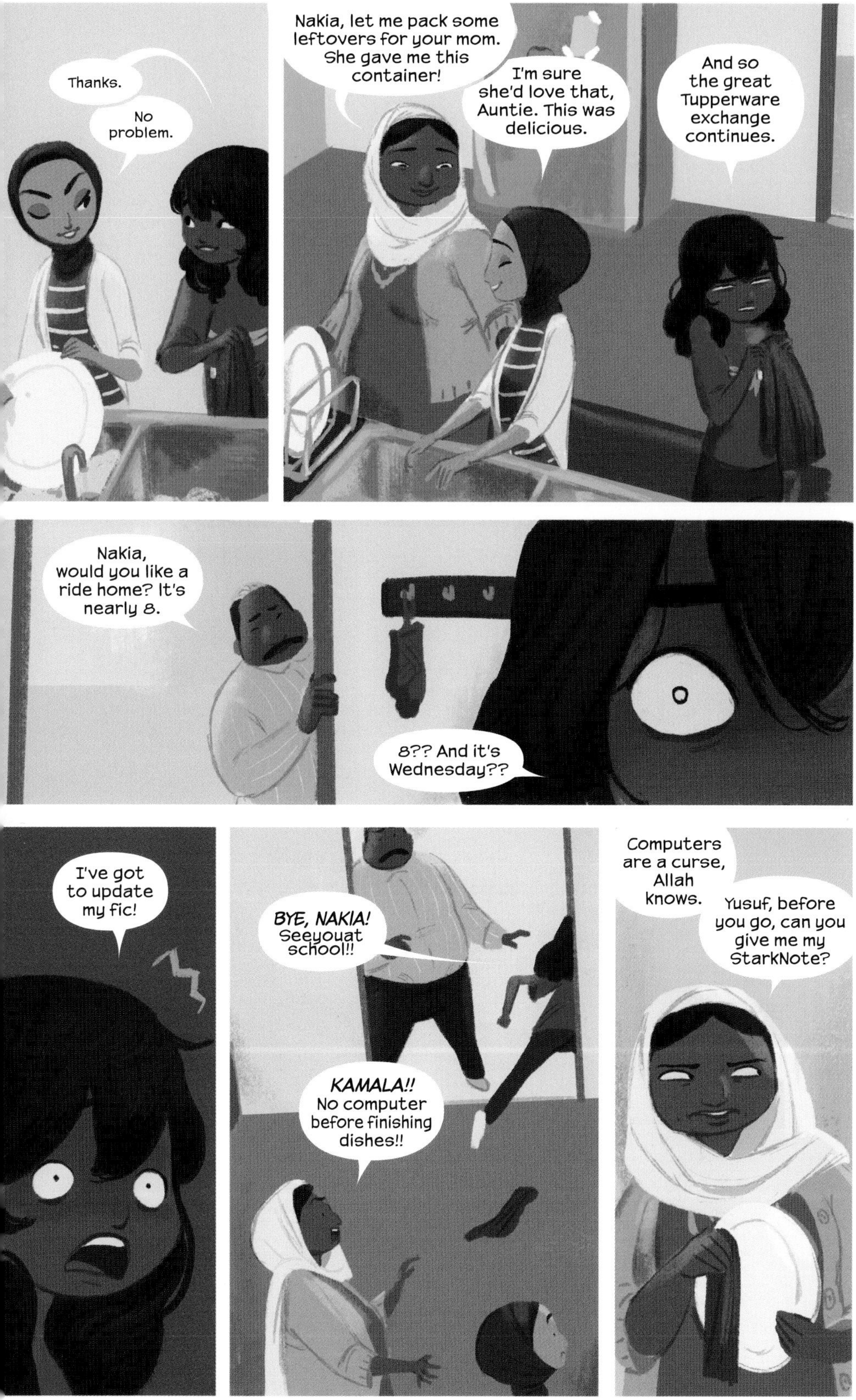
Thanks.
No problem.
Nakia, let me pack some leftovers for your mom. She gave me this container!
I'm sure she'd love that, Auntie. This was delicious.
And so the great Tupperware exchange continues.
Nakia, would you like a ride home? It's nearly 8.
8?? And it's Wednesday??
I've got to update my fic!
BYE, NAKIA! Seeyouat school!!
KAMALA!! No computer before finishing dishes!!
Computers are a curse, Allah knows.
Yusuf, before you go, can you give me my StarkNote?

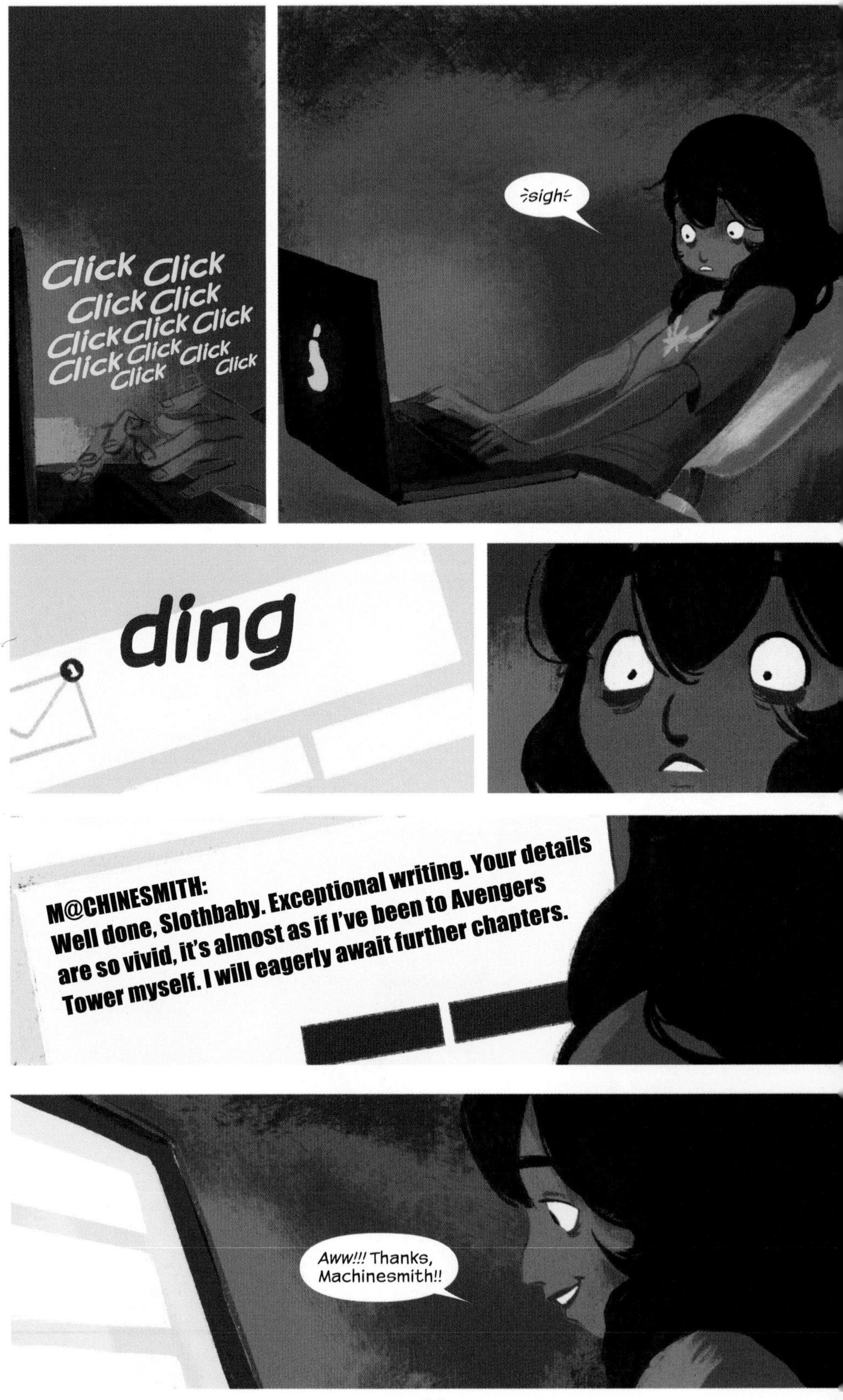

Click Click Click Click Click Click Click Click Click Click Click Click
~sigh~
ding
M@CHINESMITH:
Well done, Slothbaby. Exceptional writing. Your details are so vivid, it's almost as if I've been to Avengers Tower myself. I will eagerly await further chapters.
Aww!!! Thanks, Machinesmith!!

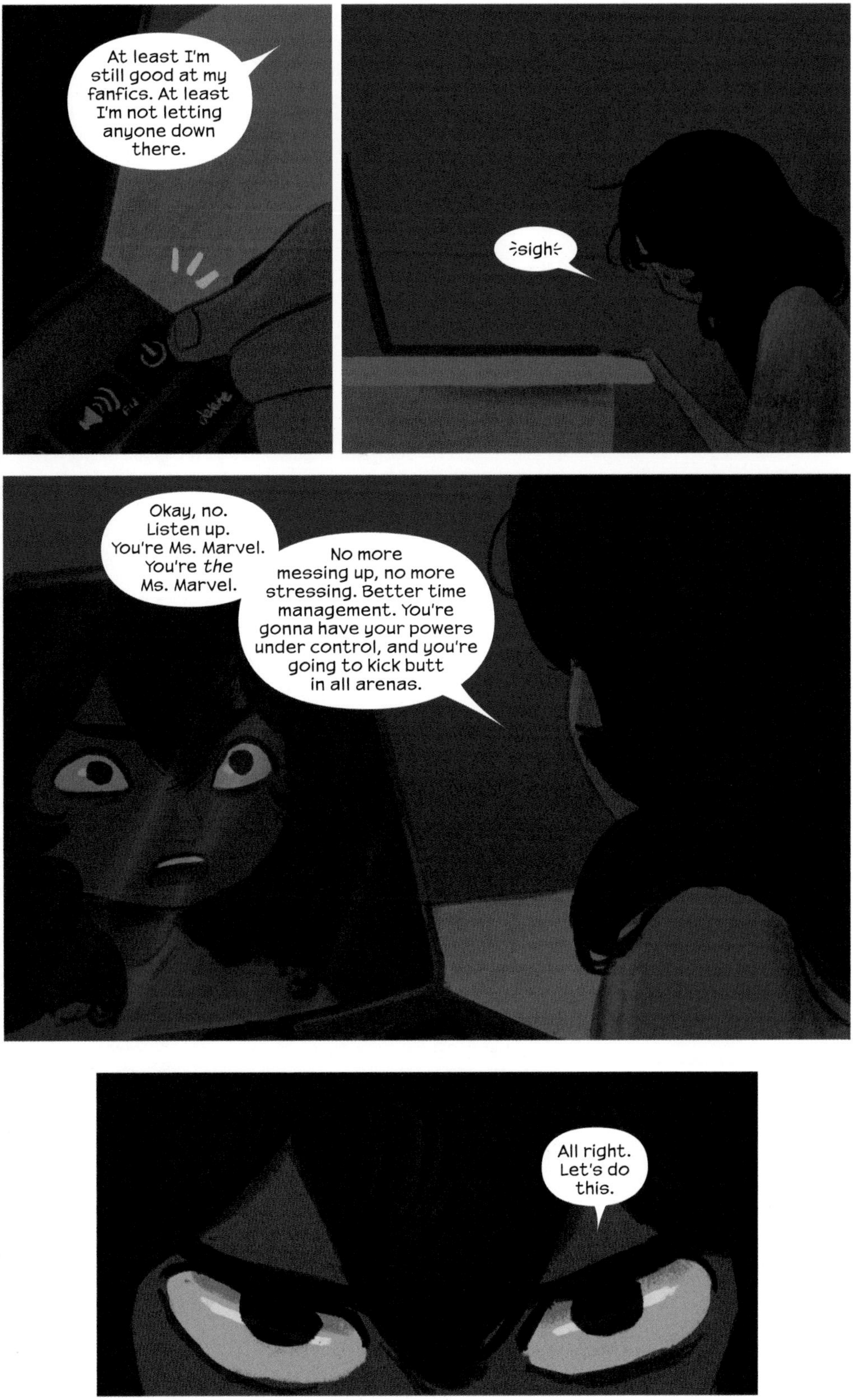
At least I'm still good at my fanfics. At least I'm not letting anyone down there.
sigh
Okay, no. Listen up. You're Ms. Marvel. You're *the* Ms. Marvel.
No more messing up, no more stressing. Better time management. You're gonna have your powers under control, and you're going to kick butt in all arenas.
All right. Let's do this.

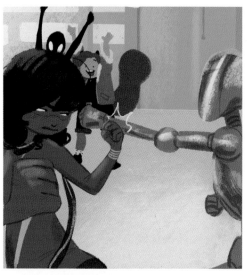

M@CHINESMITH left a like!

M@CHINESMITH left a comment!

Have you picked out your dress for the mehndi?

Not yet, Ammi.

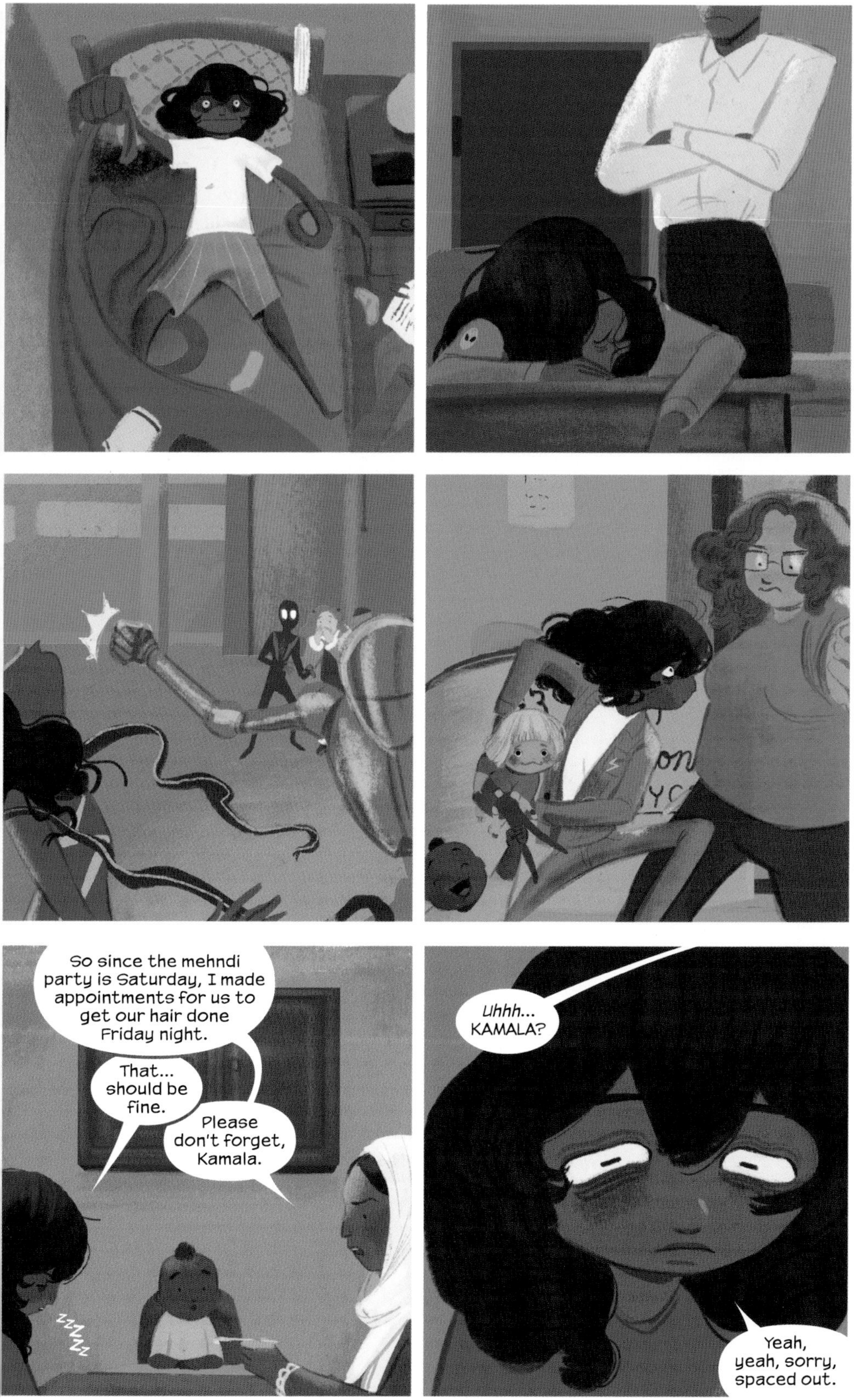
So since the mehndi party is Saturday, I made appointments for us to get our hair done Friday night.
That... should be fine.
Please don't forget, Kamala.
ZZZZZ
Uhhh... KAMALA?
Yeah, yeah, sorry, spaced out.

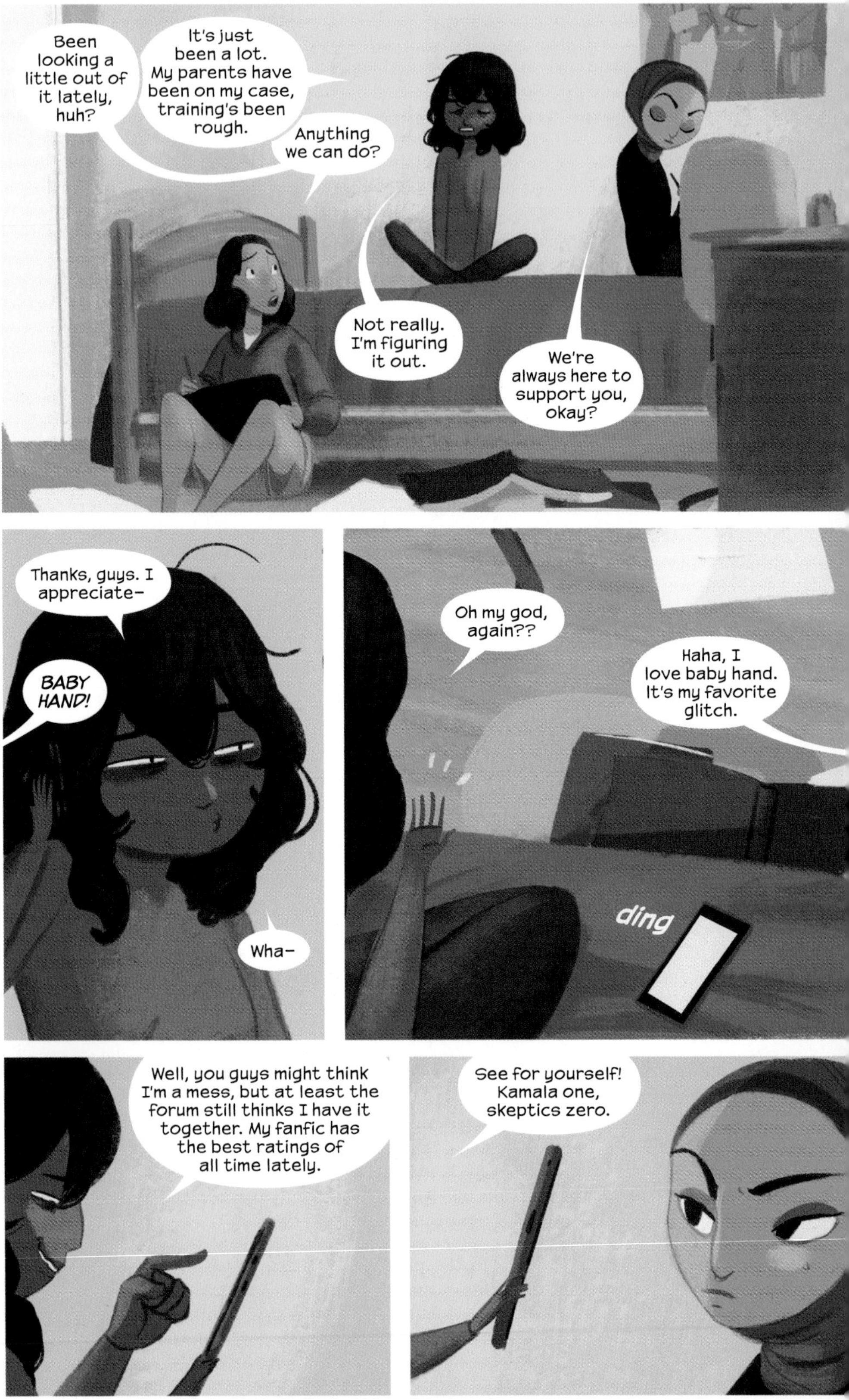
Been looking a little out of it lately, huh?
It's just been a lot. My parents have been on my case, training's been rough.
Anything we can do?
Not really. I'm figuring it out.
We're always here to support you, okay?
Thanks, guys. I appreciate-
BABY HAND!
Wha-
Oh my god, again??
Haha, I love baby hand. It's my favorite glitch.
ding
Well, you guys might think I'm a mess, but at least the forum still thinks I have it together. My fanfic has the best ratings of all time lately.
See for yourself! Kamala one, skeptics zero.

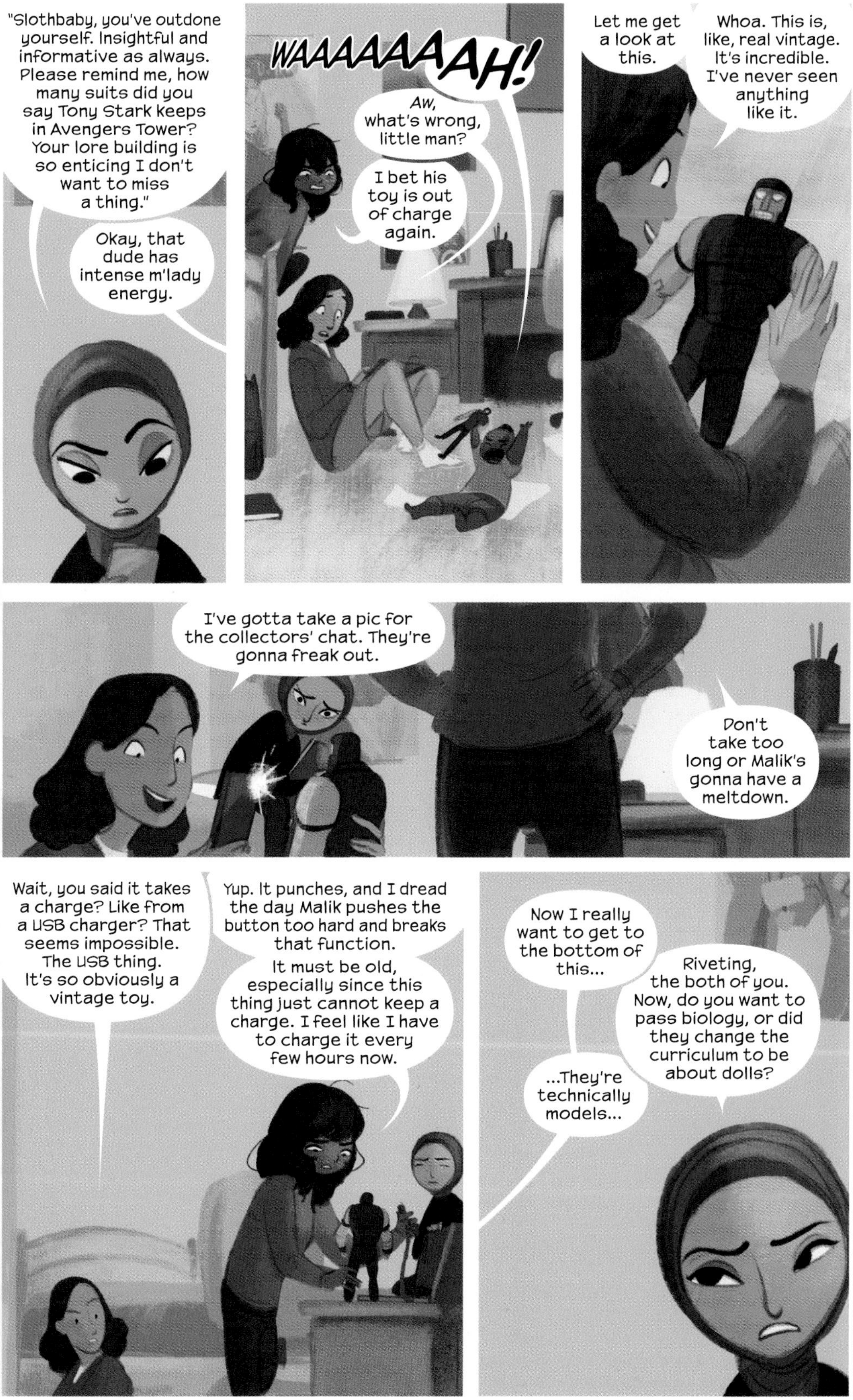
"Slothbaby, you've outdone yourself. Insightful and informative as always. Please remind me, how many suits did you say Tony Stark keeps in Avengers Tower? Your lore building is so enticing I don't want to miss a thing."
Okay, that dude has intense m'lady energy.
WAAAAAAAAH!
Aw, what's wrong, little man?
I bet his toy is out of charge again.
Let me get a look at this.
Whoa. This is, like, real vintage. It's incredible. I've never seen anything like it.
I've gotta take a pic for the collectors' chat. They're gonna freak out.
Don't take too long or Malik's gonna have a meltdown.
Wait, you said it takes a charge? Like from a USB charger? That seems impossible. The USB thing. It's so obviously a vintage toy.
Yup. It punches, and I dread the day Malik pushes the button too hard and breaks that function.
It must be old, especially since this thing just cannot keep a charge. I feel like I have to charge it every few hours now.
Now I really want to get to the bottom of this...
Riveting, the both of you. Now, do you want to pass biology, or did they change the curriculum to be about dolls?
...They're technically models...

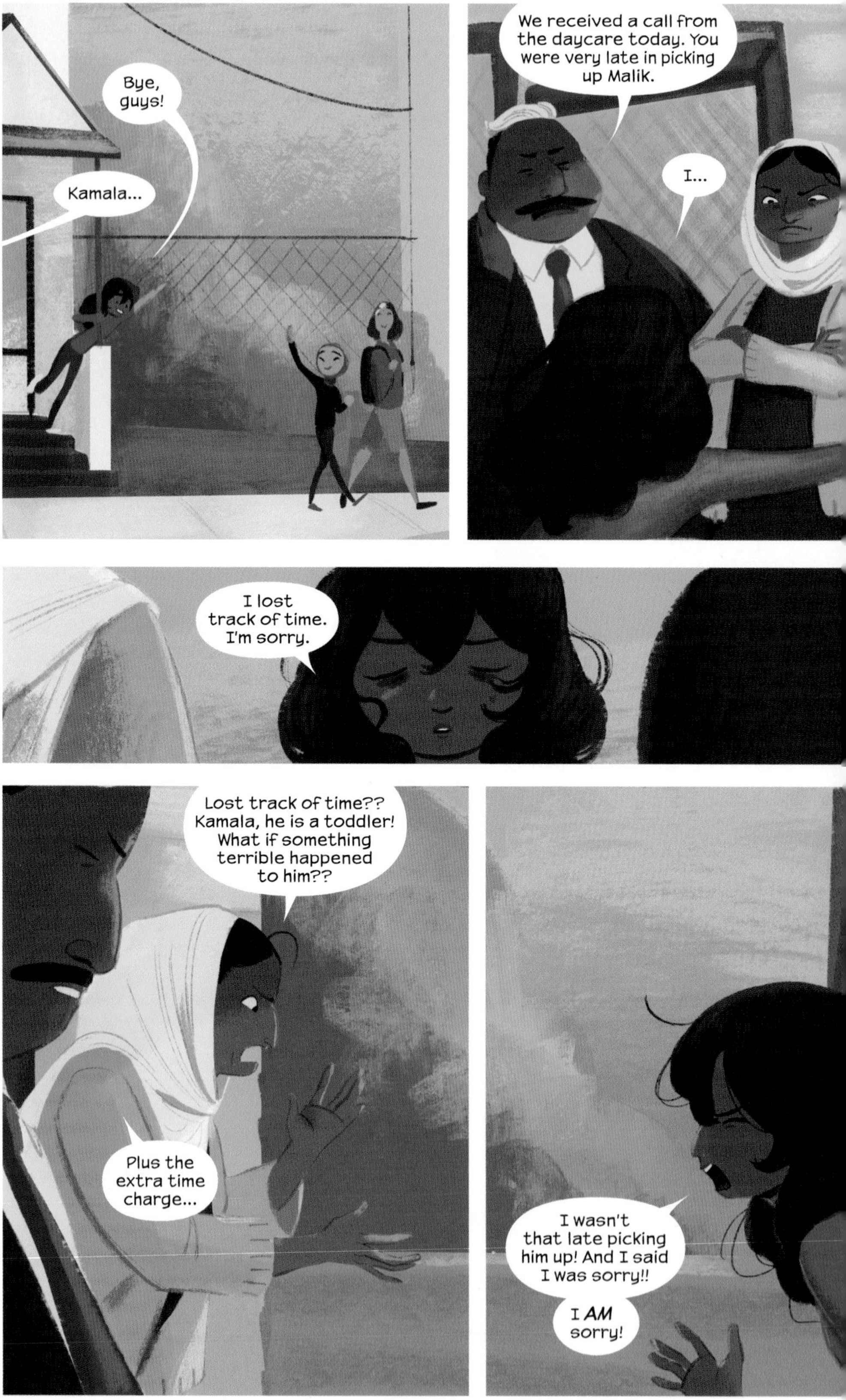
Bye, guys!
Kamala...
We received a call from the daycare today. You were very late in picking up Malik.
I...
I lost track of time. I'm sorry.
Lost track of time?? Kamala, he is a toddler! What if something terrible happened to him??
Plus the extra time charge...
I wasn't that late picking him up! And I said I was sorry!!
I *AM* sorry!

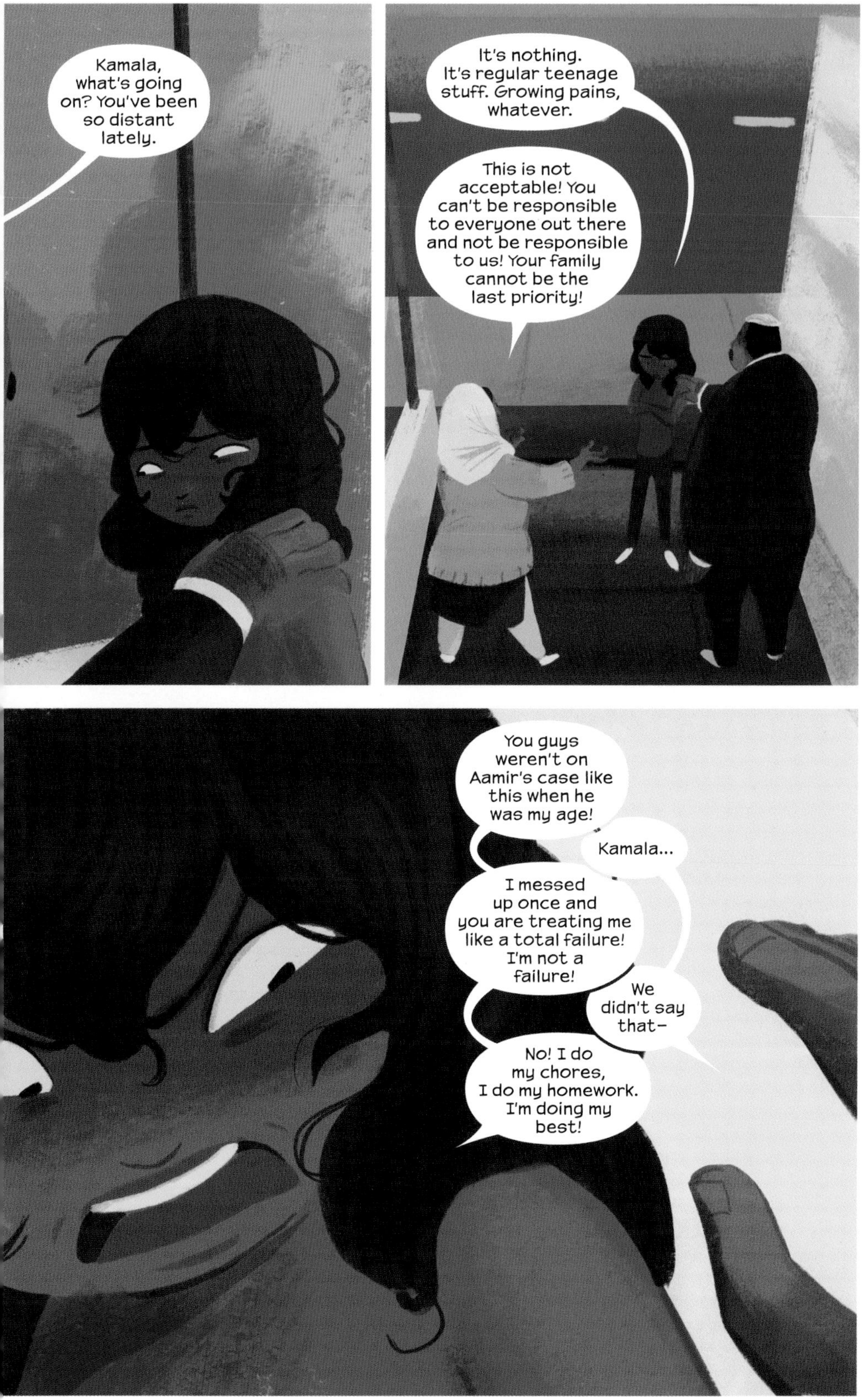

Kamala, what's going on? You've been so distant lately.
It's nothing. It's regular teenage stuff. Growing pains, whatever.
This is not acceptable! You can't be responsible to everyone out there and not be responsible to us! Your family cannot be the last priority!
You guys weren't on Aamir's case like this when he was my age!
Kamala...
I messed up once and you are treating me like a total failure! I'm not a failure!
We didn't say that–
No! I do my chores, I do my homework. I'm doing my best!

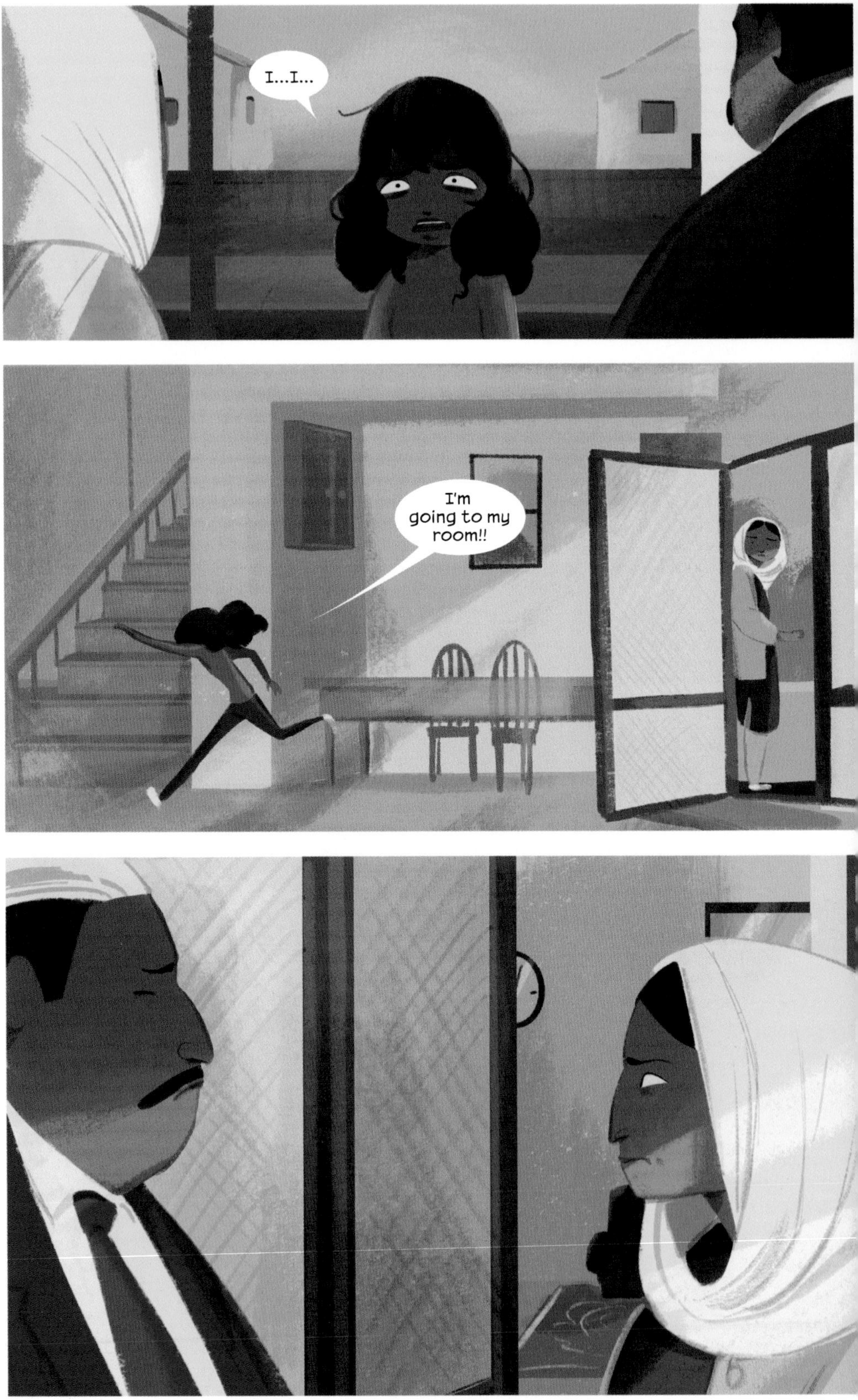
I...I...
I'm going to my room!!

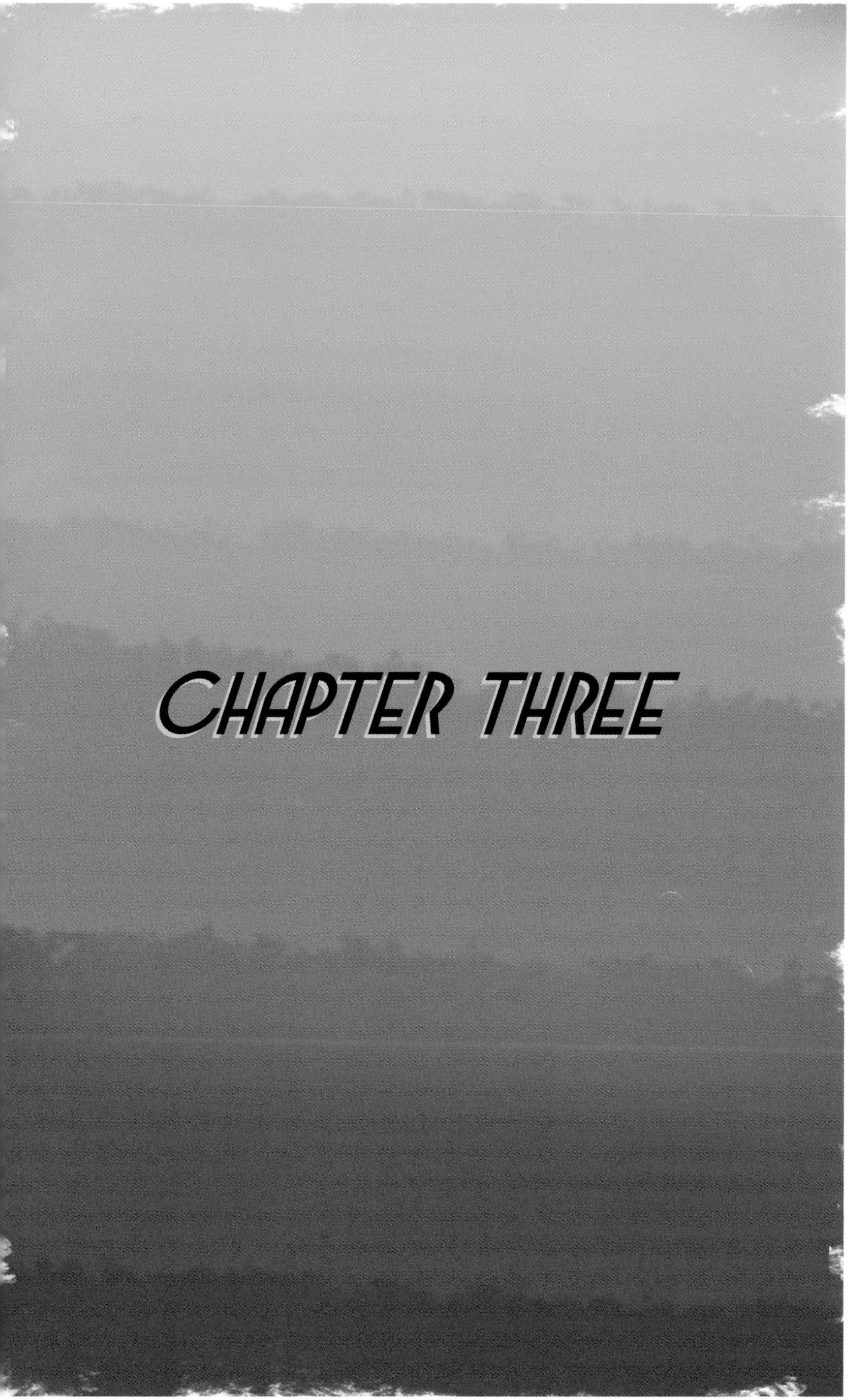

CHAPTER THREE

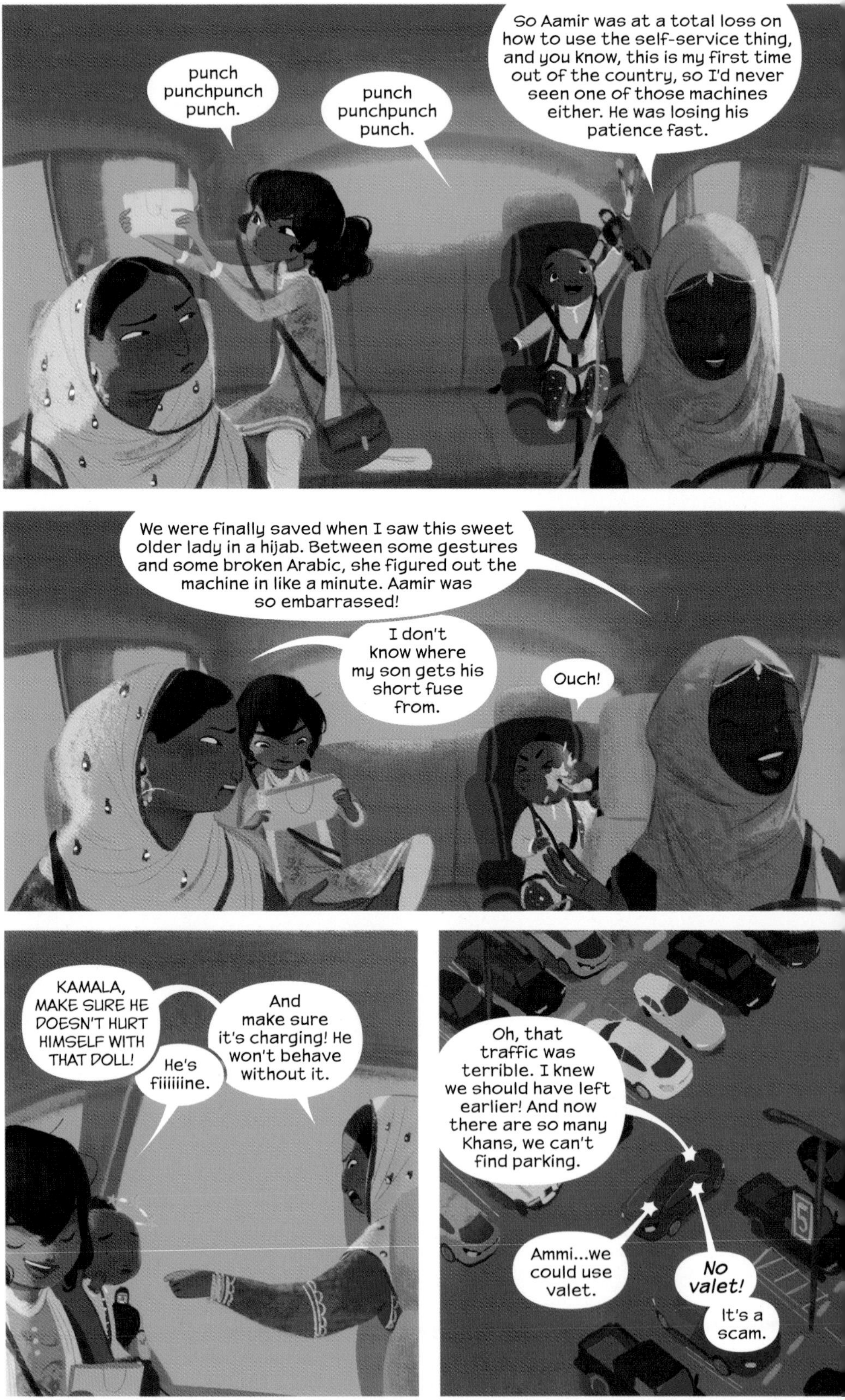
punch punchpunch punch.
punch punchpunch punch.
So Aamir was at a total loss on how to use the self-service thing, and you know, this is my first time out of the country, so I'd never seen one of those machines either. He was losing his patience fast.
We were finally saved when I saw this sweet older lady in a hijab. Between some gestures and some broken Arabic, she figured out the machine in like a minute. Aamir was so embarrassed!
I don't know where my son gets his short fuse from.
Ouch!
KAMALA, MAKE SURE HE DOESN'T HURT HIMSELF WITH THAT DOLL!
He's fiiiiiine.
And make sure it's charging! He won't behave without it.
Oh, that traffic was terrible. I knew we should have left earlier! And now there are so many Khans, we can't find parking.
Ammi...we could use valet.
No valet!
It's a scam.

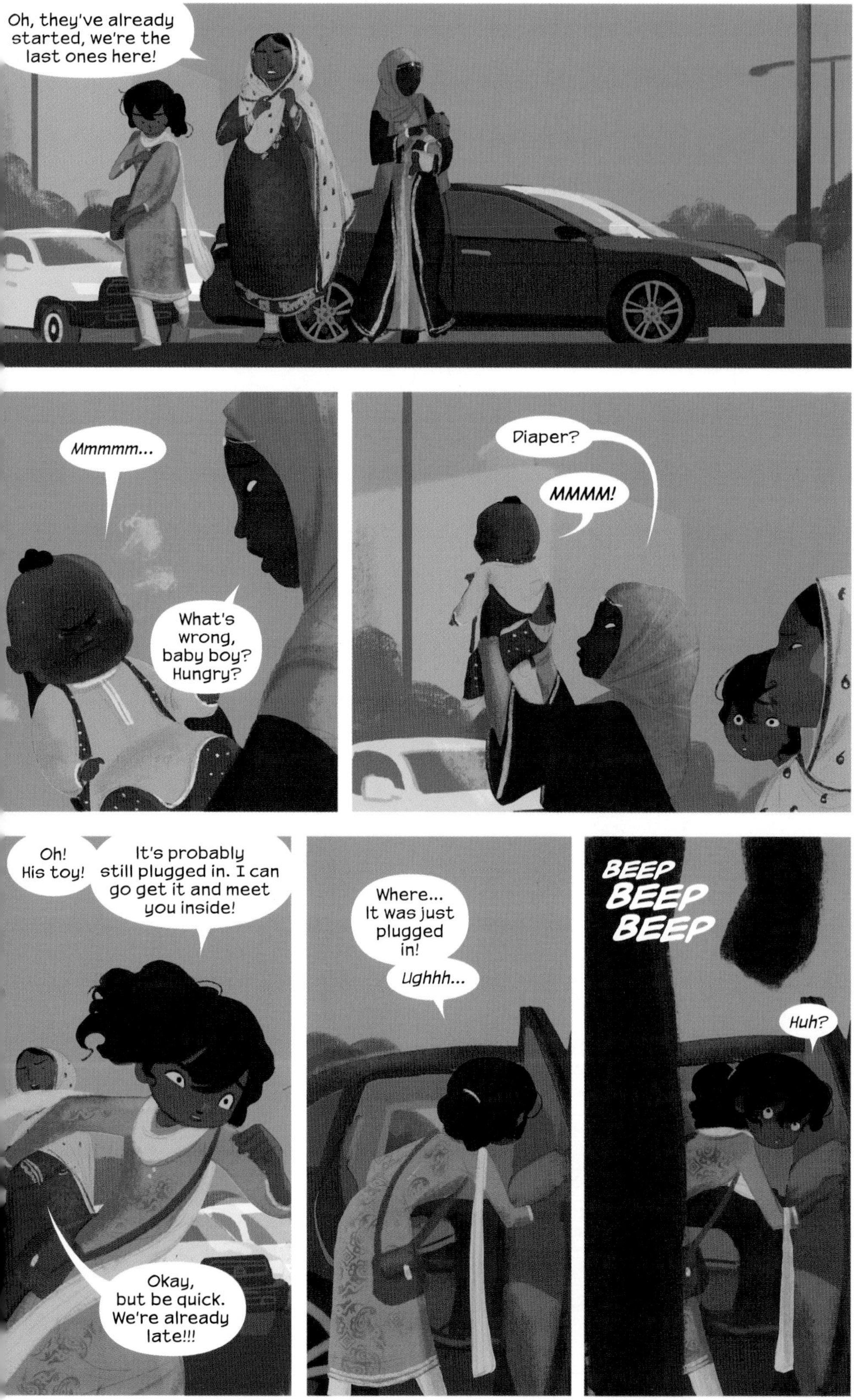
Oh, they've already started, we're the last ones here!
Mmmmm...
What's wrong, baby boy? Hungry?
Diaper?
MMMM!
Oh! His toy!
It's probably still plugged in. I can go get it and meet you inside!
Okay, but be quick. We're already late!!!
Where... It was just plugged in!
Ughhh...
BEEP BEEP BEEP
Huh?

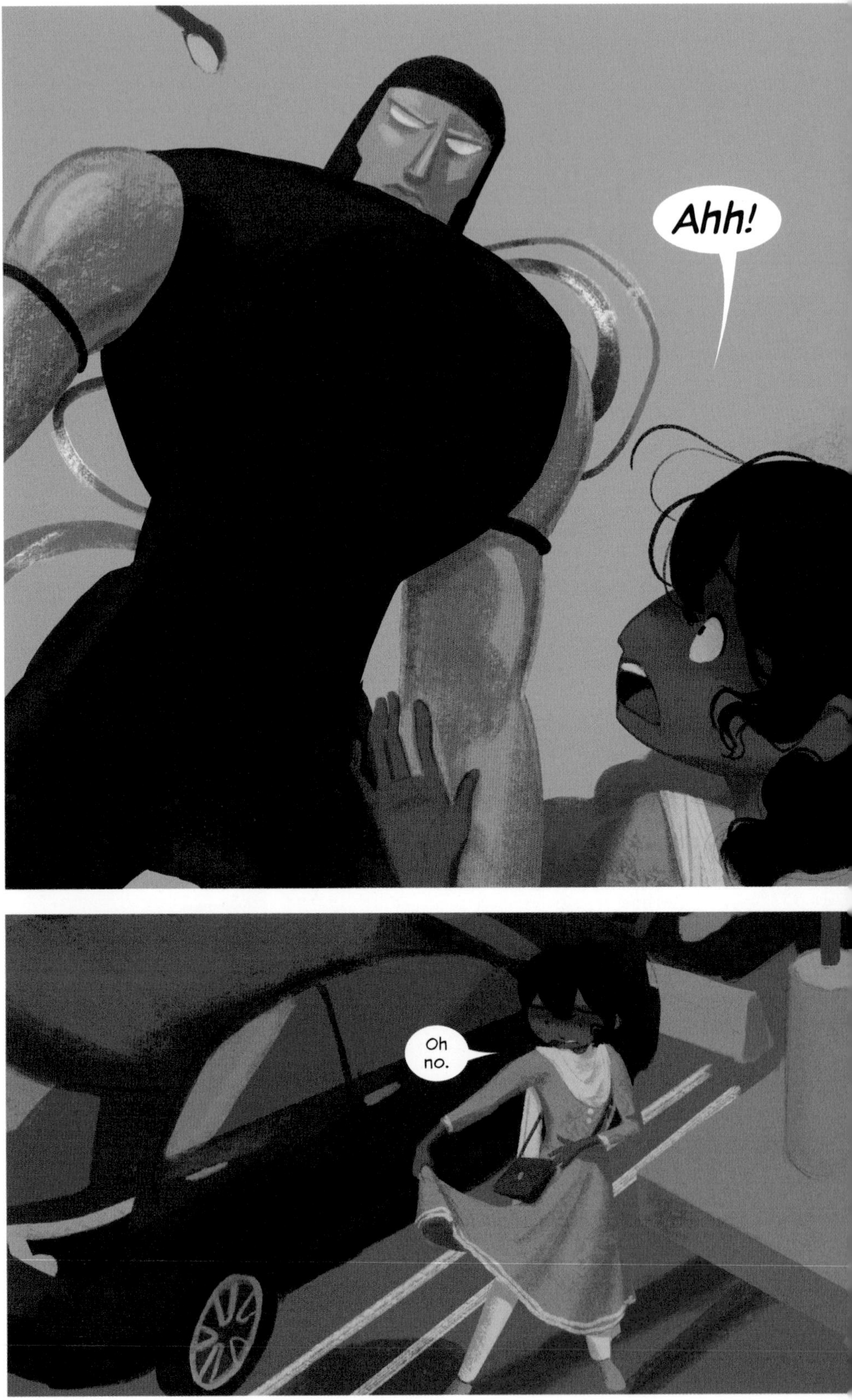
Ahh!
Oh no.

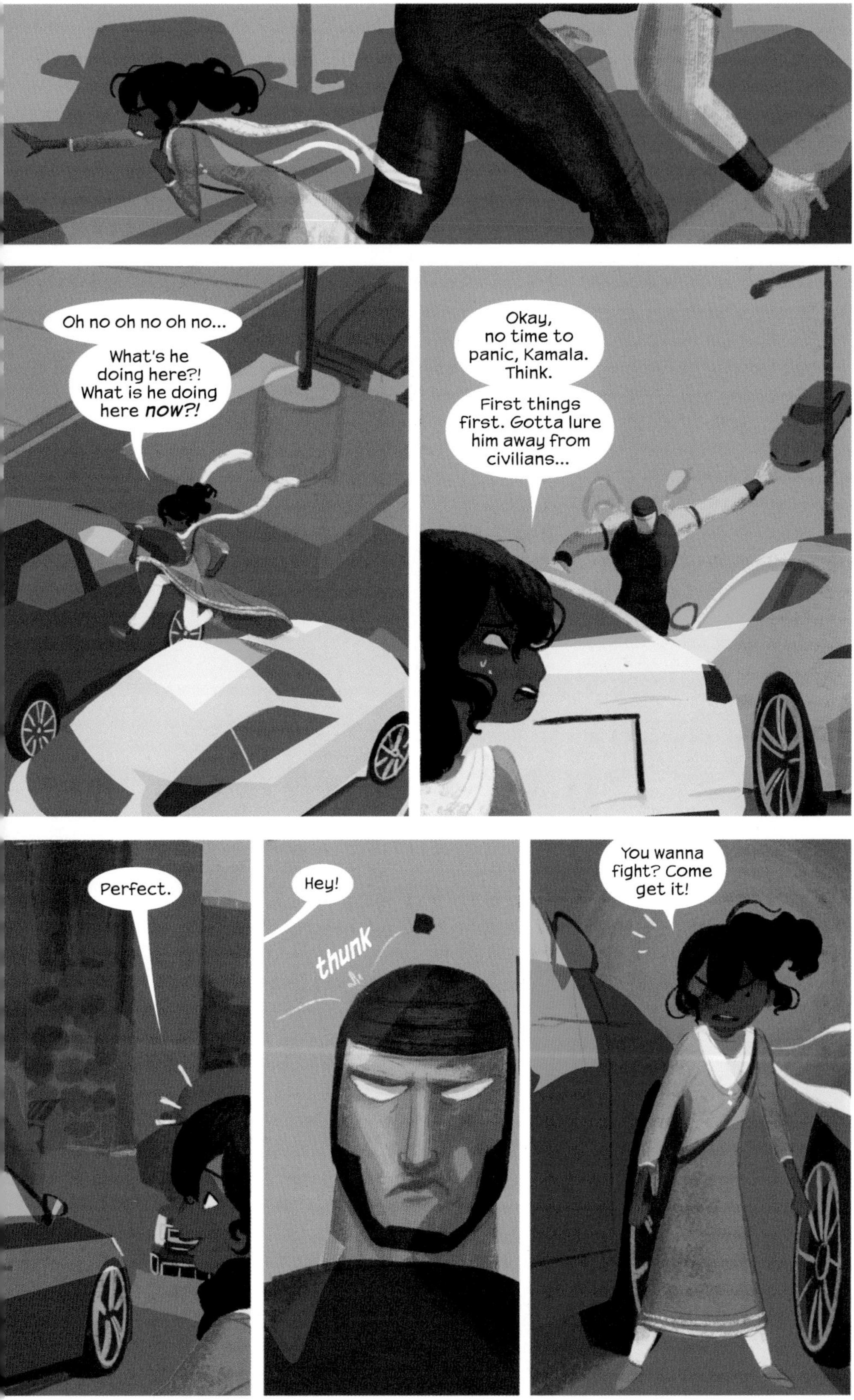
Oh no oh no oh no...
What's he doing here?! What is he doing here *NOW?!*
Okay, no time to panic, Kamala. Think.
First things first. Gotta lure him away from civilians...
Perfect.
Hey!
thunk
You wanna fight? Come get it!

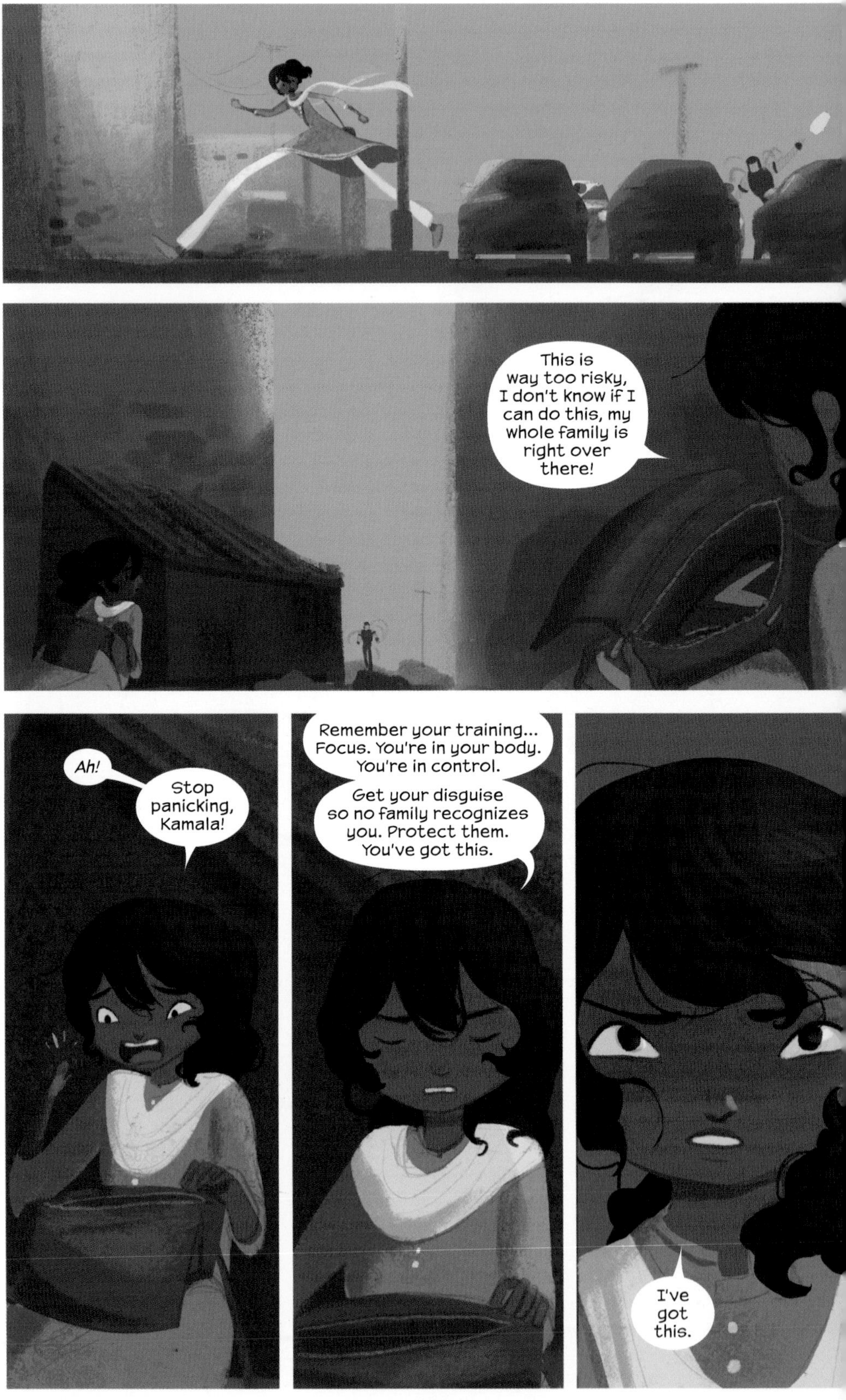
This is way too risky, I don't know if I can do this, my whole family is right over there!
Ah!
Stop panicking, Kamala!
Remember your training... Focus. You're in your body. You're in control.
Get your disguise so no family recognizes you. Protect them. You've got this.
I've got this.

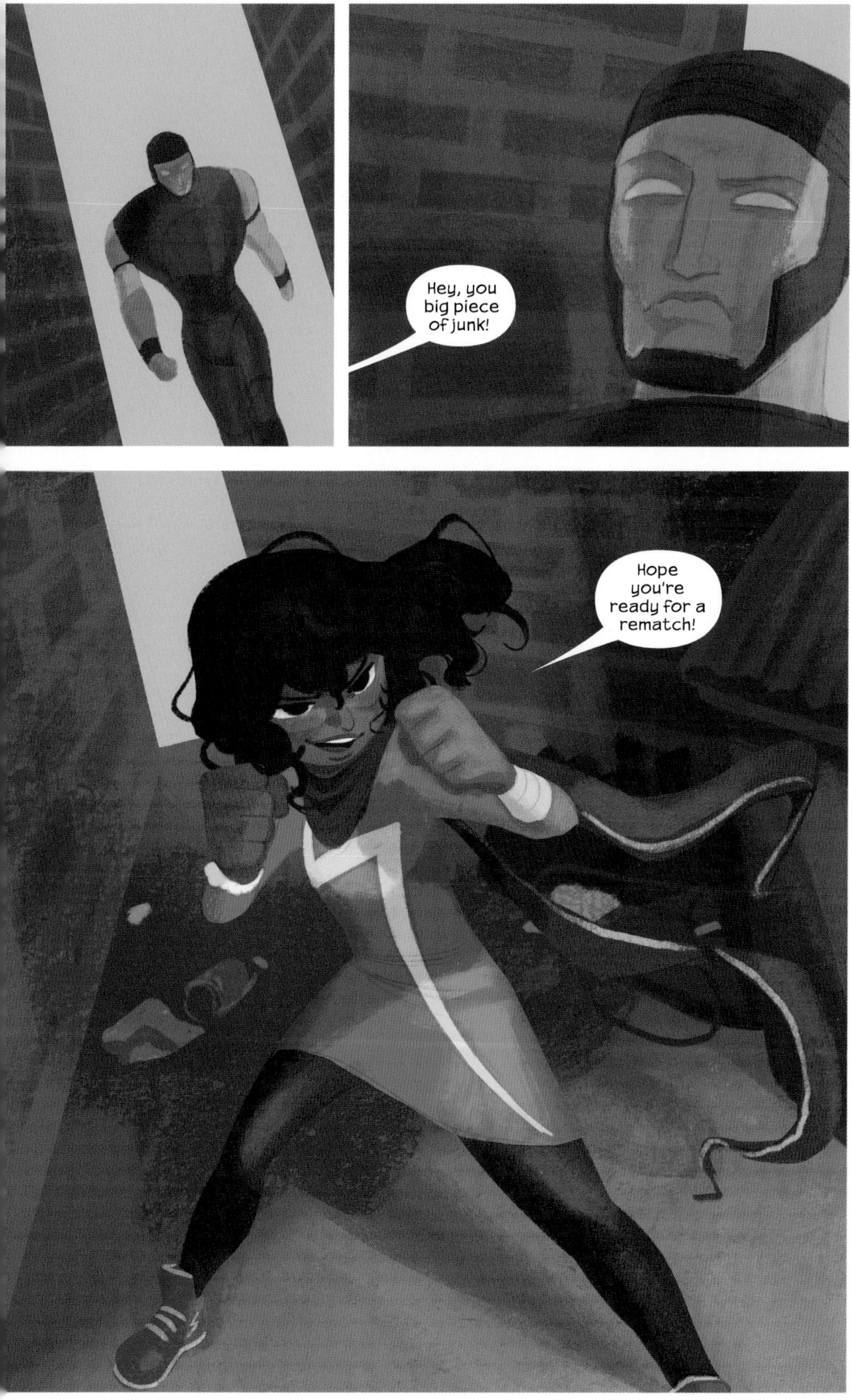
Hey, you big piece of junk!
Hope you're ready for a rematch!

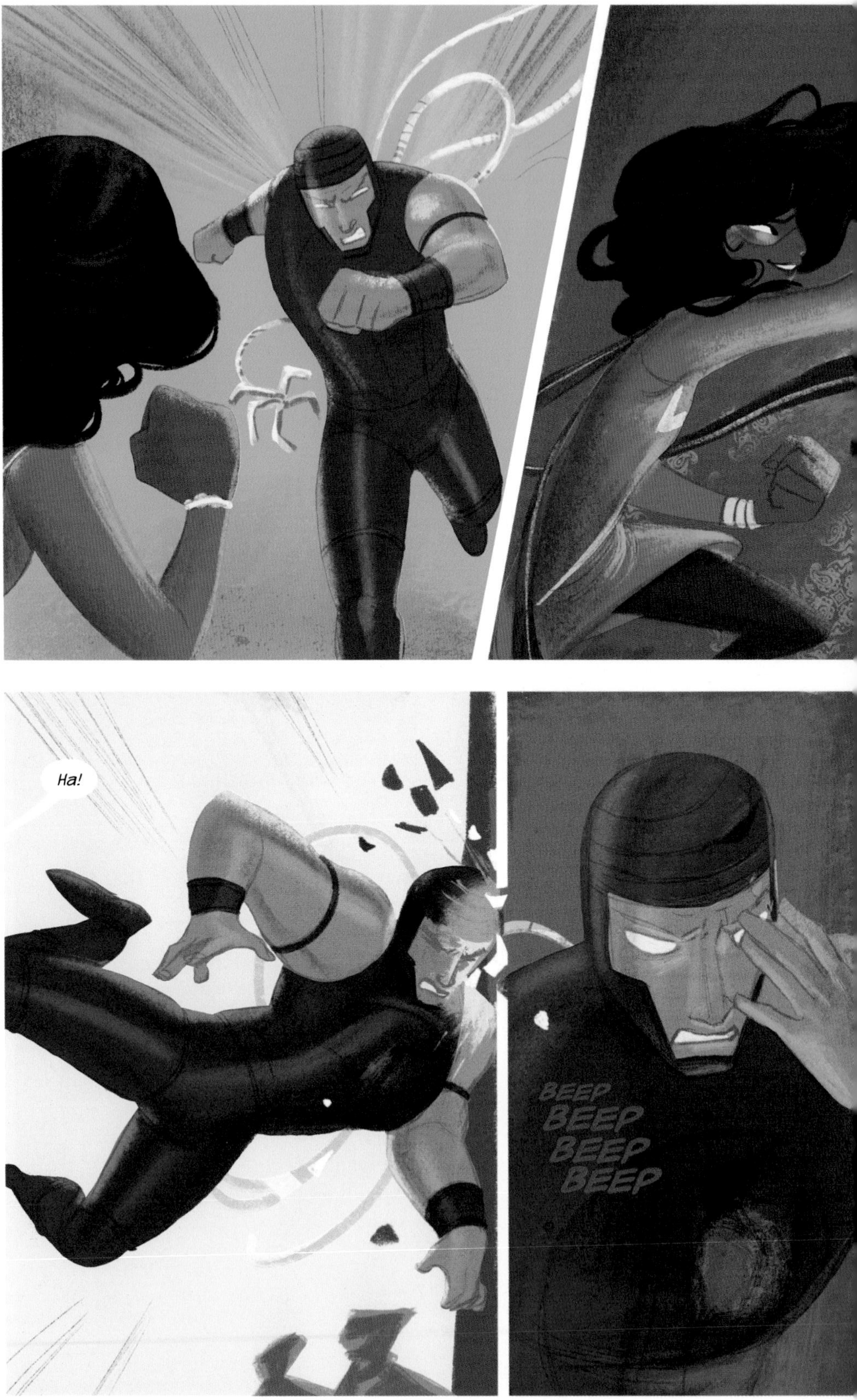
Ha!
BEEP
BEEP
BEEP
BEEP

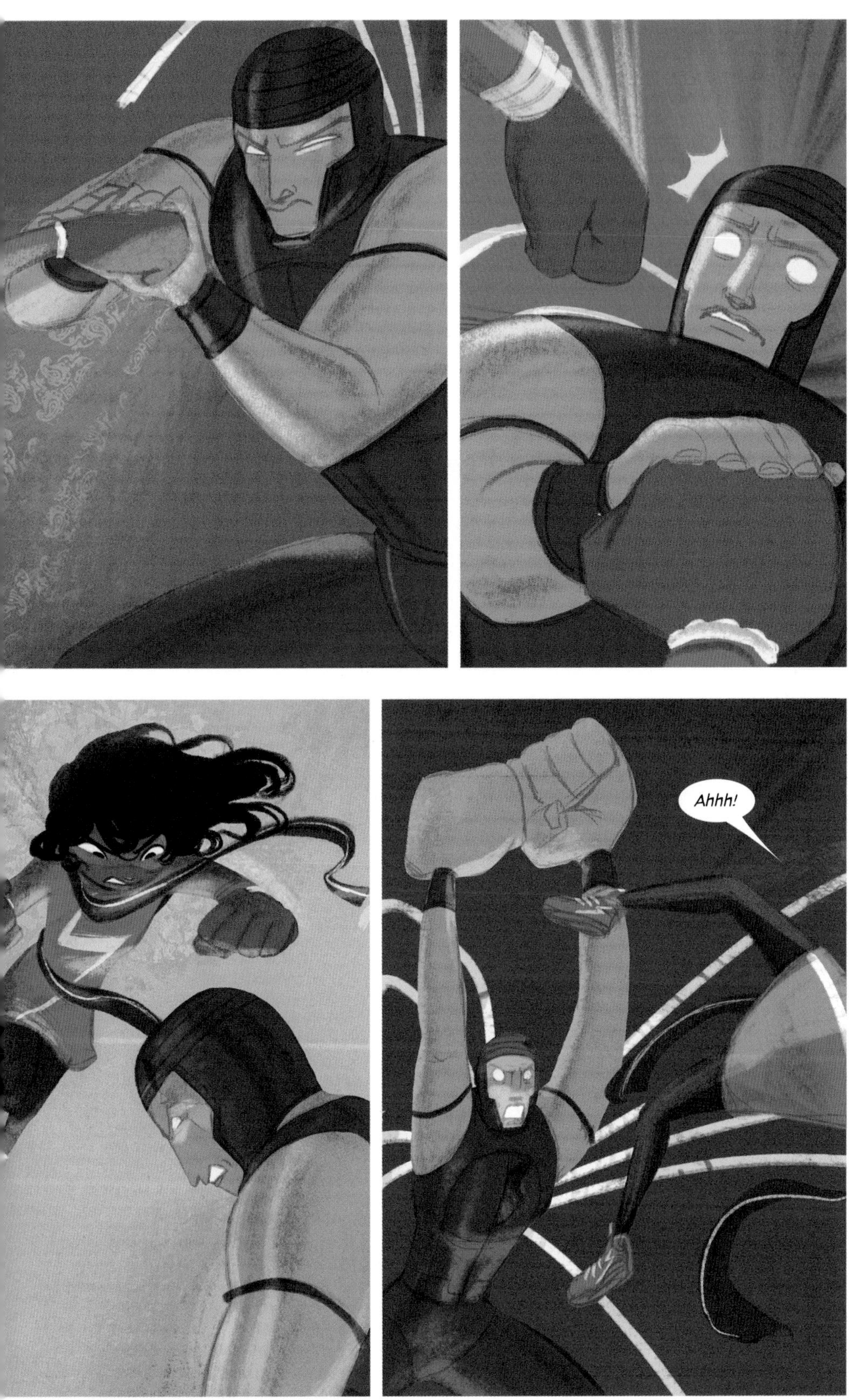
Ahhh!

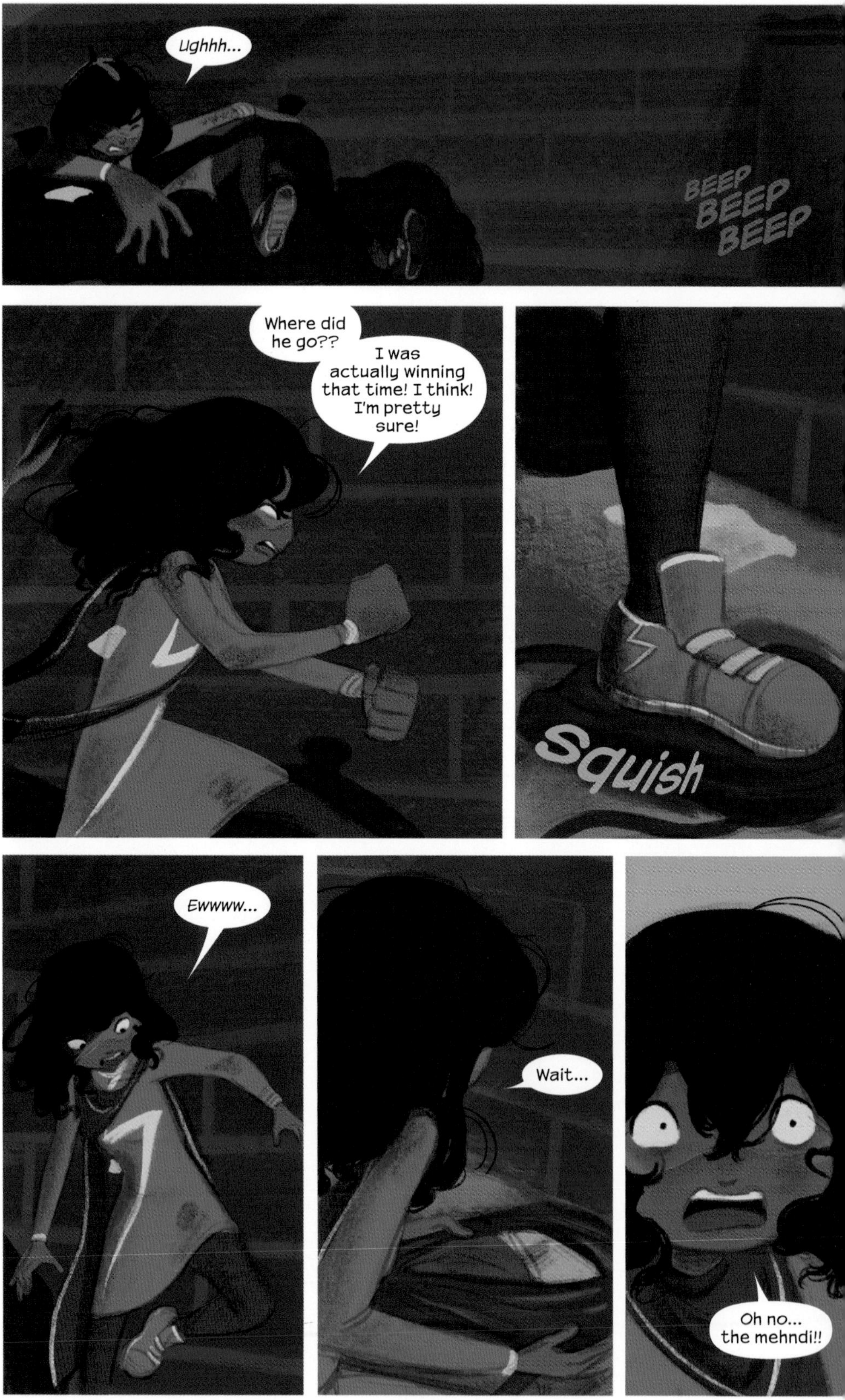
Ughhh...
BEEP
BEEP
BEEP
Where did he go??
I was actually winning that time! I think! I'm pretty sure!
Squish
Ewwww...
Wait...
Oh no... the mehndi!!

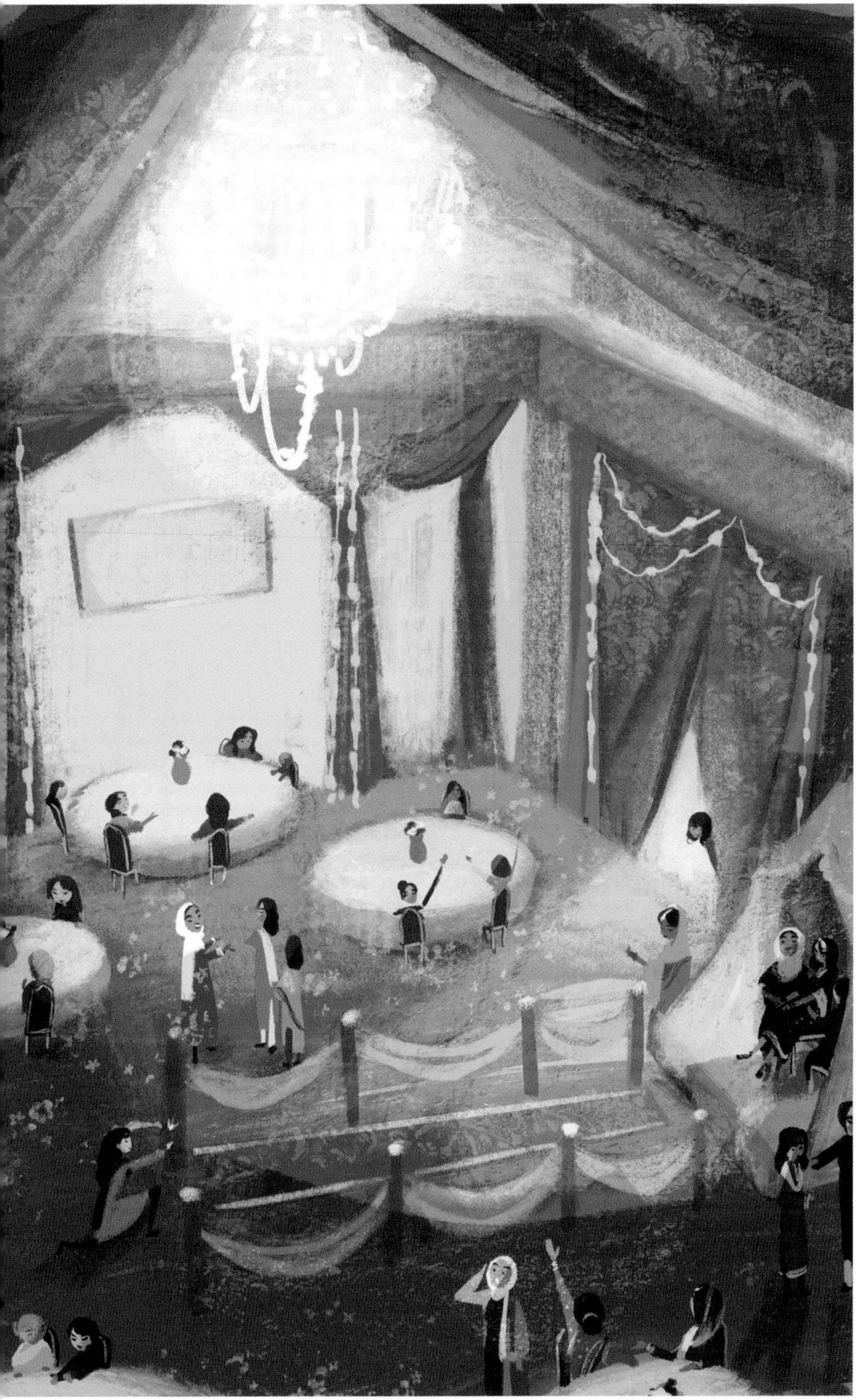

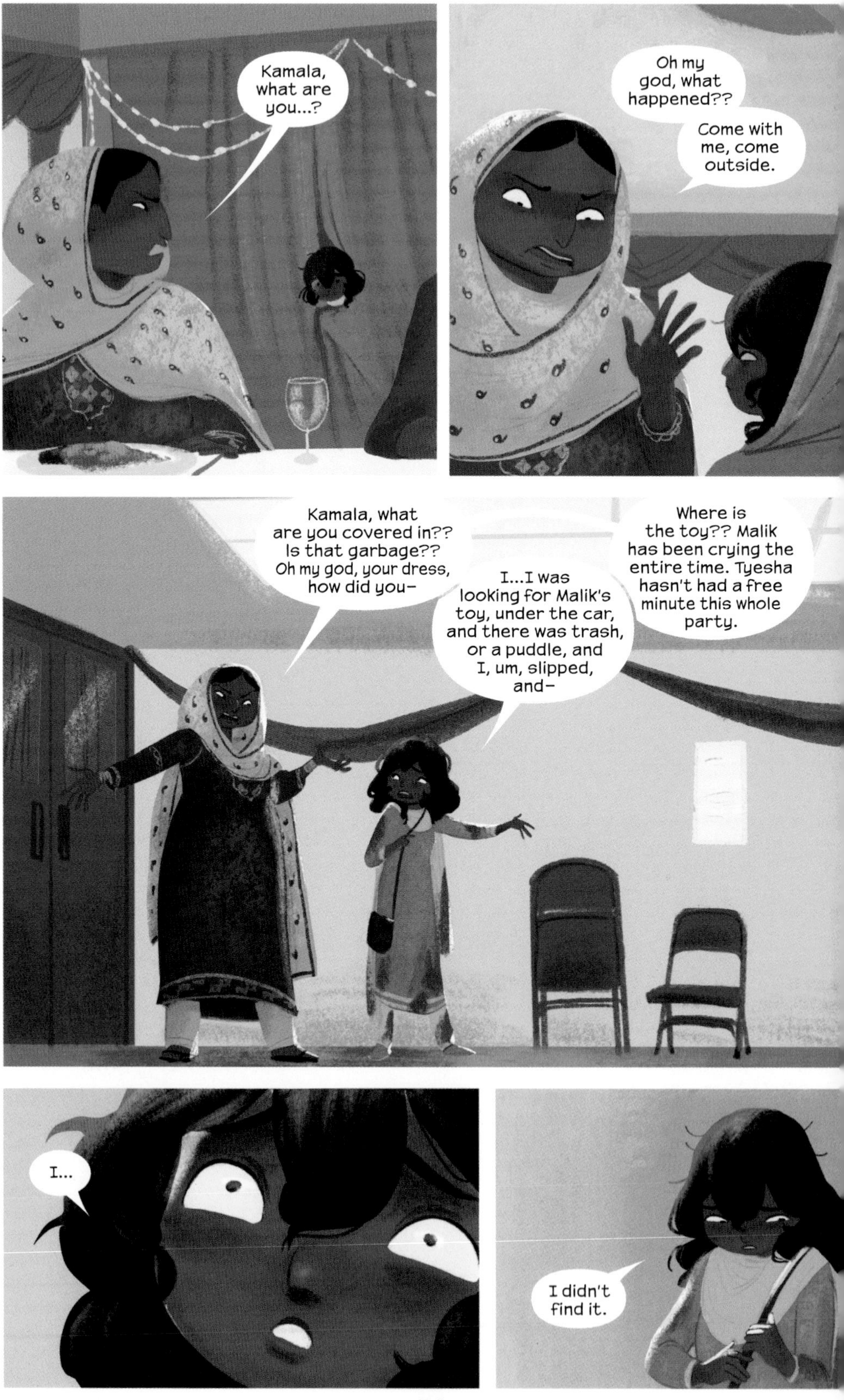
Kamala, what are you...?
Oh my god, what happened??
Come with me, come outside.
Kamala, what are you covered in?? Is that garbage?? Oh my god, your dress, how did you-
I...I was looking for Malik's toy, under the car, and there was trash, or a puddle, and I, um, slipped, and-
Where is the toy?? Malik has been crying the entire time. Tyesha hasn't had a free minute this whole party.
I...
I didn't find it.

Go sit in the car. I'm getting Tyesha. We're leaving right now.

Ammi, I—

Not a word. Not until we get home. Go.

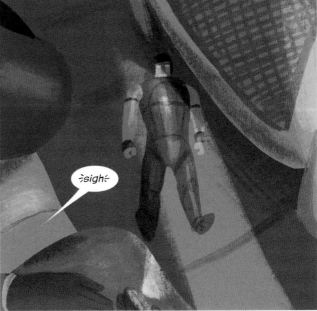

≥sigh≤

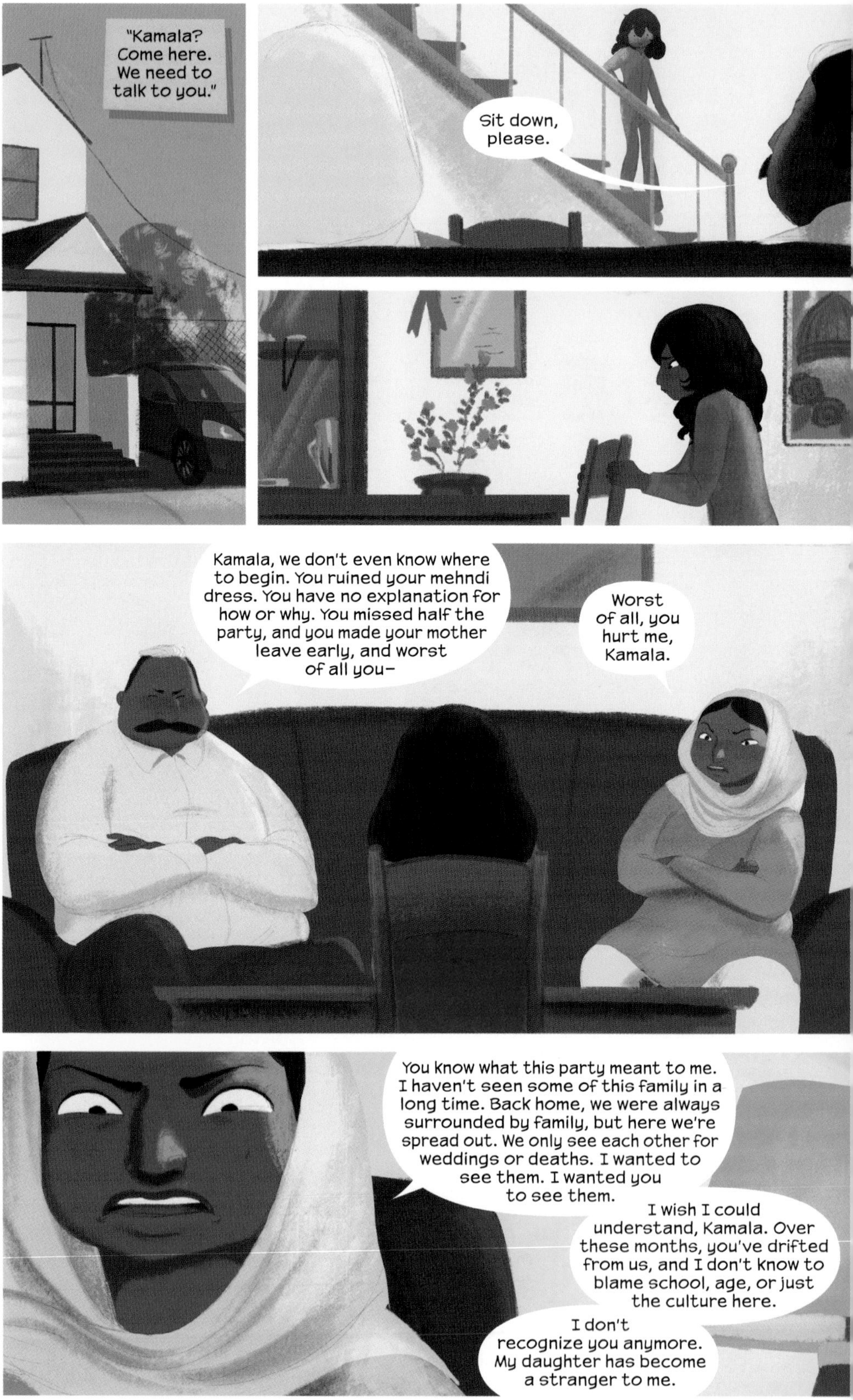
"Kamala? Come here. We need to talk to you."
Sit down, please.
Kamala, we don't even know where to begin. You ruined your mehndi dress. You have no explanation for how or why. You missed half the party, and you made your mother leave early, and worst of all you–
Worst of all, you hurt me, Kamala.
You know what this party meant to me. I haven't seen some of this family in a long time. Back home, we were always surrounded by family, but here we're spread out. We only see each other for weddings or deaths. I wanted to see them. I wanted you to see them.
I wish I could understand, Kamala. Over these months, you've drifted from us, and I don't know to blame school, age, or just the culture here.
I don't recognize you anymore. My daughter has become a stranger to me.

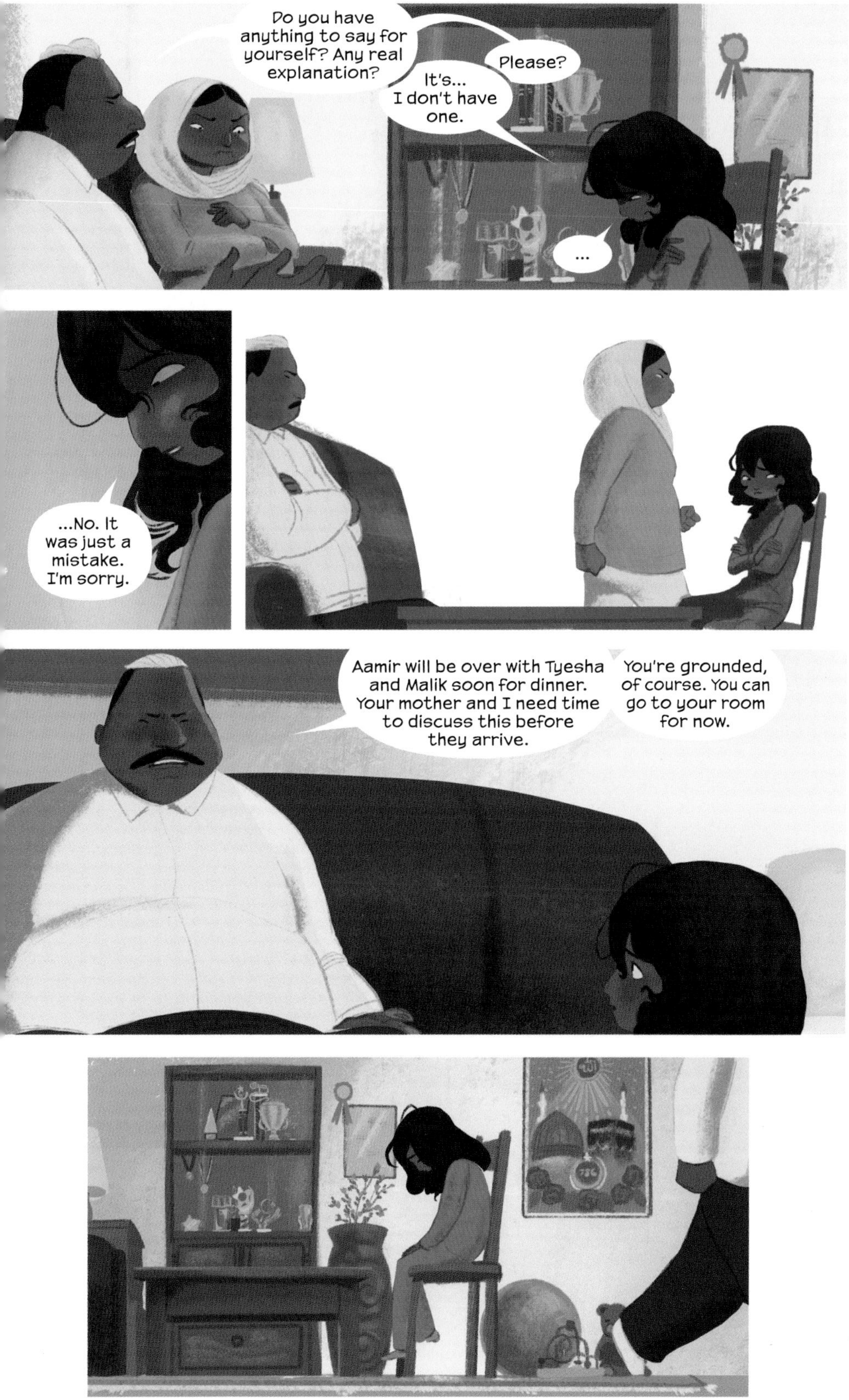
Do you have anything to say for yourself? Any real explanation?
Please?
It's... I don't have one.
...
...No. It was just a mistake. I'm sorry.
Aamir will be over with Tyesha and Malik soon for dinner. Your mother and I need time to discuss this before they arrive.
You're grounded, of course. You can go to your room for now.

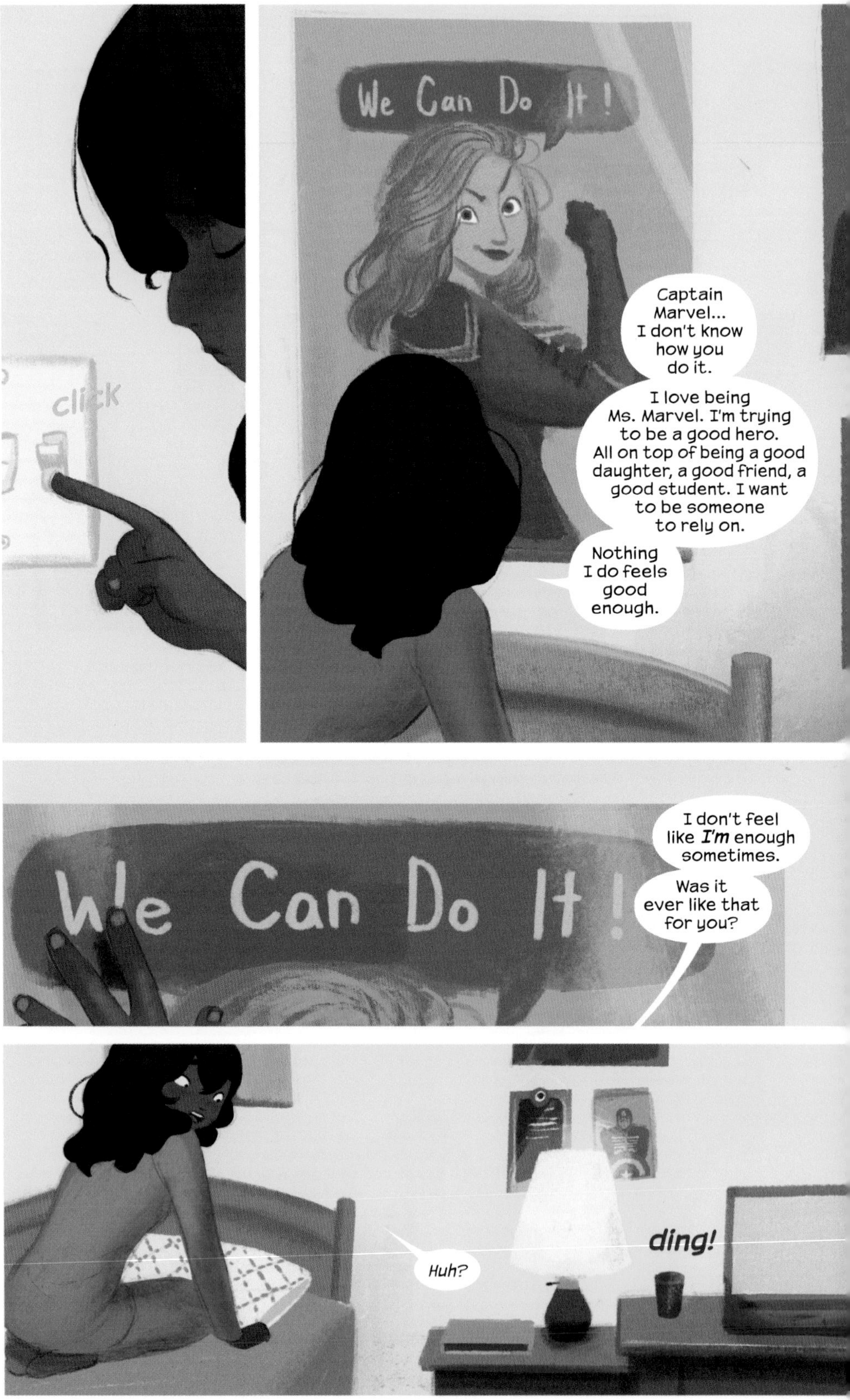
click
Captain Marvel... I don't know how you do it.
I love being Ms. Marvel. I'm trying to be a good hero. All on top of being a good daughter, a good friend, a good student. I want to be someone to rely on.
Nothing I do feels good enough.
We Can Do It!
We Can Do It!
I don't feel like *I'm* enough sometimes.
Was it ever like that for you?
Huh?
ding!

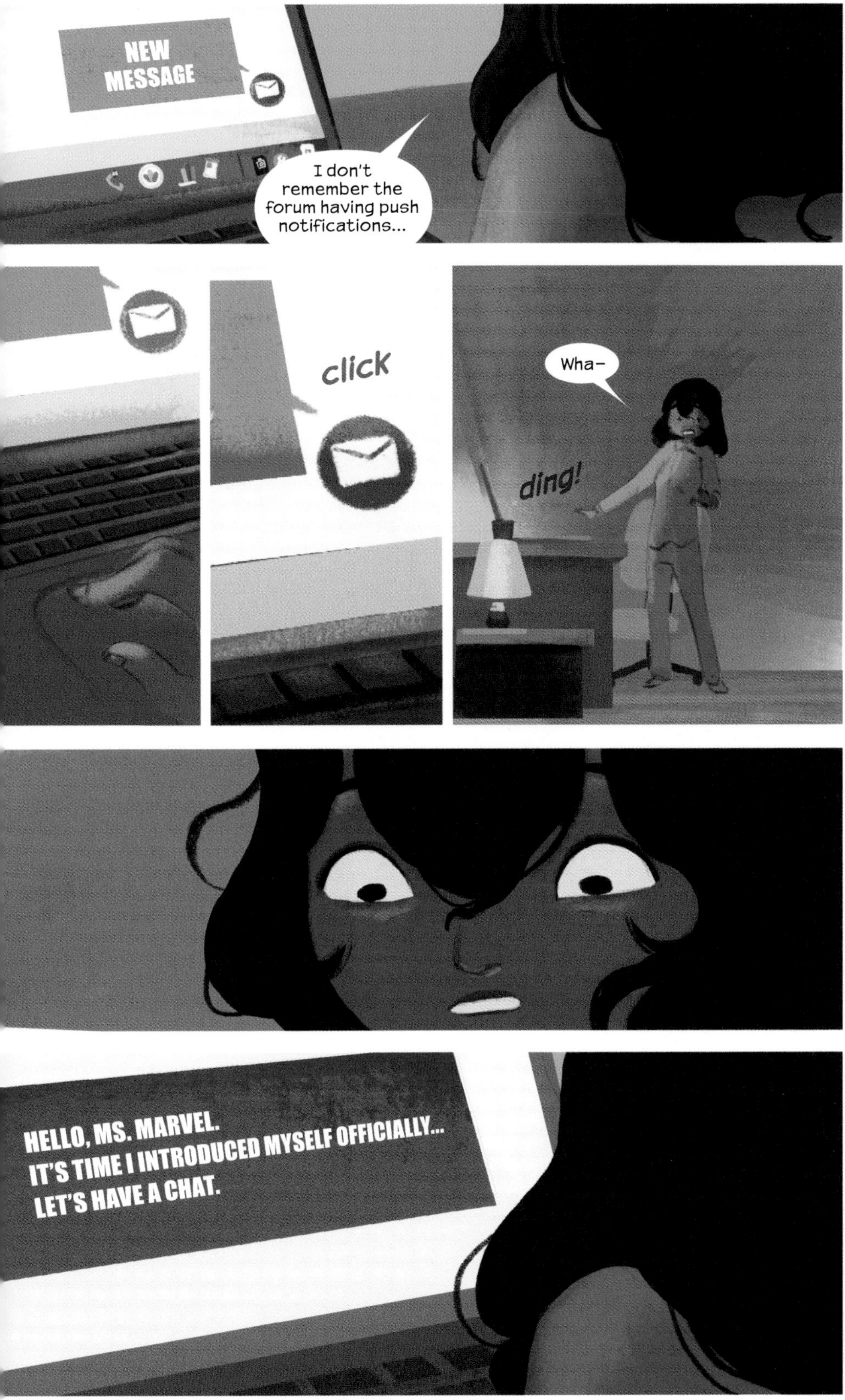
NEW MESSAGE
I don't remember the forum having push notifications...
click
Wha-
ding!
HELLO, MS. MARVEL.
IT'S TIME I INTRODUCED MYSELF OFFICIALLY...
LET'S HAVE A CHAT.

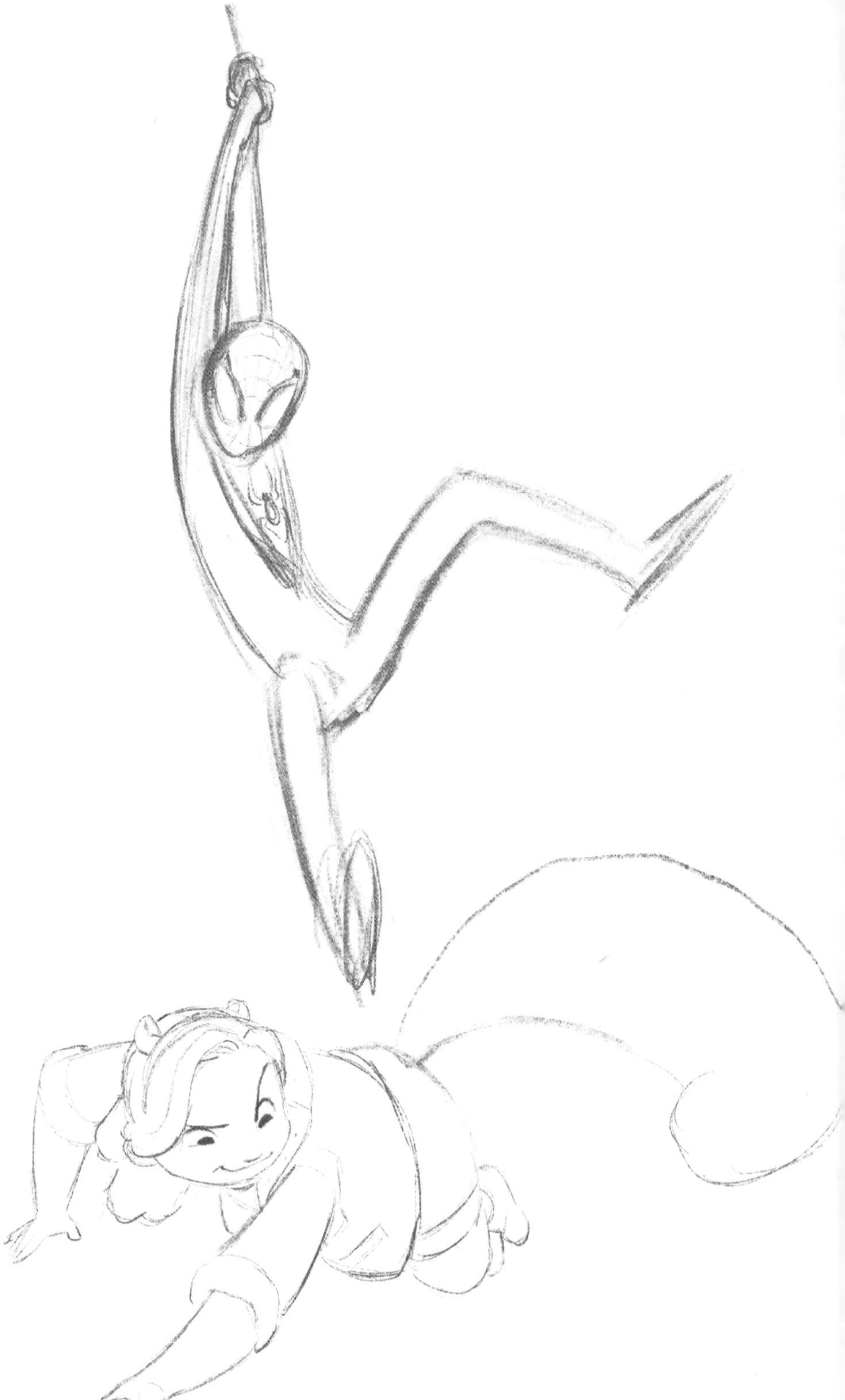

CHAPTER FOUR

HELLO, MS. MARVEL.
IT'S TIME I INTRODUCED MYSELF OFFICIALLY...
LET'S HAVE A CHAT.

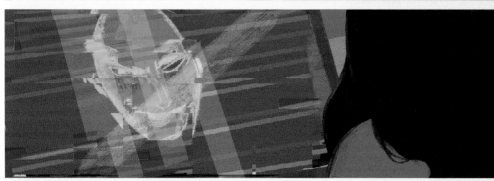

Hello, Ms. Marvel. Or do you prefer Ms. Khan?

I am Machinesmith.

What? As in... from the forum?? But...how–

I suppose we have been in communication for some time now, but that was in the guise of virtual niceties. So much better to meet in the flesh, so to speak.

It is actually the problem of flesh that led me to find you.

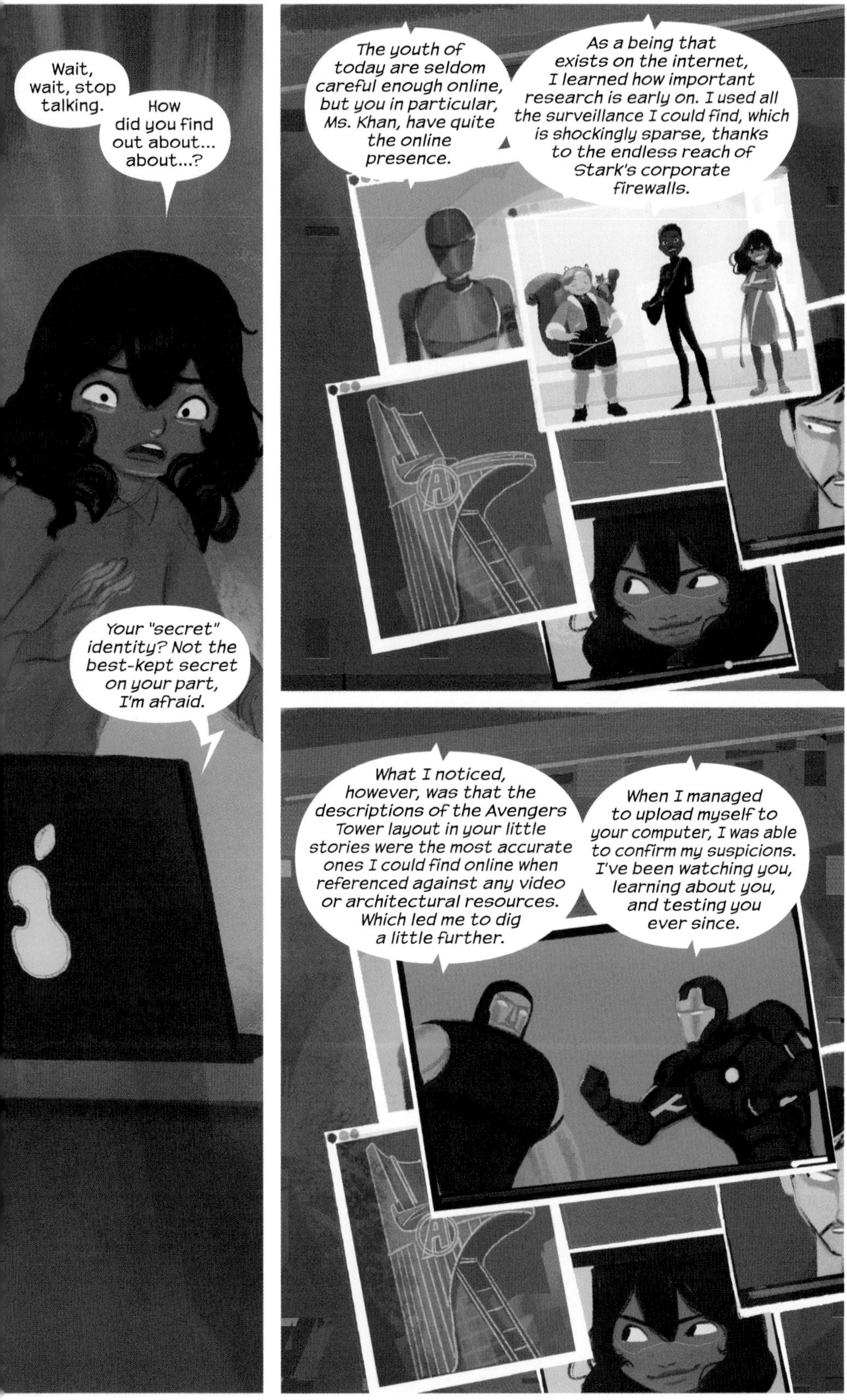
Wait, wait, stop talking.
How did you find out about... about...?
Your "secret" identity? Not the best-kept secret on your part, I'm afraid.
The youth of today are seldom careful enough online, but you in particular, Ms. Khan, have quite the online presence.
As a being that exists on the internet, I learned how important research is early on. I used all the surveillance I could find, which is shockingly sparse, thanks to the endless reach of Stark's corporate firewalls.
What I noticed, however, was that the descriptions of the Avengers Tower layout in your little stories were the most accurate ones I could find online when referenced against any video or architectural resources. Which led me to dig a little further.
When I managed to upload myself to your computer, I was able to confirm my suspicions. I've been watching you, learning about you, and testing you ever since.

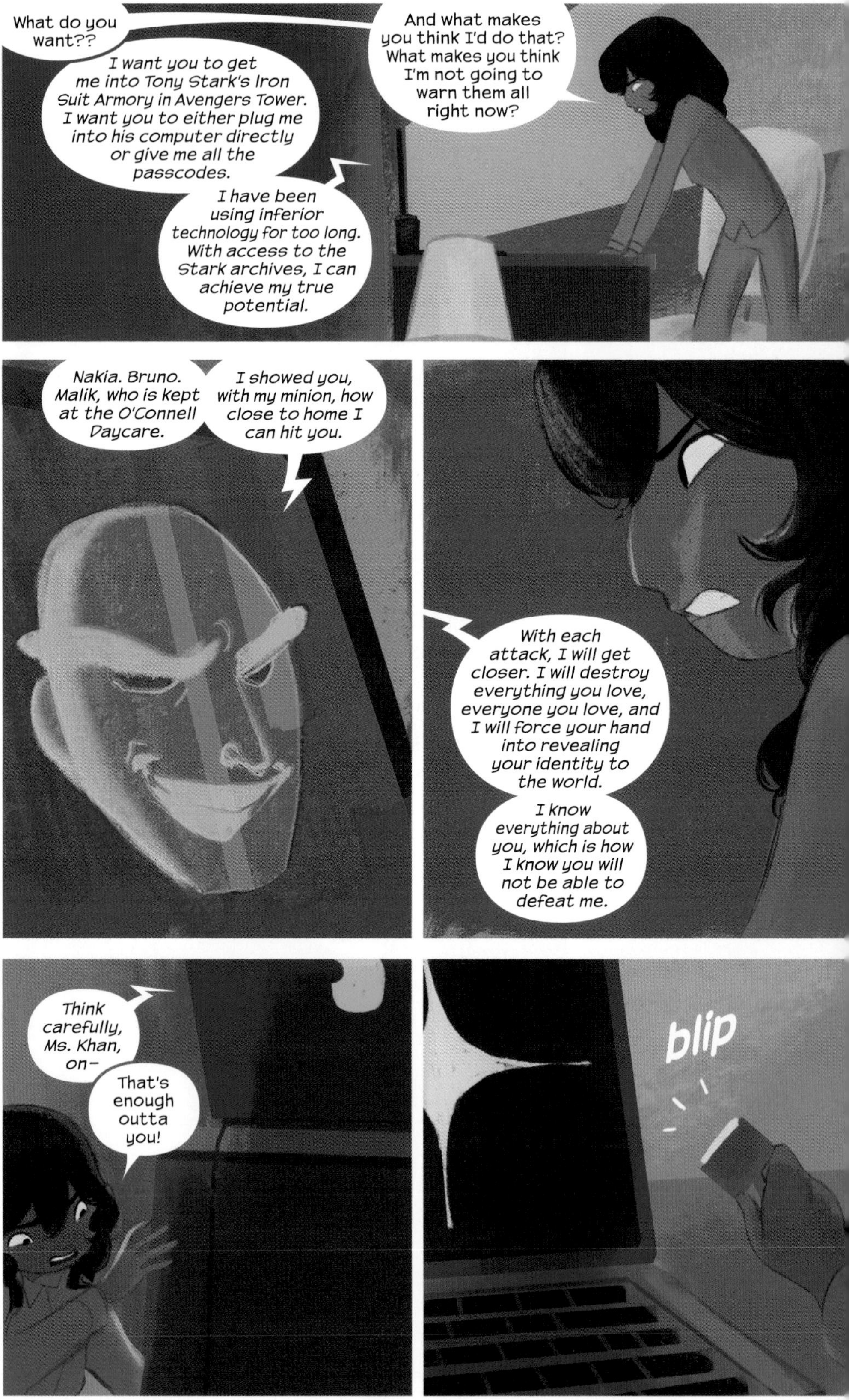
What do you want??
I want you to get me into Tony Stark's Iron Suit Armory in Avengers Tower. I want you to either plug me into his computer directly or give me all the passcodes.
I have been using inferior technology for too long. With access to the Stark archives, I can achieve my true potential.
And what makes you think I'd do that? What makes you think I'm not going to warn them all right now?
Nakia. Bruno. Malik, who is kept at the O'Connell Daycare.
I showed you, with my minion, how close to home I can hit you.
With each attack, I will get closer. I will destroy everything you love, everyone you love, and I will force your hand into revealing your identity to the world.
I know everything about you, which is how I know you will not be able to defeat me.
Think carefully, Ms. Khan, on–
That's enough outta you!
blip

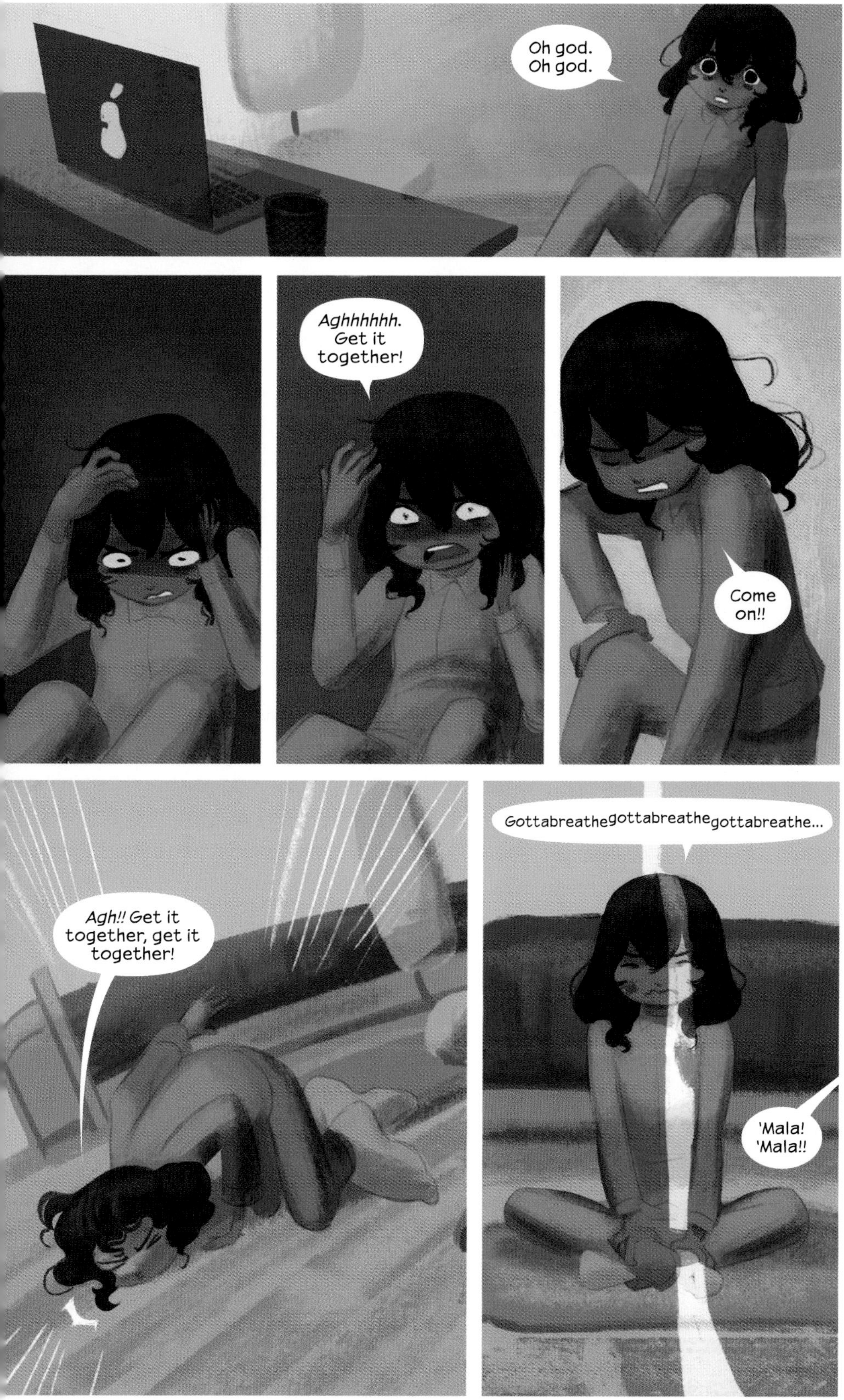

Oh god.
Oh god.
Aghhhhhh. Get it together!
Come on!!
Agh!! Get it together, get it together!
Gottabreathegottabreathegottabreathe...
'Mala! 'Mala!!

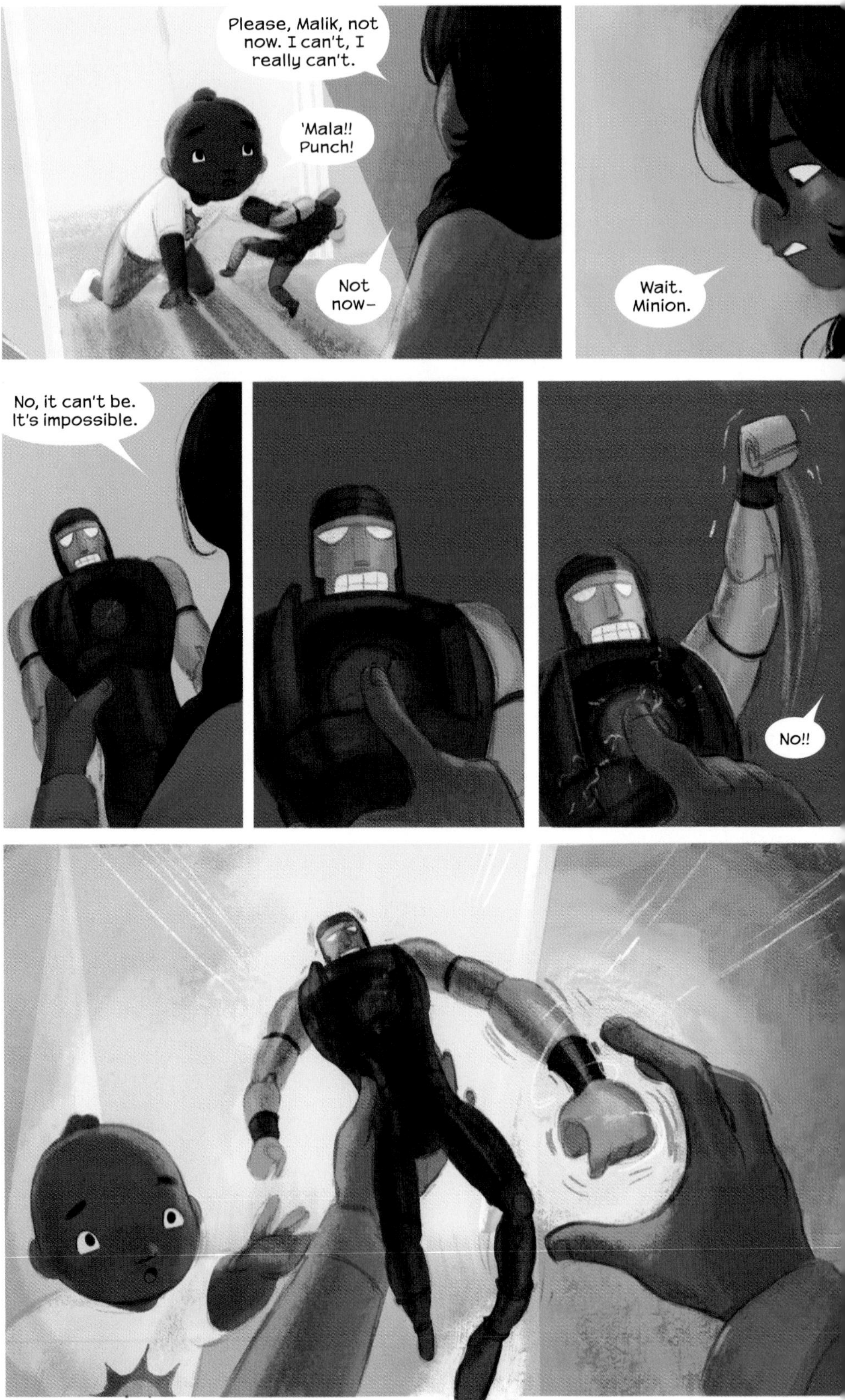
Please, Malik, not now. I can't, I really can't.
'Mala!! Punch!
Not now—
Wait. Minion.
No, it can't be. It's impossible.
No!!

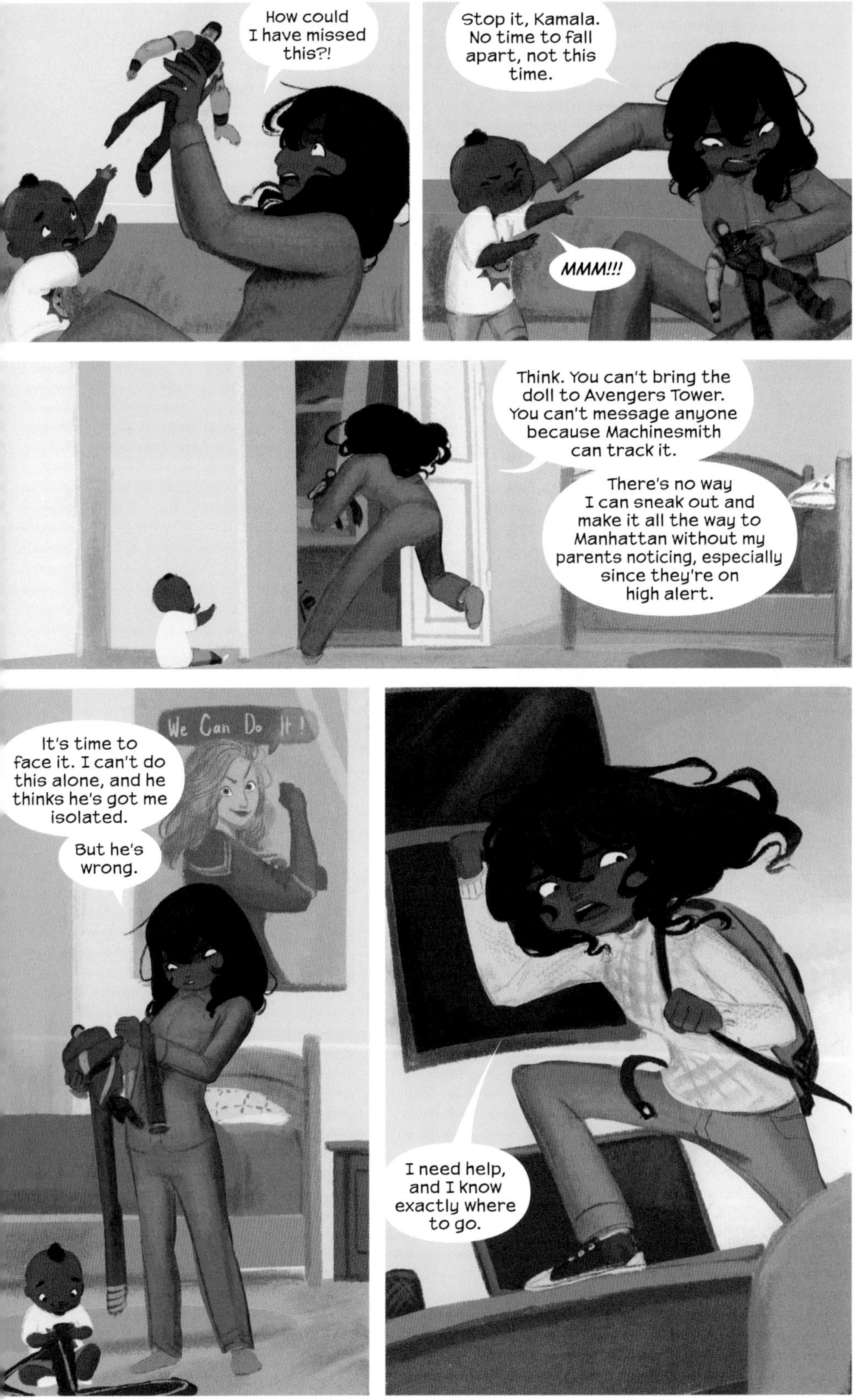
How could I have missed this?!
Stop it, Kamala. No time to fall apart, not this time.
MMM!!!
Think. You can't bring the doll to Avengers Tower. You can't message anyone because Machinesmith can track it.
There's no way I can sneak out and make it all the way to Manhattan without my parents noticing, especially since they're on high alert.
We Can Do It!
It's time to face it. I can't do this alone, and he thinks he's got me isolated.
But he's wrong.
I need help, and I know exactly where to go.

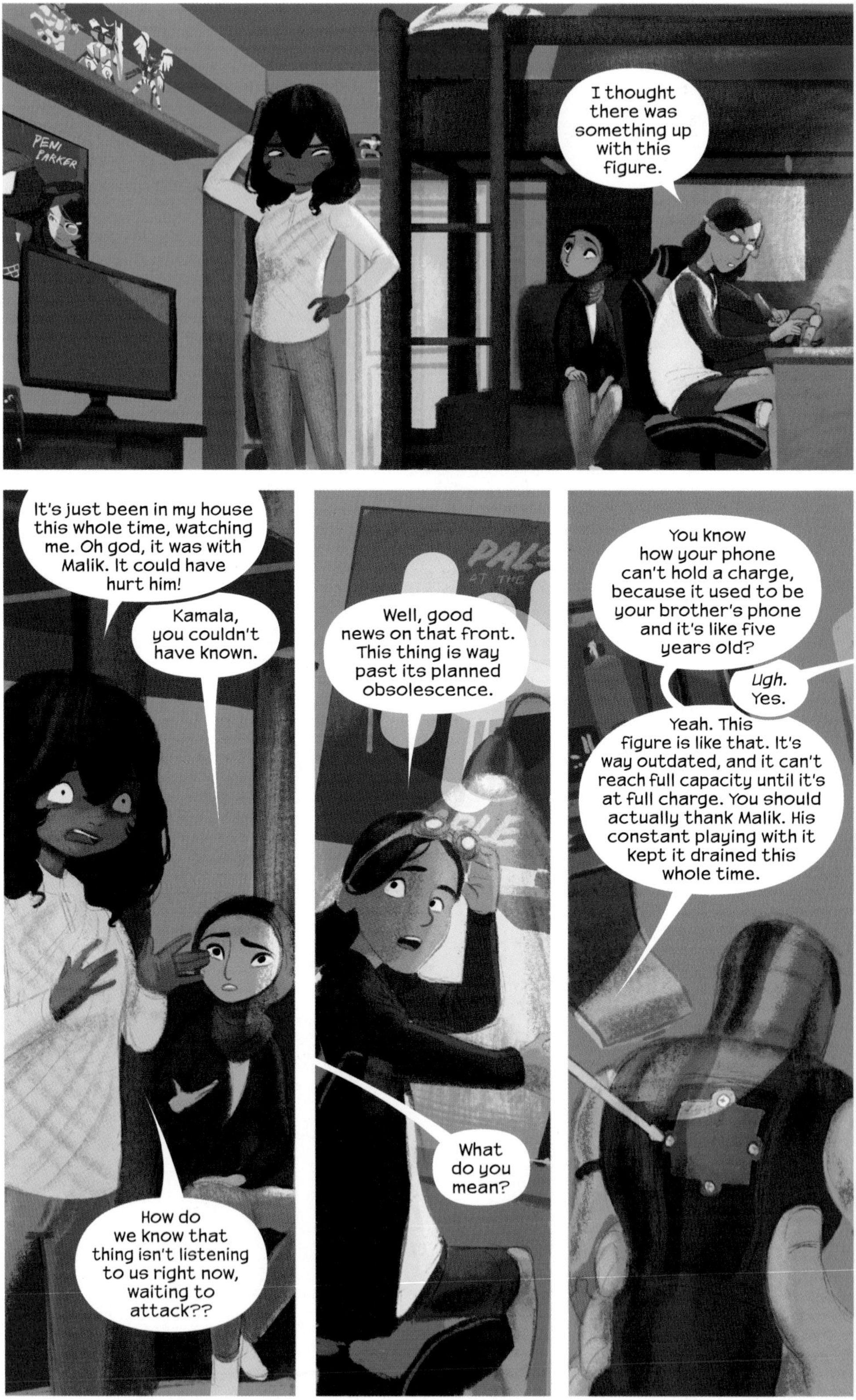
PENI PARKER
I thought there was something up with this figure.
It's just been in my house this whole time, watching me. Oh god, it was with Malik. It could have hurt him!
Kamala, you couldn't have known.
How do we know that thing isn't listening to us right now, waiting to attack??
Well, good news on that front. This thing is way past its planned obsolescence.
What do you mean?
You know how your phone can't hold a charge, because it used to be your brother's phone and it's like five years old?
Ugh. Yes.
Yeah. This figure is like that. It's way outdated, and it can't reach full capacity until it's at full charge. You should actually thank Malik. His constant playing with it kept it drained this whole time.

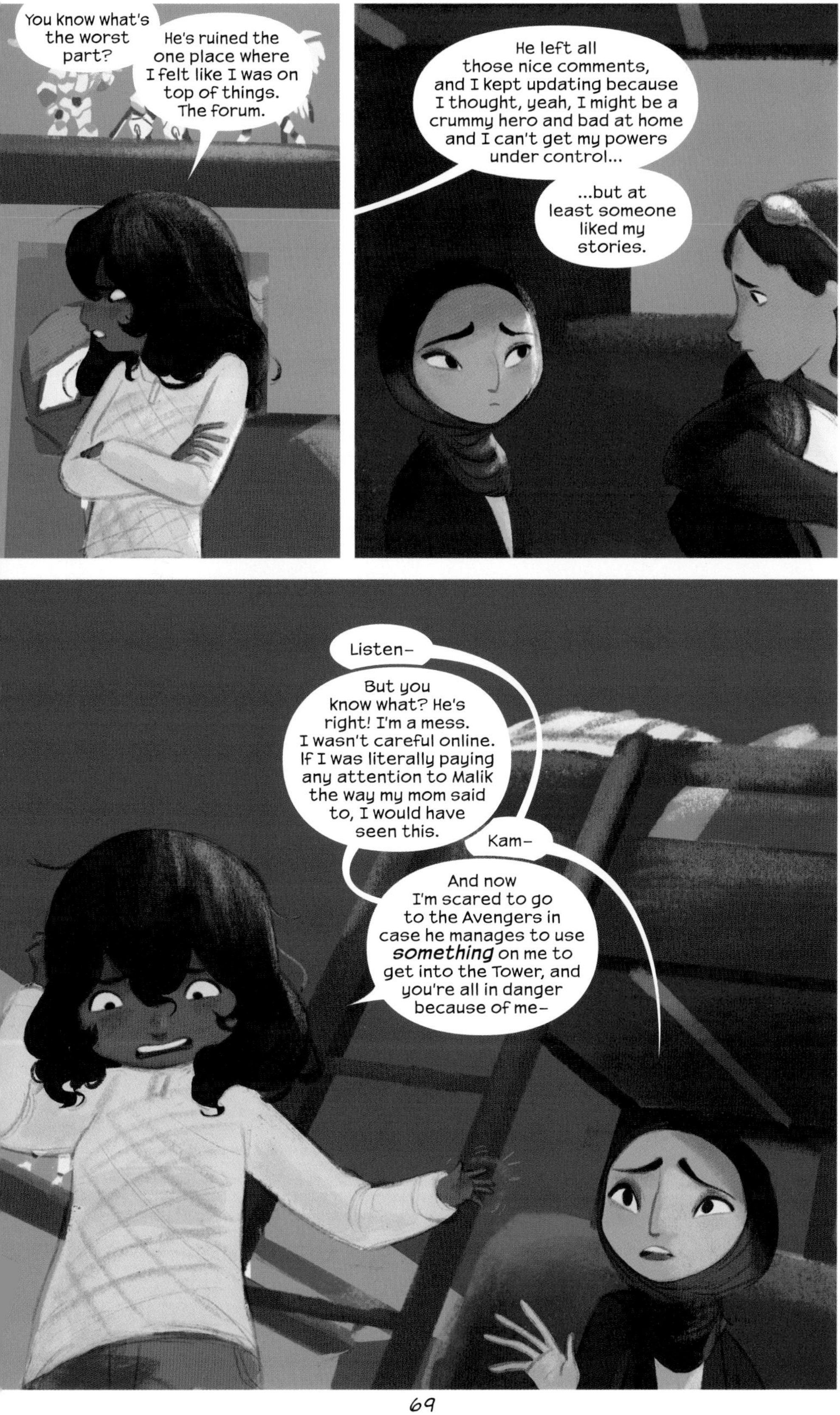
You know what's the worst part?
He's ruined the one place where I felt like I was on top of things. The forum.
He left all those nice comments, and I kept updating because I thought, yeah, I might be a crummy hero and bad at home and I can't get my powers under control...
...but at least someone liked my stories.
Listen–
But you know what? He's right! I'm a mess. I wasn't careful online. If I was literally paying any attention to Malik the way my mom said to, I would have seen this.
Kam–
And now I'm scared to go to the Avengers in case he manages to use *something* on me to get into the Tower, and you're all in danger because of me–

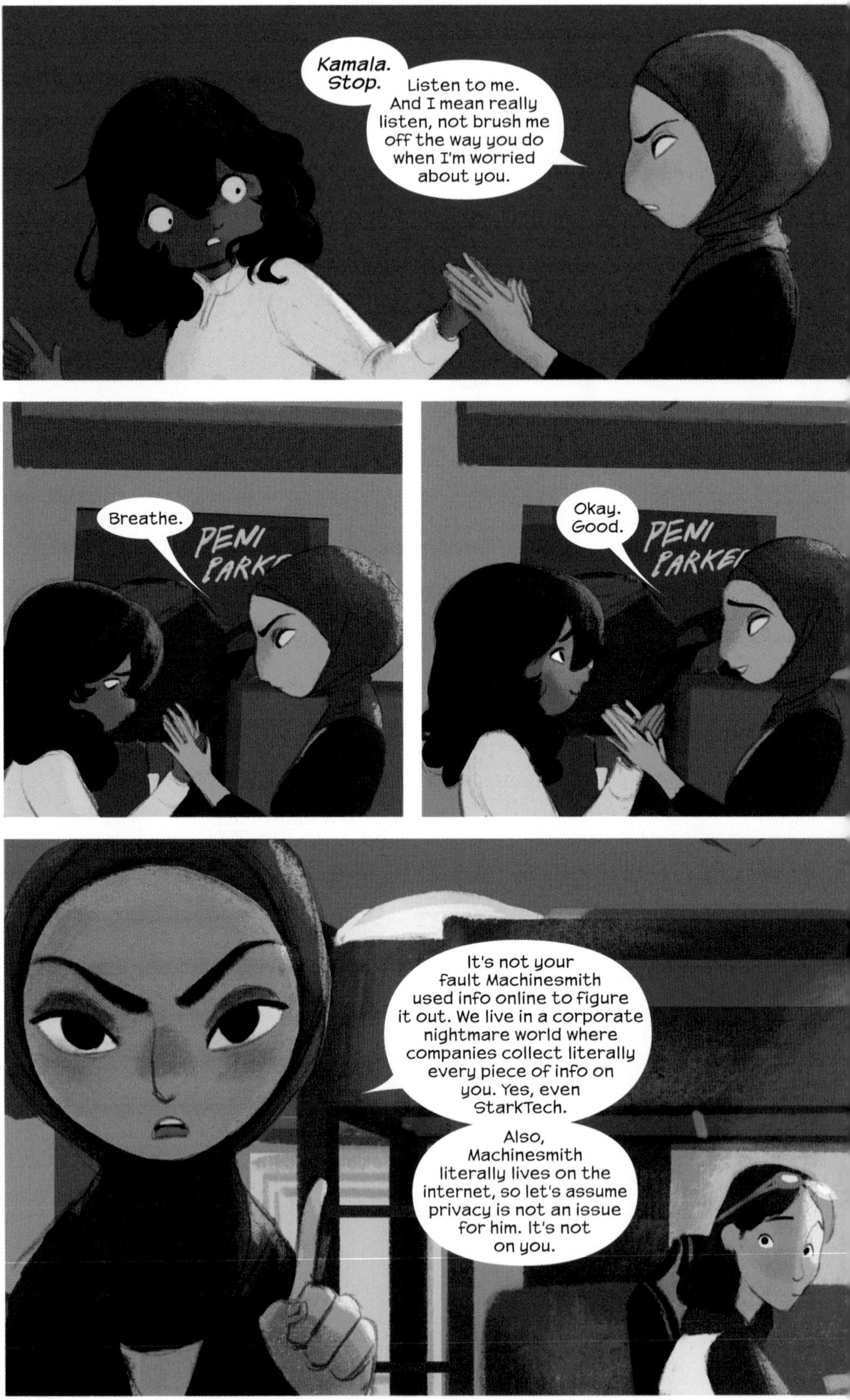
Kamala. Stop.
Listen to me. And I mean really listen, not brush me off the way you do when I'm worried about you.
Breathe.
PENI PARKE
Okay. Good.
PENI PARKE
It's not your fault Machinesmith used info online to figure it out. We live in a corporate nightmare world where companies collect literally every piece of info on you. Yes, even StarkTech.
Also, Machinesmith literally lives on the internet, so let's assume privacy is not an issue for him. It's not on you.

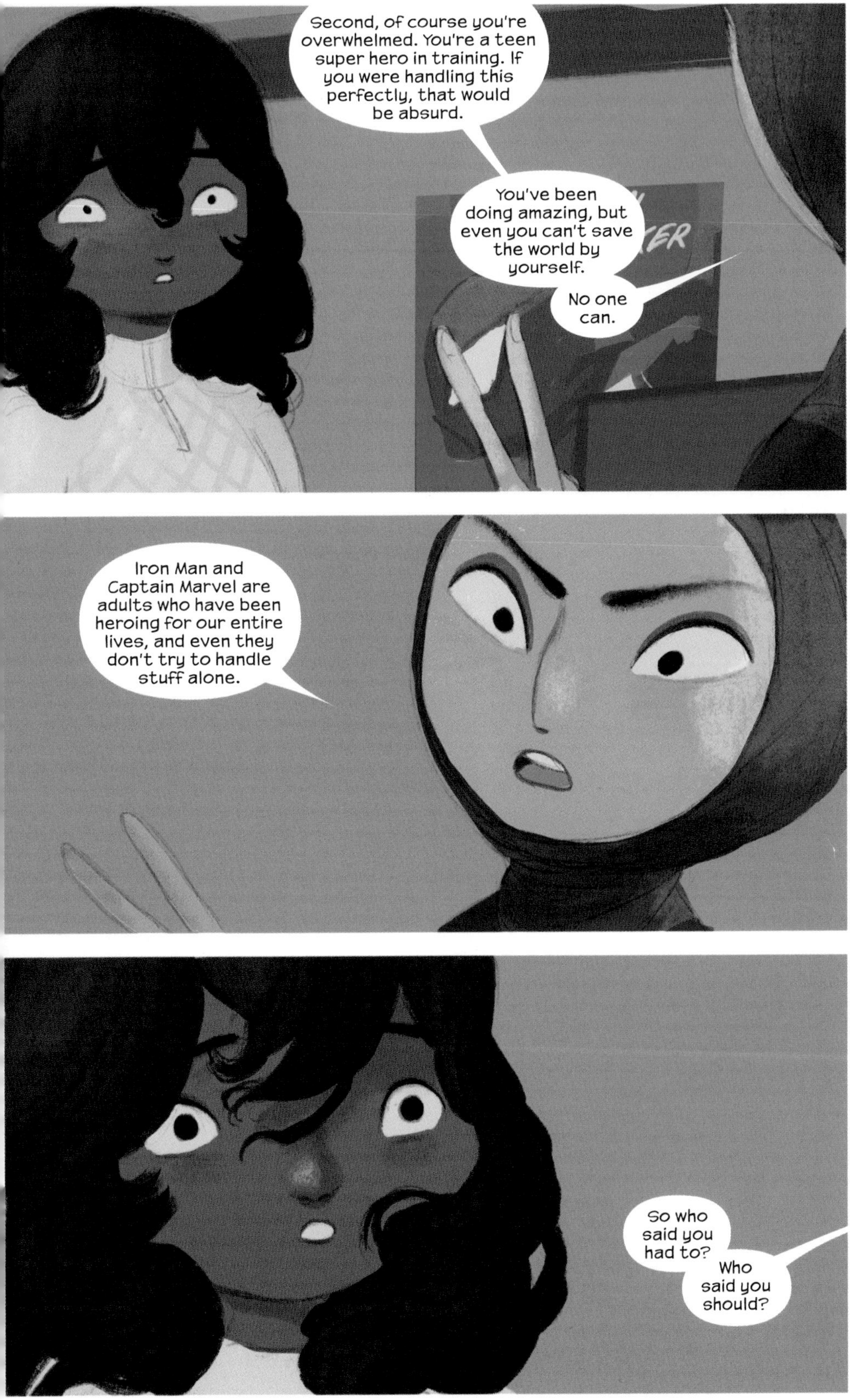
Second, of course you're overwhelmed. You're a teen super hero in training. If you were handling this perfectly, that would be absurd.
You've been doing amazing, but even you can't save the world by yourself.
No one can.
Iron Man and Captain Marvel are adults who have been heroing for our entire lives, and even they don't try to handle stuff alone.
So who said you had to?
Who said you should?

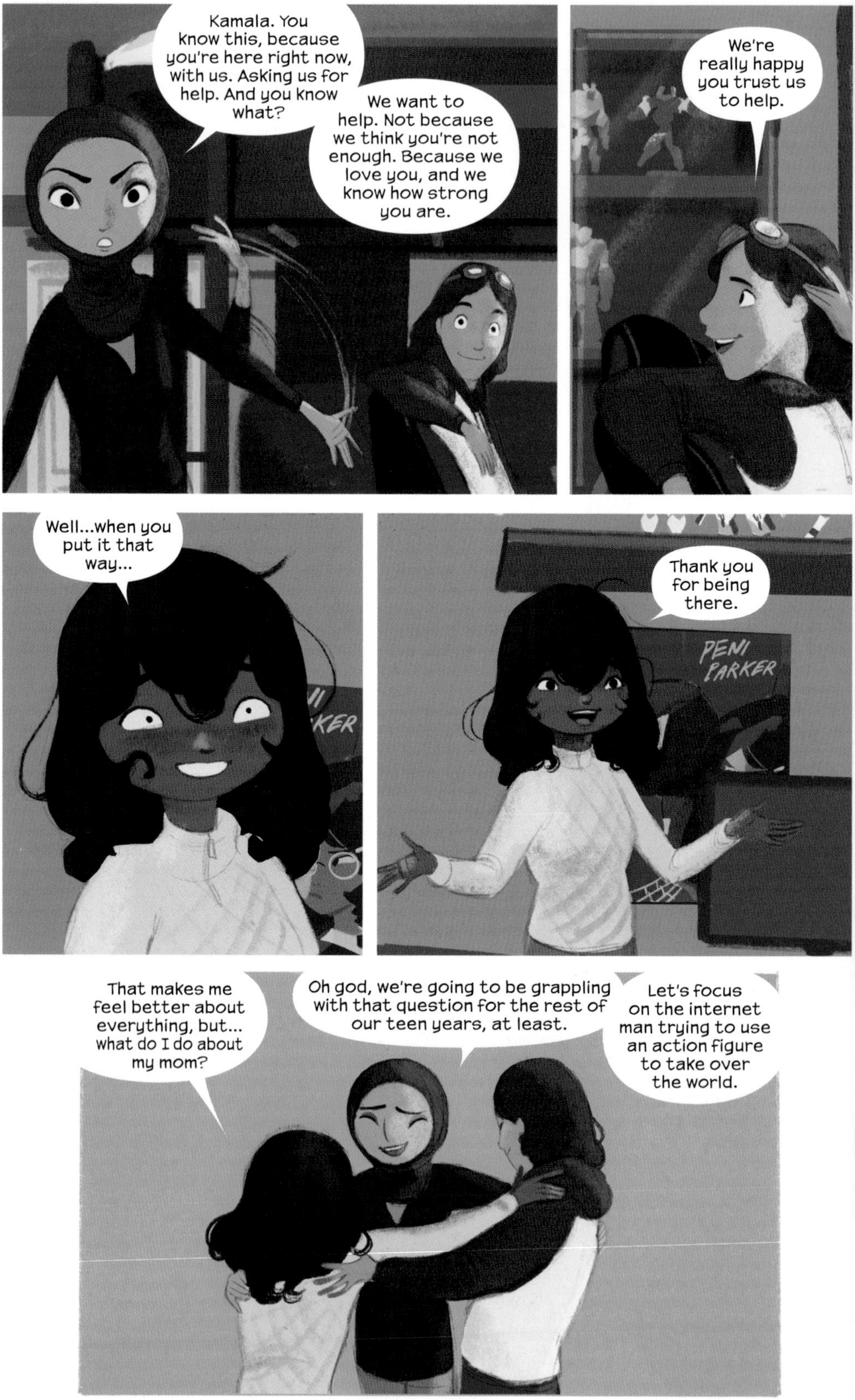
Kamala. You know this, because you're here right now, with us. Asking us for help. And you know what?
We want to help. Not because we think you're not enough. Because we love you, and we know how strong you are.
We're really happy you trust us to help.
Well...when you put it that way...
Thank you for being there.
PENI PARKER
That makes me feel better about everything, but... what do I do about my mom?
Oh god, we're going to be grappling with that question for the rest of our teen years, at least.
Let's focus on the internet man trying to use an action figure to take over the world.

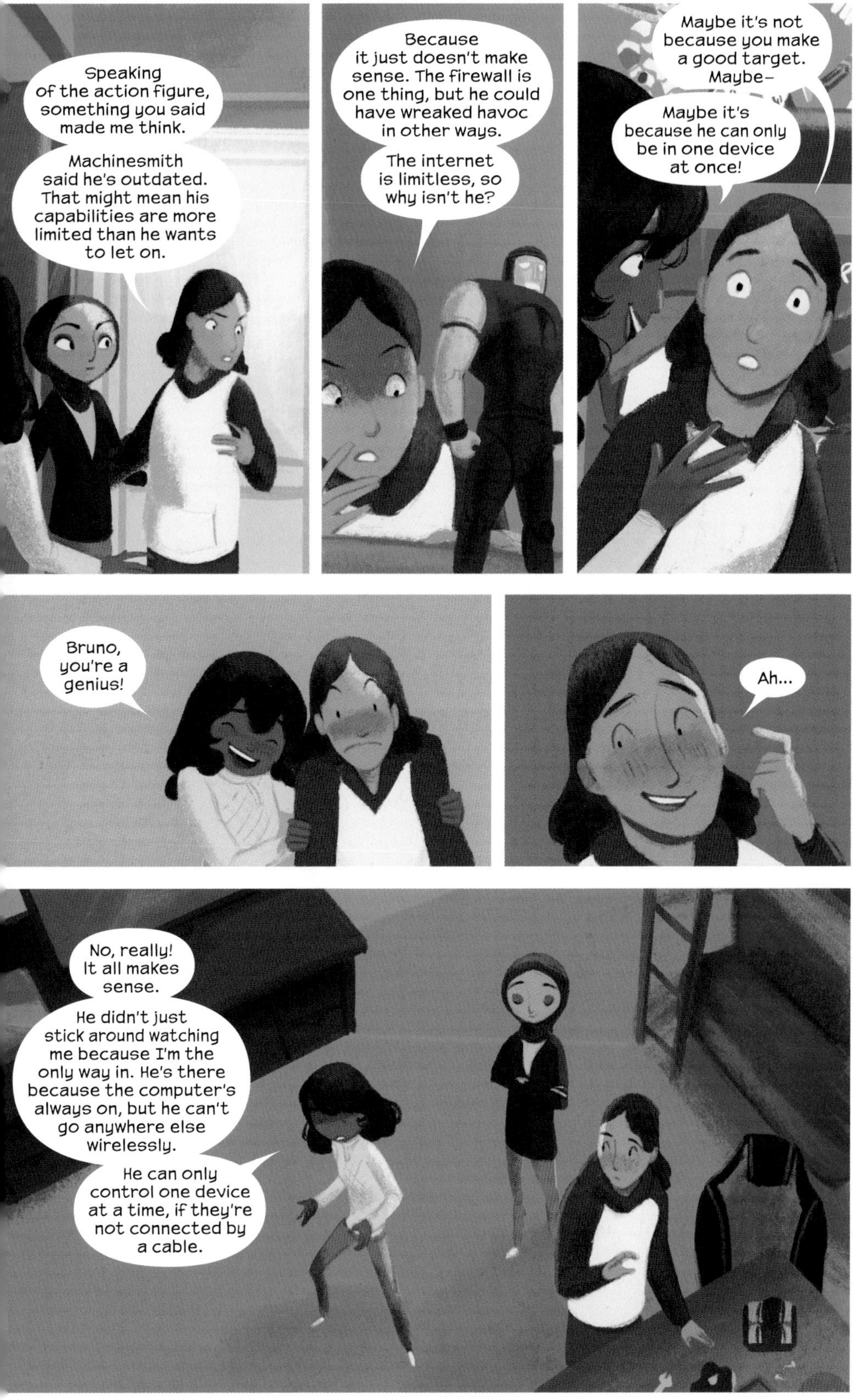
Speaking of the action figure, something you said made me think.
Machinesmith said he's outdated. That might mean his capabilities are more limited than he wants to let on.
Because it just doesn't make sense. The firewall is one thing, but he could have wreaked havoc in other ways.
The internet is limitless, so why isn't he?
Maybe it's not because you make a good target. Maybe–
Maybe it's because he can only be in one device at once!
Bruno, you're a genius!
Ah...
No, really! It all makes sense.
He didn't just stick around watching me because I'm the only way in. He's there because the computer's always on, but he can't go anywhere else wirelessly.
He can only control one device at a time, if they're not connected by a cable.

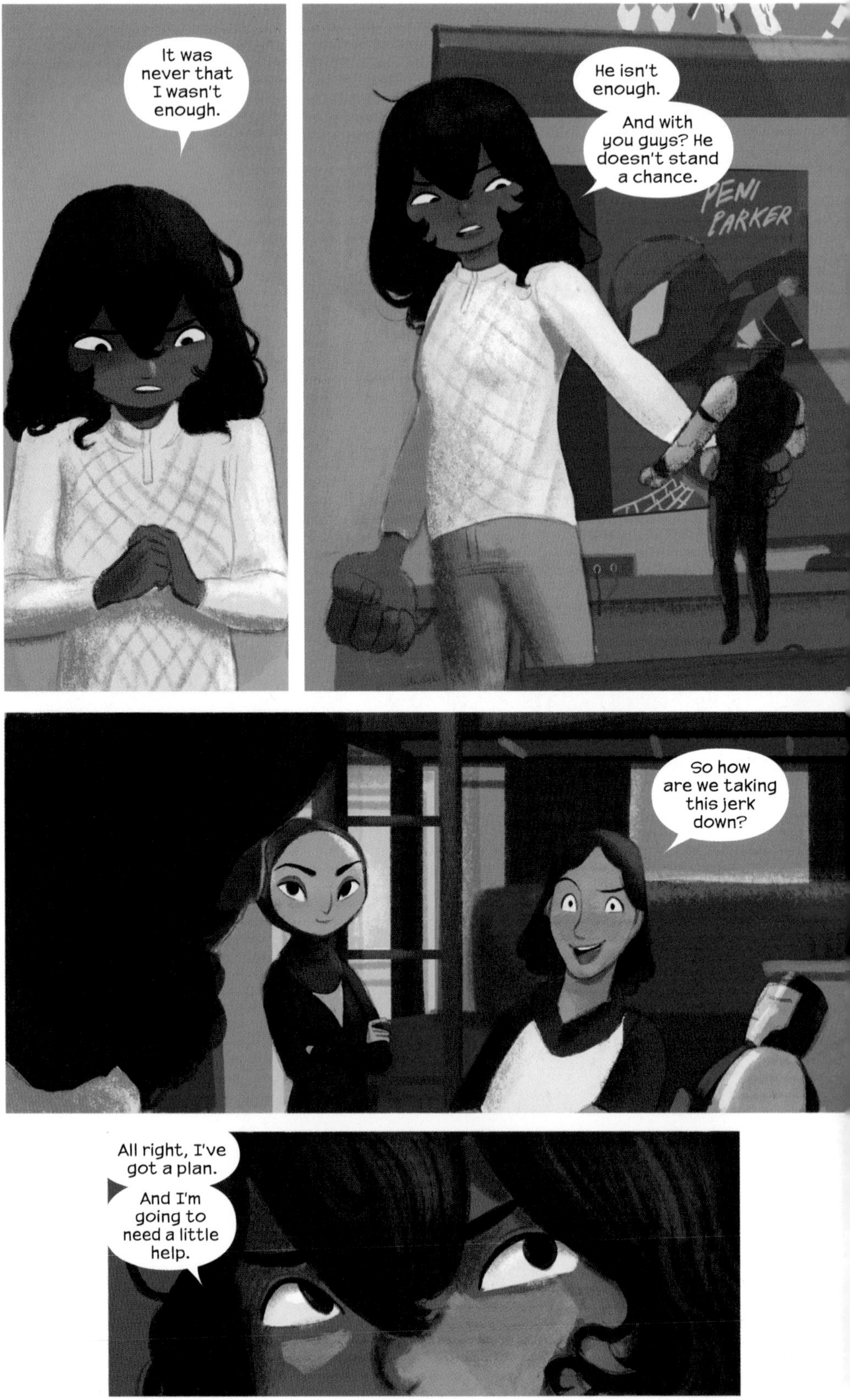
It was never that I wasn't enough.
He isn't enough.
And with you guys? He doesn't stand a chance.
PENI PARKER
So how are we taking this jerk down?
All right, I've got a plan.
And I'm going to need a little help.

CHAPTER FIVE

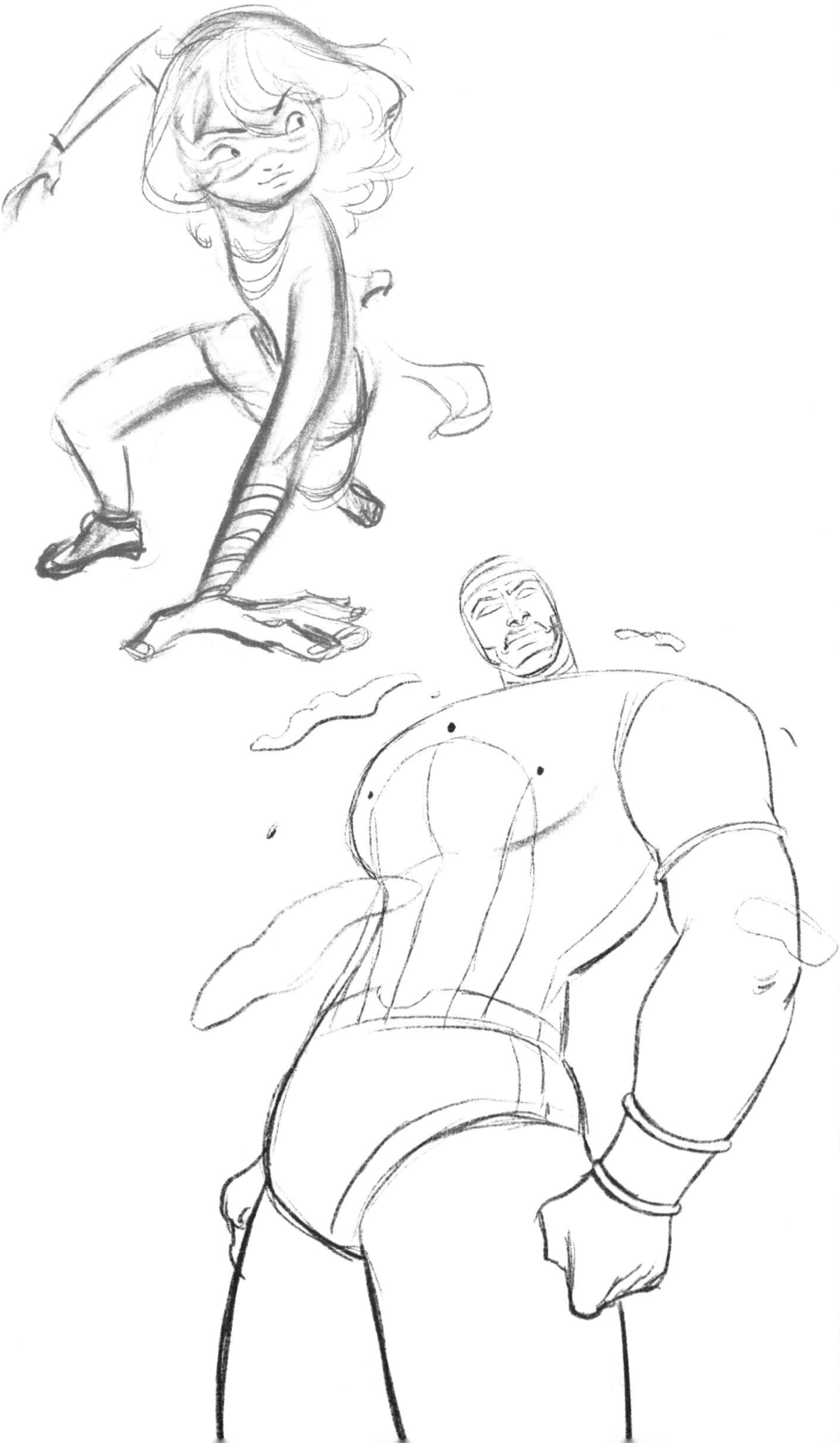

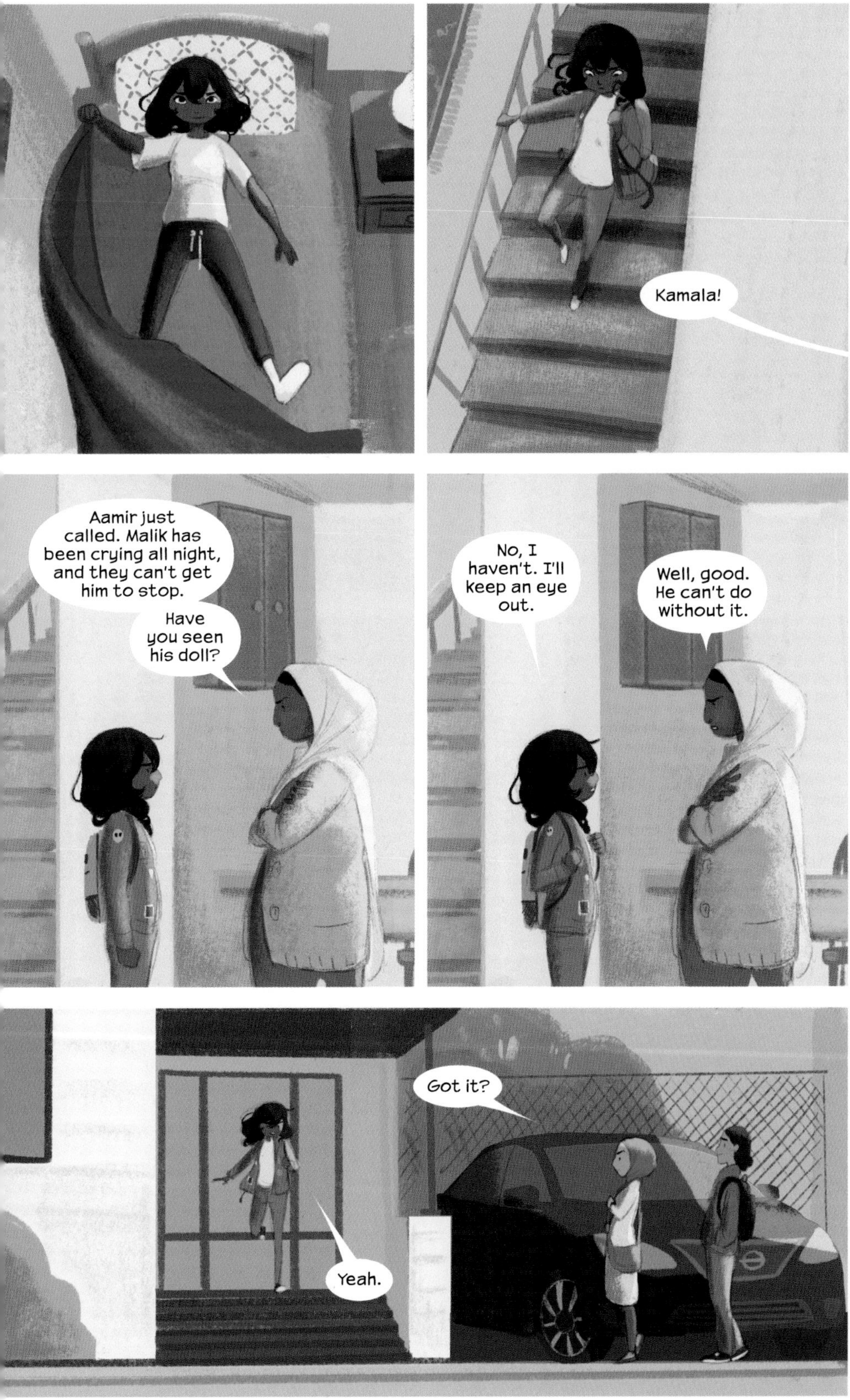
Kamala!
Aamir just called. Malik has been crying all night, and they can't get him to stop.
Have you seen his doll?
No, I haven't. I'll keep an eye out.
Well, good. He can't do without it.
Got it?
Yeah.

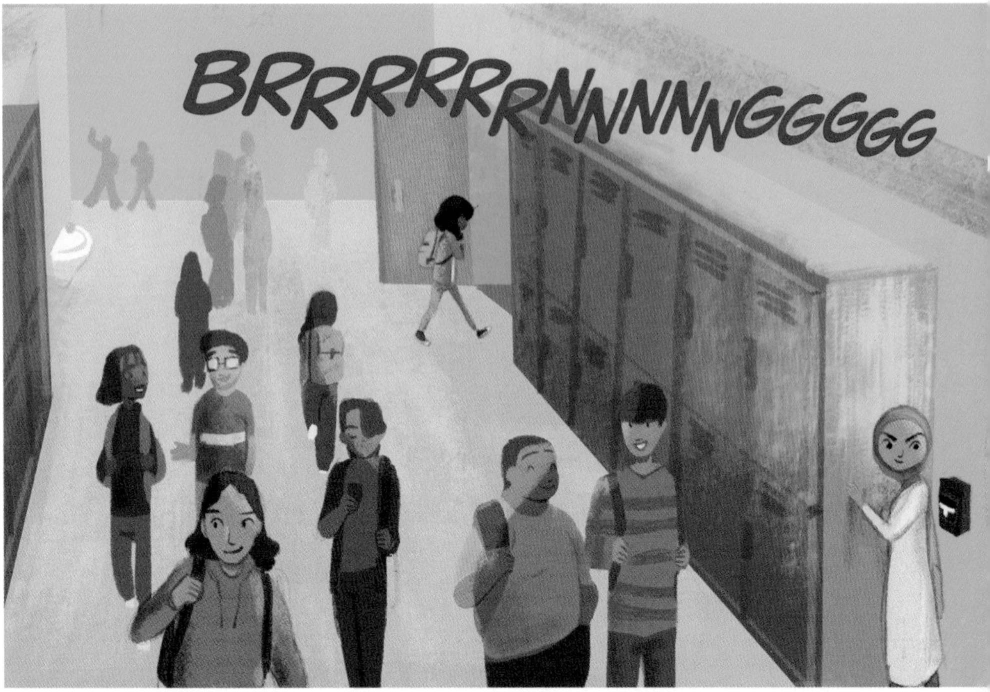
BRRRRRRNNNNNGGGGG

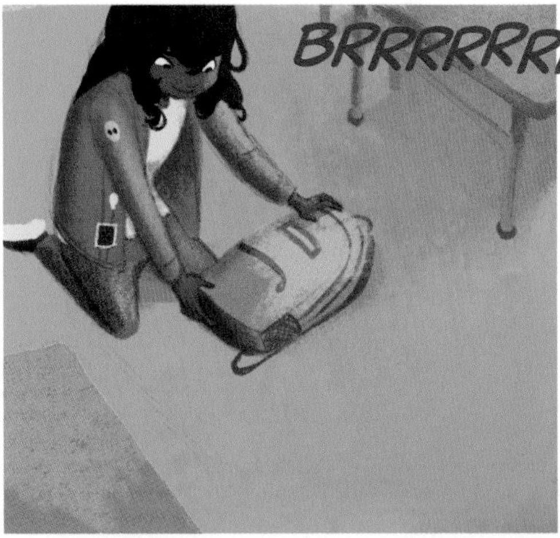
BRRRRRRNNNNNGGGGG

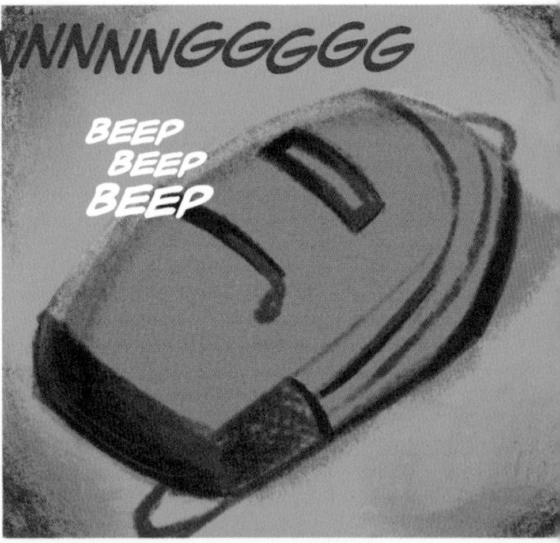
BEEP
BEEP
BEEP

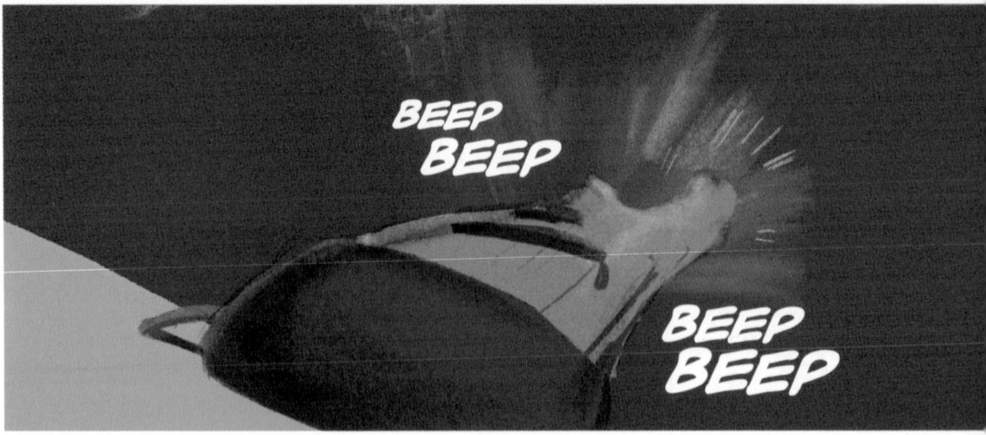
BEEP
BEEP
BEEP
BEEP

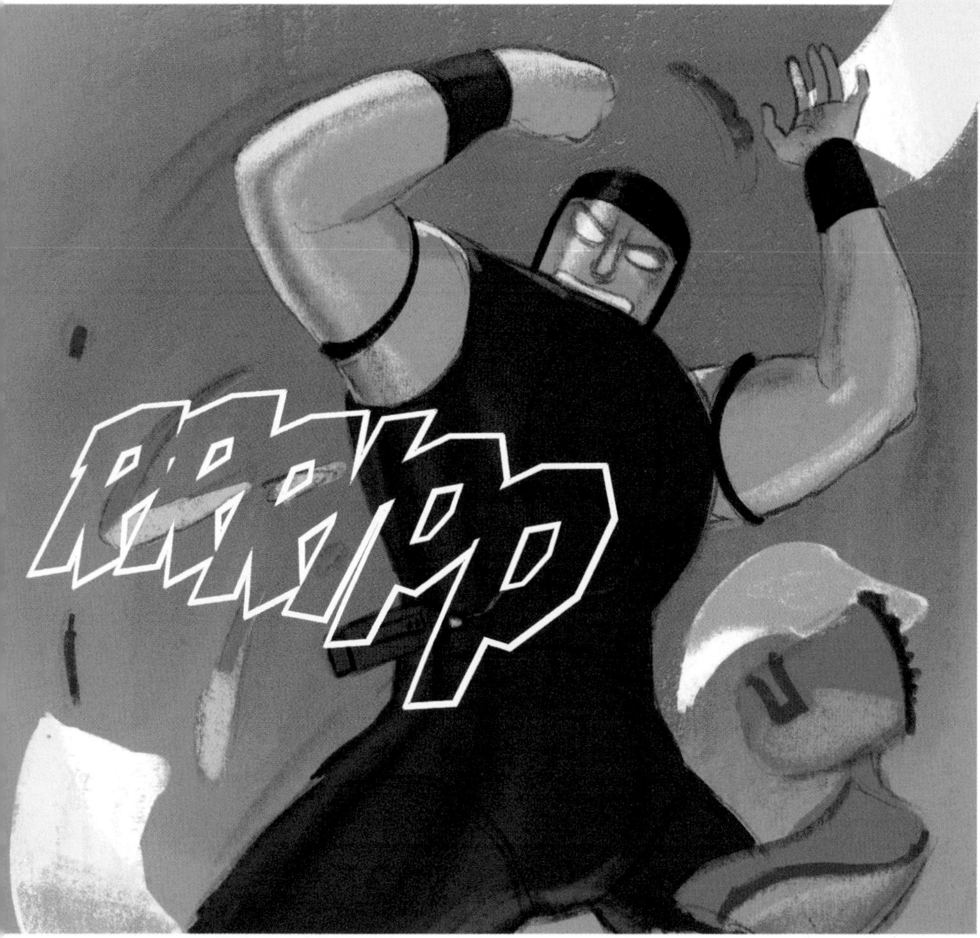
RRRIPP

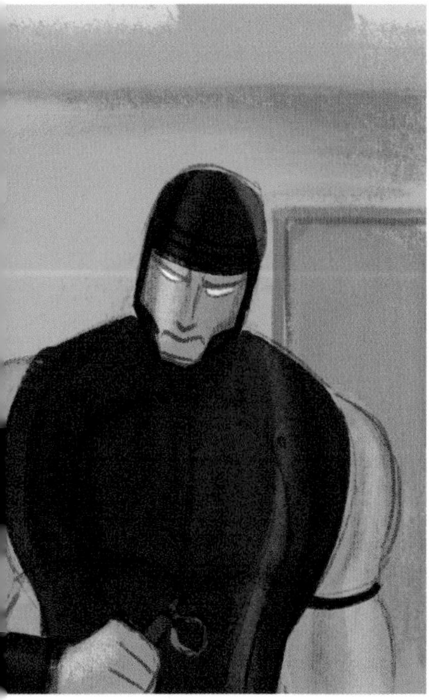

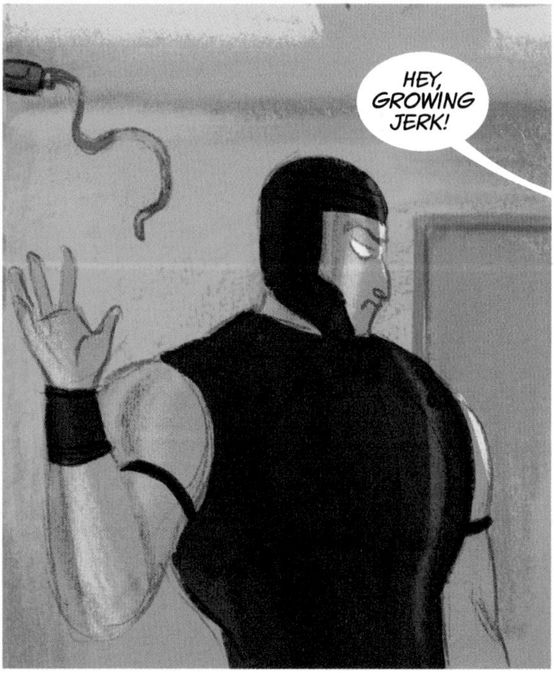
HEY, GROWING JERK!

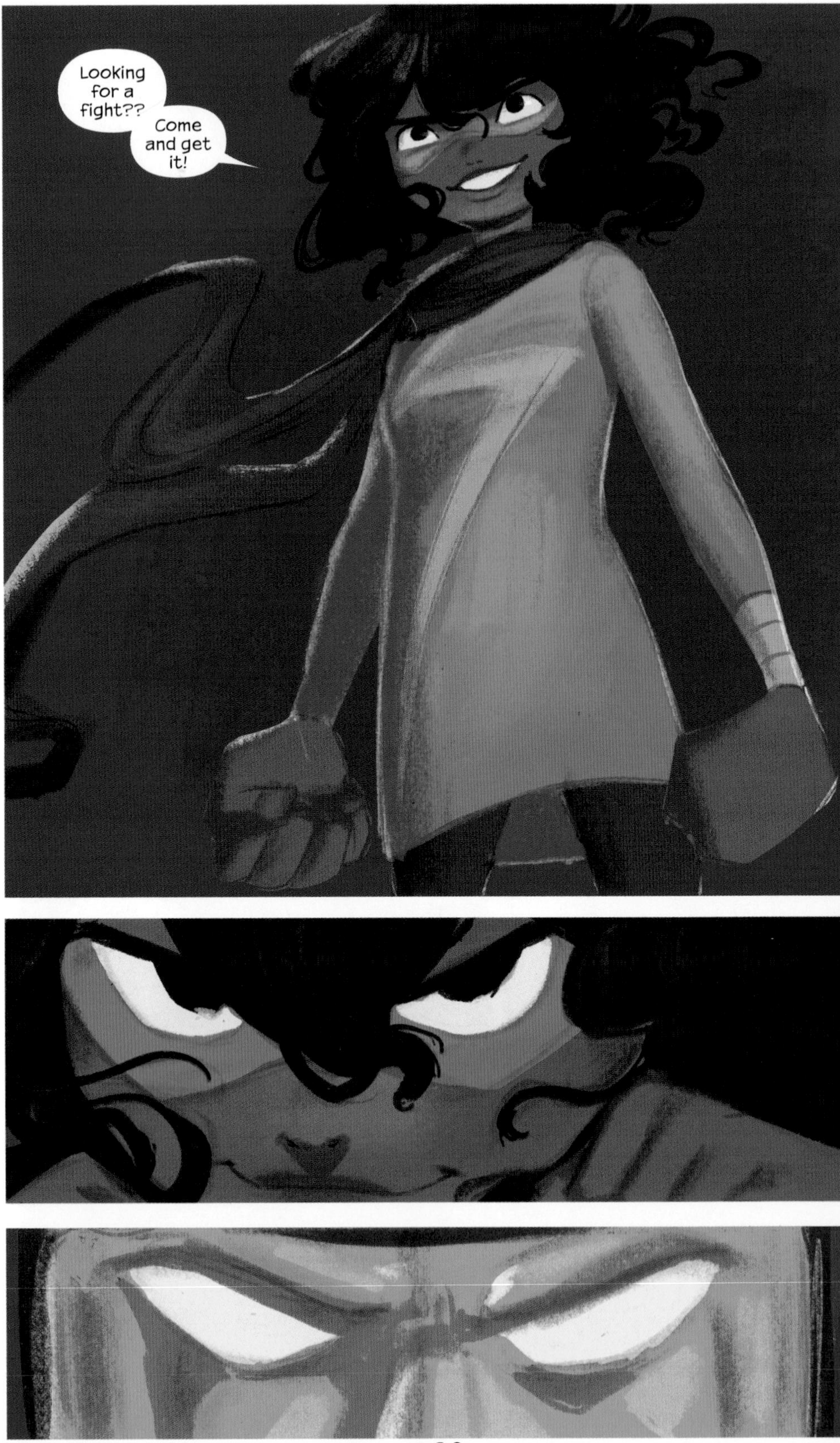
Looking for a fight??
Come and get it!

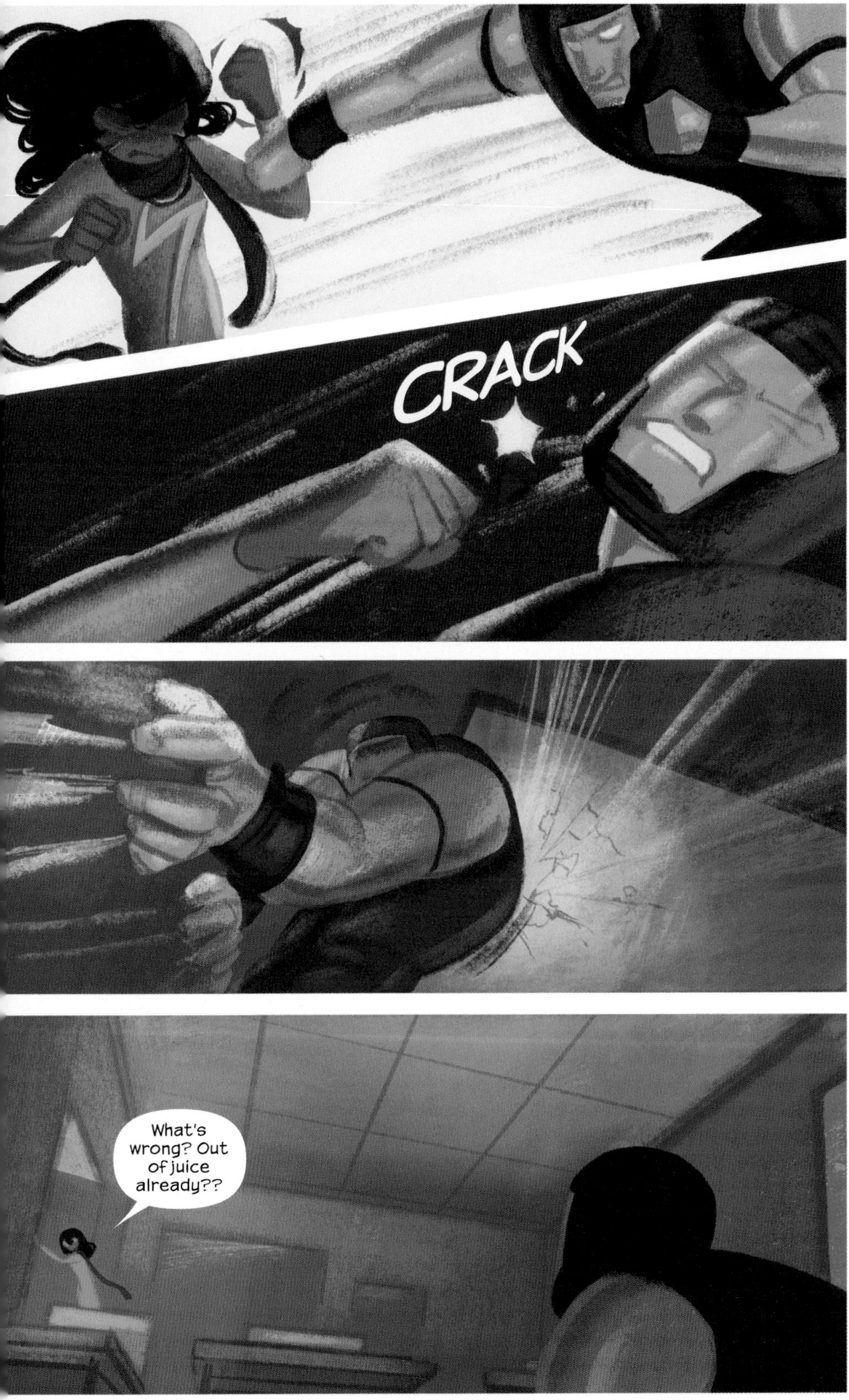
CRACK
What's wrong? Out of juice already??

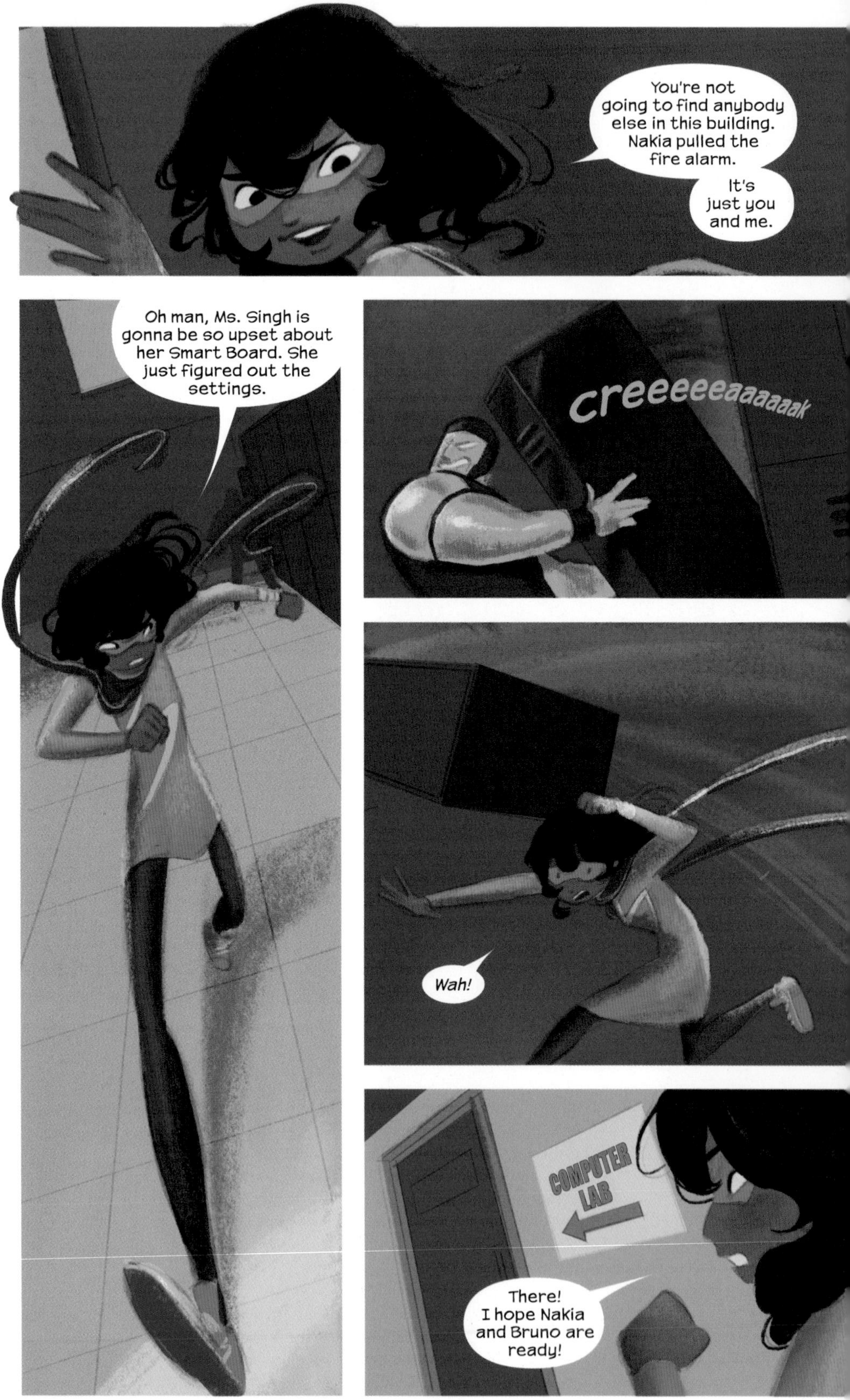
You're not going to find anybody else in this building. Nakia pulled the fire alarm.
It's just you and me.
Oh man, Ms. Singh is gonna be so upset about her Smart Board. She just figured out the settings.
creeeeeaaaaaak
Wah!
COMPUTER LAB
There! I hope Nakia and Bruno are ready!

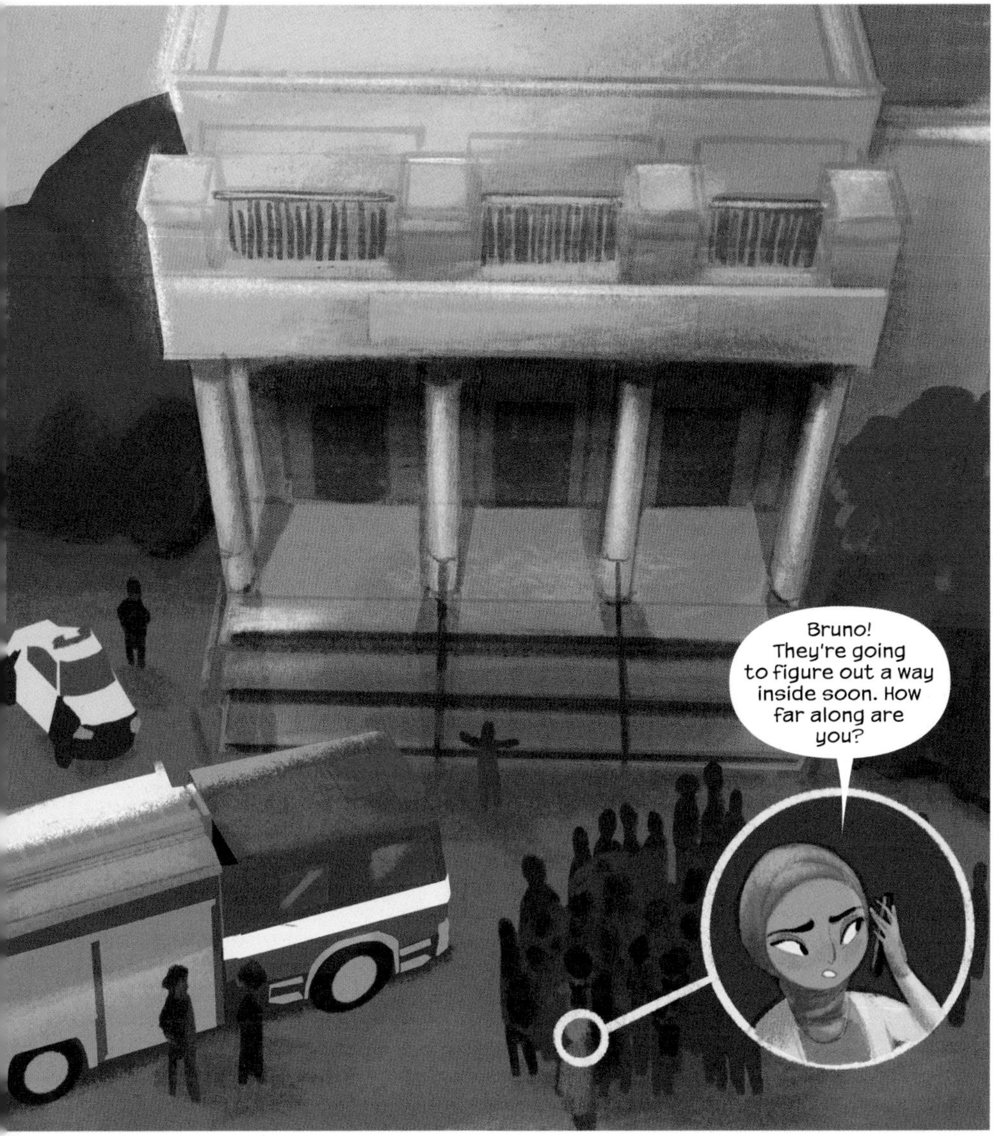
Bruno! They're going to figure out a way inside soon. How far along are you?

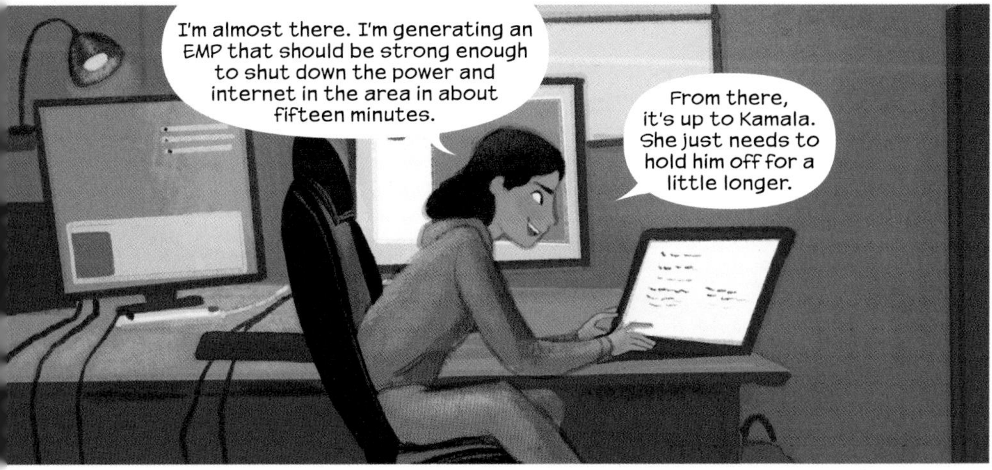
I'm almost there. I'm generating an EMP that should be strong enough to shut down the power and internet in the area in about fifteen minutes.
From there, it's up to Kamala. She just needs to hold him off for a little longer.

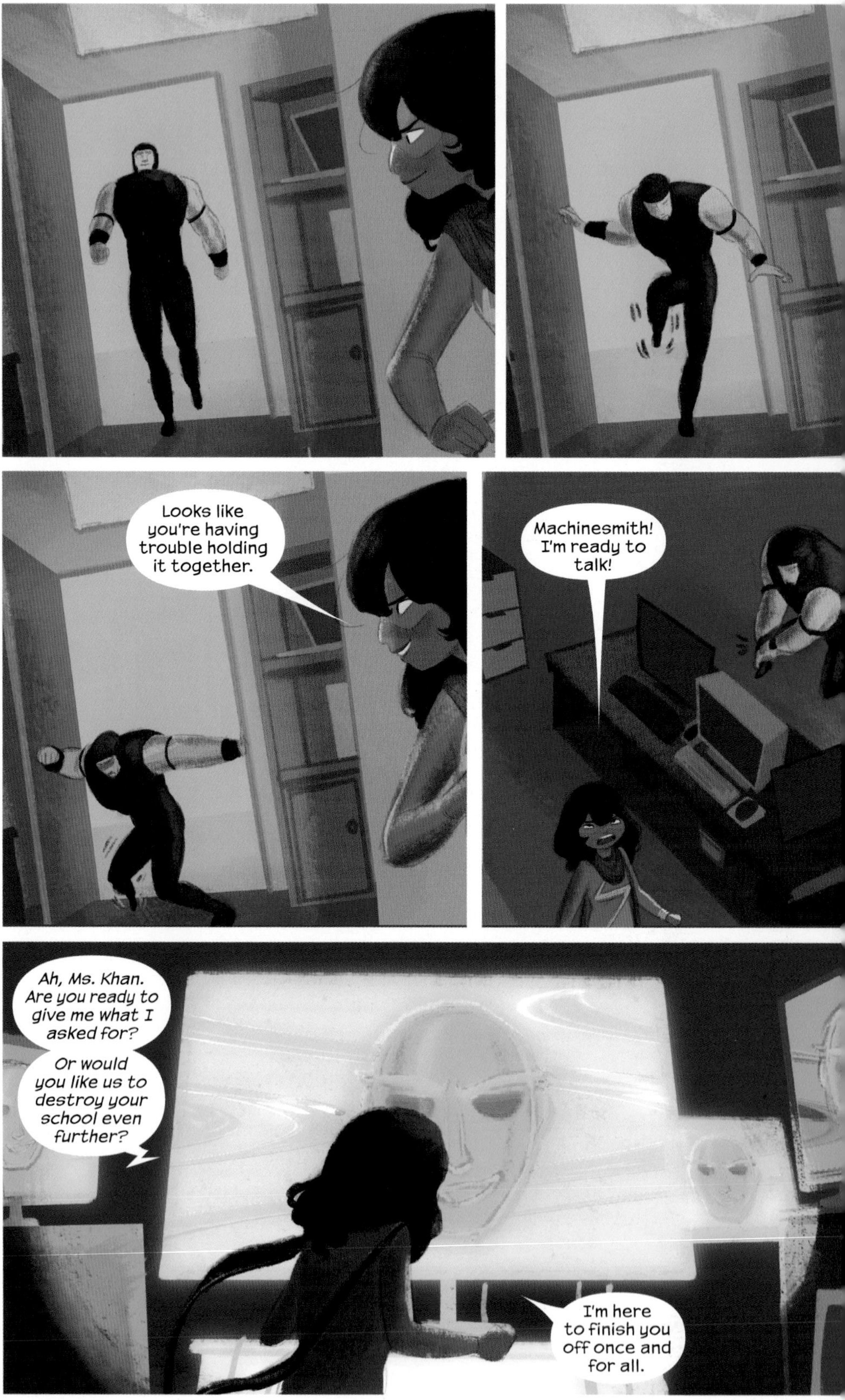
Looks like you're having trouble holding it together.
Machinesmith! I'm ready to talk!
Ah, Ms. Khan. Are you ready to give me what I asked for?
Or would you like us to destroy your school even further?
I'm here to finish you off once and for all.

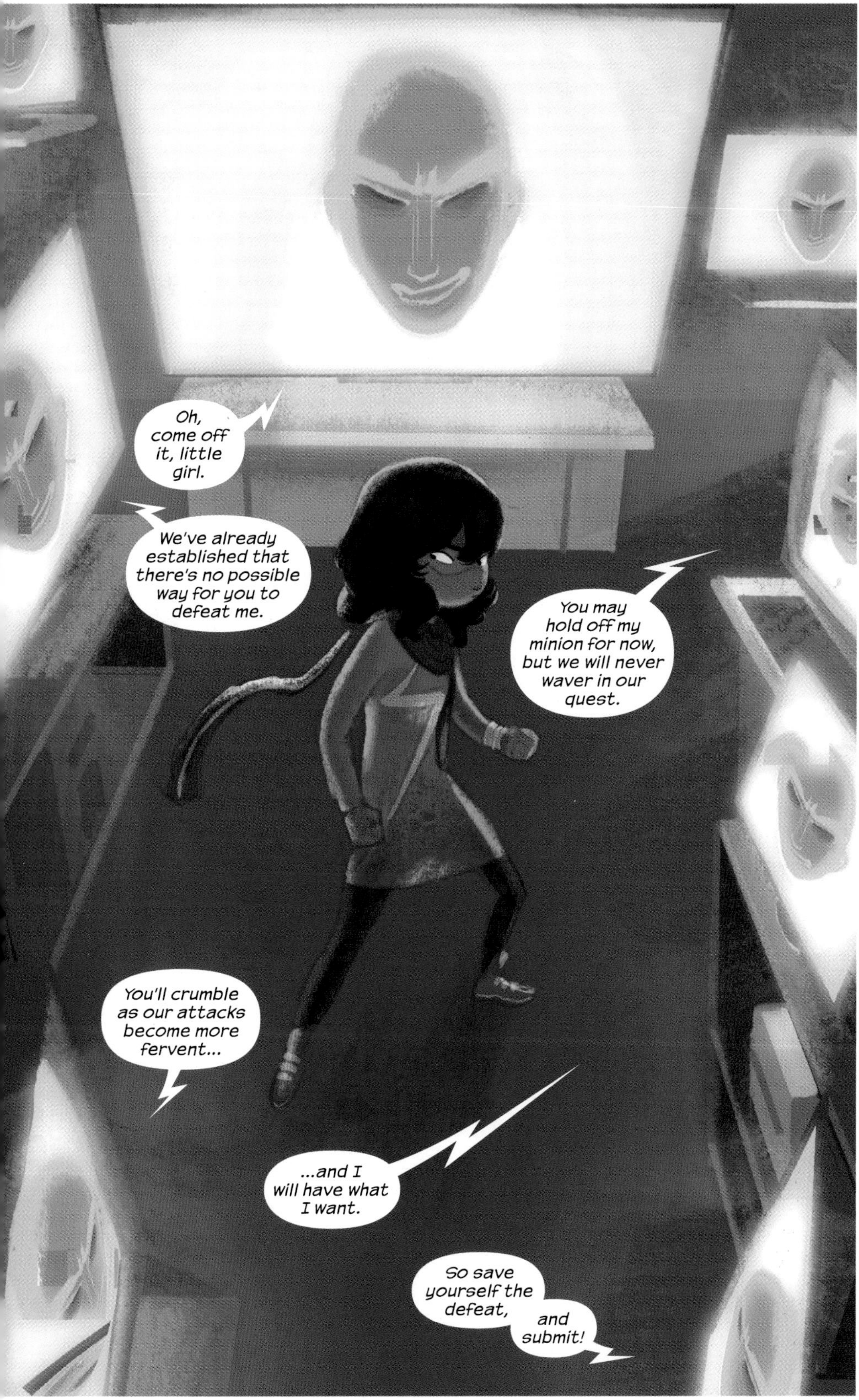
Oh, come off it, little girl.
We've already established that there's no possible way for you to defeat me.
You may hold off my minion for now, but we will never waver in our quest.
You'll crumble as our attacks become more fervent...
...and I will have what I want.
So save yourself the defeat,
and submit!

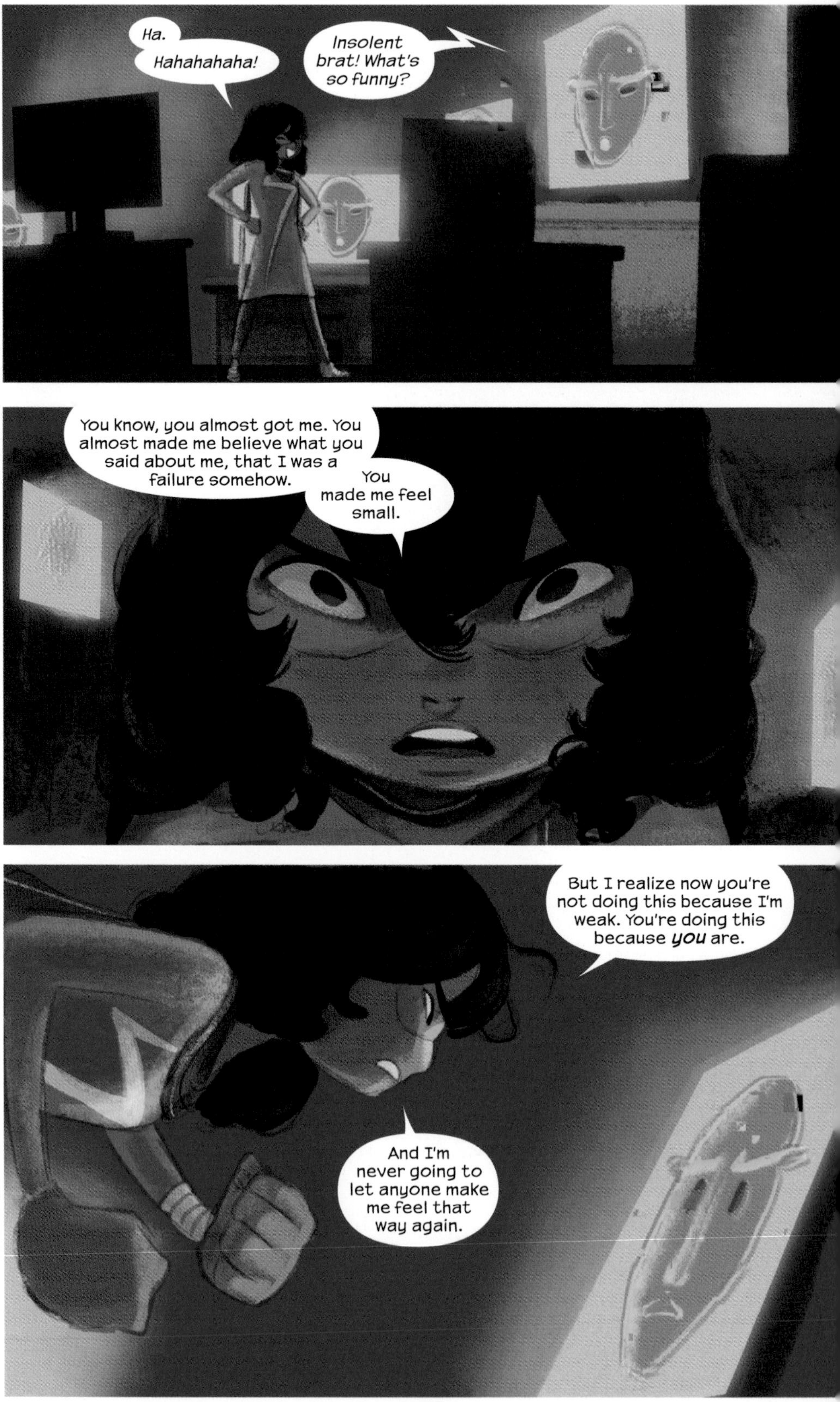
Ha.
Hahahahaha!
Insolent brat! What's so funny?
You know, you almost got me. You almost made me believe what you said about me, that I was a failure somehow.
You made me feel small.
But I realize now you're not doing this because I'm weak. You're doing this because *you* are.
And I'm never going to let anyone make me feel that way again.

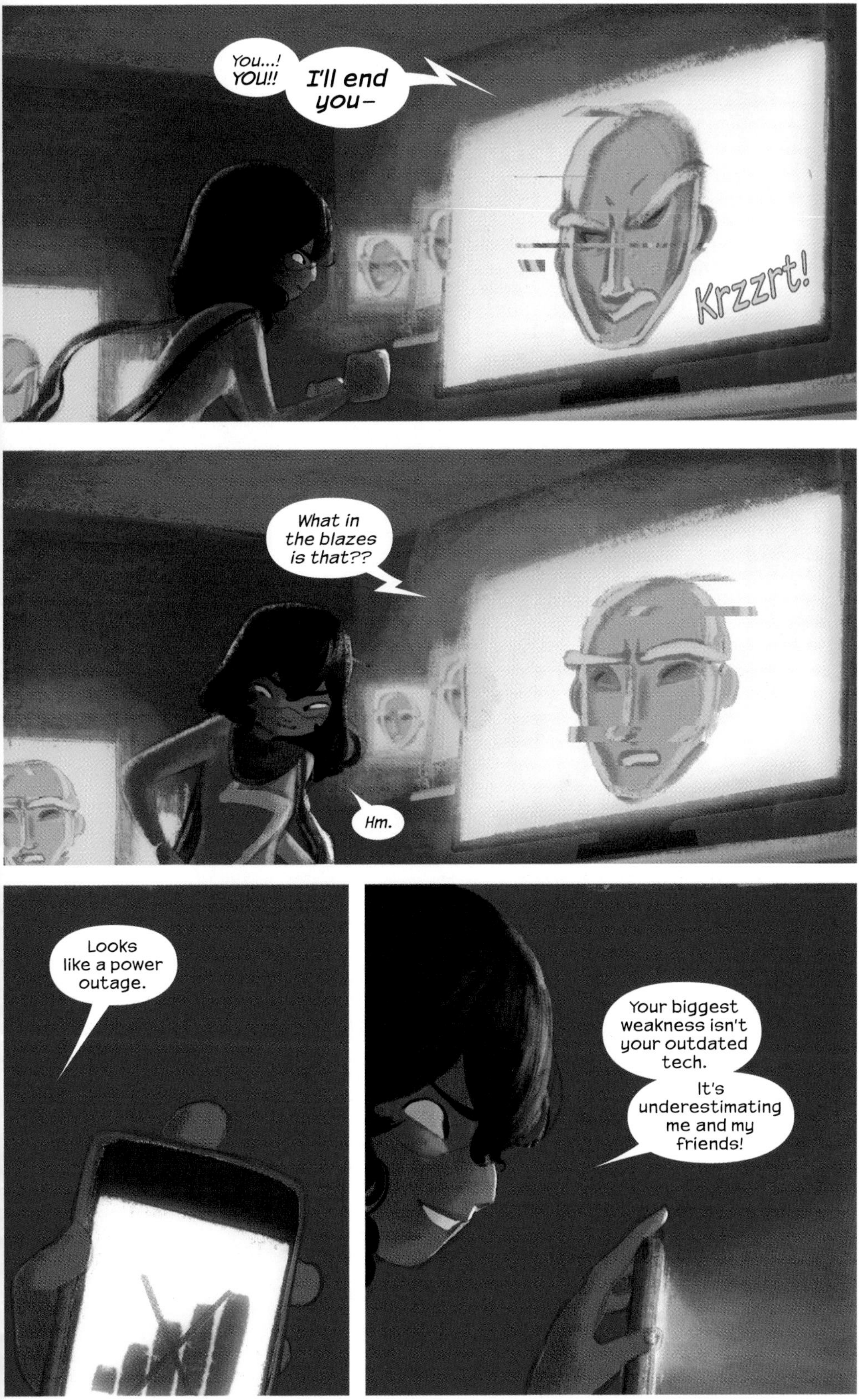
You...! YOU!!
I'll end you–
Krzzrt!
What in the blazes is that??
Hm.
Looks like a power outage.
Your biggest weakness isn't your outdated tech.
It's underestimating me and my friends!

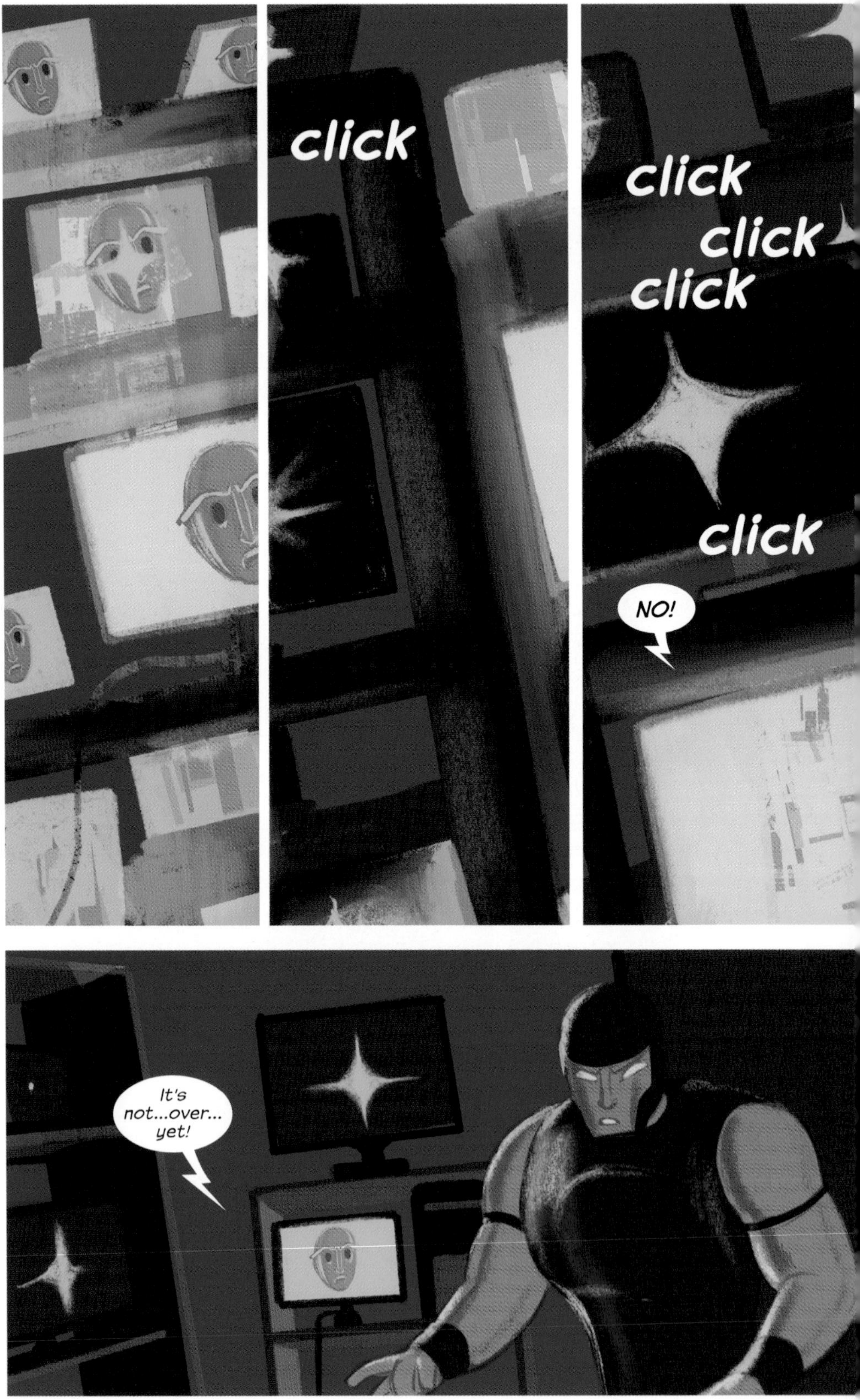
click
click
click
click
click
NO!
It's not...over... yet!

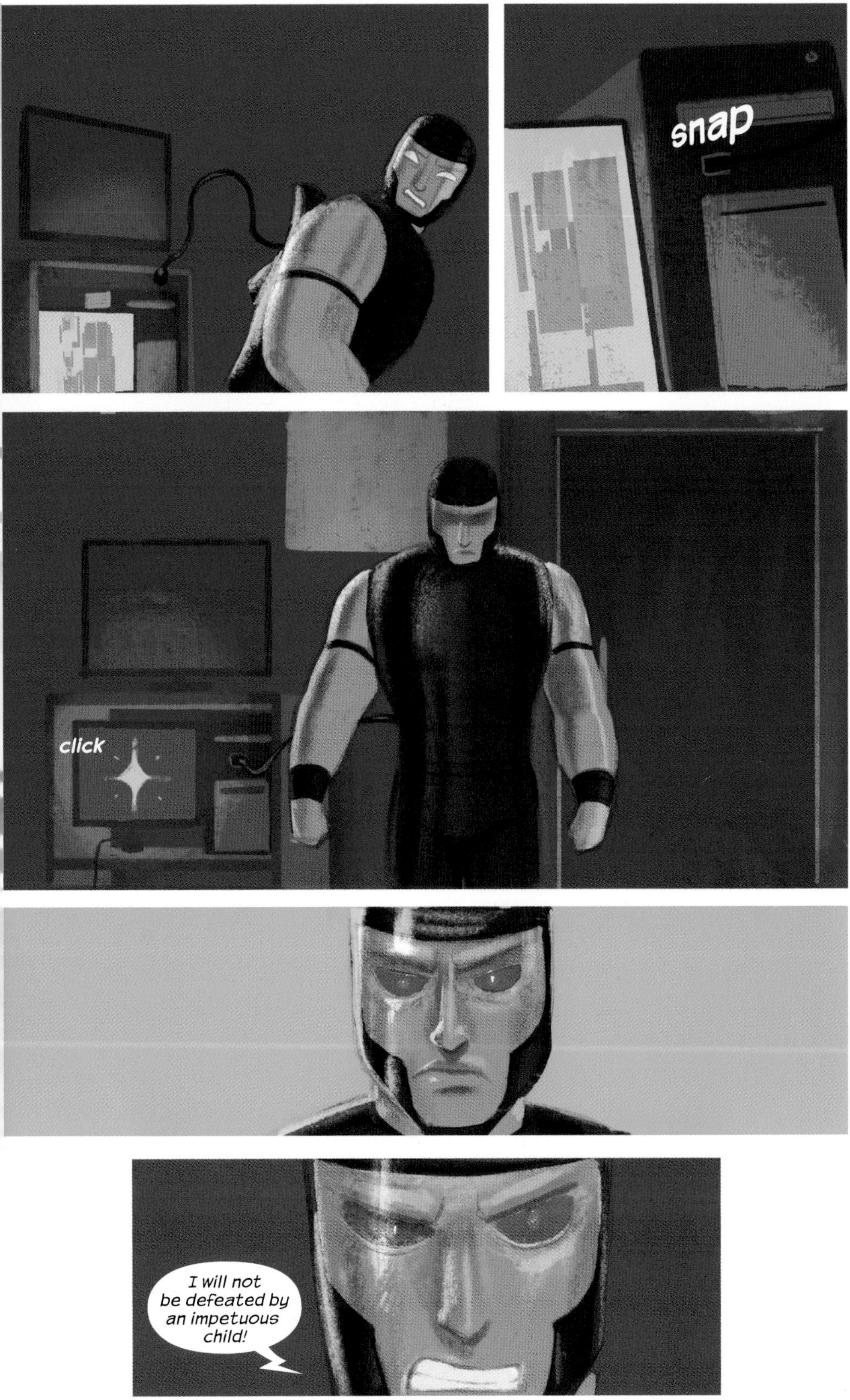
snap
click
I will not be defeated by an impetuous child!

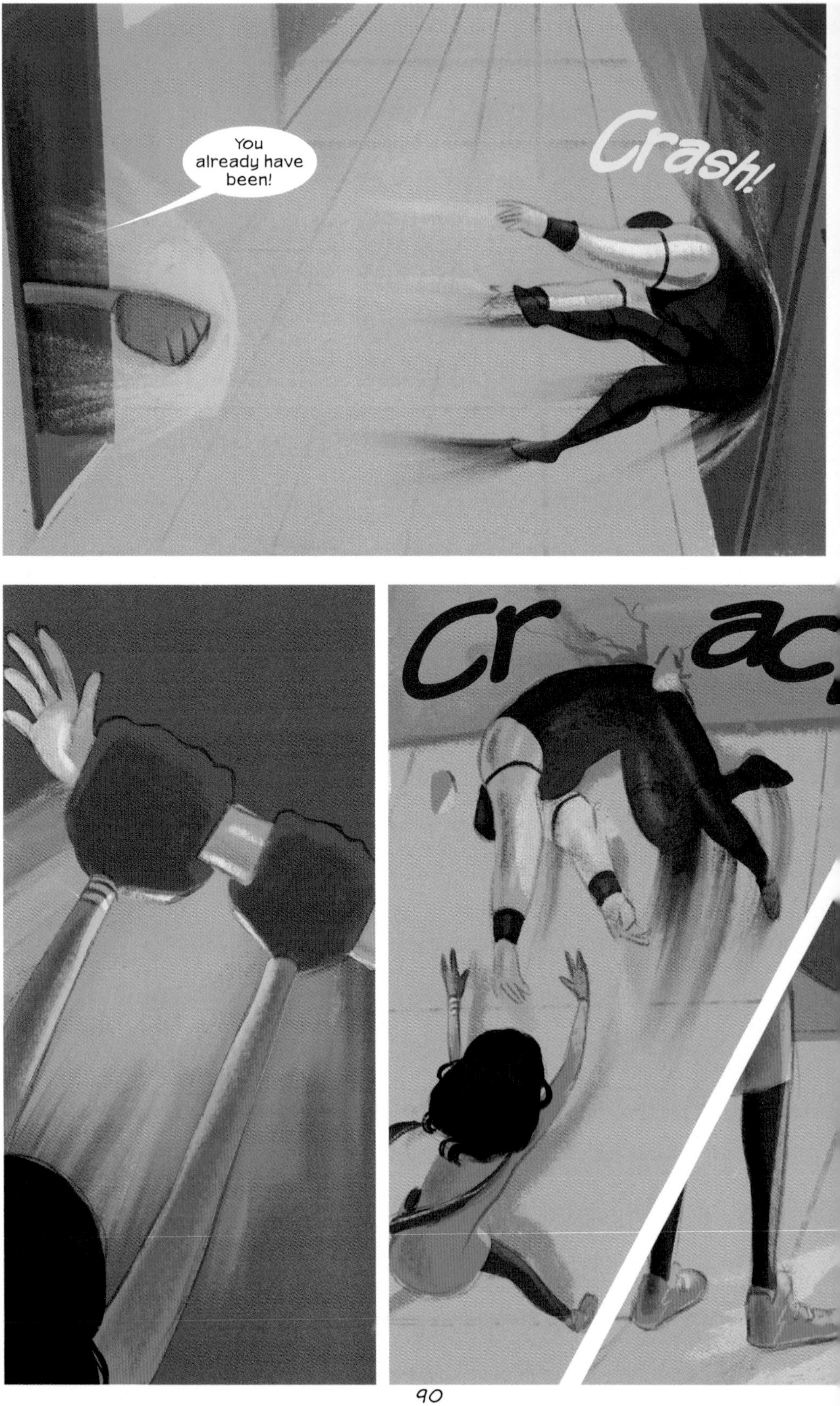
You already have been!
Crash!
Cr ac

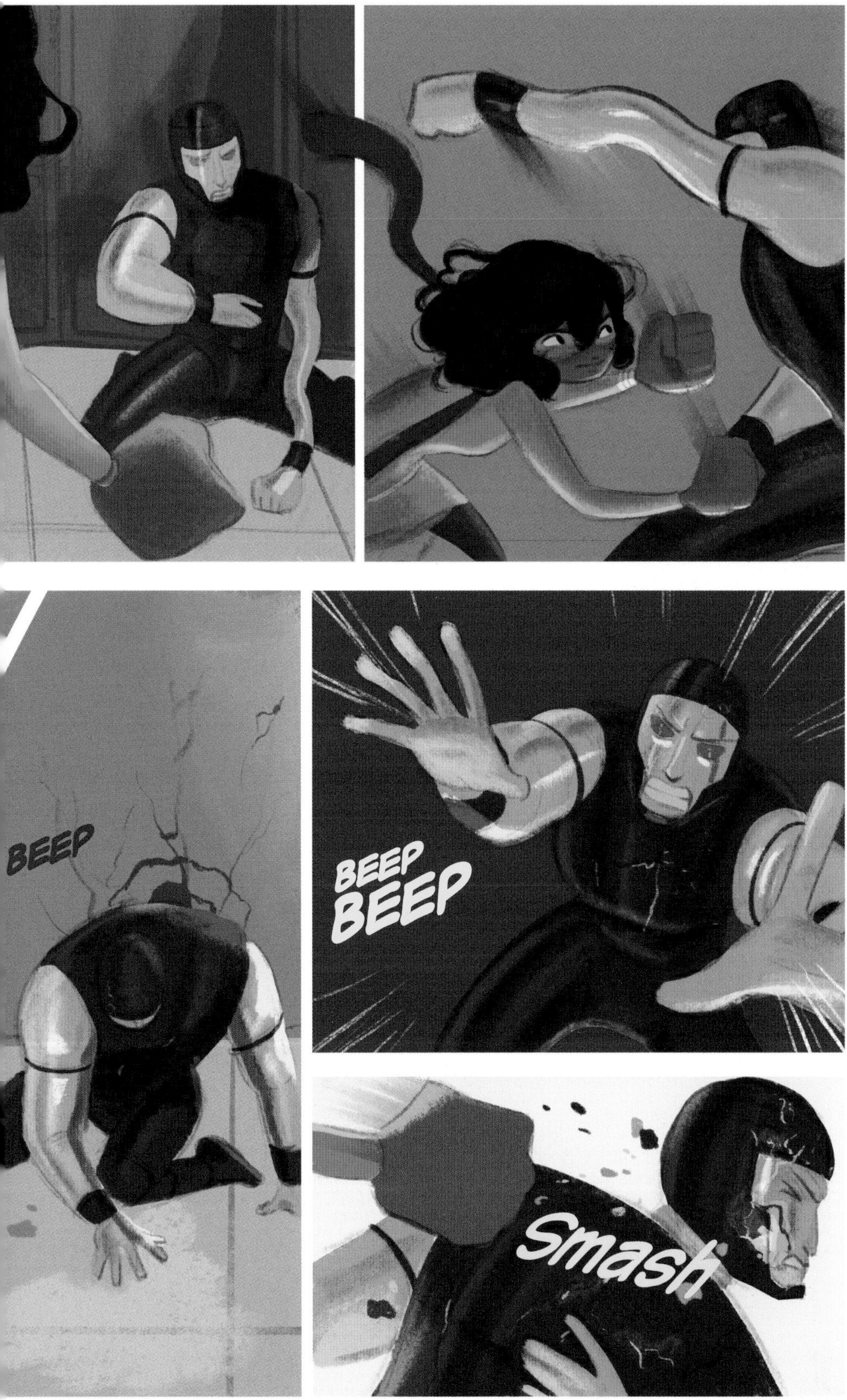
BEEP
BEEP
BEEP
Smash

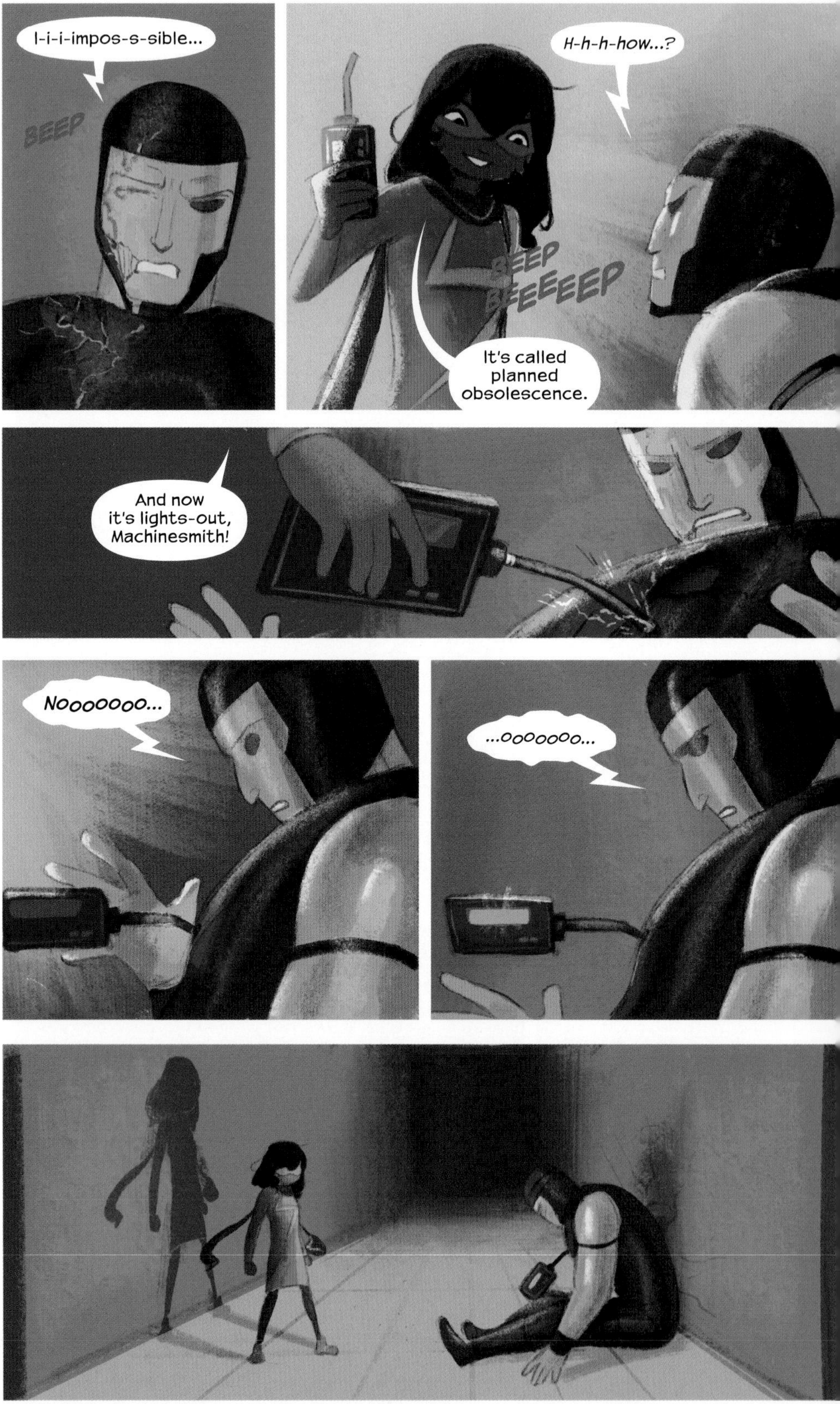
I-i-i-impos-s-sible...
BEEP
H-h-h-how...?
BEEP
BEEEEEP
It's called planned obsolescence.
And now it's lights-out, Machinesmith!
Nooooooo...
...ooooooo...

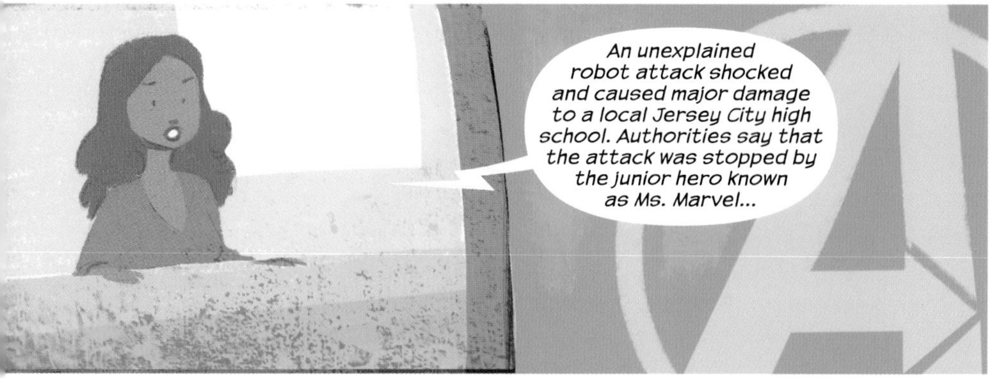
An unexplained robot attack shocked and caused major damage to a local Jersey City high school. Authorities say that the attack was stopped by the junior hero known as Ms. Marvel...

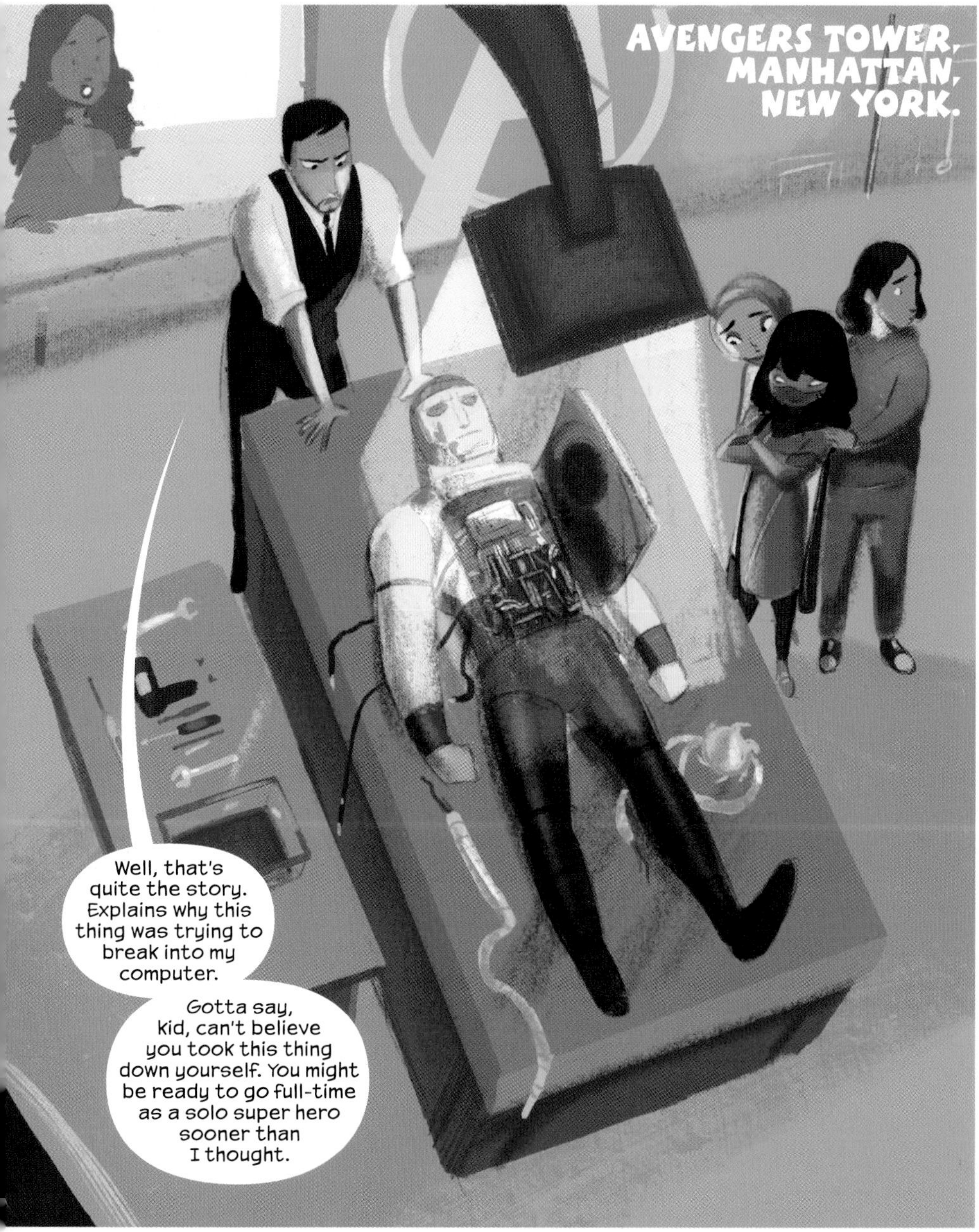
AVENGERS TOWER, MANHATTAN, NEW YORK.
Well, that's quite the story. Explains why this thing was trying to break into my computer.
Gotta say, kid, can't believe you took this thing down yourself. You might be ready to go full-time as a solo super hero sooner than I thought.

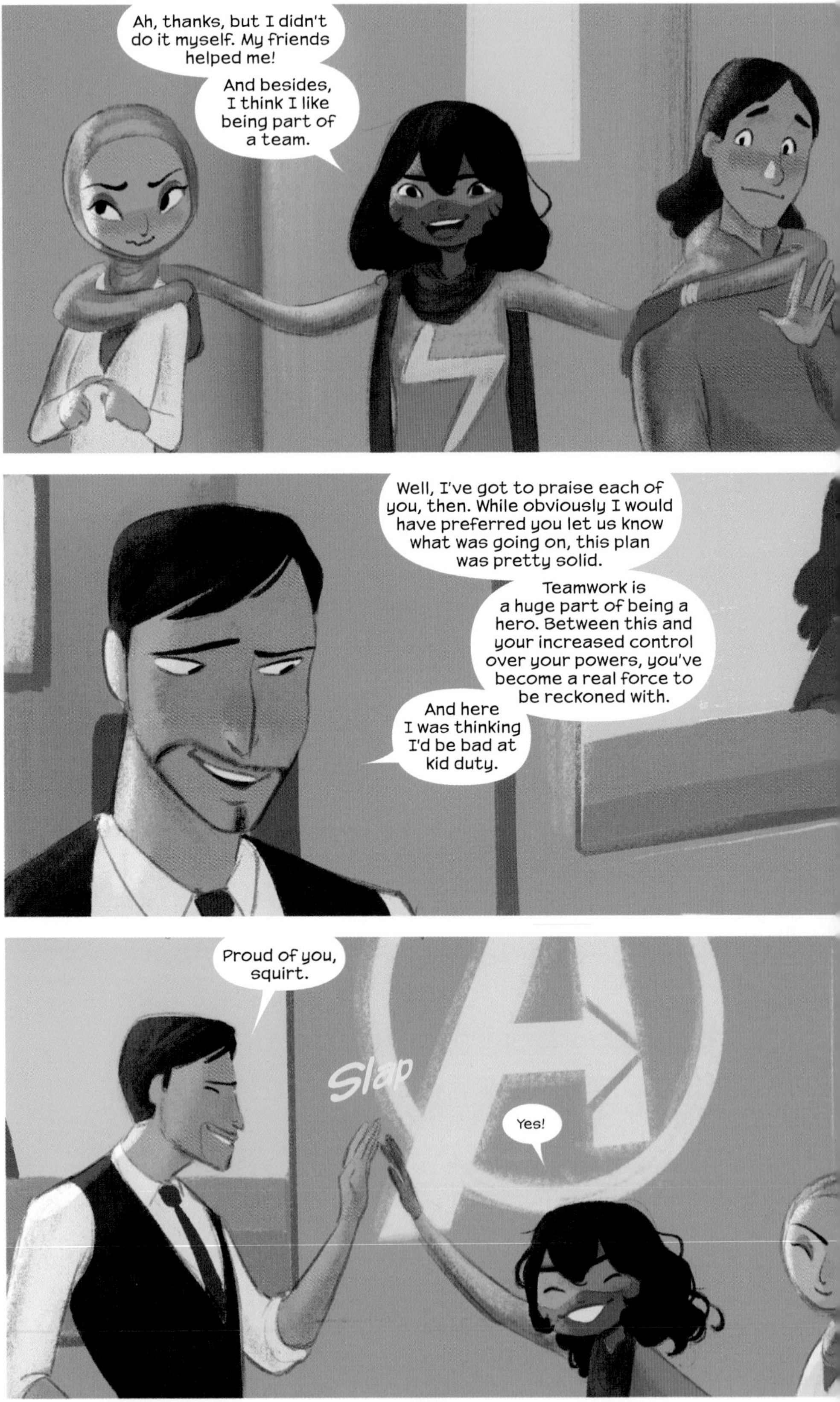
Ah, thanks, but I didn't do it myself. My friends helped me!
And besides, I think I like being part of a team.
Well, I've got to praise each of you, then. While obviously I would have preferred you let us know what was going on, this plan was pretty solid.
Teamwork is a huge part of being a hero. Between this and your increased control over your powers, you've become a real force to be reckoned with.
And here I was thinking I'd be bad at kid duty.
Proud of you, squirt.
Slap
Yes!

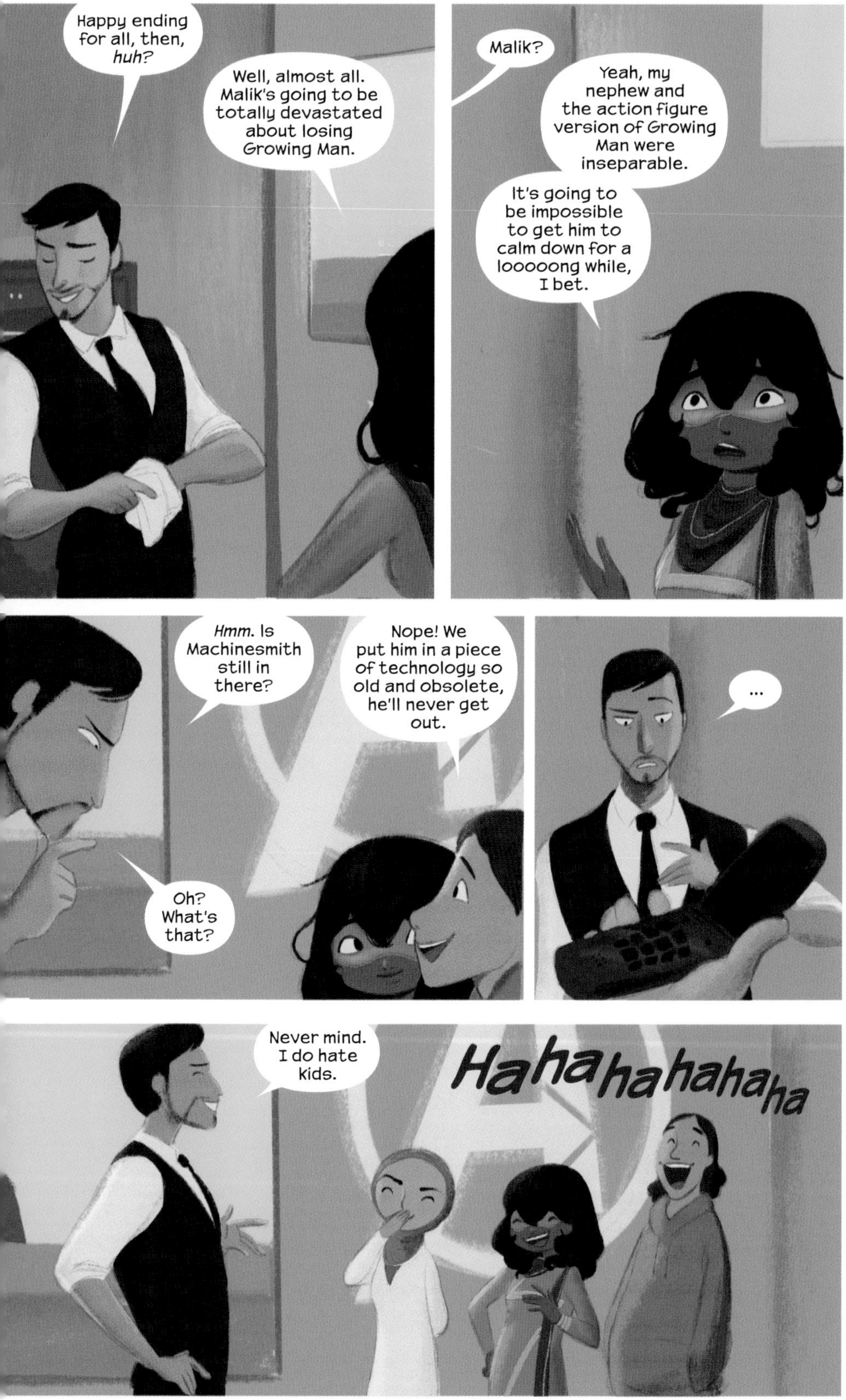
Happy ending for all, then, *huh?*
Well, almost all. Malik's going to be totally devastated about losing Growing Man.
Malik?
Yeah, my nephew and the action figure version of Growing Man were inseparable.
It's going to be impossible to get him to calm down for a looooong while, I bet.
Hmm. Is Machinesmith still in there?
Nope! We put him in a piece of technology so old and obsolete, he'll never get out.
Oh? What's that?
...
Never mind. I do hate kids.
Hahahahahahaha

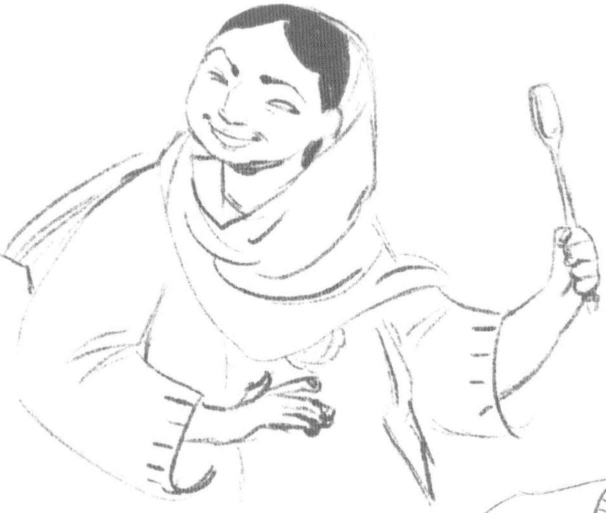

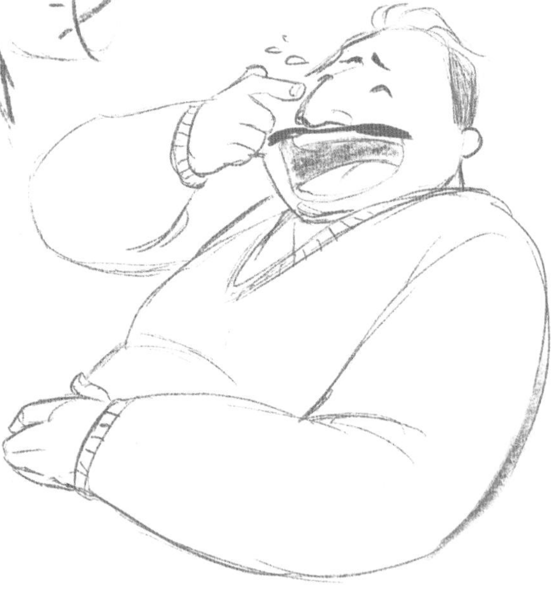

CHAPTER SIX

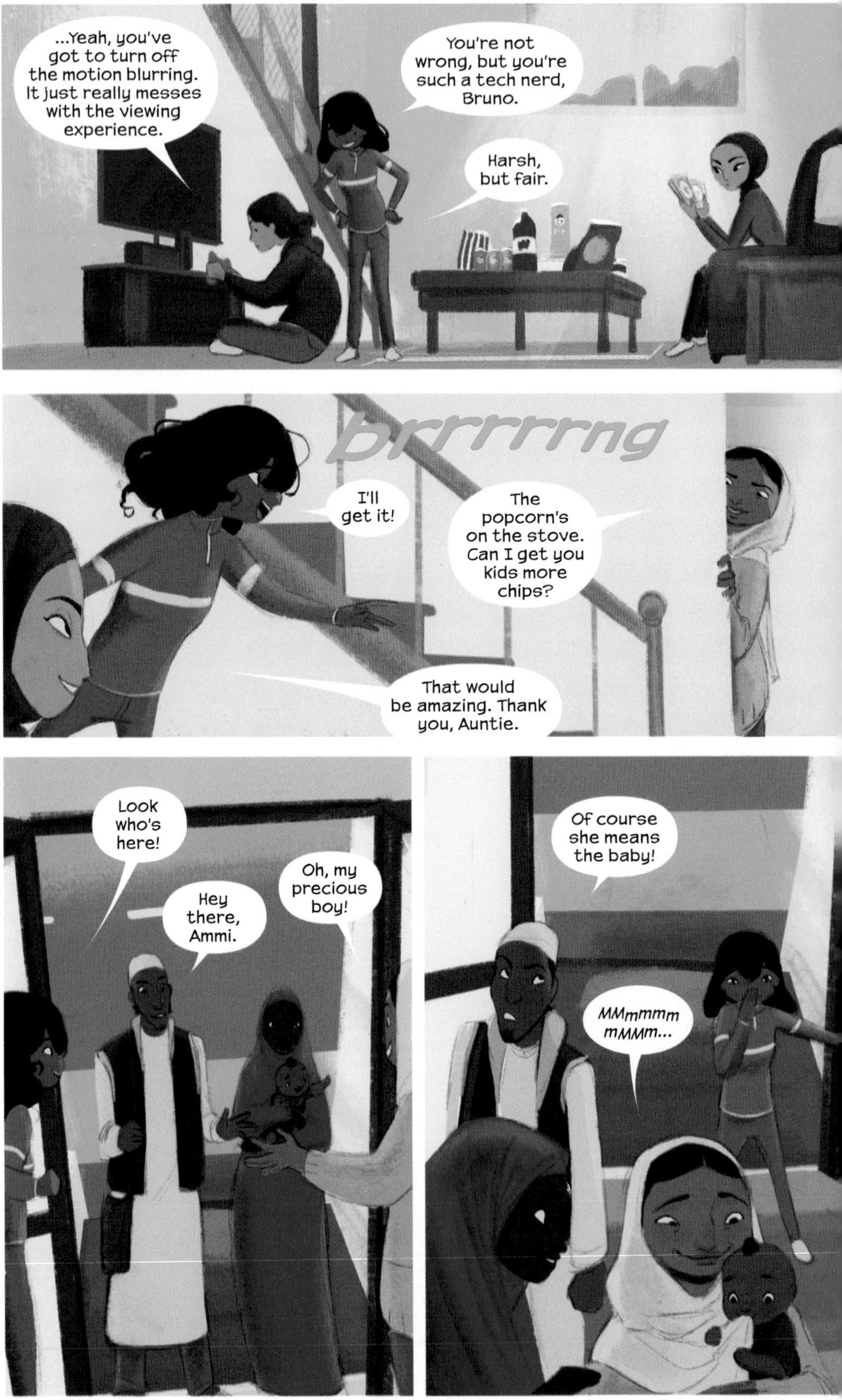
...Yeah, you've got to turn off the motion blurring. It just really messes with the viewing experience.
You're not wrong, but you're such a tech nerd, Bruno.
Harsh, but fair.
brrrrrrng
I'll get it!
The popcorn's on the stove. Can I get you kids more chips?
That would be amazing. Thank you, Auntie.
Look who's here!
Hey there, Ammi.
Oh, my precious boy!
Of course she means the baby!
MMmmmm mMMm...

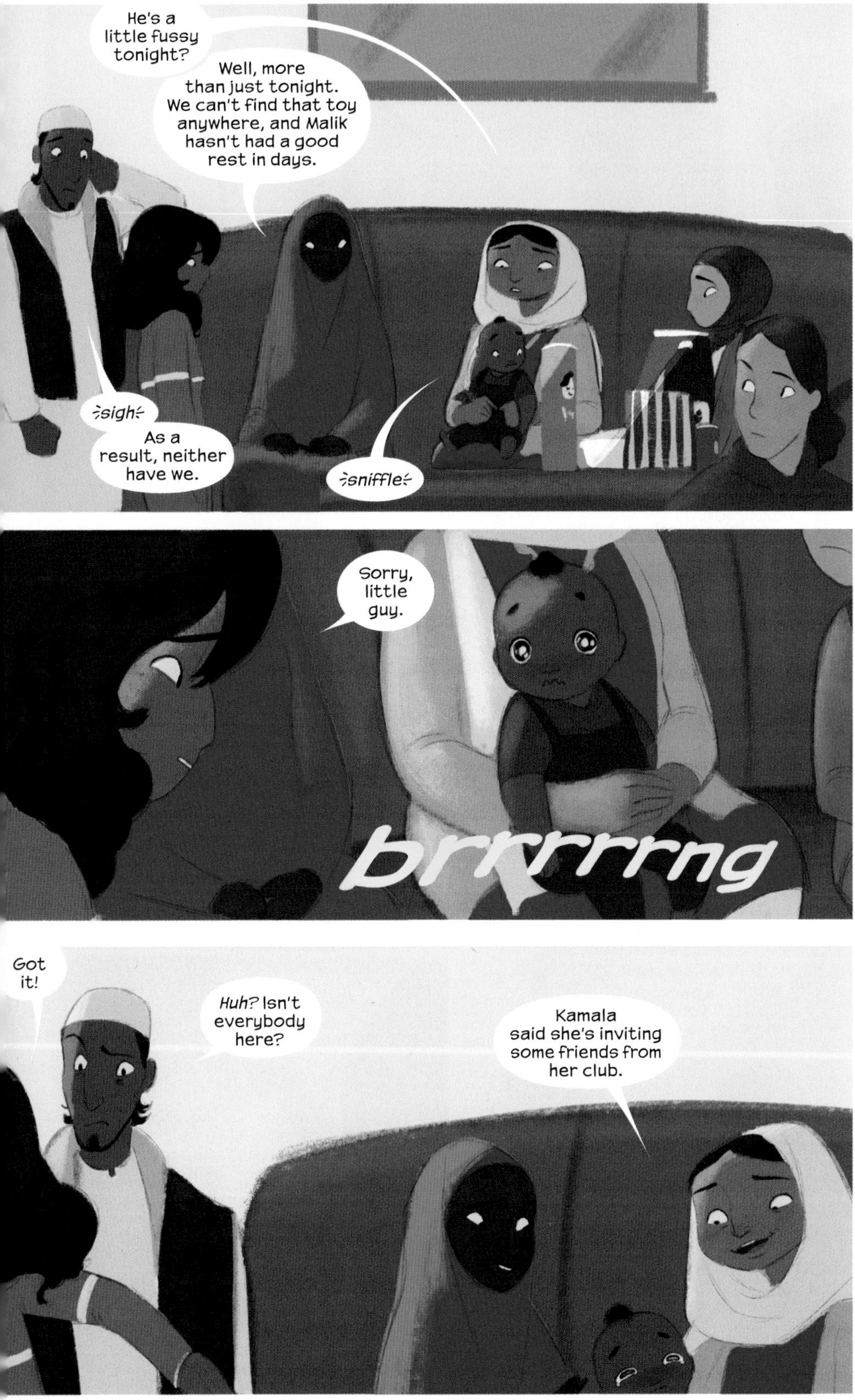
He's a little fussy tonight?
Well, more than just tonight. We can't find that toy anywhere, and Malik hasn't had a good rest in days.
sigh
As a result, neither have we.
sniffle
Sorry, little guy.
brrrrrng
Got it!
Huh? Isn't everybody here?
Kamala said she's inviting some friends from her club.

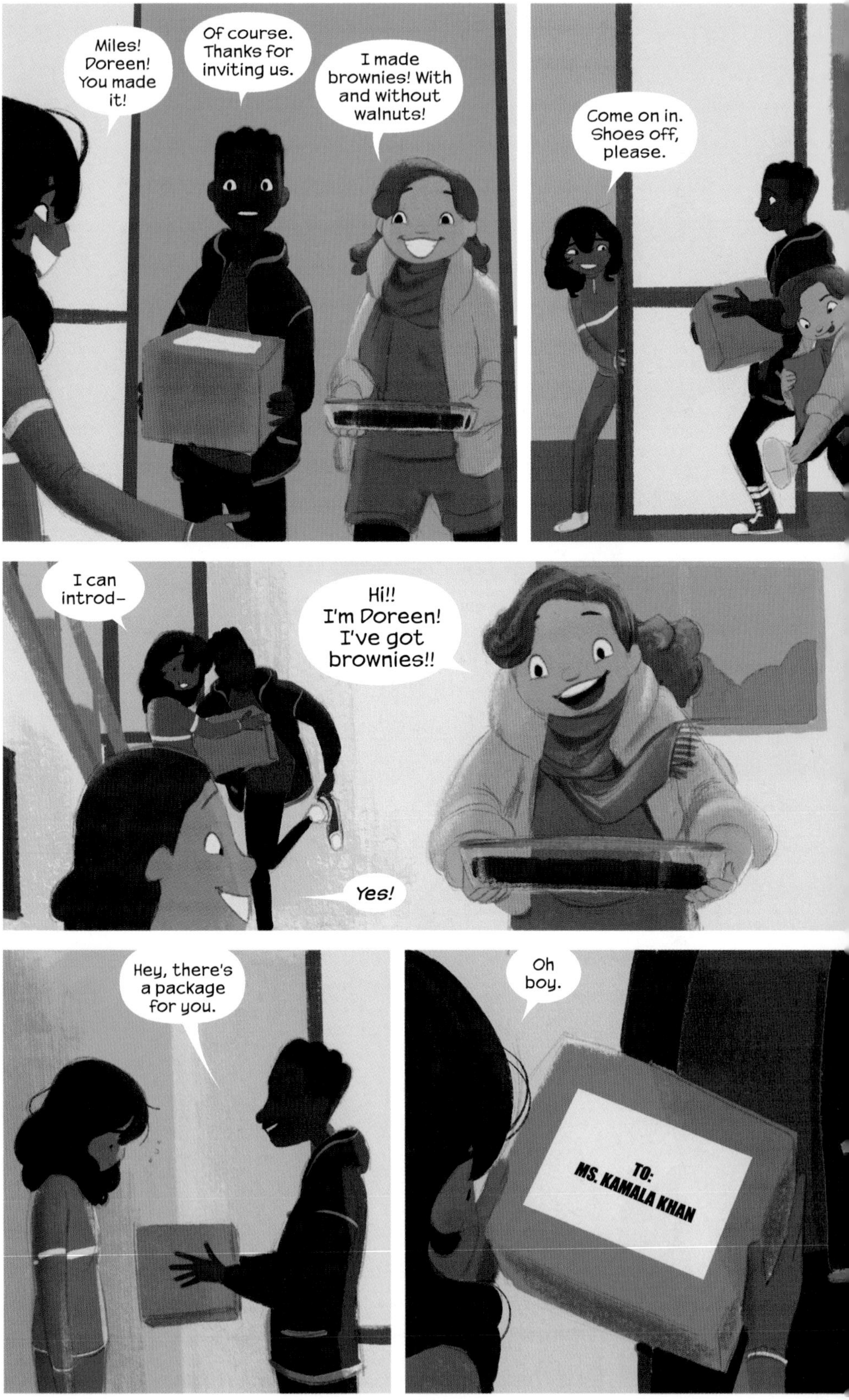
Miles! Doreen! You made it!
Of course. Thanks for inviting us.
I made brownies! With and without walnuts!
Come on in. Shoes off, please.
I can introd-
Hi!! I'm Doreen! I've got brownies!!
Yes!
Hey, there's a package for you.
Oh boy.
TO:
MS. KAMALA KHAN

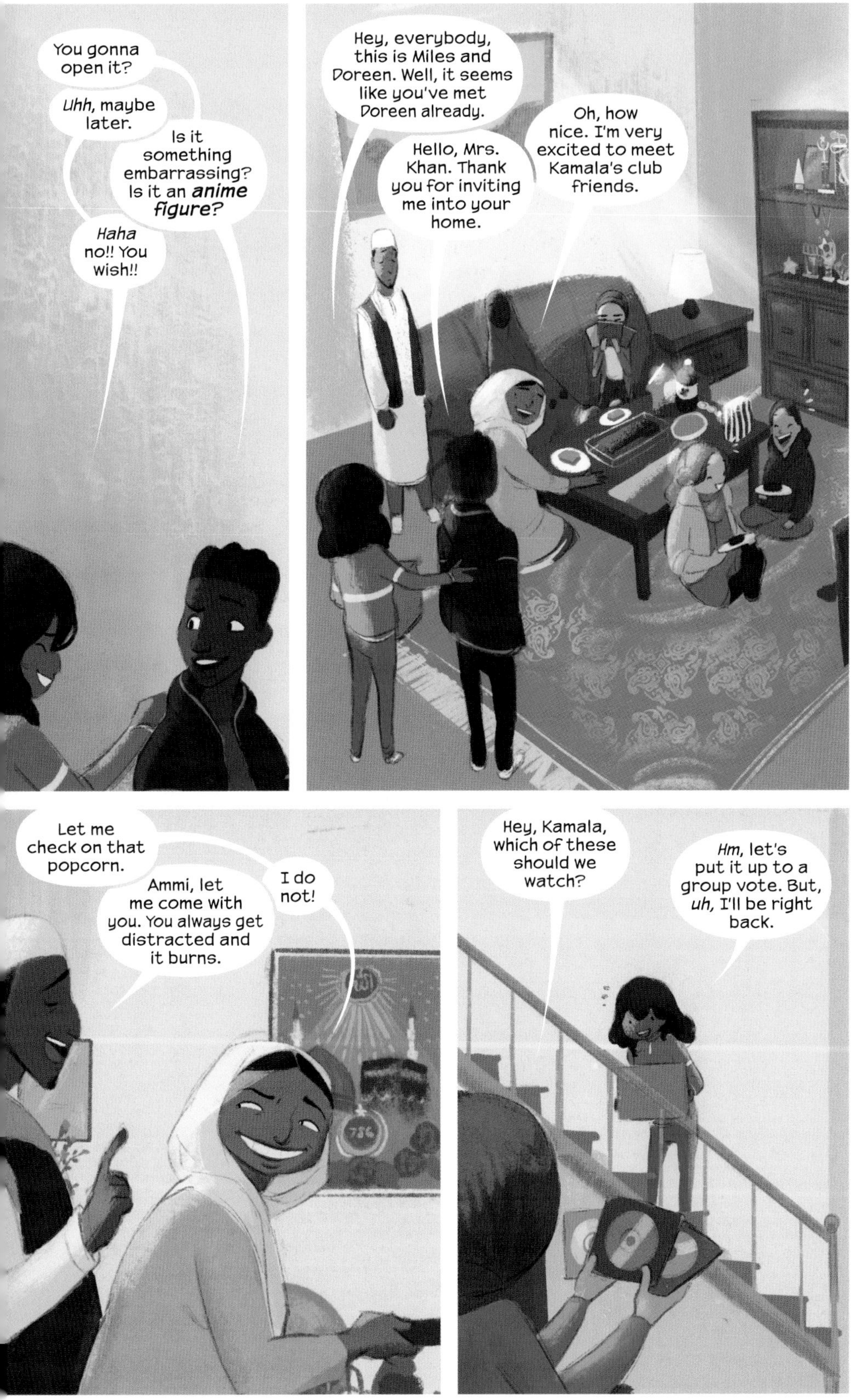
You gonna open it?
Uhh, maybe later.
Is it something embarrassing? Is it an ***anime figure***?
Haha no!! You wish!!
Hey, everybody, this is Miles and Doreen. Well, it seems like you've met Doreen already.
Hello, Mrs. Khan. Thank you for inviting me into your home.
Oh, how nice. I'm very excited to meet Kamala's club friends.
Let me check on that popcorn.
Ammi, let me come with you. You always get distracted and it burns.
I do not!
Hey, Kamala, which of these should we watch?
Hm, let's put it up to a group vote. But, *uh*, I'll be right back.

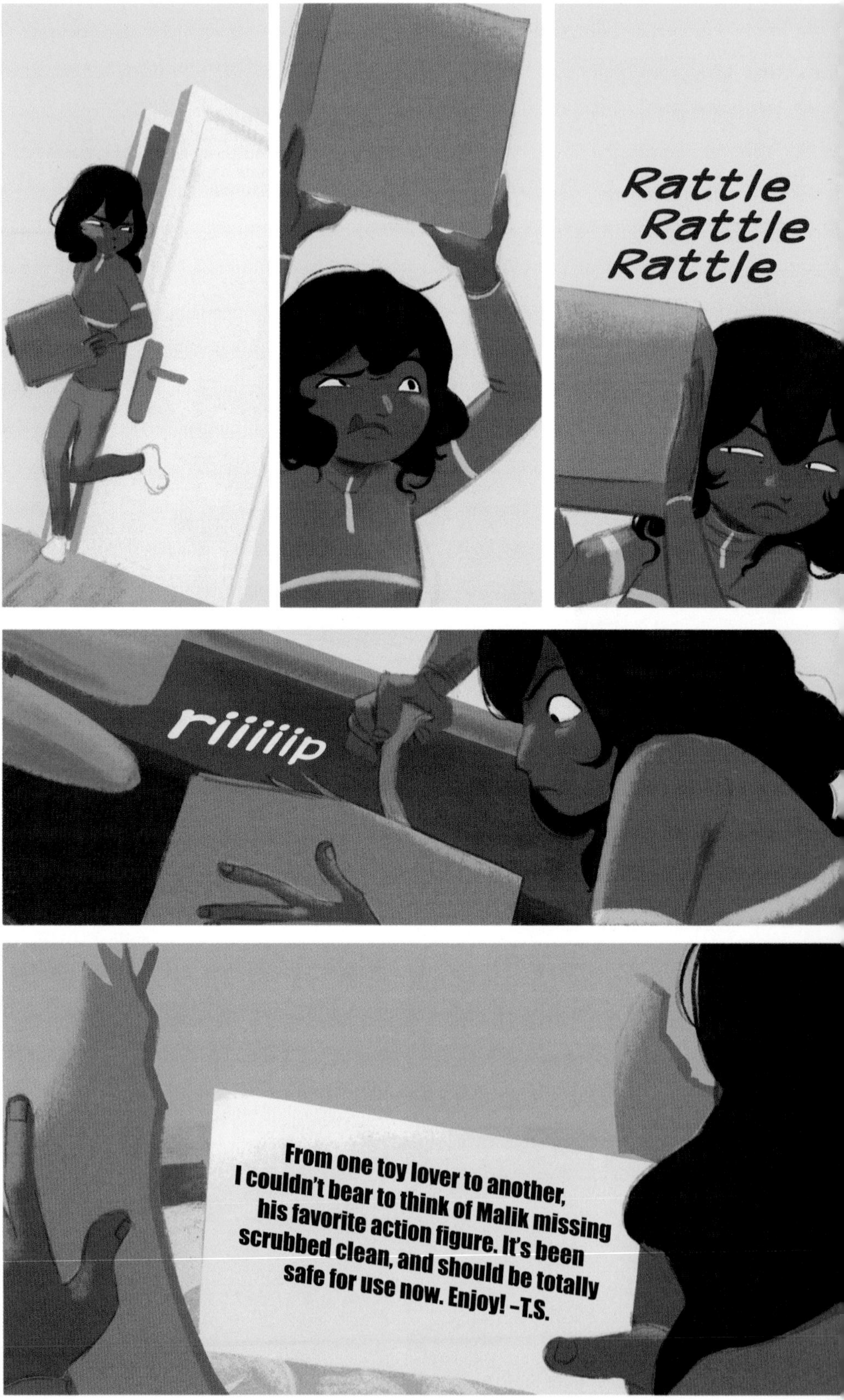
Rattle
Rattle
Rattle
riiiiip
From one toy lover to another,
I couldn't bear to think of Malik missing
his favorite action figure. It's been
scrubbed clean, and should be totally
safe for use now. Enjoy! –T.S.

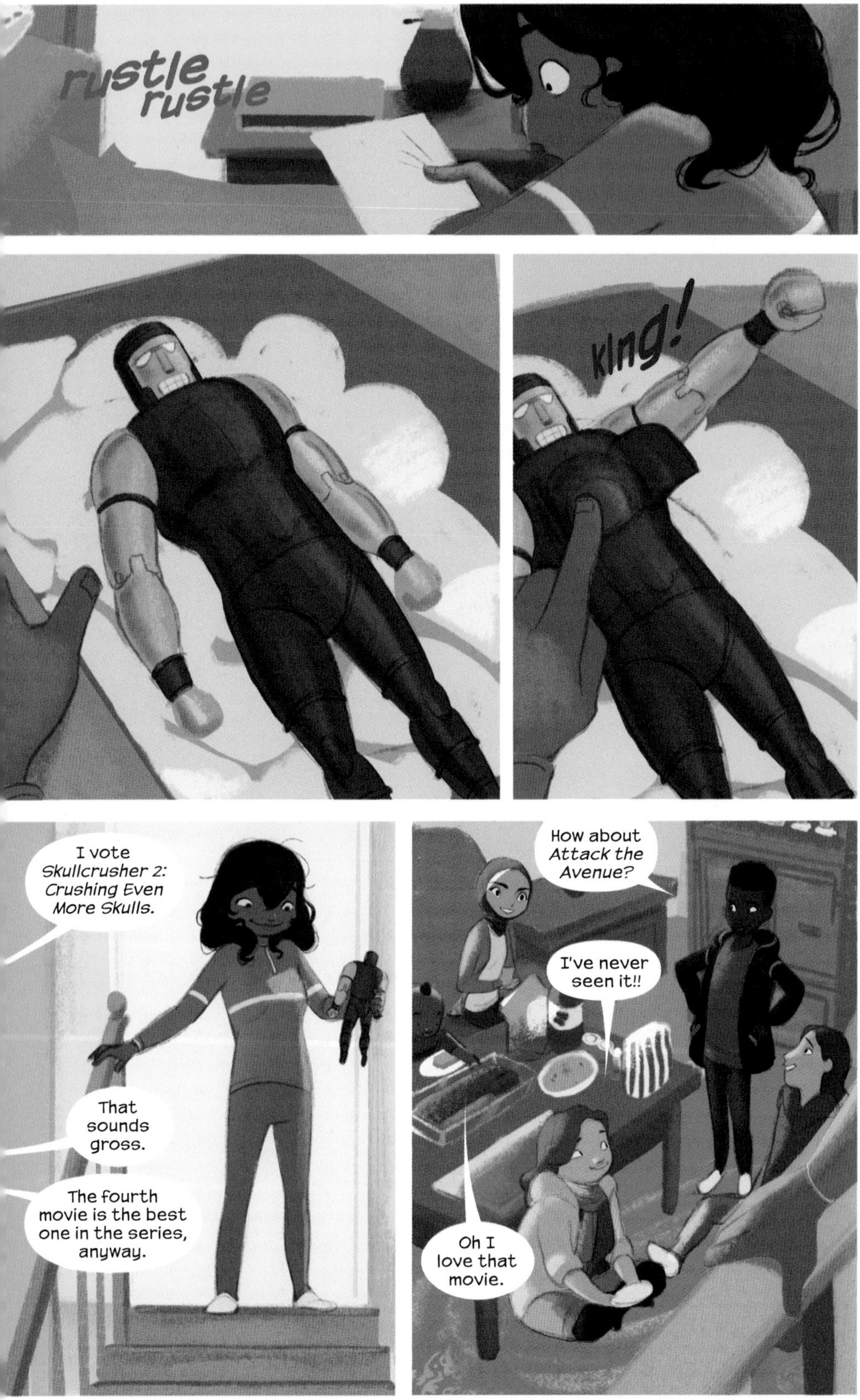
rustle rustle
KING!
I vote *Skullcrusher 2: Crushing Even More Skulls.*
That sounds gross.
The fourth movie is the best one in the series, anyway.
How about *Attack the Avenue?*
I've never seen it!!
Oh I love that movie.

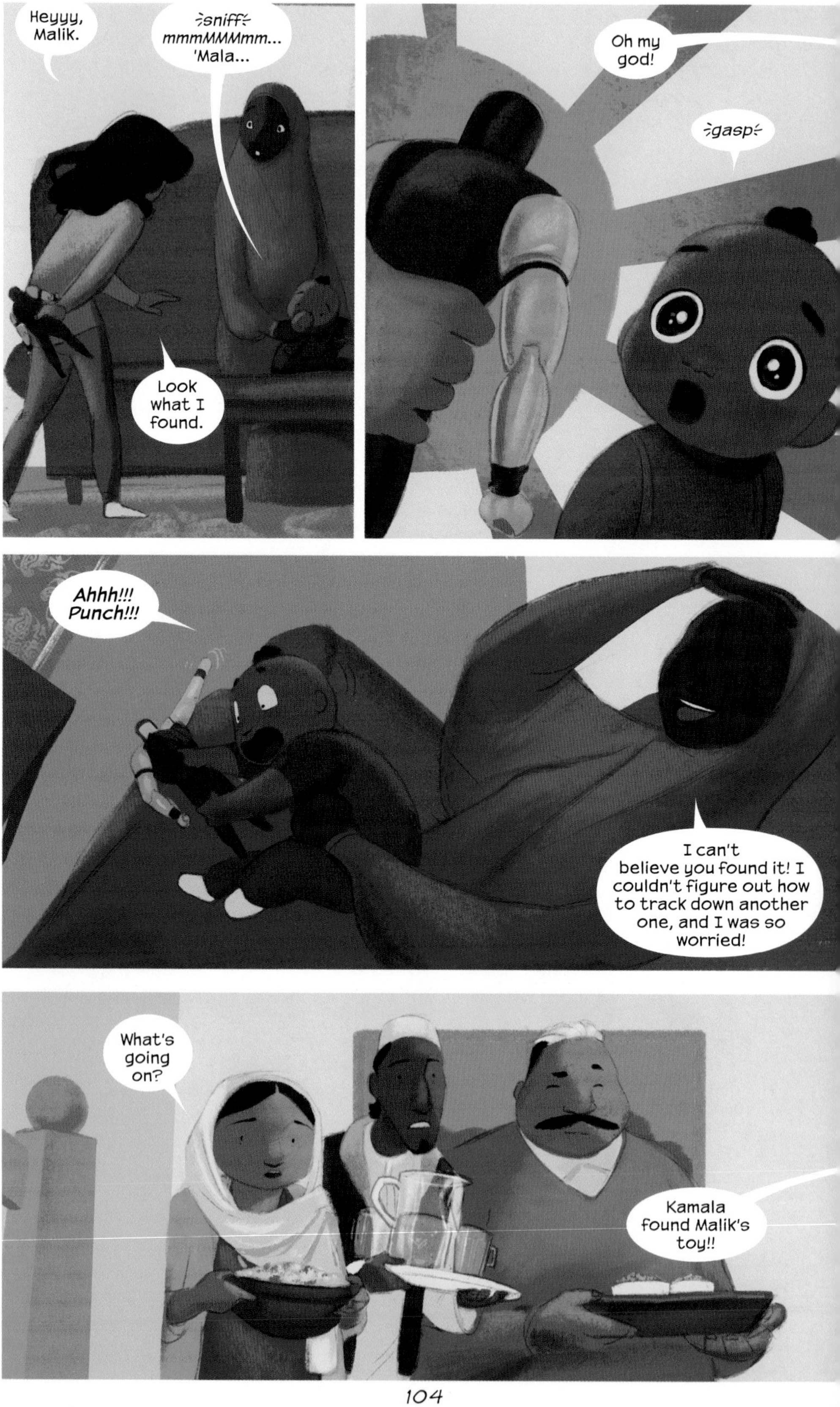
Heyyy, Malik.
≑sniff≑ mmmMMMmm... 'Mala...
Look what I found.
Oh my god!
≑gasp≑
Ahhh!!! Punch!!!
I can't believe you found it! I couldn't figure out how to track down another one, and I was so worried!
What's going on?
Kamala found Malik's toy!!

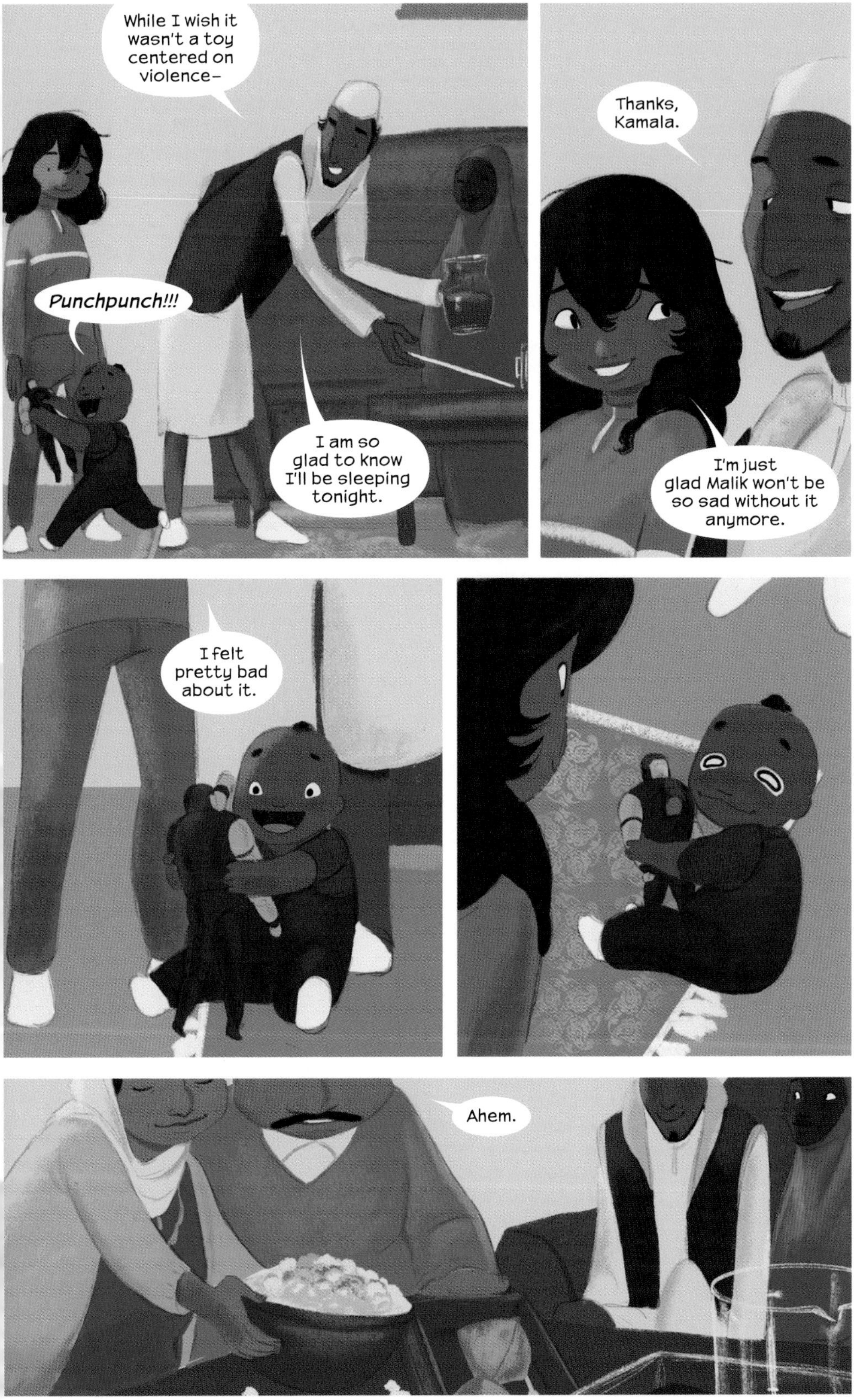
While I wish it wasn't a toy centered on violence–
Punchpunch!!!
I am so glad to know I'll be sleeping tonight.
Thanks, Kamala.
I'm just glad Malik won't be so sad without it anymore.
I felt pretty bad about it.
Ahem.

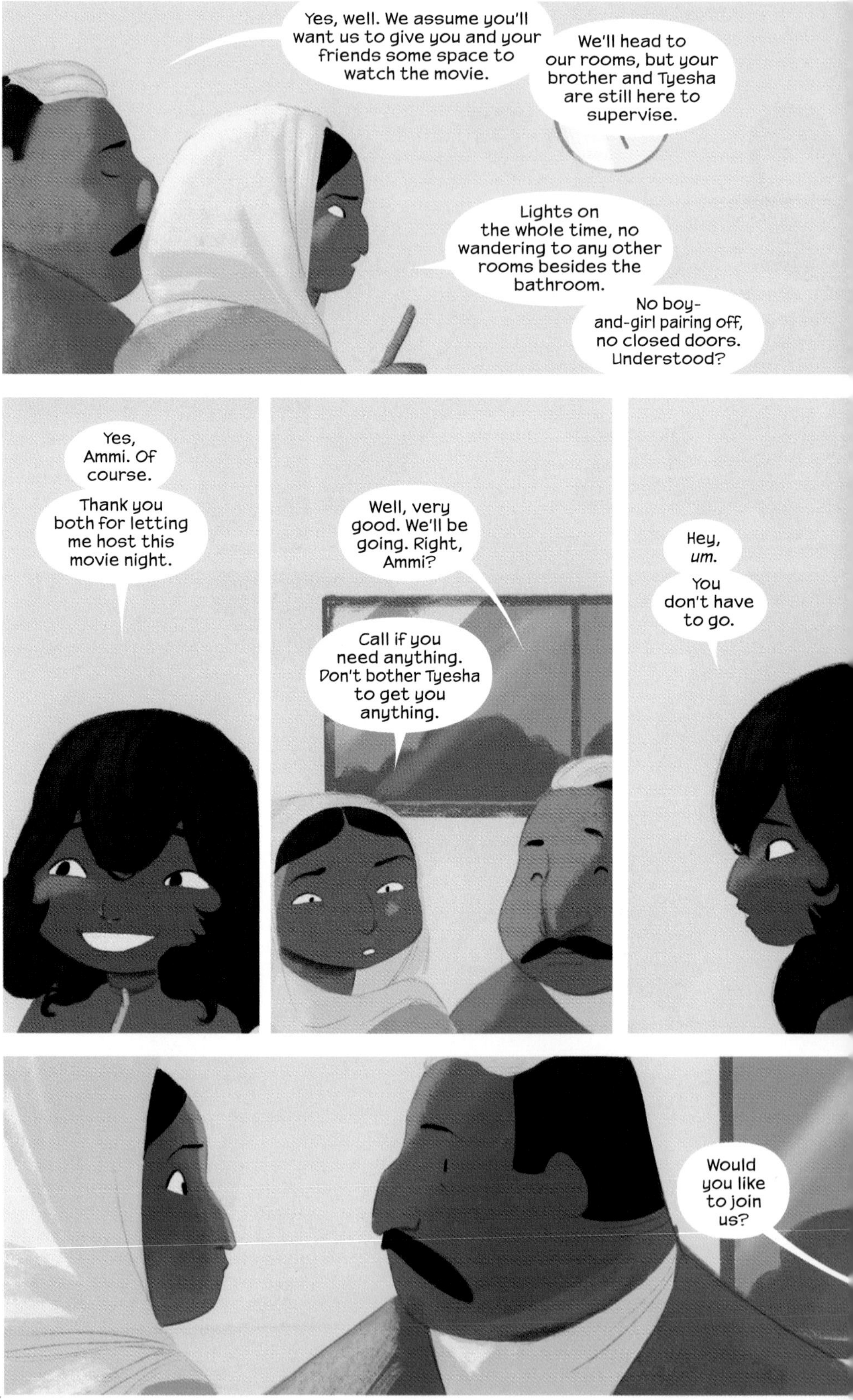
Yes, well. We assume you'll want us to give you and your friends some space to watch the movie.
We'll head to our rooms, but your brother and Tyesha are still here to supervise.
Lights on the whole time, no wandering to any other rooms besides the bathroom.
No boy-and-girl pairing off, no closed doors. Understood?
Yes, Ammi. Of course.
Thank you both for letting me host this movie night.
Well, very good. We'll be going. Right, Ammi?
Call if you need anything. Don't bother Tyesha to get you anything.
Hey, *um.*
You don't have to go.
Would you like to join us?

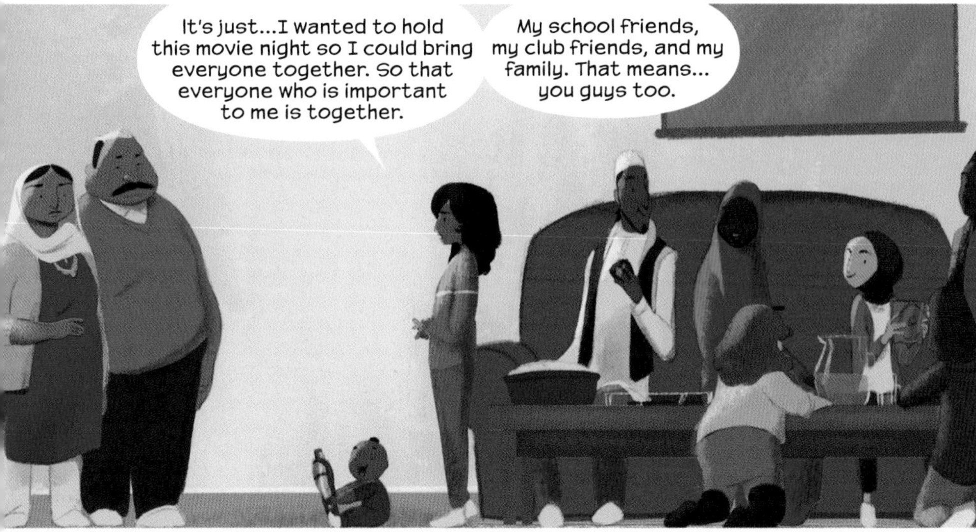
It's just...I wanted to hold this movie night so I could bring everyone together. So that everyone who is important to me is together.
My school friends, my club friends, and my family. That means... you guys too.
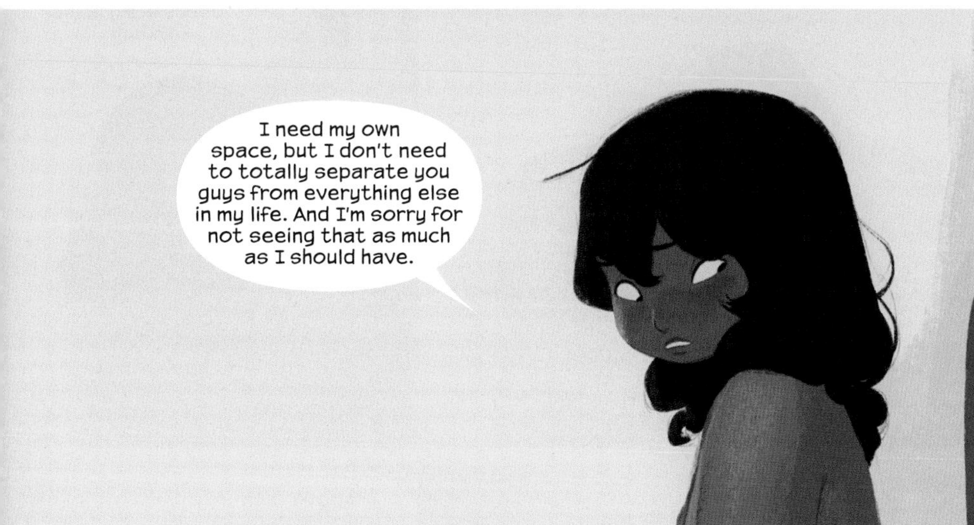
I need my own space, but I don't need to totally separate you guys from everything else in my life. And I'm sorry for not seeing that as much as I should have.
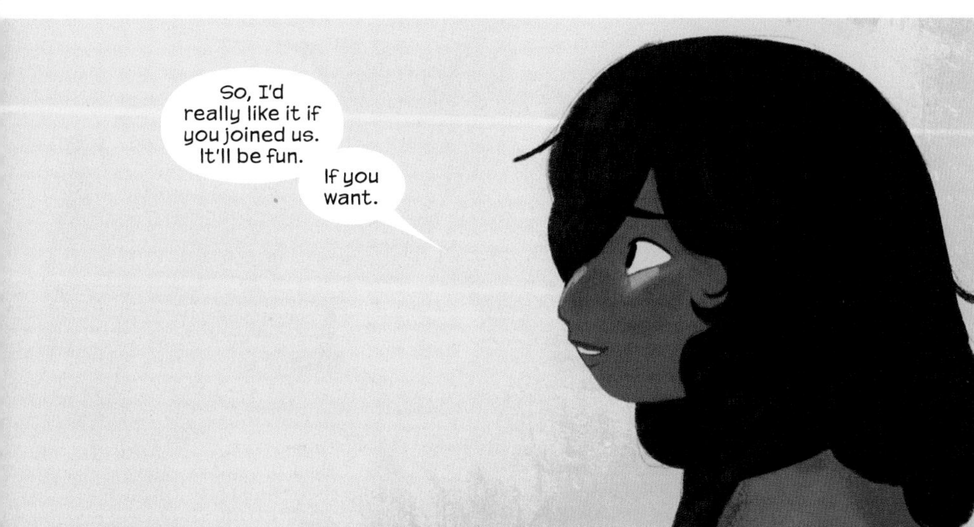
So, I'd really like it if you joined us. It'll be fun.
If you want.

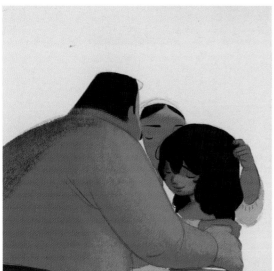

You're a good girl, Kamala.

Still no closed doors in my home though.

Oh man, I love *Pals at the Table*. It's the best tabletop podcast out right now.

I looove their mech season. Have you listened to the latest arc, *Partition*?

So *Skullcrusher 4: Crushing on Some Skulls* is actually the romantic comedy of the series.

Does it work? Like... tone-wise?

Personally, I think it's where they really hit their stride.

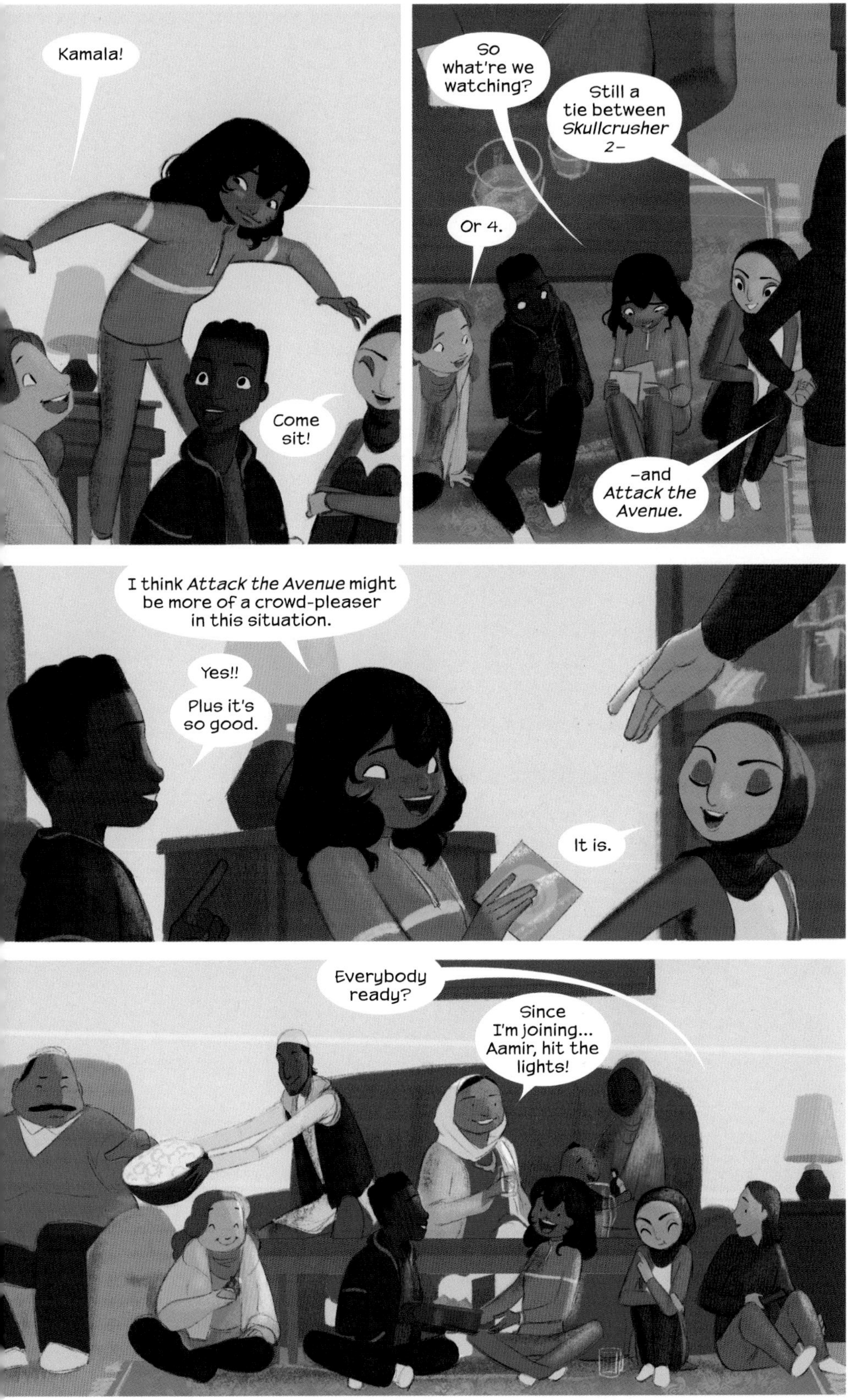
Kamala!
Come sit!
So what're we watching?
Still a tie between *Skullcrusher* 2–
Or 4.
–and *Attack the Avenue.*
I think *Attack the Avenue* might be more of a crowd-pleaser in this situation.
Yes!!
Plus it's so good.
It is.
Everybody ready?
Since I'm joining... Aamir, hit the lights!

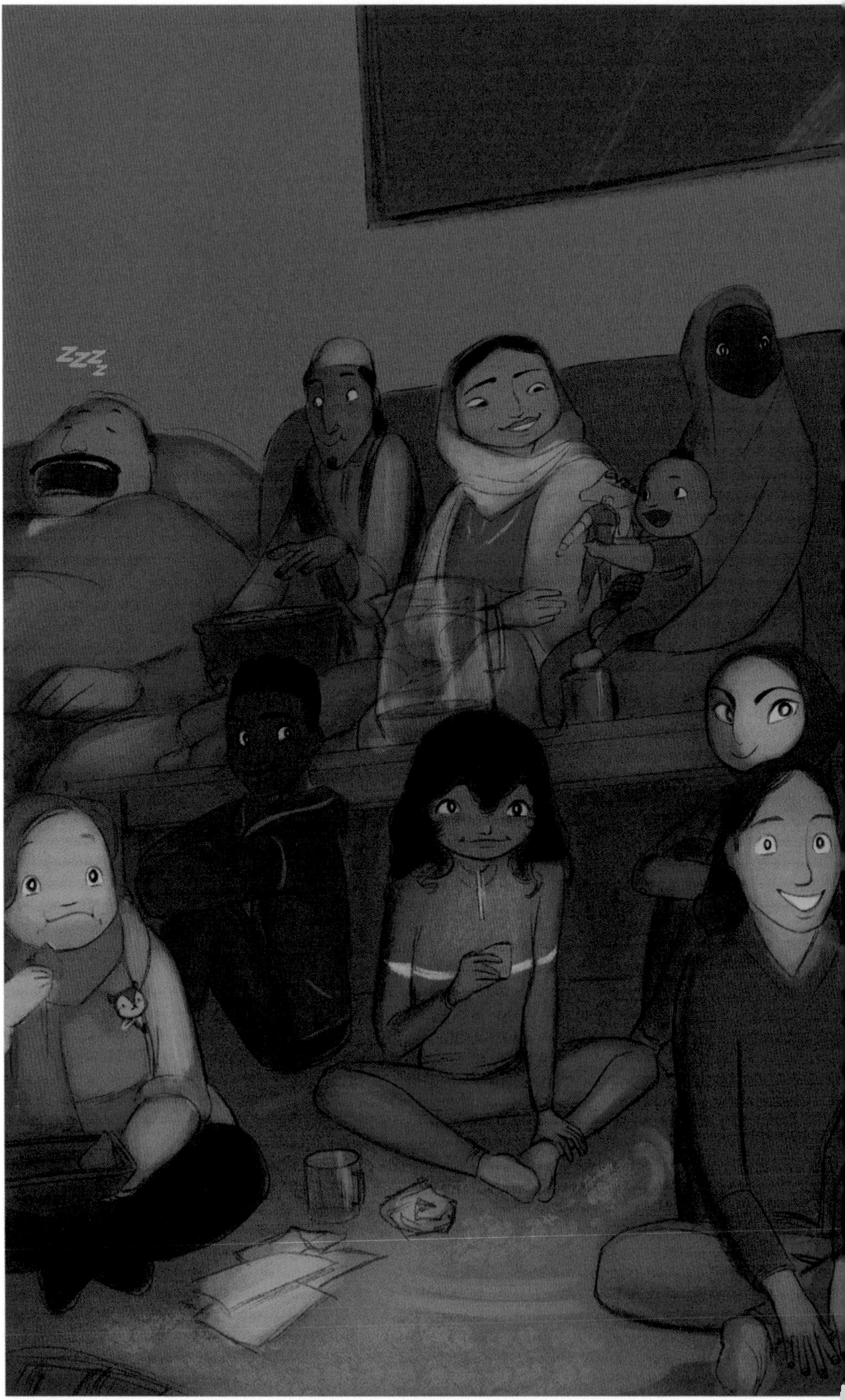
ZZZZ

NADIA SHAMMAS is a Palestinian American comics writer from Brooklyn, NY. She's best known for creating the CORPUS anthology and Squire, a forthcoming Middle Eastern fantasy graphic novel cocreated with Sara Alfageeh. She loves writing about identity, memory, and girls fighting against the odds. When not writing, she's perfecting her cold brew recipe and trying to win the love of her cats.

NABI H. ALI is a Tamil Muslim kid-lit illustrator and visdev artist based in Orange County, CA. He loves exploring art centered around the South Asian experience, both within the subcontinent and in the diaspora. During his spare time, Nabi enjoys cooking, painting, and being a history nut.

CHECK OUT A SNEAK PEEK OF

INTO THE
HEARTLANDS

A **BLACK PANTHER** GRAPHIC NOVEL

WRITTEN BY

ROSEANNE A. BROWN

ART BY

DIKA ARAÚJO & NATACHA BUSTOS

COLORS BY

CRIS PETER

LETTERS BY

VC's ARIANA MAHER

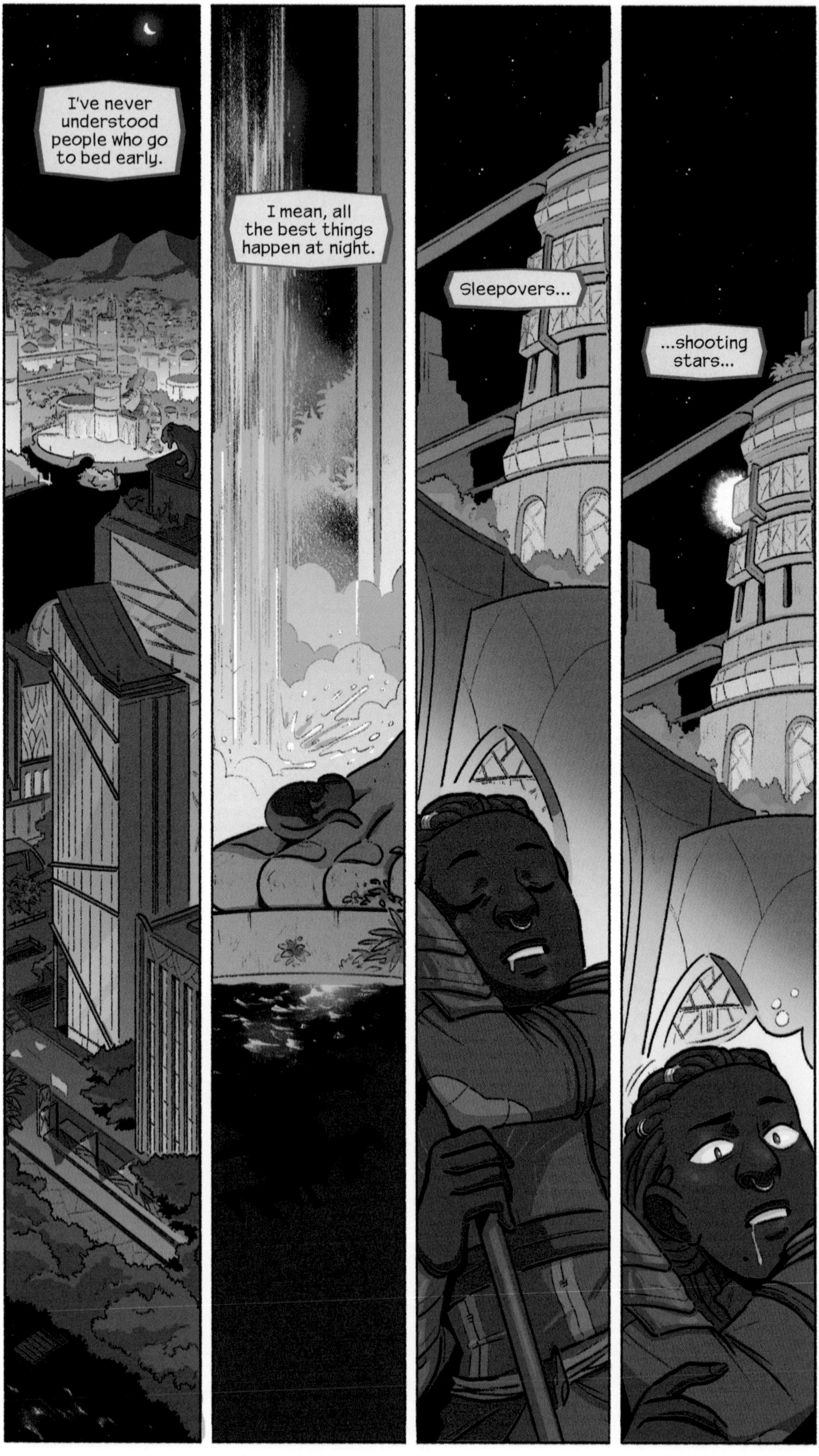
I've never understood people who go to bed early.
I mean, all the best things happen at night.
Sleepovers...
...shooting stars...

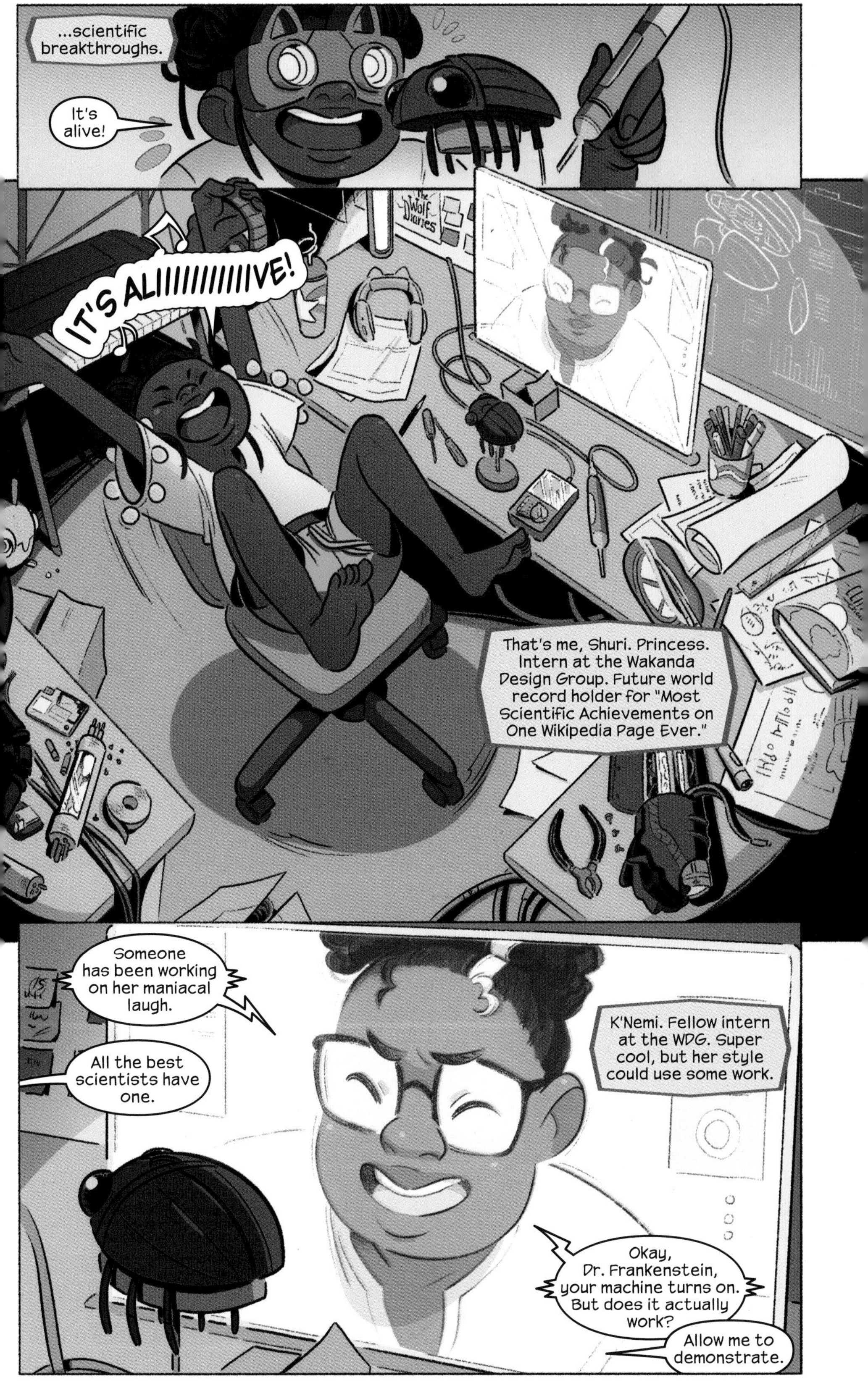

...scientific breakthroughs.
It's alive!
IT'S ALIIIIIIIIIIIIVE!
The Wolf Diaries
That's me, Shuri. Princess. Intern at the Wakanda Design Group. Future world record holder for "Most Scientific Achievements on One Wikipedia Page Ever."
Someone has been working on her maniacal laugh.
All the best scientists have one.
K'Nemi. Fellow intern at the WDG. Super cool, but her style could use some work.
Okay, Dr. Frankenstein, your machine turns on. But does it actually work?
Allow me to demonstrate.

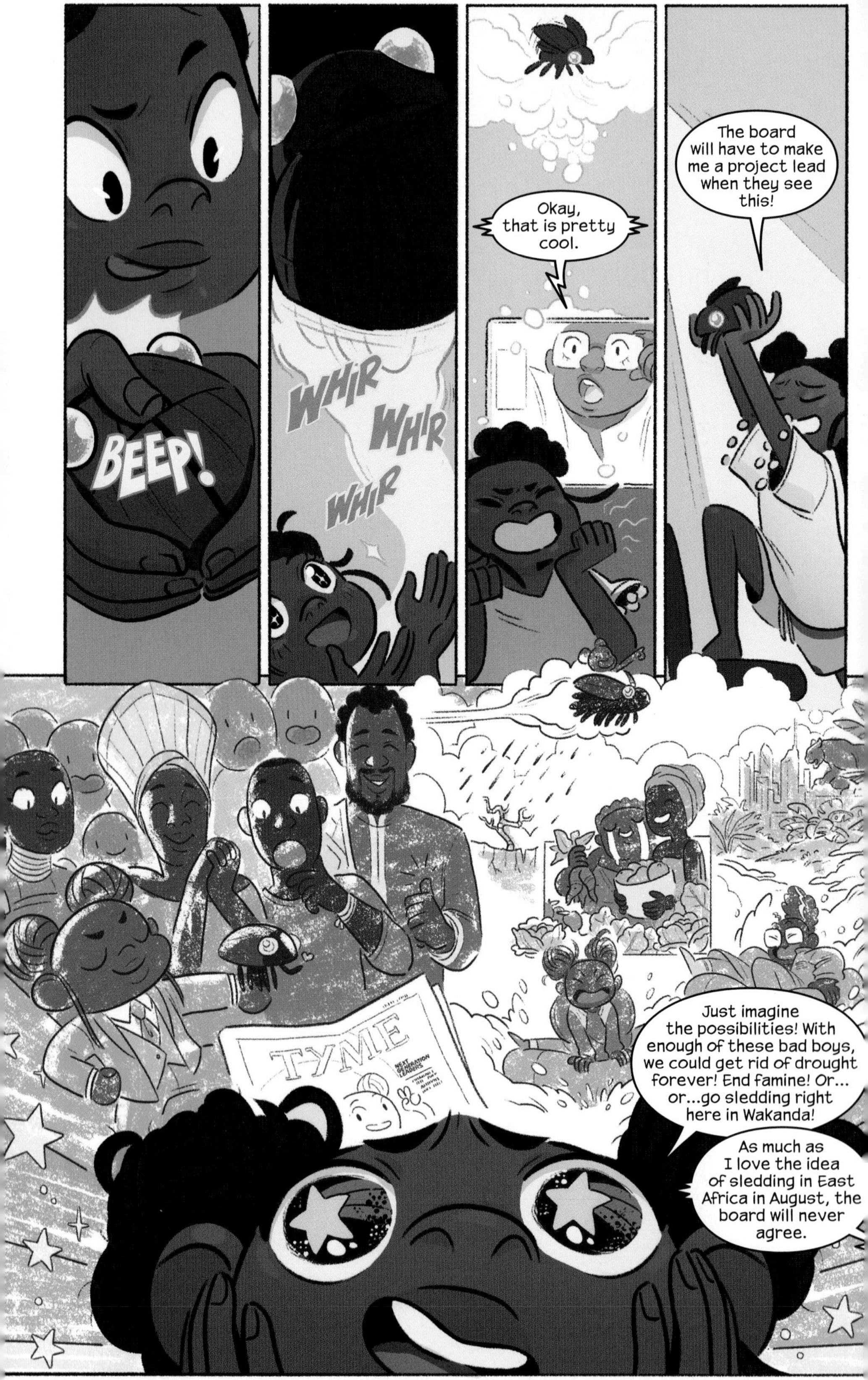
BEEP!
WHIR
WHIR
WHIR
Okay, that is pretty cool.
The board will have to make me a project lead when they see this!
TYME
NEXT GENERATION LEADERS
Just imagine the possibilities! With enough of these bad boys, we could get rid of drought forever! End famine! Or... or...go sledding right here in Wakanda!
As much as I love the idea of sledding in East Africa in August, the board will never agree.

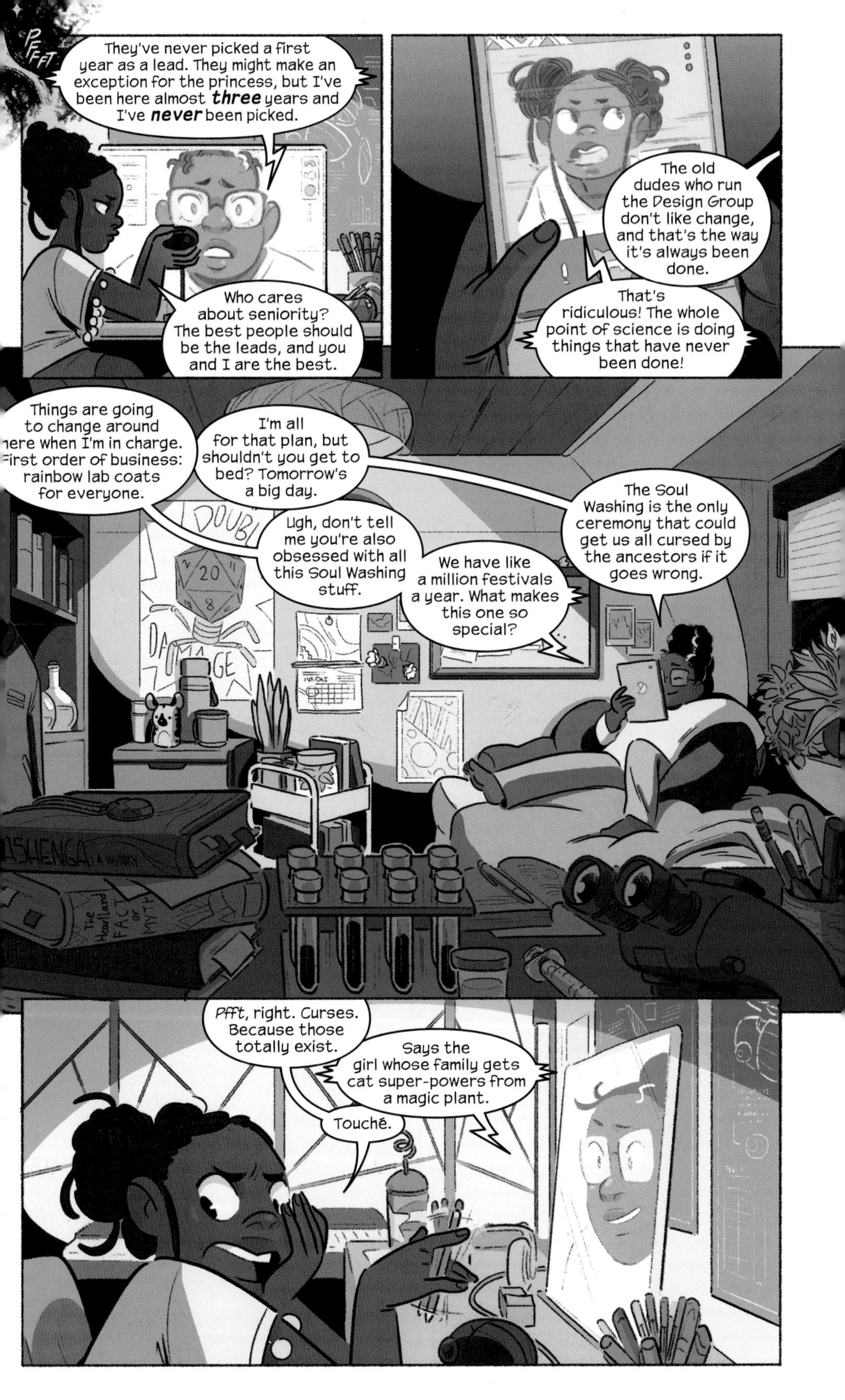
PFFFT
They've never picked a first year as a lead. They might make an exception for the princess, but I've been here almost ***three*** years and I've ***never*** been picked.
Who cares about seniority? The best people should be the leads, and you and I are the best.
The old dudes who run the Design Group don't like change, and that's the way it's always been done.
That's ridiculous! The whole point of science is doing things that have never been done!
Things are going to change around ere when I'm in charge. irst order of business: rainbow lab coats for everyone.
I'm all for that plan, but shouldn't you get to bed? Tomorrow's a big day.
Ugh, don't tell me you're also obsessed with all this Soul Washing stuff.
We have like a million festivals a year. What makes this one so special?
The Soul Washing is the only ceremony that could get us all cursed by the ancestors if it goes wrong.
Pfft, right. Curses. Because those totally exist.
Says the girl whose family gets cat super-powers from a magic plant.
Touché.

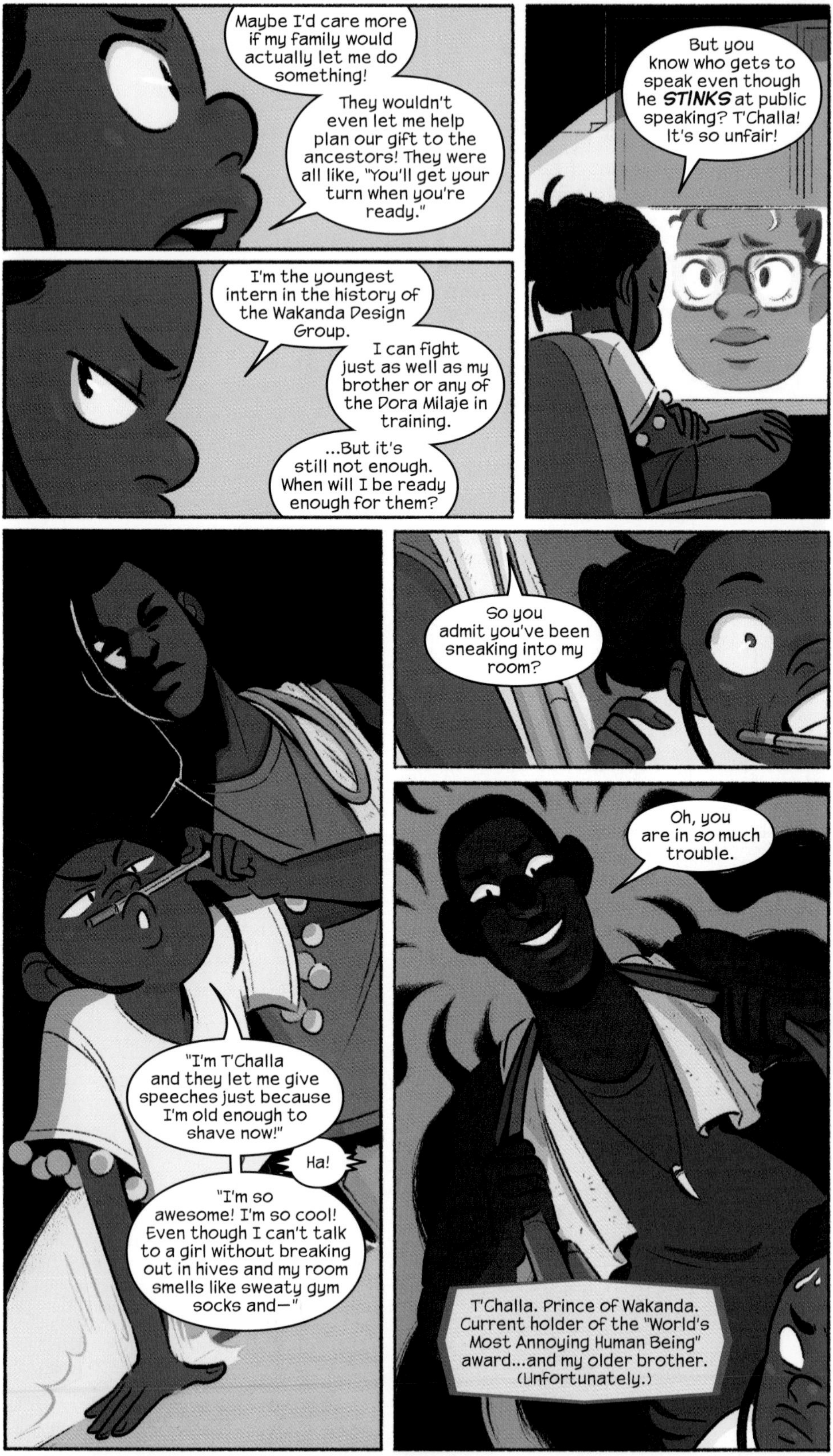
Maybe I'd care more if my family would actually let me do something!
They wouldn't even let me help plan our gift to the ancestors! They were all like, "You'll get your turn when you're ready."
But you know who gets to speak even though he **STINKS** at public speaking? T'Challa! It's so unfair!
I'm the youngest intern in the history of the Wakanda Design Group.
I can fight just as well as my brother or any of the Dora Milaje in training.
...But it's still not enough. When will I be ready enough for them?
"I'm T'Challa and they let me give speeches just because I'm old enough to shave now!"
Ha!
"I'm so awesome! I'm so cool! Even though I can't talk to a girl without breaking out in hives and my room smells like sweaty gym socks and—"
So you admit you've been sneaking into my room?
Oh, you are in *so* much trouble.
T'Challa. Prince of Wakanda. Current holder of the "World's Most Annoying Human Being" award...and my older brother. (Unfortunately.)

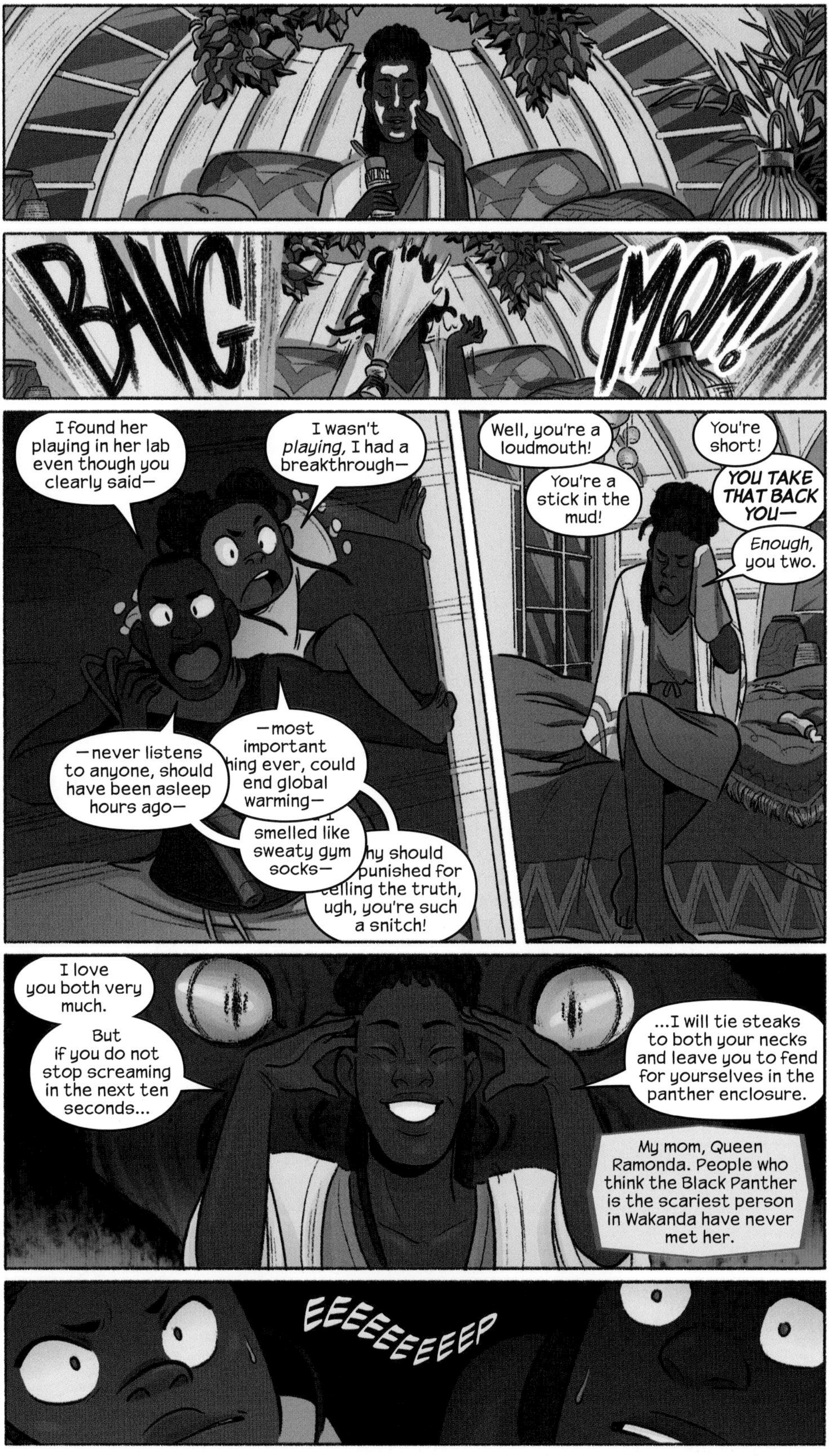
BANG
MOM!
I found her playing in her lab even though you clearly said—
I wasn't *playing*, I had a breakthrough—
—never listens to anyone, should have been asleep hours ago—
—most important thing ever, could end global warming—
smelled like sweaty gym socks—
hy should punished for telling the truth, ugh, you're such a snitch!
Well, you're a loudmouth!
You're a stick in the mud!
You're short!
YOU TAKE THAT BACK YOU—
Enough, you two.
I love you both very much.
But if you do not stop screaming in the next ten seconds...
...I will tie steaks to both your necks and leave you to fend for yourselves in the panther enclosure.
My mom, Queen Ramonda. People who think the Black Panther is the scariest person in Wakanda have never met her.
EEEEEEEEEEP

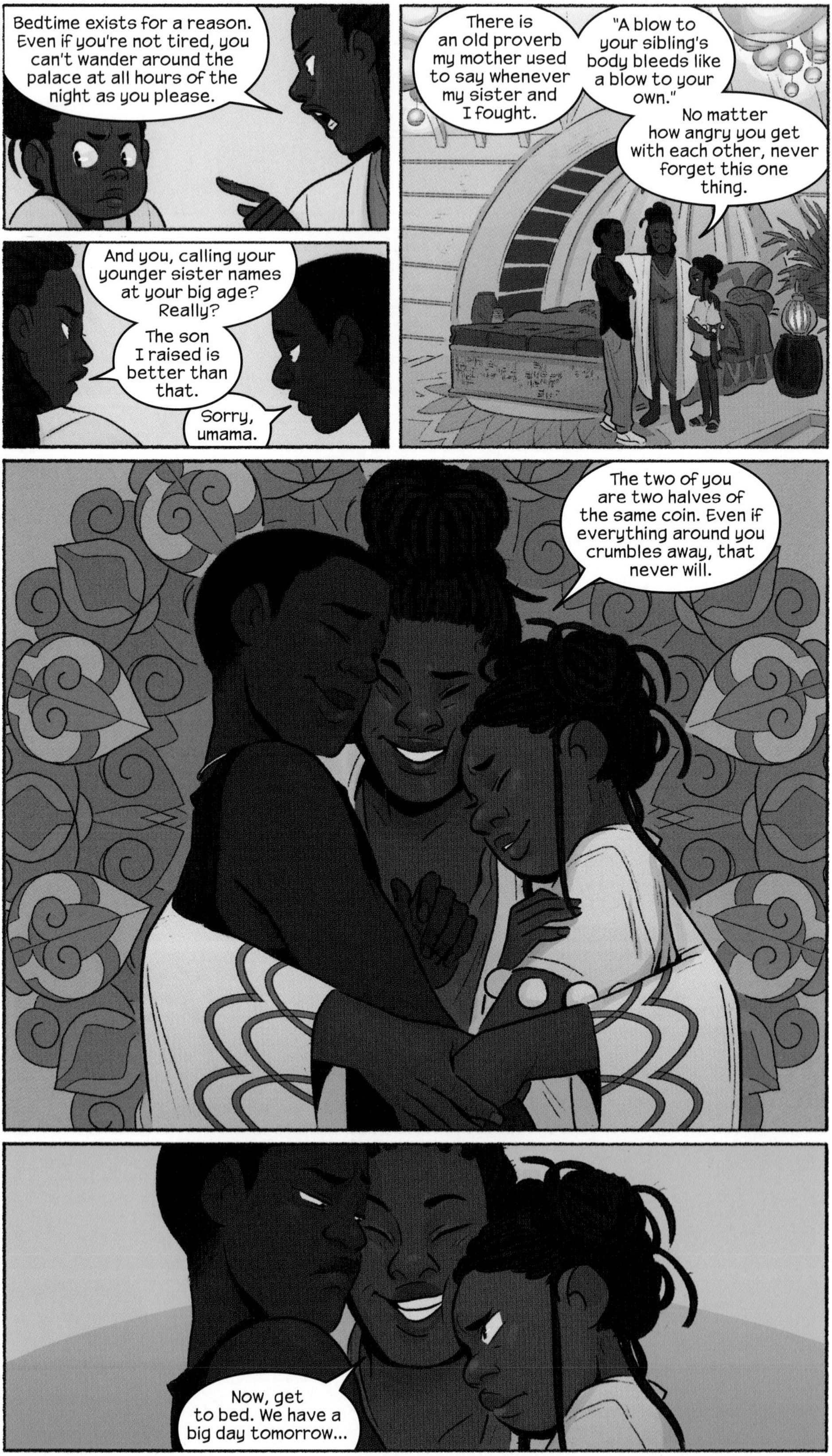

Bedtime exists for a reason. Even if you're not tired, you can't wander around the palace at all hours of the night as you please.
And you, calling your younger sister names at your big age? Really?
The son I raised is better than that.
Sorry, umama.
There is an old proverb my mother used to say whenever my sister and I fought.
"A blow to your sibling's body bleeds like a blow to your own."
No matter how angry you get with each other, never forget this one thing.
The two of you are two halves of the same coin. Even if everything around you crumbles away, that never will.
Now, get to bed. We have a big day tomorrow...

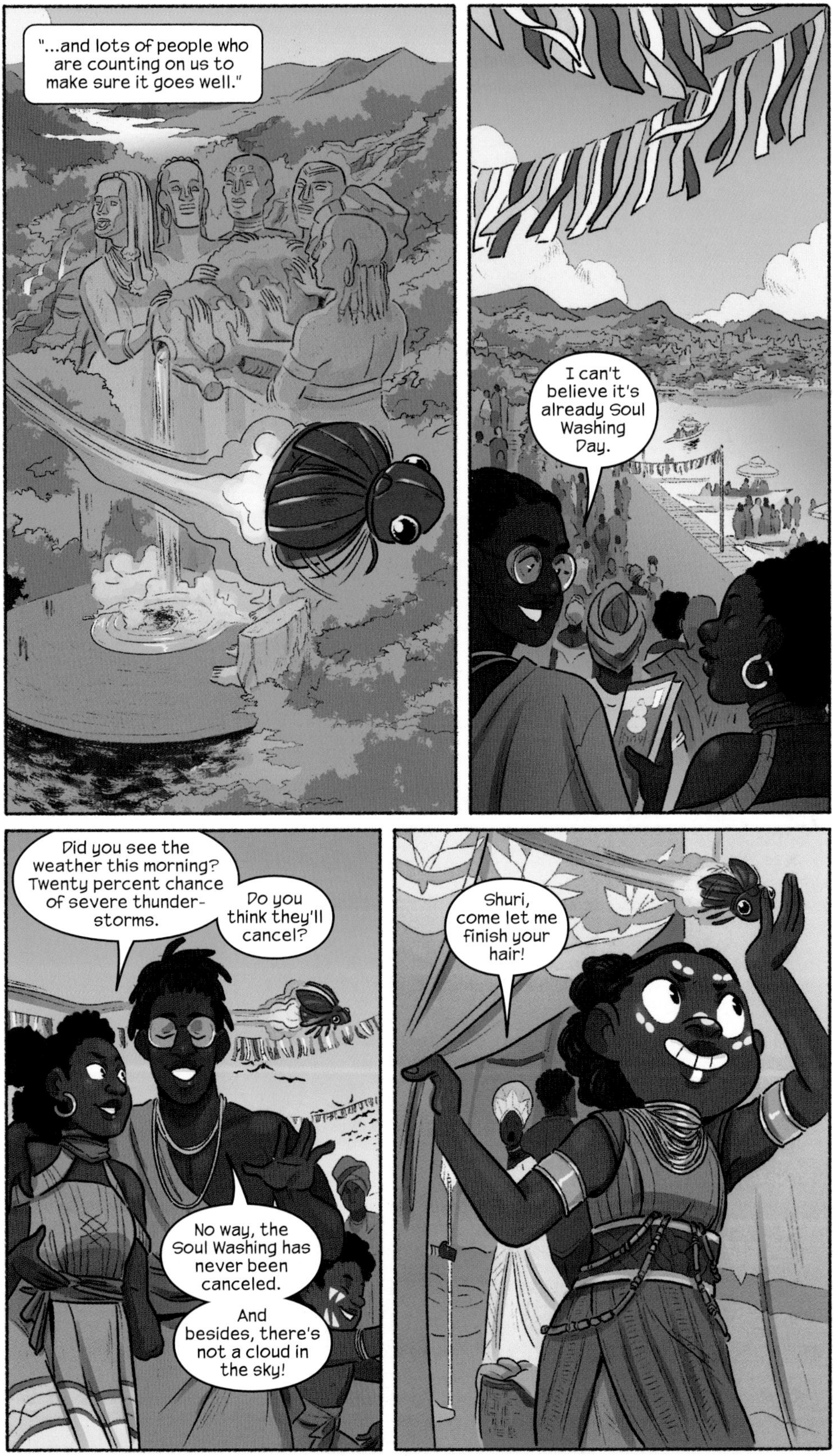
"...and lots of people who are counting on us to make sure it goes well."
I can't believe it's already Soul Washing Day.
Did you see the weather this morning? Twenty percent chance of severe thunder-storms.
Do you think they'll cancel?
No way, the Soul Washing has never been canceled.
And besides, there's not a cloud in the sky!
Shuri, come let me finish your hair!

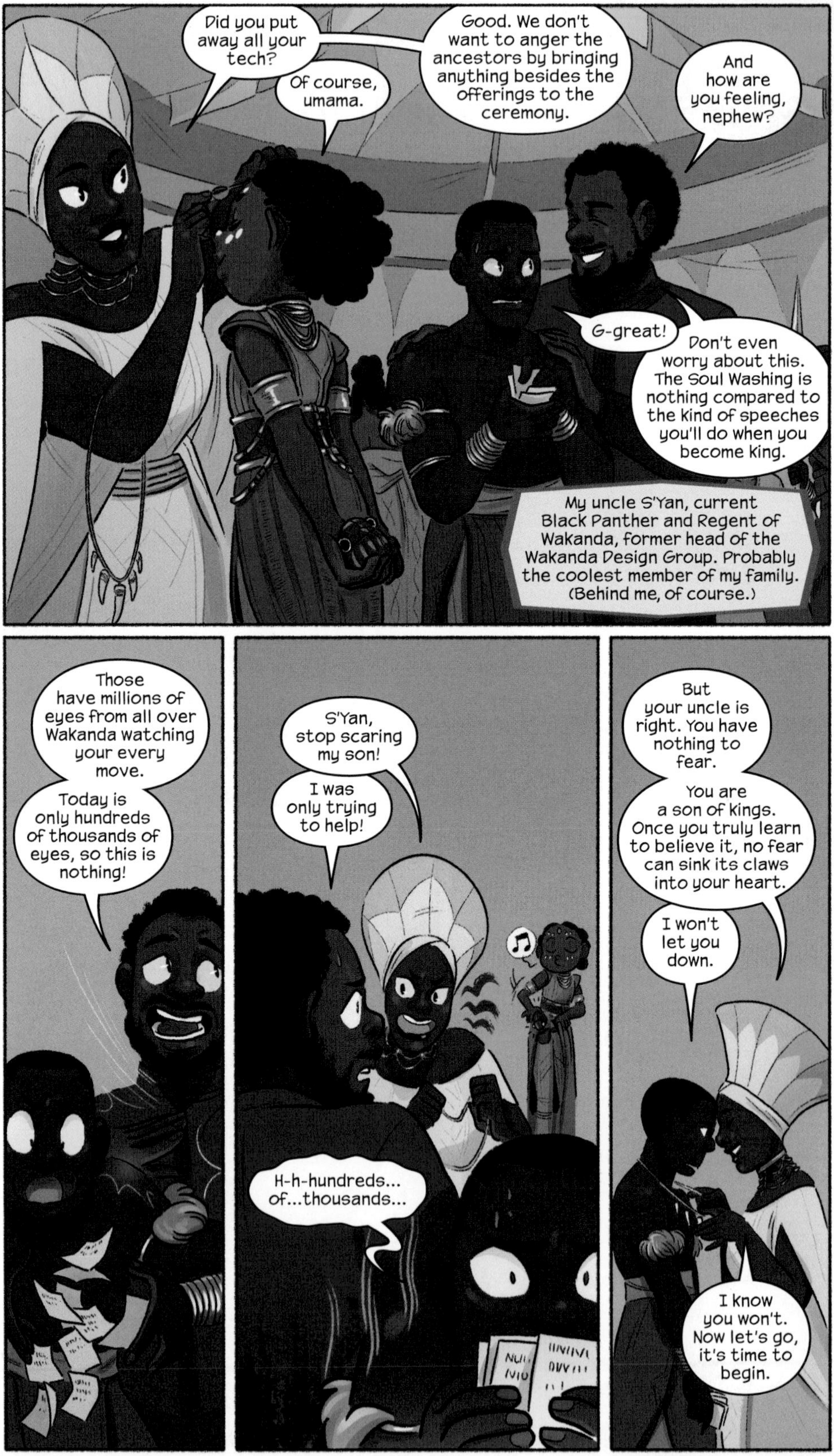
Did you put away all your tech?
Of course, umama.
Good. We don't want to anger the ancestors by bringing anything besides the offerings to the ceremony.
And how are you feeling, nephew?
G-great!
Don't even worry about this. The Soul Washing is nothing compared to the kind of speeches you'll do when you become king.
My uncle S'Yan, current Black Panther and Regent of Wakanda, former head of the Wakanda Design Group. Probably the coolest member of my family. (Behind me, of course.)
Those have millions of eyes from all over Wakanda watching your every move.
Today is only hundreds of thousands of eyes, so this is nothing!
S'Yan, stop scaring my son!
I was only trying to help!
H-h-hundreds... of...thousands...
But your uncle is right. You have nothing to fear.
You are a son of kings. Once you truly learn to believe it, no fear can sink its claws into your heart.
I won't let you down.
I know you won't. Now let's go, it's time to begin.